FLIGHT
PATH

FLIGHT PATH

E J PEPPER

Matador
9 Priory Business Park,
Wistow Road, Kibworth Beauchamp,
Leicestershire. LE8 0RX
Tel: 0116 279 2299
Email: books@troubador.co.uk
Web: www.troubador.co.uk/matador
Twitter: @matadorbooks

ISBN 978 1838594 657

British Library Cataloguing in Publication Data.
A catalogue record for this book is available from the British Library.

Printed and bound in Great Britain by 4edge Limited
Typeset in 11pt Minion Pro by Troubador Publishing Ltd, Leicester, UK

Matador is an imprint of Troubador Publishing Ltd

For Andrew

ACKNOWLEDGEMENTS

My warmest thanks to:

Alison MacLeod for her encouragement and interest in the book.

Fellow author, Sarah Hegarty, for helpful feedback and support.

The Exeter Novel Prize, especially Broo Doherty, Cathie Hartigan, Margaret James and Sophie Duffy.

Readers Linda Anderson and Sue Rawlings.

Chris Hanson for checking the legal facts. Any errors that remain are mine.

The team at Troubador for their efficiency and expertise.

ONE

A BEFORE AND AN AFTER. WITH ANY CRISIS, IT IS the same. One moment, things are going along much as they have always done. A satisfying balance. And in the next, along comes an event that threatens to destroy everything we have ever worked or cared for. The world tilts. All our bearings are gone.

Sometimes, of course, you see the crisis coming, and avert it in the nick of time. Sometimes it is transitory: an errant husband or wife returns to the fold. A person's reputation is not, after all, irretrievably tarnished.

So at what point do you stop agonising over what you might have done differently? At what point can you relax, safe in the knowledge that it is truly over?

*

A man stands by a window, watching the early light seep through the gap in the curtains. The room has the deadened feel of many luxury hotels. No doubt the bathroom's velvety towels and gold taps, the quilted bed cover, the deep pile carpet – like wading through cotton wool, Miles thinks – are all designed to make one feel pampered and indulged. Instead, he feels hemmed in, cornered.

He parts the curtains, and glances into the lamp-lit street. This is a quiet part of London, the plane trees lending it a deceptively bucolic air, but still along each pavement the cars are parked nose to tail, and in a doorway opposite litter is piled in an unruly heap.

He wishes he were away from here – as, God willing, he soon will be – striding through the Oxford landscape. But no – he brings himself up short. Not Oxford. He'll never feel completely safe there again. Cornwall, then, and beside him the only woman he has ever loved.

She lies sleeping in the bed behind him. Were he to turn, he would make out her rounded outline, the spread of her hair, the curve of her fingers against the pillow, like that of some Renaissance Madonna.

But he doesn't turn.

In the street below, two women in coats and white caps – hotel waitresses no doubt – have their heads bent in conversation, the smoke from their cigarettes forming a grey shroud about them. As he watches, they throw the stubs to the ground, releasing a brief shower of sparks, before disappearing into a doorway opposite.

This is the start of a new chapter, he tells himself, so what use in looking back?

Yet it seems he can't help himself, because he's there once more on that wet January morning. Less than a year ago, but already it seems a lifetime away.

*

How still the place is! With no radio blaring out the day's news, and no burble of the coffee machine, it's as if the house too has had the breath knocked out of it. He pauses in the kitchen doorway, listening to the beat of rain on the tiles that forms a counterpoint to the thudding of his own heart.

He's had the kitchen done up only the previous year, the stained work surfaces and chipped cupboards replaced by pale wood and chrome. Never something he'd have gone for himself, and it's certainly left an uncomfortable hole in his savings. But of course it wasn't for him, it was for Sophie, who has been unusually muted since the twins started university. She's always been a first-rate cook, so what better way to cheer her up?

At the time, her effusive thanks made it all worthwhile, but now as he looks about him, he realises the folly of his creation, which seems as sterile and forbidding as an operating theatre.

He scoops instant coffee into a mug, and reaches into the fridge for some milk.

Through an open window comes the sound of tyres along the driveway and then, sharp as a ringtone, a blackbird's alarm-call. Later, he will recall the sound as a warning.

The hall is also hushed, as if it needs the clang of a bell, or the click of a switch, to get things going. He stares about him, knowing that he should be taking action of some kind, but the exact nature of this eludes him.

The house is an elegant Edwardian affair, with large airy rooms, and high ceilings rimmed with flower and leaf cornices. On the wall beside him, a gilt-framed mirror throws a wavering reflection on the polished floor. Opposite is a set of hunting prints – the riders, self-important in their scarlet jackets, mounted on varnished-looking horses – a long-ago wedding present that he always feels adds a sense of gravitas to the place.

He squares his shoulders, and glances into the mirror. A man with round cheeks and a fringe of dark hair stares back at him. Is this how he really looks to others? No hint of grey yet, so younger than his sixty-two years, surely? He studies the face, trying to draw strength from this stranger. Yet behind the brown-rimmed spectacles, the eyes are watery and uncertain.

He tweaks the knot in his tie – the one with the maroon circles he bought several years ago in M&S. 'You're so uncool, Dad!' he can hear the twins saying. It was meant as a tease, of course, but he refuses to enter into the modern mania for discarding the perfectly serviceable in favour of some latest trend. And "uncool" – what sort of a word is that?

'You're ready?' a voice says, so that for a split second Miles thinks it's the mirror speaking.

Laing is in the far doorway. How long has he been there? His surprise must show on his face, because Laing adds, 'Just trying to avoid any wee hitches.'

With that pretentious Edinburgh accent, Miles has always found him hard to take seriously. He's very short, only coming up to Miles's ear, and although in his early forties, he looks far younger, with a smooth babyish face and bright blue eyes.

Now, without waiting for a reply, he walks forward, stopping a few paces away.

'I thought,' Miles says, 'you know – that some of the others might...' His voice tails off.

'Oh, I hardly think so.'

Miles's stomach plummets. He was expecting a better show. If Murdo were here, he would be standing by him, would never have let it come to this.

Laing holds out his hand, which is decent of him in the circumstances. But when Miles goes to grip it, Laing says, 'I'll take that.'

Looking down, Miles sees he's still clutching the empty coffee mug. He holds it out, and Laing's small fingers prise it from his grasp.

'Well, goodbye then.' His voice doesn't sound like his own, and something odd is happening with his breathing.

Laing nods before walking over to the front door, and pulling it open.

He should be following, but he can't seem to shake off the sense of being caught up in some improbable nightmare. All he can do is stand, staring down at his shoes, gleaming up at him from the extra brushing Sophie gave them earlier.

She must be there waiting because he can hear the Rover's engine give a splutter before gasping into life.

'Sixty ciggies a day transport!' one of the girls had joked. He's had it over twelve years – was planning to replace it in the autumn.

He has no recollection of carrying down his overnight bag, but there it is by the door. He picks it up and, lifting his chin in the air, brushes past Laing with what he hopes is the right degree of insouciance.

Outside a steady drizzle is falling and as he walks across the front garden, he sees the caretaker's ginger tom crouched under the laurels, staring past him, amber eyes fixed on some unseen prey.

Then he is through the gate, hearing it swing shut behind him with a click. He looks along the curve of the drive. It is deserted. The world tilts. No one will be coming now.

He can see the back seat of the Rover piled with boxes and carrier bags – at least they've been able to leave the furniture and other bulky items in the house. A pot plant with cream flowers and broad, tapering leaves leans precariously against the side window. The passenger door is open and from the driver's seat, Sophie calls, 'Do get a *move* on, Miles!'

There's nothing for it but to climb in beside her.

Her knuckles are white against the steering wheel. 'Seat belt!' she orders, her voice bright.

He fumbles for the strap and they set off down the drive, the car sluggish, weighed down by the luggage in the boot.

He stares out of the window.

They're passing the long line of the beech hedge that borders the gravelled drive. In a couple of months, the soft green of the new leaves will be showing through in the first adolescent fuzz of spring. Beyond are the rookery, and the stand of chestnuts, with the fields and woodland stretching into the distance. He has walked every inch of it in his time.

As they approach the gatehouse at the bottom of the slope, he can see Carter, in a brown sweater and red knitted hat, stooped over the vegetable patch. He glances up, and Miles forces his lips into some sort of rictus. No doubt the man is registering the fact that here are the two of them heading off on a Monday morning to God knows where. Some family crisis perhaps? He'll be in touch with any gossip doing the rounds, but by the time word gets out, they should be well out of reach.

Miles's stomach gives another lurch.

They are turning into the Oxford Road, following the route south before picking up the signs to the A40. Easy enough to imagine they're off to the Cornish house again.

'I really need to know, Miles.' Sophie's voice makes him jump.

He should tell her more, but his head is too full of the images spinning around in it: rows of empty desks, a towel tossed across a bench, the curious look of satisfaction on Laing's face. '*Please*, Sophie. Let's wait until we're well and truly away from here.'

She lets out the ghost of a sigh. 'All right then. But we can't put off telling the girls for much longer.'

Thank God it's not a year ago, when they were still at home, gearing up for their A levels.

The car smells fuggy. He presses the window control and the glass slides down a short distance.

Suddenly, Murdo's reedy voice is in his ear. *Exilium – banishment, the state of being expelled from one's native land. That's part of the human condition, wouldn't you say, Miles? Curious how so many spend their lives trying to discover a sense of home, only to find themselves in free fall at the end. Now Diogenes had an interesting account of...*

'By the waters of Babylon I sat down and wept,' Miles murmurs, only now fully grasping the gist of it.

Sophie turns towards him. He can see the streaks of grey in her hair and the way the collar of her blouse – the blue flowered one that he's always liked – has started to fray. 'Did you say something?'

He shakes his head, keeping his gaze fixed on the windscreen. At least the rain has stopped.

They're passing a petrol station with a striped awning tacked on one end. 'Where is this?'

'For heaven's sake, Miles! We've driven past here umpteen times.'

'Of course,' he murmurs again. He's never been much good with directions – leaves all that side of things, including the actual driving, to her.

The traffic has built to a steady stream. A lorry overtakes, enveloping them in a spray of muddy water. Sophie brakes sharply, muttering something under her breath. Then the smooth rhythm of the journey is resumed, the only sounds the shush of tyres on the wet road, and the steady beat of the wipers.

He reaches forward and pushes a CD into the slot. The opening chords of the *Pastoral Symphony* – light-hearted, full of optimism – fill the space.

Slowly, he feels his shoulders relax. He's hardly slept for the past couple of nights, but at least when they get to the other end he'll be able to have a decent night's sleep. Sophie has said the new place is small. He pictures some cosy mews house, with window boxes and a bistro round the corner.

God, how exhausted he feels! His head nods forward.

*

He's aware of the distant crash of waves. He opens his eyes, and sees to his surprise that they're at the bottom of a granite cliff. He blinks, and the cliff transforms itself into a skip piled with old mattresses, leaning towards him at an impossible angle. Why, any minute now they'll start toppling over, and –

'Oh, good. You're awake.' Sophie shoves her mobile under his nose. 'Can you read the map? I think it's a right turn here – but then what?'

He takes the phone, trying to make sense of the criss-cross of lines dancing before his eyes.

'Glasses, Miles!' Her voice is sharp.

He pats his pockets, trying to remember where he's put them.

She sighs. 'Give it here then.'

He watches her study the map, biting her lower lip and running her fingers through her hair in that way she has whenever she's under pressure.

'I've got it. Second left, under a railway bridge, first right before a junction, third left. But we may need to stop again.'

They pull out into the traffic, passing a row of Victorian houses, three-storeyed and with decent front gardens. Then, after a series of further turns, the architecture becomes pre-war, interspersed with flat-roofed modern blocks. Some front directly onto the pavement, others have rickety fences, behind which he glimpses patches of balding lawn.

'I think we must have overshot the—' Sophie begins.

High on a building, Miles spots a road name. Pleased with himself, he points up. 'Look! Stephen's Close!'

It's a long cul-de-sac, with cars parked bumper to bumper on either side. The houses are semi-detached, with pebble-dash walls, picture windows downstairs and glass-panelled front doors. Fairly grim, but at least they seem well kept. A man in a hooded top walks past, leading a large German shepherd on a chain. As Miles watches, the man stops and the dog cocks its leg against a fence, the urine running down the wood.

He averts his gaze.

The road is narrowing and the properties becoming shabbier. 'Number 49 must be at the far end.' For the first time, her voice is uncertain.

He feels a flutter of panic in his stomach.

They pull up outside the last pair of houses. She gets out and stands on the pavement. Miles follows more slowly.

In silence, they stare at the flaking paintwork, the front door with its smeared bottle glass, like the eye of some diseased Cyclops, and the yellowing net over the downstairs window. A rust-coloured stain runs in a zigzag down the wall, presumably from the broken guttering that juts out from under the roof.

He feels a rising sense of disbelief. Surely no one can be expected to spend even one night in a dump like this? As if giving voice to his unspoken protest, the roar of an aircraft fills the air, before fading into the distance.

He looks at Sophie. Perhaps this is just some ghastly mistake? But already she is crossing the patch of cracked concrete between the pavement and the house, and is stooped over a plastic urn by the front door.

She straightens, turning towards him and holding up a small bunch of keys. 'At least they're where they said they'd be.'

When he doesn't answer, she says, 'Better get our things out of the car.'

TWO

BY THE TIME HE REACHES HER SIDE, SOPHIE IS already pushing at the door, which opens with a creak. She clicks on the light, and he follows, fighting the queasiness in his stomach.

They are in a narrow hall, little more than a passageway, the floor covered in faded lino, the walls a dirty cream. The smell of damp is overpowering.

'Phew!' Sophie wrinkles her nose. 'This can't have been lived in for months.'

'Years, more like!'

She leads the way along the passage. At the far end a door opens into a small, dark kitchen with a Formica-topped table, a sink with a worm-eaten draining-board and a four-ringed gas cooker encrusted with grease. Through the glass panel of the back door, Miles glimpses a shed, half-buried in dead grass.

They retrace their steps to the front room, papered in trailing yellow and green roses. Two sagging armchairs and a sofa, covered in orange bobbled material, are arranged in front of an ancient gas fire.

It's all perfectly ghastly. 'Surely we could have found something better than this?'

'I'm truly sorry, Miles. I never imagined...' Her voice trails away.

They climb the steep stairs, with its strip of worn carpeting, to the three bedrooms and bathroom. She points to the tear-like stains under the taps. 'Haven't seen those since my student days. All that's missing is the immersion heater.' She pushes a strand of hair from her face. 'I don't know about you, but I'm parched! See to the car, would you, and I'll get the kettle on.' As he turns to go downstairs, she adds, 'At least it won't be for long.'

Even a minute is too bloody long, he feels like saying, but bites the words back.

As he hoists the first suitcase out of the boot, a young woman emerges from the adjoining house, carrying a folded pushchair, a child tucked under one arm. She has shoulder length glossy hair and a trim figure. Barely out of the sixth form. She calls a cheery 'Morning!' to him, but he pretends not to hear, lugging the case across the concrete and bumping it up the narrow stairs to the main bedroom, the muscles in his arms aching. He lingers in the bathroom having a much-needed pee, and by the time he goes out to the car again, the girl has gone.

When he's emptied the boot, he sits at the kitchen table while, just as at the start of their summer holiday, Sophie bustles about, washing surfaces and lifting things out of boxes. He recalls the light-filled rooms of the Cornish house with its views over the Helford River. Of course they'll be back there in August as usual. He can picture them joking about this place. Why, any moment now, there will be a phone call from Alan Sanderson to say the whole thing has been a terrible mistake.

He checks his watch. 1.30. School lunch will just be finishing – lamb korma, made with the leftovers from Sunday's roast, and crumble to follow.

'Here we are.' Sophie unpacks plates and cutlery from their picnic hamper and places ham and a jar of Stilton on the table. She begins slicing a loaf with almost medical precision, her hair swinging as she moves.

He spears a piece of ham onto his fork. His stomach is still unsettled, but he'd better eat something.

Sophie must have located the boiler switch, because the ancient radiator in the corner creaks into life. At least it will help get rid of the damp.

A thought comes to him. 'The let here is, for how long? Six months?'

'No – I already told you – a year.'

'For God's sake, Sophie!' The words ricochet round the cramped room. 'There's little enough in the building society as it is.'

'I'm really sorry, Miles – it was the minimum the landlord would agree to.'

He sighs. 'But surely you checked out the state of this place before taking it on?'

She puts down her knife and fork. 'There was no *time*, Miles. Remember?'

As if he could forget.

*

Alan Sanderson's call came as he and Sophie were finishing breakfast. 'Sorry to bother you so early, Miles, but I wondered if you could pop over?'

'Now?'

'If you wouldn't mind. Something rather urgent has cropped up.'

'Of course, Alan. Be with you shortly.' He clicked off the phone pleased and, if he were honest, relieved. This was only Sanderson's second term as head, and up to now, he'd barely consulted Miles on any issue. Something that, as Murdo's right-hand man, Miles found hard to take.

'Seems my help is wanted after all,' he said, in answer to Sophie's raised eyebrows. He swallowed the last of his coffee. 'I'll go straight to my first class. See you later.'

He kissed her goodbye, before walking briskly across to the main building. It was an icy morning, the lawn silvered with frost, twigs crackling under his feet as he cut along the side path. As he passed the refectory, he could hear a hubbub of voices – the boys were still at breakfast. He entered the main building, nodding a greeting to Carter, who was sweeping the hall floor, and taking the stairs two at a time.

The first surprise came when Alan ushered him, not into his study, but into the room used for governors' meetings. Miles had always found its oak furniture, mullioned windows and diamond-patterned carpet a reassuring reminder of a more civilised and mannered world. Even more of a surprise, however, was seeing the people seated behind the long table: Hugo Paget, the current chair of governors, the deputy head, Cosgrave, Burrows, the school solicitor, and the diminutive geography master, Laing.

Sanderson nodded Miles towards the single chair that was placed facing them, and after a moment's hesitation, he settled himself onto it, nodding across to indicate he bore no ill will over having to leave his breakfast at short notice.

No one met his eye, and there was some shifting in seats, almost as if they were about to be interviewed by *him*.

Paget, one of those large-boned, broad-shouldered men, who looked as if they'd been reared on steak and claret, was the first to speak. 'We wondered what comments you have, Miles, about the incident last Tuesday?'

'Last Tuesday?' he echoed, trying to gather his thoughts. 'But hasn't Alan explained?'

Alan coughed. 'Unfortunately, there have been certain...' he paused, 'developments.'

'We agreed no further action was needed.' Miles struggled to contain his frustration. 'We all know what boys can be like.'

Through the open window, the raucous call of a magpie broke the silence.

Alan coughed again. He was in his early fifties, with an aquiline nose and dark hair silvered at the edges. 'The whole thing is most unfortunate.'

'But surely you can't imagine—?'

'If I may?' The interruption came from Burrows, a short, balding man with a droning voice. Miles had encountered him at various school functions. 'Before you say anything further, Mr Whitaker, I have to advise you that the father of the Remove Year boy is demanding an enquiry.'

Miles opened his mouth to speak, but the solicitor held up his hand. 'Best you say nothing further at this stage, Mr Whitaker, not until you've obtained legal advice.'

'Legal advice?' Miles stared.

Sanderson pushed back his chair. 'The board has unanimously agreed, Miles. It would be in the best interests of all concerned for you and your wife to leave the school premises. Until this whole business is cleared up.' He paused. 'You have the weekend in which to pack your belongings. I'm sure you don't need any reminder about leaving South Lodge in good order. Obviously your furniture and other possessions will be looked after in your absence.'

Miles stared at the portrait of the school's founder. Above the black frock coat and cravat, the bewhiskered face, its expression stern, gazed back at him.

'The school will be in touch in due course, through your legal representative,' Sanderson continued. 'Laing has kindly offered to oversee things – give you and Sophie whatever help is needed to...' he paused, 'facilitate your departure.'

The geography master gave a supercilious sniff, reminding Miles that his had been one of the faces that had appeared after the incident on Tuesday.

He banged his fist on the table, the enormity of what was happening sweeping over him. 'I think you've all taken leave of your senses! Putting the Cunningham boy's word above mine.'

'It's not just his—' Laing began, but the solicitor cut him short.

'I urge you very strongly again, Mr Whitaker, to seek legal advice.'

He was filled with a mixture of dismay and outrage. 'This would never have happened in Murdo's time. There's no way he—'

'Murdo is no longer the head,' Alan said, his tone curt. He got to his feet and, as if drawn by an invisible thread, Miles followed. Alan held the door for him, making it clear that Miles was dismissed.

A few moments later, he was crossing the lawn on his way back to the house, wondering how on earth he was going to break the news to Sophie that they had three days in which to pack up their belongings and go Christ knew where.

*

Sophie looks across at him. 'I think it's time you told me.' He gives a start. They are sitting at the Formica table finishing their ham and salad, but for a moment he forgot they were actually here, in this god-awful house.

'I have to know what's going on, Miles.' She's looking across at him, grey eyes wide, the vertical crease that has recently formed between her eyes more pronounced.

But what *can* he tell her, when he doesn't as yet know the full facts? Better to fend her off until he's sorted it out with his solicitor. He sighs. 'The Cunningham boy has accused me of bullying him.'

'What sort of bullying?'

'I don't know the precise details yet.' He takes a sip of water.

'But that's absurd.' She frowns. 'They'd never make you leave for something as vague as that.'

He reaches for her hand. 'I'm afraid there is more to it than that.'

She puts down her knife and fork. 'I'd much rather know.'

He strokes her fingers. 'Apparently the boy is saying it's not just verbal bullying. He says that I've actually been assaulting him.'

'How ridiculous! And why on earth would he do that?'

'God knows. He's not exactly a pupil one warms to, but I'd never have thought even he would have stooped so low.' He takes another sip of water. 'He's claiming that I've been kicking him, hitting him – that sort of thing. Unfortunately, the father has now filed a formal complaint.'

'Without talking to you direct?'

'You know what parents can be like.'

She nods, because of course she *does* know. As deputy matron, she also has had dealings with mothers who scream and shout, with fathers who threaten violence if their sons do badly in exams, or are not given their first choice of university.

'But I still don't understand why they've suspended you without evidence.'

He sighs. 'The whole thing's a bloody nuisance. But Alan insists on playing it by the book.'

'In a way Murdo would never have done.'

'Quite.'

Sophie studies him, and he feels his stomach tighten.

'Wasn't Justin Cunningham part of the group who've been giving you all that gyp? The boy who's had all those detentions?'

'The very same.'

She gives a smile of sympathy. 'Oh, Miles – and after all your years at the school. We must get onto the solicitors right away.'

'I meant to say – I've already spoken with Rupert Marshall's office. I'm just waiting for them to come up with a date for a meeting.'

'Oh.' She looks taken aback. 'I wish you'd said something sooner. But at least we can now fight this together.'

He smiles. 'I promise you don't need to be too concerned. It'll all get sorted out, and we'll be back at Fordingbury in no time.' He pushes away his half-eaten food.

'Would you mind terribly if I put my feet up?'

She scrapes back her chair. 'You do look done in – and no wonder, poor love.' She holds out a box of matches. 'Why don't you light the fire in the front room, and I'll bring some coffee.'

'Thanks.' He stands up, overcome with relief.

He takes the matches from her and walks along the narrow passage to the sitting-room. The smell of damp has lessened, but it still feels chilly. He bends over the fire, which is the old kind with a mantle. Aren't these things illegal? He twists the tap and there's a hiss of gas that lights with a popping noise.

He sinks into one of the sagging chairs. Christ! He could do with a drink!

As if on cue, the door opens and Sophie appears round the side of the chair, with a glass. 'I thought some of our Bordeaux might hit the spot.'

He reaches up, giving her hand a grateful squeeze.

'Goodness, it's dark in here!' She clicks on the lamp in the corner. 'When you're more rested, might it be an idea to write down your recollection of events? For when we meet the solicitor.'

'You're right.'

'I'll be upstairs. There's our bed to make up, and I need to start getting the worst of the grime off this place.' She leans over and kisses the top of his head. Then the door closes behind her and he hears her steps echoing back along the lino.

He gulps his wine. God, how good it tastes!

His watch says two thirty. Almost time to take the Lower Fourths – a rowdy group, though not a bad one. Not like Cunningham and his lot. The little shits.

He can see now that the trouble must have been brewing for a while. He'd mentioned it to Sophie, of course, but only in passing. Should he have seen it all coming? Would someone else in his position have done so? Cosgrave, the deputy head, wasn't a bad sort. Perhaps Miles should have confided in him?

21

He can hear Murdo's voice. *Twenty-twenty vision after the event is no bloody use, Whitaker. On Your Toes is the motto if we want to keep ahead of the game!*

Except it wasn't a game, Miles thinks now. Or if it started as one, it certainly hasn't ended that way. Sophie's right – he needs to set out his version of events – the one any right-minded person will give credence to over the vengefulness of some adolescent boy.

He fishes in his blazer pocket for the notepad and fountain pen he always carries. The pen was a sixtieth present from Murdo. He unscrews the top, stretching his feet towards the fire. The room is warming up. On the other side of the window, the winter afternoon is drawing in, mercifully blurring the view of the broken fence and the road.

He takes another swig of his drink and begins to write.

As from South Lodge,
Fordingbury School,
Oxford
January 2015

I have been a master at Fordingbury School for over forty years. I attended the school as a boy and having gained my degree in Literature and the Classics, returned there to teach a range of subjects under the auspices of the then headmaster, Murdo MacPherson, who retired last summer after a long and distinguished career.
On Tuesday afternoons I take the Remove boys for

drama. There are fourteen in the class, and it is expected that the majority will gain a good grade in the end of year examinations.

Although academic qualifications are by no means the whole story – we have always prided ourselves on giving the boys a rounded education – we have had notable successes, with a number of pupils gaining a place at Oxford or Cambridge.

The Tuesday we are speaking of was no different from any other...

THREE

SOPHIE DIPS THE BRUSH INTO THE BUCKET, AND starts scrubbing. Forty-eight hours in the place, and she still can't believe the levels of dirt. What kind of person would allow things to get into this state? The skirting boards are ingrained with specks of fried food, and grease is spread under the gas stove in a translucent layer of yellowed wax.

She hasn't seen these levels of grime since her student days. Earlier, she caught sight of a large brown insect scuttling into a corner. She hopes it was a beetle, not a cockroach.

Dip, scrub, wipe. Dip, scrub, wipe.

The events of the past few days seem increasingly unreal. One moment, she and Miles are immersed in the ordered life of Fordingbury, with its rituals, timetables and bells, and the next here they are, in a cold and filthy house, in a run-down part of London.

No wonder Miles remains white-faced and silent. If she's finding it too much to take in, God knows what it's like for him.

She reaches for a cloth. If only she and Miles had picked up something from that breakfast phone call of Alan Sanderson's. At least that would have given them more time to prepare themselves. Miles wouldn't have been so easily wrong-footed that morning. They wouldn't have been so easily ousted. Yet no matter how hard she searches her memory she can't recall anything that gave cause for alarm.

'It seems I'm wanted at some board meeting.' Miles had gulped the last of his coffee. 'Pretty early, so there's obviously some panic on.' He'd smiled, no doubt pleased to be going to help.

'I'm off to the town,' she called after his retreating back. 'See you at coffee time!'

She was only gone a couple of hours, and it was as she re-entered the empty house, and placed her bag on the hall table, that she heard a noise from the study. 'Is that you, Miles?' No answer. The noise came again. A harsh sound that she couldn't identify. She felt a moment's unease. She didn't remember closing the study door. The noise came once more. Perhaps Carter's cat had got itself shut in again?

She eased open the door.

At first glance, the room seemed empty, the light from the window revealing Miles's desk, piled with papers, and the shelves of books, floor to ceiling, that ran around the remaining walls. Then she spotted him, slumped into a chair in the far corner. 'Miles?'

He looked up at her, his face ashen and, for one dreadful moment she thought: my god – a heart attack!

She moved over to him. 'What on earth's the matter?' A thought struck her. 'The girls…?'

He shook his head. 'They're fine. Listen, Sophie – I'll explain – later – for the – moment – just – do –as I – ask.' The harsh tone, the words coming out in staccato bursts, were so unlike him that she stood staring.

He ran his tongue over his lips. 'We have to leave Fordingbury. On Monday. We have to—'

She sank into an armchair. '*Leave*?' She ran her fingers through her hair, struggling to take in what he was saying.

'Alan assures me it's the only way. The board has to follow – procedures.' He hesitated. 'I'm not sure of the details yet. But I promise you, whatever's being said, is totally unfounded.'

She continued to stare at him.

'The school solicitor suggests I consult the union, but you know I never joined of course.' He was fighting back tears. 'So the upshot is, Sophie, we need to pack up our personal stuff and find somewhere to stay. They were quite insistent about it, even though it is only temporary. It needs to be in London, so I can be within easy reach of Marshalls. Oh – and we need to keep this under our hat.'

She listened, appalled. 'You'd never hurt a fly. How can they do this after all you've done for the school?'

He lowered his head again, moaning like some creature in pain. It frightened her to see him like this.

She went over and put her arms round him. 'Come

on now, darling. It's not *that* bad. Of course you must go along with what Alan Sanderson suggests.' She was using her most reassuring voice, the one reserved for sickbay emergencies. 'I'm sure he'll have your best interests at heart.'

'You're right.' He got unsteadily to his feet. His wan smile turned her heart over. 'Can I leave you to sort out the accommodation? I need to work out what books and papers to take.'

'Of course.'

'Nothing too pricey. The coffers are a bit low at the moment.'

She nodded. He was still very pale. 'Let me make coffee first. And then we can run through what needs doing.'

She remembers later that morning phoning Rachel in a panic, and the two of them huddled together in the empty sickbay.

'I've known you both over ten years.' Rachel's round face was soft with concern. 'It's unthinkable Miles would bully anyone.' She handed Sophie a tissue.

'Thanks.' Somehow she had to stay strong – too much was depending on her. 'He's taking it very badly, as you can imagine.'

'I'm surprised they're allowed to treat you like this.' She looked hesitant. 'What else has Miles told you?'

'Only what I've said. That he's been accused of bullying. And you can imagine how upset he is.' She sighed. 'It would be easier if he weren't insisting on London. I've made umpteen phone calls, and the rents are *exorbitant*. He says he'll continue to get his pay, so of course we'll

27

manage. But this has come just when the girls need our support through uni.'

'What an idiot I'm being!' The Welsh lilt in Rachel's voice always became more pronounced when she was excited. 'One of Brian's cousins rents out property. In South London, I think. Probably not a very salubrious area, but at least it would fill the gap. Would you like me to get on to him?'

'Oh, *could* you, Rach? That would be really great.'

She squeezed Sophie's arm. 'I know Alan's a new broom and all that, but for him to treat a staff member like this…'

Sophie blew her nose again. 'At least Miles's solicitors have a good reputation.'

'There you are, then. You'll be back here before you know it! Now, I must push on, but I'll phone through those details the moment I get hold of Brian.' She gave Sophie another hug. 'Promise to keep in touch. Don't go disappearing into the big smoke, even if it is only for a few weeks!'

Later, the promised phone call from Brian's cousin came. The rent seemed exorbitant, and for a longer letting period than they wanted, but what option did they have?

She found Miles sorting papers in the study. The afternoon was drawing in, the desk lamp throwing long shadows across the walls. He had removed a quantity of books from their shelves, the spaces as disconcerting as missing teeth.

'Oh, good,' he said, rather vaguely, when she told him she'd sorted the house problem.

Now was not the time to worry him with the rental

terms. 'Of course we need to tell the girls and Aunt Harriet.'

'Tell them what?' he snapped. 'All I know is there's a complaint against me. Let's wait till we're away from here and have more information.'

'But—'

'*Please,* Sophie.'

She bit her lip. They were talking about family, after all. But he was still so pale – it felt risky to upset him further.

The rest of the weekend was spent cancelling grocery deliveries, and deciding what to pack.

Miles had been instructed not to have further contact with either staff or boys, and neither of them went near the main building.

So the only person they saw was Hamish Laing, the geography master, who arrived on the doorstep on the Sunday evening.

Sophie let him in. 'How good of you to visit, Hamish. Miles will be so pleased to see you – he's in the study.'

'Hello, Laing,' Miles called. 'Come to give a hand?' He waved at the boxes on the floor. 'Would you believe the amount of stuff one accumulates?'

'This is not a social visit, Whitaker,' Laing said in his precise voice, never smiling or looking either of them in the eye. 'I am here to ensure that you leave by eight thirty in the morning, as directed.'

Up to now, Sophie had viewed him as someone who hid his vulnerability under a somewhat cocky exterior. His wife had walked out on him the previous year, and although never talked of openly, as always at Fordingbury the information seeped through the staffroom, as if by osmosis.

Now she felt torn between a desire to laugh – because really Laing was being quite ridiculous – and outrage. Obviously he was here at Alan Sanderson's behest.

Miles was silent – with shame? Indignation?

'Better keep to the timetable then, Hamish,' she said, 'interruptions permitting.'

Miles gave one of his wide smiles. 'I thought we might grab a spot of lunch en route, Sophie?'

'Good idea. Maybe that new place in Woodstock? Now, we've both got plenty to be getting on with. *If* it's all the same to you, Laing.'

*

From overhead comes the creak of a board. Miles must be awake.

She tips the bucket of water into the sink, watching it swirl down the plughole. Then turns, as Miles comes in, and they exchange a good morning kiss. She's used to seeing him smartly dressed in blazer and cords. Today, his breath smells sour, and he's still in yesterday's shirt.

'I've hung your clean clothes in the wardrobe.'

'I'll change later.' He seats himself at the Formica-topped table. 'Did we bring any bacon?'

'We certainly did.' She bustles around.

They eat in a silence she feels hesitant to break. It's only when they are on the last of their coffee that she leans across the table. 'I know what a terrible shock this has been, Miles, but we really do need to discuss what to tell the girls.'

He sips his drink. 'What do you suggest?'

'Perhaps just that you've been asked to leave while an inquiry takes place.' She pauses. 'Except I'm still not sure exactly what's going on.'

He gives a short laugh. 'Believe you me, you're not the only one.'

She pulls at a thread on her blouse. Surely the board wouldn't have been as vague as this. 'So, where does that leave us?'

He runs a hand over his face, its pallor accentuated by the dark smudges under his eyes.

'If I could just finish that report, it'll help get my thoughts in order.'

It's a reasonable enough request. 'Fine. I'll bring more coffee through when I've finished clearing up.'

He smiles, the lines around his eyes crinkling in the way she finds so endearing. 'We'll be back at Fordingbury by the end of the month, Sophie. I promise.'

It's an effort to return his smile and, once on her own, she's suddenly desperate for fresh air. She pushes back the metal bolts on the back door, and steps into the small garden. A fine drizzle is falling on the dilapidated shed and the waist-high winter grass. Another job that needs tackling, but by someone else, thank God!

There's a strong smell of tomcat, but at least she's in the open. She stands for a moment, face turned upwards, enjoying the rain on her skin.

Beyond the fence, a block of flats looms over the

31

surrounding rooftops. Most are in darkness, but several squares of orange light spill into the overcast morning. They resemble some large ship at anchor, she thinks, and it gives her a strange feeling to realise that the trip to New Zealand with Aunt Harriet is over a quarter of a century ago.

Suddenly she can see Alastair's green sports car driving away; can hear his: 'You'll be fine, Sophie,' echoing in her ears.

She wasn't, but when she returned to London, Miles was there, waiting. She always intended to tell him the reason for her abrupt departure, but somehow it never happened. And he never asked, she thinks, disconcerted by the memory.

There's a movement at one of the windows and, feeling watched, she turns and goes back inside.

She lights the gas under the milk saucepan, and tries to marshal her thoughts.

Surely the school has acted illegally? The board's treatment of Miles seems inexcusable. Yet it's odd that none of the staff has phoned to commiserate, and after that discussion with Rachel, Sophie's heard nothing further from her. She supposes they've all been instructed to have no contact. Perhaps there are even rumours of a tribunal?

They have lived at South Lodge for over twenty years, raised the girls there, and looked on it as their home. It's only over the past few days that the painful reality of their position has hit her, because of course, South Lodge is not theirs. It is part of the employment package that Miles negotiated with Murdo – a reduced salary in return for their accommodation and keep.

She remembers suggesting to Miles a while back that they buy a small flat. 'As a safety net.' He shook his head. 'Murdo will see us right. And, anyway, it would just be one more thing to manage.'

Why hadn't she pressed him further?

There's a hissing noise followed by a smell of burning. Blast! Sophie plucks the saucepan off the ring.

The kitchen stinks of burned milk. Their microwave is still in South Lodge, along with the rest of the kitchen gadgets. It would be good to send for it, but perhaps such a request will give the wrong message? Imply that they expect to remain here for more than a short time?

She looks at her watch. It's just after half ten – the time on school weekdays when Miles returns to the house for a quick coffee. She arranges some of his favourite shortbread on a plate. It's important to keep up some semblance of normality. Maybe she'll be able to persuade him to walk up to the shops with her?

She finds him slumped in one of the sagging chairs in the front room, papers strewn around him.

'How's it going?'

'I'm almost through that report for Rupert Marshall.'

'Well done!'

She hates to see that haunted look in his eyes. 'Once you've finished, let's go through it together. Two heads, and all that.'

He looks up, his mouth working, as if there aren't the words; as if she has him on some horrible hook.

FOUR

A FEW DAYS LATER, ON THE FRONT DOORSTEP, Sophie is still adjusting to being back in London after all these years. A light aircraft is skimming the rooftops – for a few moments drowning out the muted hum of traffic. In the distance, a car alarm sounds, and further along the road, someone shouts – a greeting? A warning?

But it's an urban myth, she thinks, to believe that the countryside is silent. Early morning at Fordingbury, for instance, is filled with the cooing of wood pigeons, the piercing call of blackbirds, and the raucous squabble of magpies.

If circumstances were different, she could enjoy being here. The ghosts of the past are long laid to rest and would, under different circumstances, leave her free to sample all the city has to offer. Miles's only wish is to escape. Despite all her pleading, he's still not been out of the house, and for the past twenty-four hours, she's barely had two words out of him.

The previous night, as they lay side by side on the lumpy mattress – stained from heaven knows how many ancient encounters – she reached through the semi-dark, running her fingers across his throat and chest. He turned away, as if half asleep already, and she felt more shut out than ever.

She looks up as a young woman emerges from the adjoining house, manhandling a pushchair. Two small boys pile out on either side. The youngest runs across the front area before catching his foot on the kerb and falling headlong. There's a silence, followed by a roar.

Sophie rushes over, picking him up and setting him on his feet. He looks to be about eight, skinny, with spiky hair and brown eyes too big for his face. One of his cheeks is grazed and, as she bends to take a closer look, he wriggles free of her.

She looks around and catches the mother frowning.

She's so used to dealing with children when there are no parents about, she half expects a master to emerge to sort things out. 'Sorry – I didn't mean to interfere.'

'No, you're all right.' The woman sighs. 'Ben's always falling over himself.' She's slim, wearing jeans and a leather jacket, with sleek, dark hair tucked behind her ears.

She turns to the boy. 'How many times do I have to say it? Watch where you're going!'

'Obviously no harm done,' Sophie says, as he begins trading punches with his brother.

'Henry's my eldest,' the woman says, cramming plastic bags in the space under the pushchair, 'and Leo's the one asleep, or he'd be screaming his head off too.'

'I'm Sophie – Sophie Whitaker.' She wonders whether to hold out her hand, but the young woman is still stooped over the pushchair, tucking a cover around the child.

She straightens up. 'Kirsty. You moved in earlier in the week?'

Sophie nods.

She looks at Sophie with undisguised curiosity. 'Stopping long?'

The face is narrow, not unattractive although the large jaw stops her being conventionally pretty.

'Only a month or so.' She pauses. 'We were let down over a house. Just waiting to get into our new place.'

'I said to Mike it'd be something like that. Number 49's a bit of a dump. No one stays longer than they can help.' She nods towards the Rover. 'Nice car. Should be safe enough up this end, though I'd still keep an eye on it, if I were you.'

'Thanks. And you? Have you been here long?'

'We moved in over a year ago. Used to be up at Victory House.'

Sophie looks blank.

'One of those tower blocks near the Tube. Couldn't wait to get away.' She pauses. 'You wouldn't want to know what goes on up there.'

Over thirty years since her days in A & E, but Sophie can still picture the drunken fights, and the pools of vomit and blood. 'I can imagine.'

'By the way, hope the boys' racket doesn't bother you?'

She shakes her head. 'My two girls were a handful at that age. I really miss them now they've left home.' She wants to say how proud she is they've both got into good universities.

Kirsty purses her lips. 'Your partner doing OK?'

How she hates that word! It makes marriage sound like some business arrangement.

'Yes, he's fine.'

'He isn't very friendly, if you don't mind my saying so. Looked straight through me the other morning.'

'Oh, I'm sorry. I'm sure he didn't mean to be rude.'

'Men, eh? Well, I'd best get some food in, or my three will bawl the frigging roof off.' Kirsty's smile softens her features.

Sophie watches as the young woman – a jaunty spring to her step – pushes the buggy away up the road.

Her account of Miles' behaviour was surprising. She's used to parents telling her how charming he is, and she thinks also that he'd find Kirsty attractive. She must remember to say something to him. Even if they're only here a short time, it doesn't do to go upsetting people.

It's begun spitting with rain, but she can't stay cooped up in that house a moment longer. She turns up her collar, just as her mobile rings. She clicks it on.

'Mum? Got hold of you at last! I was just starting to worry. How's the term going?'

'The thing is, Miranda, we're not at South Lodge. We're in London.'

'Don't tell me you've managed to drag Dad up to the bright lights? Good for you!'

'It's not quite like that, darling. You see your dad's been—'

'What did you say, Mum? This signal's awful, and I've a lecture starting any minute.'

'But this is really—'

'Catch you later.' And she's gone.

Just as well it's Miranda who's rung, Sophie thinks, as she starts walking up the road. Helena has always been the more astute – she'd have picked up something from my tone of voice.

For a moment, she is filled with longing to be back at South Lodge with the girls still at home. During their A level years, the three of them used to go for an early morning run, leaving the house just after six, jogging down the drive and along the track through the beech woods. From there they crossed the deserted sports fields, looping past North Lodge – occupied by Murdo, until his retirement – round the main school building and back down the gravel drive. It was too early for any of the boys to be about, though sometimes they heard the rising bell, followed by shouts and laughter from the dormitories. She was touched by the way the twins slowed their pace for her, abandoning their usual chatter. Looking back on it now, there had been something very special about that time.

Already the school seems a universe away. Impossible to imagine that this week she and Carter were due to discuss the planting of the summer beds. She'd like to phone him, but is it all right to do so? And once more her thoughts go back to the girls – how on earth will they react to hearing that their father has been suspended?

She must try and stop this needless worrying. She's never known Miles break his word, and if he's promised they'll be back at Fordingbury in a matter of weeks, then that is what will happen.

The rain finishes as suddenly as it started, and she's aware for the first time of the smell of the city – traffic fumes and the sour tang of wet pavement that she finds energising. She lengthens her step, passing the man walking his German Shepherd that she recalled from when they arrived; two women clothed from head to foot in black; a youth on a bicycle pedalling furiously along the pavement towards her, and swerving onto the road at the last minute.

As she waits to cross the main road, she thinks how lucky it is that everything they'll need for their short stay is here: a grocery shop, a chippie – though Miles of course won't touch fried food; and, beside it, Patel's, the newsagents. She'll pick up *The Telegraph* for Miles, and maybe some chops for supper.

Once over the road, she skirts round a group of hooded youths, who are standing, smoking and talking, and enters the shop.

An Indian woman, presumably Mrs Patel, is stacking magazines, but when she catches sight of Sophie, she moves behind the counter, shoulders slumped, feet shuffling in green sandals. Sophie holds out her newspaper. The headlines are full of the dreadful massacre in Paris. Those poor people, she thinks, their worlds and bodies ripped apart.

In response to Sophie's, 'Good morning!' the woman gives a weary smile. Sophie would like to say something more, but other customers have come in and are waiting to be served.

Outside on the pavement, she hesitates, an idea forming in her mind. She begins walking up the road, towards the spire she can see poking above the rooftops. The shops beside her are now even scruffier, some with steel shutters, the rest filled with second-hand goods and cheap clothing. She passes knots of men talking in doorways, young mothers with pushchairs and the ubiquitous youngsters in their hooded tops. She's aware suddenly of her too-smart raincoat, and her black Gucci bag – a Christmas present from the girls. She clutches it to her.

After a ten-minute walk, the church comes into view – late Victorian, set in a corner plot, and surrounded by conifers. A sign facing the main road gives the name: St Saviour's, and the times of the services. Miles always sets such store by his weekly attendance at chapel – it will do him good to come here on Sunday. Get him out of himself. Her own thoughts on God are vague and fleeting. A part of her feels that He – or She – is too vast to be crammed into a series of buildings – a view that at Fordingbury she keeps to herself.

She glances up at the church clock, and is surprised to see it's still only just after nine. At school, she would be sorting the weekly linen with Rachel, as well as seeing to the boys in sickbay. Already flu is going the rounds.

This break is only for a couple of months, but already she's relishing a sense of freedom.

She follows the sign to the entrance, turning a corner and going through an ivy-covered lych-gate, its surface crusted with dark, worm-eaten wood. She recalls Miles one summer holiday explaining to the girls, who must have been about twelve at the time, its use as a coffin rest. 'Lych – from the Anglo-Saxon "lichen" – a corpse,' he'd said. Helena raised her eyebrows. 'For heaven's sake, Dad! We're not in one of your classes!'

As she draws closer, Sophie can see the church walls are blackened by years of exposure to London grime, as are the stone figures set into niches. The scale of the place surprises her. She supposes people must have flocked here in its Victorian heyday. Nowadays they're probably lucky to get a dozen. 'O tempora O mores!' she can hear Miles saying.

The traffic in the road is muffled by shrubs and trees, giving the spot a tranquil feel. Half-a-dozen rooks circle overhead, wings flapping. As she watches them swoop onto the branches of a conifer, she feels her spirits lift.

She turns towards the porch, the outer door of which stands ajar. Stepping inside, she finds herself in a small area with a stone bench set against each wall. To her surprise, there's a noticeboard, plastered with brightly-coloured pieces of paper. It seems they have a thriving children's class here.

The inner door is oak, with brass studs. Reaching forward, she twists the iron handle and steps inside. The place is unlit – only the dim light from the window behind the altar revealing the outline of the pulpit and the rows of pews. She edges forward, taking a seat at the back, and allowing the silence to wash over her.

But the moment she closes her eyes, the face of the Cunningham boy appears before her. Rachel described him as a "toe rag", and it's true that there's something about him that is difficult to warm to. Not hard to believe, then, that he's concocted this preposterous charge because he has a grudge against Miles. That he—

'About to lock up, I'm afraid,' a voice behind her says.

'Oh!' She swings round, making out the figure of a tall man.

'Didn't mean to startle you.'

'Sorry. I didn't realise.' She moves outside and stands blinking in the light.

He joins her on the path, waving an arm towards the area of grass and trees. 'The churchyard is for everyone to enjoy. But I'm afraid the building itself has to remain closed most of the time – too much vandalism about.'

'That's a shame.'

He must be well over six foot – in his early forties, she guesses. Above the dog collar, the face is narrow and intelligent. A stretch of trousered ankle protrudes from beneath his surplice. It makes him seem slightly vulnerable.

'It's a popular place for all that,' he continues. 'We get all sorts in here – retired folk, down-and-outs, courting couples.' The accent is – Yorkshire? Lancashire? She always finds it hard to tell them apart.

'I should introduce myself.' He holds out a hand. 'Seb Webster. The vicar – in case you've not already worked it out!'

'Sophie Whitaker.' She returns his handshake, aware of the dry warmth of his skin. 'I was just looking up the times of the services. My husband and I are staying in the area for a short while. We're regular churchgoers, you know.'

Goodness, I sound pompous, she thinks, but he's smiling, and his eyes, a curious shade of chestnut, are warm. 'Good news indeed. You'll double the congregation.' Then seeing her expression, he adds, 'Only joking. My sermons aren't *that* bad.'

She tries to imagine David Wilson, the over-earnest Fordingbury chaplain, making a similar joke. The boys make fun of him behind his back. *Dave the rave; Willie Wonka.*

She realises instinctively that, despite his apparent flippancy, they would never take such liberties with the man standing before her. Too much of a live wire, she thinks, noting the expressive eyes that seem to absorb everything around him.

From nowhere, she finds herself saying, 'Making time for ourselves is pretty important, isn't it?'

He gives a vigorous nod. 'Without it, we're no good to anyone. But I'm a fine one to talk.' He laughs. 'I must away. Hospital visits, followed by a parish meeting.' He studies her for a moment. 'Hopefully we'll link up again on Sunday. You'll be most welcome, whenever you can make it.'

She watches him go off down the path, his surplice flapping round his ankles. What a relief he never asked about how she's come to be in London. There again, she senses that whatever she said, he'd understand. But no doubt that was being fanciful.

She wonders what Miles will make of someone so different from David Wilson. She herself is already looking forward to Sunday.

She glances up at the church clock – nearly quarter to. By now, any boys in sickbay will have been attended to, so it's as good a time as any to call Rachel. Sophie's already left several messages, but still hasn't had a response. Doubtless, she realises, with a pang of guilt, because *Rachel is having to do all my work as well as her own.*

She moves round the corner of the building, furthest away from the traffic noise, and takes out her mobile. She must try not to bombard her friend with questions, but she's the one person who can shed light on things. At the very least, she can tell her how the other staff members are reacting to Miles's departure.

The number rings. *Pick up, oh please pick up,* Sophie silently begs.

She listens to the voicemail message, before leaving her own. 'Rach – hello, it's me, Sophie. Hope all's well. I'm sorry to bother you again, but I'd love a quick word.' She pauses, fighting off her growing sense of unease. 'Give me a call when you get a moment. *Please.*'

FIVE

MILES STRETCHES HIS FEET TOWARDS THE FIRE, trying to summon up energy. His boxes of books are stacked in the corner, with that plant of Sophie's propped at an angle on the top. He's yet to make a start on unpacking them. Then there are his notes for Rupert Marshall, the solicitor, to go through again. Their meeting is only three days away.

When Sophie was out the other morning, he took himself up to the nearest off-licence and bought a supply of Scotch – just to help steady his nerves. He flips through the pages of yesterday's paper, wondering if he might sneak a small whisky. Sophie is still busy upstairs, so the coast is clear.

He's halfway along the passage when his phone starts to ring. He snatches it up. Perhaps it's Alan Sanderson, with an apology from the board?

'Ah, Miles. There you are!'

He can see the uncompromising stare and beaky nose. 'Aunt Harriet. How *are* you?'

'Don't give me any of that nonsense, Miles. Sophie's message said you were taking a short break. She doesn't answer any of my calls, and when I try ringing the school, there's an interminable wait and then that new headmaster – Alan whatshisname – informs me you're "not currently residing at South Lodge".'

He feels panic rising. 'What else did he say?'

'I'd have thought that was quite enough to be going on with.'

He draws in his breath. 'I'm sorry, Aunt Harriet. We should have told you earlier.'

'Told me *what* exactly?'

'Just that there's been a spot of bother.'

'I gathered *that*.'

Overhead comes the sound of running water – Sophie must be having a bath.

'The thing is, one of the boys has lodged a complaint against me.'

'What sort of complaint?' The voice sounds suspicious.

He feels his face redden. 'An allegation of bullying.'

'Bullying?' The old lady's voice has risen.

'There's nothing in it, of course. The Remove Year has always been tricky, but these days, schools have to follow protocol. You know how it is…' His voice tails away.

There's a sniff at the other end of the line and then to his relief Aunt Harriet says,

'Well, rules *are* rules, I suppose. Still, it seems a strange way to go about things.'

'As Alan Sanderson may have told you, it *is* only temporary. So Sophie and I decided to take a short break.' He stares at the faded wallpaper, and the sagging orange sofa. 'Make hay, and all that.'

'Is she there?'

'Sorry. She's just popped out for some milk.'

'Oh, well. As long as things are all right. For a moment I thought—'

'No – everything's fine. And you? I hope you're keeping well?'

There's a grunt at the other end of the line. 'Knee playing up. Last cold snap almost did for the big cherry tree. Both past our sell-by date, but mustn't grumble.'

'I'm afraid I have to dash, Aunt Harriet. Sophie wants to have a look around the shops. I'll get her to call you.'

'You do that, Miles.'

He clicks off the phone. One problem out of the way, at least for the time being. He lifts the net curtains – still a depressing grey despite the repeated washing Sophie has given them – and stares into another overcast morning.

It's almost ten o'clock – time for Sunday chapel. He's always loved the chanting of the Lord's Prayer and the hymns – two hundred boys lifting the roof off the place. Thankfully, his days as a junior master, having to lunch with the boys in the dining hall are long gone. Now, there's sherry with the head and the rest of the senior staff before a return to South Lodge for Sophie's Sunday roast.

He stares into the fire, remembering the recent memo from Alan, suggesting they drop the pre-lunch drink. As Miles pointed out in his response, not only was it the one time in the week when the staff could meet socially, it was also a tradition going back to the school's foundation. A great pity to do away with it, he added, with what he thought was remarkable restraint. He never received a reply, but surely he couldn't have been the only one to protest?

The memory of that Sunday sherry reawakens his need for a drink.

Murdo's voice: *Extremis malis extrema remedia, Whitaker!*

In the kitchen, he stoops over the corner cupboard, reaching past an assortment of chipped crockery and lifting out the whisky. He's not sure why he's hiding it away like this. Perhaps because, at Fordingbury, Sophie and he rarely touch the stuff.

He pours himself a generous slug, adding a splash of tap water. He drains the glass in a series of swift gulps, the heat snaking down his gullet.

Better have some coffee though. He doesn't want to smell of alcohol. As he switches on the kettle, he hears Sophie's steps, and turns as she comes into the room. She's wearing one of her pleated skirts and a cream blouse, above which her hair, in its neat bob, shines in the dim light. Somehow just the sight of her, moving with such an air of assurance, makes the world all right again.

'I slept like a log.' She comes towards him for a good morning kiss. 'How about you?'

'Fine.' He turns away, not wanting her to catch his whisky breath. 'Coffee?'

There's the slightest of pauses.

'Thanks.'

'Was that the phone?'

Now is obviously the time to tell her about Aunt Harriet's call. But suppose that leads to Sophie phoning her aunt back? Sophie's mother died when she was fifteen, since when Aunt Harriet has been like a mother to her. Any talk between them will inevitably lead to more awkward questions. No, he needs this meeting with the solicitor to work out what to tell everyone.

'Just one of those annoying marketing people,' he says. 'Toast?'

She shakes her head. 'I had some earlier.'

'I'll get back to my paperwork then. Could you be an angel and bring some coffee through?'

She regards him, unsmiling. 'You've not forgotten, Miles?'

'Forgotten?'

She folds her arms across her front in a gesture that indicates she means business. 'Church. You know we agreed to go.'

He pulls a face. 'Would you mind awfully if I didn't come this time? Next week, perhaps.'

She's glaring across at him. 'Dammit, Miles – *No!*'

He sighs in resignation, recognising that this is one of the few times when she's not going to give in.

Twenty minutes later, they let themselves out of the house and begin walking along the close. Overhead the sky is the same scratched grey as the pavement. From behind front rooms comes the blare of morning television, but to his relief there's no one about.

Deep down, he knows his reluctance to go outside is not due solely to his almost physical revulsion for these surroundings. There's also a fear that some perfectly ordinary stranger will take one look at him and know that there in front of him stands a man accused of breaking the laws of decency.

He glances at Sophie, but she's striding out, her gaze fixed on the pavement ahead. Sooner or later, he's going to have to tell her the full story – or as much as he himself knows – but not now, not today.

If only there were some way of finding out what his colleagues think – what they've been told.

'Did you manage to get hold of Rachel?' He tries to keep his voice casual.

Sophie has obviously been wrapped in her own thoughts, for she turns to him in surprise.

'Rachel. Have you spoken to her?'

'Oh – no. I'll try again this afternoon. I've left a couple of messages, but obviously she'll be up to her eyes.' She pauses. 'Doing my work as well as her own.'

Is there a note of reproach in her voice?

Now they're across the main road and, to his relief, the pavement outside the parade of shops is deserted. Sophie mentioned all the youths she's seen hanging about. 'No work, and little prospect of any.' There was sadness in her voice.

Yet most of those youths would have been out all hours, binge drinking, dealing drugs and God knows what else. It was nonsense to believe they couldn't make more of themselves. Anytime he's had one too many, he's always managed to pull himself together. He can hear Murdo's voice: *Show some backbone, Whitaker.*

'Not much further,' Sophie is saying.

They're passing a junk shop, its window crammed with an assortment of brass jugs, and crudely carved animals. He can't imagine anyone actually buying them.

'We'd better leg this last bit,' Sophie says, quickening her step.

A few moments later the church comes into view – a splendid example of late-Victorian architecture, with a fine perpendicular tower. They go through a lychgate and along a weed-filled path. Already they can hear singing. They creep in through the open door, choosing a seat halfway back in the vast nave.

It's then he has his first surprise. Although there are rows of empty pews, the congregation is larger than he imagined. Nearly forty parishioners, he reckons, and although it can't come up to the packed chapel at Fordingbury, nonetheless it's a respectable turnout, with the singing tuneful and robust.

'That's him!' Sophie whispers, as a lanky, surplice-clad man leads the prayers. At least it's not a woman vicar.

He only half follows the service. Well, he knew from the start he wouldn't take to the Alternative version. As they sit for the sermon, he glances at his watch. David Wilson never speaks for longer than ten minutes and is invariably upbeat, emphasising the importance of team spirit, fair play, and pulling one's weight. A sound fellow.

This man Webster, rather predictably Miles feels, begins banging on about inner-city poverty and bonuses. 'If each of us just listened to our consciences,' he declaims, 'then we would know the action we must take.'

Miles shifts in his seat, noting the heads craned forward to listen. Beside him, Sophie never takes her eyes off the man. Miles's view is partially blocked by a large black woman in a shiny pink jacket. There are only a handful of other men, mostly middle-aged or older.

He closes his eyes, letting the words wash over him. Not long to go until he can be back in that front room, perhaps treating himself to another whisky. He must stop hiding the bottle from Sophie, before it becomes too late to joke about it.

And then a truly appalling thing happens. As the organ plays the opening bars of the final hymn, to his horror Miles feels tears prick his eyes. "Fight the Good Fight" is the school hymn, and the last thing he'd have expected to hear in this place. The words and tune carry him back to the Fordingbury chapel. For a moment he can smell the polish and candle wax, can see the pews crowded with boys, and hear the roar of their voices. He digs his nails into his palm.

In desperation, he turns to Sophie, wondering if she's noticed, but she's looking ahead, singing in an unrestrained way that she's never displayed at Fordingbury. He blinks back tears.

'So, what did you think?' she whispers, as they make their way outside. She sounds elated.

He blows his nose. 'It was OK.'

The vicar is waiting by the porch entrance, greeting the members of the congregation as they file past. 'Ah, Sophie!' he says, when he catches sight of her. 'Great you could make it.'

'I thought your sermon was truly inspired. Oh, and this is my husband, Miles.'

He mumbles a greeting and, after a brief handshake, makes for the lych-gate.

He expects Sophie to follow, but when he glances over his shoulder, he sees that she's joined a group, all women, apart from one shaven-headed youth with a nose-stud, clustered round the clergyman. Webster says something that makes them laugh, waving his hands about in that irritating way he has.

He's desperate to head back to Stephen's Close, but Sophie has the house key. He tries catching her eye, but she's deep in conversation with the woman in the pink jacket.

'Miles!' To his dismay, Webster is beckoning him over. 'Come and join us!'

There's nothing for it but to walk over.

The black woman extends her hand and says in a rich, melodious voice, 'Hello, there. I'm Ruth Madiebo.'

The rest of the group introduce themselves, and Miles mutters something in reply.

If this were a sports day or a school concert, he'd be the one putting *them* at their ease, telling stories about his own time as a pupil, answering questions about the syllabus and the extracurricular activities. Now he feels paralysed.

At least there are no awkward questions. Everyone is obviously too caught up in what the clergyman has to say. Miles lets the talk carry on around him.

Only when Sophie is at last ready to leave, does

he have a final moment's discomfort. She beams her goodbye to Webster, who covers her hand with both his own. Then he turns to Miles. 'Good to meet you. I'm around, if you ever feel like a chat.' His eyes, an unusual shade of amber, remind Miles of the cat belonging to the caretaker, Carter, and suddenly he has the terrible feeling that Webster has seen right through him. He feels sick.

He and Sophie begin walking along the main road. He wants to say something about his instinctive mistrust of the man – what a people-pleaser he seems to be – but she's humming under her breath, her face animated.

Not that any of this matters, he reminds himself. The solicitor will soon have this whole damn mess sorted, and he and Sophie will be sharing a bottle of fizz, while he tells her his plans for a trip to Tuscany, where they honeymooned all those years ago. He's always intended for them to return, and this will be a way of making up for all the recent upheaval.

They're crossing the road opposite the newsagents, and she's saying something.

'What?'

'Such an interesting man!' She turns towards him. 'And what a varied bunch of people. That woman I was talking to, Ruth Madiebo, is a psychologist. Apparently she and Seb met in Africa – Zimbabwe, I think it was.'

So it was "Seb" already.

'I thought we might go again next week.'

Over my dead body, Miles thinks.

They walk the rest of the way in silence.

SIX

H E WAKES WITH A START TO THE ROAR OF A PLANE, and squints at the clock. It's not even half five. Will he never get a decent night's sleep?

He rolls onto his back. In the orange glow from the street light, he can make out the plywood chest of drawers, the wicker chair piled with clothes, and the open door of the wardrobe, a gaping mouth in the semi-dark.

A dead leaf blows towards him out of nowhere. Except it isn't a leaf, but an angle shades moth – *phlogophora meticulosa* – pale brown, with a v-shaped patterning of green and pink. He's never spotted one this early in the year. Helena is always going on about this global warming business, and you only have to look at those African women on the news, trudging miles for water across a desolate landscape, the skinny children with protruding bellies trailing behind, to see her point.

Beside him, Sophie's steady breaths fill the silence.

It pains him to recall the way she's been cleaning and scrubbing away in this dreadful little house, as if her life depends on it.

He recalls the South Lodge kitchen, installed only a couple of months ago as a way of cheering her up. Brian, the husband of the school matron, runs a kitchen and bathroom shop, and helped with the design. The whole thing was arranged, with special approval from Murdo, while Sophie was visiting Aunt Harriet in Cornwall.

It was far more pricey than he'd wanted, but worth it, because when Sophie walked in and saw the oil-fired Aga, the chrome surfaces, and the concealed lighting, she was too stunned to do more than murmur, 'Oh, Miles – you really shouldn't have.' And he'd felt a glow of pride.

Now he leans over her, studying the streaks of silver in her hair, and the faint lines across her forehead. Obviously she's finding all this upheaval a strain, and he minds – Christ! How he minds – that the two of them have been put in this shameful position.

When they married all those years ago, all he wanted was to carry her off to Fordingbury and keep her safe. From what, exactly, he was not entirely sure. Something or someone had caused that look of pain he glimpsed in her eyes, but she obviously didn't want to talk about it, and somehow he never plucked up the courage to ask. Too afraid, perhaps, of driving her off, because it seemed little short of a miracle that this young woman, with her Grecian curves and curtain of blonde hair, was actually agreeing to marry him.

They hadn't slept together beforehand, something that he didn't feel able to insist on and, if he were honest, also felt a relief. For once she found out how inexperienced he was, she might well change her mind.

After the reception, they travelled to a small inn near Bridport – the recommendation of a Fordingbury colleague – arriving just before midnight. They were greeted by a landlady, who looked as if she'd walked off a stage set – bright red hair, scarlet mouth and high heels. 'Clapham and Tooting! Common stamped all over her!' he could hear Murdo saying.

The landlady handed him a pen so that he could sign the register – Mr and Mrs Whitaker – and gave a wink. He felt himself blush. He had needed to stay sober for the drive down, and what he longed for at that moment was a nightcap. A large one.

With his bride clutching his arm, he followed the landlady up the stairs.

'The honeymoon suite,' she announced, showing them into a square room at the top of the building. It had low beams on which Miles was to crack his head over the next twelve hours, and bare, uneven boards. A four-poster with a pink satin bedspread took up most of the space. She opened a door in the far corner to reveal a bathroom painted an avocado green.

Her heels clacked over to the door. 'The bar's closed.' She gave a weary smile. 'Please don't create a disturbance, Mr and Mrs Whitaker – the other residents will be wanting their rest.'

The door swung to behind her, and his new bride turned towards him, giving a very un-Grecian-like giggle. 'Do you think the whole place will be listening in?'

She sank onto the bed, flicking off her shoes, and it struck him that the very decent Burgundy that had flowed throughout the day– it had to be said that Sophie's Aunt Harriet wasn't stingy – must still be having its effect. As if to confirm his impression, she began stripping off her clothes, tossing her silk dress and jacket on the floor, before peeling off bra, stockings and panties.

'Oh blast – must have a wee!' She tiptoed unsteadily across the floor to the bathroom, breasts swinging. He stood listening to the tinkle of her urine and this, even more than her nudity, embarrassed him.

Suddenly the thought of what lay ahead felt unbearably daunting.

Put some backbone into it, Whitaker!

He rooted through his suitcase for his wash things.

Hearing the lavatory flush, he turned and watched Sophie lurch across the floor and fling herself onto the bed.

His eyes roved up and down her body. Her arms were stretched above her head and he could see the whole magnificent length of her – broad shoulders and large breasts, the right nipple slightly bigger than the left, the swelling of her belly with its triangle of blonde fuzz at its base, and the spread of shapely legs below.

'Well, come *on* then!' she cried, as if she were inviting him in for a swim. And in a way, wasn't that just what he was doing? Over thirty years old and about time too! He stripped off his clothes and dived on top of her.

He was relieved by how uncomplicated it proved to be. Entering her was as easy as pushing a knife through butter, and the moment of climax brief, but satisfying. He rolled off her with a glow of triumph, the smell of her filling his nostrils. Next moment, she turned on her side, and was asleep.

*

A thump from next door brings him back to the present. Of course – today he has his first meeting with the solicitor – the first step towards his return to the school.

The only difficulty, he thinks, watching her turn onto her side, is Sophie. Despite all his attempts to dissuade her, she seems determined to accompany him.

He swings himself out of the bed, which creaks, like everything else in this bloody house. In the bathroom he has a quick wash before pulling on his clothes and creeping down the narrow stairs.

In the kitchen, he makes tea, ignoring the ancient toaster, and settling for bread and marmalade. Perhaps after his meeting with Rupert Marshall he'll pop along to the Strand and treat himself to lunch at the Savoy Grill. Murdo always enthused about it, which reminds him – despite having sent a letter filling the old boy in on what's been happening, he's heard nothing from him. *Any advice you can give, will be greatly appreciated*, he wrote. He assumes the school will forward his mail from South Lodge, but so far nothing has come. Something else to check with the solicitor.

He also needs to work out how much to tell the girls about his suspension. Miranda isn't likely to ask awkward questions, but he wishes he could be more confident of Helena.

He gets up and, walking along to the front room, retrieves his A4 pad, tucked away behind a pile of books. Settled at the kitchen table again, he reads through his account of events. Even if he says so himself, both Fordingbury and he himself come out rather well. Yet, as he shoves the papers into his briefcase, he has a sudden picture of Cunningham's pale face and sly smile. On his return to the school, he'll ask for the boy to be transferred to another class. Let someone else deal with the little sod.

But for now there remains the problem of Sophie. He looks at his watch. It's nearly seven. But he must try not to panic.

It's as he carries his breakfast things over to the draining-board that the solution comes to him. So simple he doesn't know why it hasn't occurred to him before.

Back in the kitchen, he scribbles her a note – *Gone up to town, back around lunchtime. Will explain later* – and unhooks his coat from behind the door. He hears a movement behind him, and freezes. He turns to see her standing, bleary-eyed, in the doorway.

For a brief moment, he thinks of making a break for it, pushing past her with some muttered excuse. But even as the thought comes to him, he knows it's too late. He shoves the note into his pocket.

She eyes his briefcase. 'Don't tell me you were planning to go to this meeting without me? For heaven's sake, Miles!'

She comes towards him, putting her arms round his neck and clasping him to her.

She smells of the flowered soap she uses. 'I know you don't want to give me extra worry, but don't you see that bottling things up only makes it worse?'

She removes her arms, and he steps back. To his relief, he sees that she's smiling.

'Now, I won't hear any arguments. You've hardly touched your food all week. Take off your coat and I'll scramble us some eggs.'

He sits at the table, watching as she melts butter in a saucepan, whisks eggs and puts out plates and cutlery. All done with a brisk efficiency that makes his heart sink.

SEVEN

HE ASSUMED SOPHIE WOULD DRIVE THEM UP TO the Strand, one advantage at least of their going together, but she's refused outright. 'I honestly don't think I'd find the way, Miles, not through all these back streets. On top of that, there's the congestion charge, and then we can't be sure of the parking. You know what London's like.'

He nods, although in point of fact, he does *not* know. When the twins were growing up, the four of them went each year to a Christmas show, taking the train to Paddington and then a taxi to the theatre. Later, Sophie and the girls went to West End musicals and on shopping trips to Oxford Street and Knightsbridge, and he was happy enough to be left behind.

His mental picture of London is of somewhere little changed from his own childhood visits with his father: Madame Tussauds, the Planetarium, the Tower of London, feeding the Trafalgar Square pigeons, feeding themselves at a Lyons Corner House. All taken in at such a breakneck rate that Miles wonders in hindsight if his father had not shared a similar aversion to the city.

Now, as he closes the door of the house behind him, he can feel his stomach churn.

It's spitting with rain.

'Never mind, we've got brollies.' Sophie turns up the collar of her raincoat.

'I can get us to the Tube all right, and I've got the map on my phone just in case.'

Miles is only half listening. Now that he's outside, he feels disorientated. It takes a moment to realise that the faint rumble in the distance is from the traffic up on the main road.

He catches up with Sophie, and she puts her arm through his. 'Let's get a move on. It looks as if the heavens are about to open!'

As several large drops of rain fall, Miles opens his umbrella and holds it over them, immediately feeling shielded from any curious stares, although of course it's ridiculous to think that a couple like them would attract attention or curiosity.

As he expected, the main road is filled with traffic. There's the row of shops opposite: the Patels, a shop selling second-hand furniture, a bookmakers, and further along a fish and chip place. The rain has now turned into a steady downpour and outside the bookies, a knot of young men huddle together, their heads concealed by the hooded jackets they all wear. The traffic cuts off their lower bodies, making them resemble a band of medieval monks.

He risks a quick glance at the other pedestrians, and feels another twinge of unease. Most are scruffily dressed in padded jackets and his Austin Reed raincoat, and Sophie's Burberry seem old-fashioned and out of place. He looks across at her, wondering if she feels the same, but she's busy dodging puddles, weaving her way between the other walkers. He hangs onto her arm, feeling like a ship being towed towards port, the umbrella an unwieldy sail above their heads.

They pass under a dank metal railway arch before climbing the steps to the Tube. They buy their tickets, and then there's another slow-moving escalator, with a swirl of people moving in both directions.

As they stand on the crowded platform waiting for their train to pull in, he realises he's forgotten how London *smells* – metallic and dusty. Staring at the tiled walls, the advertisements for cheap loans and the passengers staring blankly ahead, he thinks: *l sol tace* – where the sun is silent.

When their train pulls in, they find seats, jolting along for what seems an eternity, emerging into the glare of each station before plunging once more into the darkness. He's relieved when, eventually, Sophie leads the way out of the carriage and up a succession of escalators.

They come out into the daylight and begin walking along the Embankment. It's stopped raining and beside them the Thames reflects patches of faded blue. A sharp wind slaps waves against the arches of Hungerford Bridge. Men, all younger than he, walk past, either in conversation with a colleague, or with mobiles clasped to their ears. He glances at his watch. Eleven thirty-five – Greek translation with the Upper Sixth. Now *there's* a promising group – more than one of them headed for Oxbridge, if he's not mistaken. No doubt Miller, the junior master, still in his thirties and a bit full of himself, will have been asked to step into Miles's shoes. Still, he seems competent enough, and Miles can make up any gaps on his return.

'Is this it?' Sophie has come to a halt in front of a Georgian building. Steps lead up to a cream panelled door with a row of brass plates on one side. The place has been done up since they were last here for the reading of his father's will in old George Marshall's time – fifteen years ago it must be.

He lets Sophie go ahead, willing himself not to panic.

Inside, a young woman in a silky top and grey jacket sits behind a modern reception desk. She shows them into an empty waiting room with comfortable chairs, a glass-topped table with an array of glossy magazines, and still-life paintings on the walls.

He doesn't recognise any of it.

'Mr Marshall won't keep you long.' The accent is impeccable – Roedean or Cheltenham Ladies, perhaps. The girl waves a manicured hand towards the coffee machine in the corner. 'Do make yourselves at home.'

He sits in the nearest chair, aware of his dry mouth and increased heart rate. He still hasn't thought of what to say to Sophie. She's settled in a chair and is flicking through a magazine. The carriage clock on the side table says twenty to the hour, so now's the time. He opens his mouth to speak, but at that moment the receptionist comes back in.

'Mr Marshall realises it's a little early, but he's ready for you now.'

He stands and, as he'd expected, Sophie makes to follow him. He turns to her.

'I'll start things off, shall I, sweetheart?'

She stares in surprise.

'You can join us when the preliminaries are done.'

For one ghastly moment, he thinks she's going to protest. Then, unexpectedly, the receptionist comes to his rescue. 'I'll fetch you the moment your husband sends word, Mrs Whitaker.'

Sophie is looking at him with disbelief. He avoids her eye, following the girl out of the room. They walk past the desk and along a short passage to a door at the far end. She knocks and, without waiting for a reply, pushes it open. The room, large and square, contains a desk and chrome chairs with brown leather seats. The row of filing cabinets that was there in George's time has gone. Through the window Miles glimpses the winter skeletons of plane trees, with a modern office block behind.

Rupert Marshall gets up from his desk, and he and Miles shake hands. In his late fifties, Miles guesses, Rupert is a shorter, thinner version of the father, but with the same receding hairline and slight stoop to the shoulders. 'Here, let me take your coat.'

'Your father's keeping well?' Miles asks, as he hands it over.

'All things considered.'

'My father often spoke of him. You know they met up regularly at Round Table dinners?'

'Indeed. Have a pew.'

Miles waits to see if more information is forthcoming, but the solicitor has seated himself behind the desk and is leafing through a folder. Not a computer in sight, Miles notes with approval.

'Now,' Rupert Marshall begins, 'I've read through the account you sent.' He pushes his glasses further onto his nose in a way that is reminiscent of the older man. 'Let me see. A preliminary letter came in from the school's solicitors two days ago. Fordingham, isn't it?'

'Finding*bury*,' Miles says, thinking that old George would never have made such a mistake.

'Yes. Well.' Rupert peers at Miles again. 'We need to go over several points, Mr Whitaker.'

'Miles – please.'

He nods, and there's a silence, while he studies the papers in front of him.

Miles relaxes in his seat, confident he's done a pretty good job in setting things out.

Rupert Marshall unscrews the top of a pen and draws a pad towards him. 'For a start, we need to have an actual date in here.'

Miles leans forward. 'Oh, I thought I'd included it. Two weeks into the new term. The twentieth it would have been.'

'And the location of the incident?'

He feels himself blush. 'The changing rooms. The ones in the block by the sports pavilion. There are three blocks in all – the other two are in the main building – one for the juniors and the other for the—'

'Quite so.' Rupert peers across the desk again. 'I take it you still don't want to consult anyone at the ATL?'

'The union? Good god, no.'

Rupert gives a thin smile. 'That's what I thought.'

'I have written to the former headmaster, Mr MacPherson, to ask for his advice. He's a sound man.'

'Excellent idea. Now, let's go over the details, shall we?' He leafs through his papers. 'Although your information about the school is all very interesting, Miles – the way it's modelled on Eton, and so forth – we do need to focus only on what's relevant. There'll be time enough for you to explain your position more fully when you give your evidence.'

'Evidence?' Miles leans forward. 'You're not saying it's going to come to that?' He wonders if his voice sounded as panicky as he feels. 'Surely once they've read my account of events, they'll realise the whole thing's a pack of lies?'

The eyes regarding Miles are shrewd, but not unkind. 'That's a Not Guilty plea, I take it?'

Miles has nothing against the man – it's just he's not George, who would by now be making sympathetic noises. 'Poor show! What a bad business,' Miles can imagine him saying. Now he's starting to feel as if he's being put through a rigorous exam in which, if he's very lucky, he might just scrape a pass.

'It probably won't come to court. These cases often collapse at an early stage.' The solicitor pauses. 'I take it you still haven't heard anything from the police?'

Miles shakes his head.

'That's good news for us. They must still be assessing the boys' evidence.'

'The *boys*?'

'Yes.' The solicitor studies the folder again. 'Here we are. Justin Cunningham, Luke Owen and Christopher Webb. We are awaiting their statements. They may, of course, be so much hot air, but we do need to be prepared.' He gives a slight cough. 'But I just wanted to make one thing perfectly clear, Miles. You do realise that the charge against you is not straightforward bullying? That it is in fact a sexual one?'

He nods.

'Good – if we could just run through these points then.'

Owen and Webb also, Miles thinks. Cunningham has always been a devious little bastard. But why those two? He digs his nails into his palms, letting the solicitor's talk drift over him.

'So,' Marshall is saying, 'Section 9s are used when the evidence is presented in written form, and Plea Bargaining is the deal we can strike with the prosecution.' He leans back in his chair. 'I think that just about covers it for today.' He looks across at him. 'Any questions for me?'

'The whole thing's ridiculous,' he manages to get out. 'As I keep telling you, nothing whatever happened. But how does anyone prove a negative?'

The solicitor regards him. 'That is my job.'

He wishes the man's tone were less formal. 'I've promised my wife we'll be back at Fordingbury by the start of next term. That seems reasonable enough, doesn't it?'

'Let's see how it goes, shall we?' Marshall pushes back his chair. 'In the meantime, I must advise you to have no contact with the school.' He peers at Miles over his glasses. 'That way we won't go digging any holes for ourselves.'

'Oh – yes.' He wishes things were clearer in his mind, yet as in that dreadful boardroom meeting, he's left even more confused. What exactly is going to happen next? *If* it happens? He'd like to ask Marshall to recap, but perhaps that will only make him look more guilty as well as stupid?

'My secretary will arrange a convenient time for your next appointment,' Marshall says. 'Oh, and by the way,' he adds, 'I understand your father had some sort of financial arrangement with mine. Obviously that is no longer appropriate.' He holds out his hand for Miles to shake. 'I'll put a copy of the firm's fees in the post. If you have any queries, meanwhile, do feel you can get in touch.'

At God knows how much a pop, Miles thinks, wishing he'd prepared himself better. He realises now he came here telling himself all this was just a formality – a matter of time before Fordingbury opened its doors to him again. But suppose it doesn't?

The waiting room has filled. There's a young couple in the corner, three elderly women and a man in his forties; all well heeled, looking up at him, assessing his not quite smart enough coat, and the slight hesitance in his manner.

Sophie rises from her chair and comes towards him.

'Let's go,' he whispers, aware of the stares directed at them.

'But the meeting?'

'Oh, no, that's finished.'

She bites her lip, then pushes ahead of him through the door.

He was hoping they might walk together so that he could tell her about his worries; receive reassurance that Rupert Marshall has it all wrong, and that things will blow over.

But Sophie is going at such a brisk rate that he has to break into a half-run to keep up.

EIGHT

THE FOLLOWING MORNING, DOING THE WASHING IN the upstairs bathroom, Sophie remains outraged.

'I felt such a fool, Miles,' she told him, the moment they were back in the house. 'Did you think me incapable of following legal niceties?'

'I didn't mean it to come to this—' he began, but his voice was so uncertain she found herself shouting.

'For God's sake, tell me what's going on! It's *my* life too!'

But he only walked through to the front room, closing the door behind him.

Since then, they've barely spoken. At mealtimes, she slams his food on the table, avoiding his gaze, which is both hesitant and hangdog – like one of the boys caught out in some misdemeanor. If only she knew what he's meant to have *done*, for she recognises that her anger is also fuelled by fear. Bullying, kicking, hitting – how could anyone possibly credit it?

As she drapes the wet clothes over the bath, she recalls the numerous emergencies they've dealt with over the years: broken bones and concussion, a fire in the kitchen – mercifully contained – a tree falling on the assembly hall one winter night. And then that dreadful time when Miranda was rushed to A & E with meningitis.

Sophie remembers sitting in the hospital waiting room, while Miles spoke with the doctor in the authoritative tones he used at the school. But away from Fordingbury, she thinks, he's like a fish out of water. Maybe the reason for all this secrecy is not that he has something to hide, but that he doesn't know *how* to talk about what he is going through. After all, the school has been his whole life.

She switches on the kettle. Whatever the truth of it, she needs to stay calm – for both their sakes. 'I didn't mean to corner you, Miles,' she'll say, 'but I do need just a *bit* more information.'

She's putting milk on the table when he appears in the kitchen.

She smiles, and a look of relief crosses his face.

'Coffee's ready.' She moves over. 'I'm sorry for shouting at you, Miles.'

'If you'd just give me a chance to explain.'

'Of course.'

They sit at the table.

He spoons sugar into his coffee. 'It's just that Rupert Marshall went through things at such a rate, there was no opportunity for you to join us.'

'So what exactly did he say?'

'That's the thing. He still doesn't even know whether any actual charges will be brought. The police haven't made contact, so he's fairly positive they won't be.'

Her phone starts to ring. 'Hang on a moment.'

'Ah – you're there.'

'Aunt Harriet! I've been meaning to call you. Everything all right?'

'Did Miles not tell you I rang?'

She raises her eyebrows at him. 'No – when?'

'A couple of days ago.'

He pushes back his chair. 'Just going for the paper,' he mouths.

'What about your coffee?'

He gives a shake of his head, before reaching for his coat. A moment later, she hears the slam of the front door.

'... and after speaking to that new headmaster, I must admit I was worried.'

'I'm sorry Miles forgot to mention your call.' Why does she always end up apologising? 'He has a lot on his mind.'

Aunt Harriet sniffs. 'Yes, and this whole bullying allegation seems most extraordinary. You're sure you're getting good advice?'

'From one of the top firms in London, Aunt Harriet.'

'Well, if you need a few days by the sea, you know where to find me.'

The happiest days of Sophie's childhood were spent in her aunt's cliff-top house in Cornwall. She could still picture the stems of pink thrift blowing in the sea wind, and herself as a small girl running down the path to the shore, the swooping cry of gulls in her ears, and the crunch of shingle under her feet.

That wonderful sense of being both carefree and cared for – before those times came to such a shocking and abrupt end.

What wouldn't she give to be back there?

She feels tears well up.

'Sure you're all right, Sophie?'

That's the thing about Aunt Harriet – under the harsh exterior is a kindness that Miles has always refused to recognise.

She swallows. The last thing she wants is to burden her aunt. 'Of course. I'll call you again soon. Promise.'

So what I must do now, she thinks, sipping her cold coffee, is to concentrate on the present crisis. Because there's still the problem of the girls, who must be told about it, and soon.

They've already texted her today. *R U OK, Mum*? From Miranda. And from Helena: *N E nuz?* And Sophie replied: *All fine. Luv U.*

Although the twins have the same dark hair and high cheekbones, Helena has a smaller, upturned nose and is the shorter of the two. 'Quite the wrong way round,' Miles said, launching into a summary of *A Midsummer Night's Dream*, and the statuesque Helena.

In one sense they'll always be my babies, Sophie thinks, although anytime she voices this, Miranda laughs, and Helena raises her eyebrows. 'Get real, Mum!'

If only there were someone she could talk things through with, but both Marcia and Connie, her two closest friends, are out of reach – one on a world cruise and the other having a knee replacement.

Of course, she has other friends at Fordingbury – women with whom she runs fund-raising events or meets up with for coffee – but they're hardly people she can confide in. Which only leaves Rachel. Sophie pictures the round face, with its mass of curly hair, can hear the Welsh lilt: 'Think *you've* got problems, *cariad*? Let me tell you about…'

So what do I want from her? she asks herself. Yet already she knows the answer. She needs someone who'll listen to her questions without judging.

For a start, surely Miles should have fought his corner a bit more? Did he do a runner, in much the same way he shot out of the house just now rather than speak to Aunt Harriet? Perhaps he caved in to Alan Sanderson when there was no need? According to Miles, it was merely a *request* to leave. Although looking back, it was surely more than that. She recalls Laing's voice: 'You have twenty minutes in which to vacate the house.' The whole thing had been humiliating, intolerable, but she'd gone along with it. Should she have put up more of a fight? Refused to go even?

She's putting rashers under the grill when Miles reappears, a newspaper tucked under one arm.

'You went out of the door pretty sharpish.'

'I'm sorry – I wanted some air.' There was a pause. 'Is that brunch I smell?'

'It is.'

'Oh, good! Would you be an angel, and bring mine through to the front room? I need to get on with my paperwork.'

And perhaps because waiting on him all these years has become such an ingrained habit, she finds herself saying, 'Of course. One egg or two?' – as if all that's happening is of no consequence.

But for now, the main thing is to keep busy. She carries his breakfast through, gives the windowsills another wipe down, and has just begun mopping the hall lino, when there's a rap on the front door. Perhaps it's Kirsty from next door?

'I'll get it!' she calls, wiping her hands on her skirt, and tugging the door open.

'Good afternoon.' The policeman is young and fresh-faced as a sixth-former. Beside him is an older woman, also in uniform. She stares at Sophie, her eyes steely.

'Mrs Whitaker?'

She feels a moment's panic. 'My daughters—?'

'It's your husband we've come to see, Mrs Whitaker. May we come in?'

Sophie gestures behind her. 'He's in here. What do you—?'

But the pair are already in the hall, flashing identity cards. She just has time to call: 'Miles!' and then they're pushing past her into the front room.

She follows behind, wishing she'd cleared away Miles's brunch, the congealed remains of which are on the table beside him. He's in one of the green armchairs, feet stretched towards the fire. A look of alarm crosses his face, and he half rises in his seat.

'Miles Whitaker?'

'Yes?'

'I'm Detective Inspector Benson, and my colleague here is Detective Sergeant Perkins.'

'Oh.' For a moment, his voice wavers, but then recovers. 'Please. Take a seat. My wife, Sophie, will make you a drink. Tea? Coffee?'

The two officers exchange a look. In this cramped room with its sagging furniture and stink of fried food, his bonhomie must surely be striking a false note.

'Would you stand, Mr Whitaker?'

'Oh – of course.'

He gets to his feet and, once again, Sophie is reminded of one of the boys facing a ticking off.

'Miles Francis Whitaker, we are arresting you on suspicion of the sexual assault of a minor. You do not have to say anything, but anything you do say will be taken down and may be used in evidence. Do you understand?'

Sophie puts out a hand to steady herself. She wants to say something, but the words won't come. She looks across at Miles, who is also silent, staring down at the floor.

'Do you understand?' the policewoman repeats.

He gives a slow nod.

'We need to ask you some questions. If you could accompany us to the police station.'

'Well, I—'

'*Now* please, sir.'

She waits for him to tell them this is all a big mistake, but when he still doesn't speak, she turns to the policewoman. 'You can't do this, can you? Just walk in here?'

The cold eyes appraise her. 'Your husband, Mrs Whitaker, is facing serious allegations.'

Miles has turned pale. 'I'll fetch my coat.'

'One more thing, Mr Whitaker. Do you possess a laptop?'

'A laptop?' Miles stares as if he's been asked to produce a rabbit out of a hat. 'The only one I use belongs to the school. I left it behind when we came here.'

There's a pause.

'If you don't believe me, you can search the place.'

But that's the truth, Sophie thinks. Why are they treating him as if he's a liar?

'Thank you, sir. I'll just take a quick look around, then.' The young sergeant examines the corner shelving of books, before going out of the room. Sophie listens to his feet pounding along the hall to the kitchen. There's the sound of drawers being opened and closed, and the scrape of furniture being shifted, before he doubles back and climbs the narrow stairs.

After a couple of minutes he returns, shaking his head at the woman officer.

'We need your mobile phone,' she says.

Miles hands it over.

'Now, if we could continue this at the station?'

Sophie has no intention of being excluded again. 'I'm coming with you,' she hisses, as she and Miles go into the hall. They put on their coats and follow the two officers outside, Sophie locking the door behind them.

The police car with its orange stripe and clear markings is unmistakable. She glances up. Kirsty, with Leo balanced on her hip, is staring out of next-door's window.

She gets into the back of the car with Miles, and they're

driven slowly out of the close. Too slowly for her liking, because already doors are opening. A young housewife, and an old man clutching a Zimmer frame, stand watching them. She resists the urge to duck down in her seat.

Miles is muttering something. She turns towards him. He's still so white.

'The number, Sophie.'

She stares uncomprehendingly.

'Of Marshalls. I don't have it on me.'

'Don't worry – I'll find it,' she whispers.

The car is turning out of the close and picking up speed.

She glances out of the window, fighting back tears.

The police don't make arrests without evidence. So why has Miles spun her this story about bullying? Though it's possible, of course, that he's done so out of sheer fright.

Any other explanation doesn't bear thinking about.

NINE

WITH THE SERGEANT AT THE WHEEL, THEY DRIVE through the maze of side streets, the car attracting impassive stares from passers-by. Neither he nor the policewoman speaks, but when the radio breaks into a harsh cacophony, in the seat beside her, Miles flinches.

They reach the main road, with the Patels, the chippie, the launderette. She sits back, feeling curiously detached from it all.

Now they're passing under the railway bridge and the entrance to the Tube. Beyond it are more shops, some with steel shutters, and, over to the right, a tower block. They turn off the main road and skirt the building. *Victory House,* a huge sign says. She cranes her neck. There must be at least twenty storeys, rimmed with concrete balconies. The only signs of life are a rusting bicycle and an overflowing litter bin. No wonder Kirsty was so glad to get away.

A few minutes later they pull up outside another modern block. In a daze, Sophie follows the two officers and Miles up a short flight of steps, and in through double doors.

The crowded reception area could be that of a hospital. There's the same smell of pine disinfectant, the same underlying trace of urine and vomit. An untidy queue has formed by the desk, and the row of plastic seats along the far wall is almost full. Behind the desk, uniformed officers ask questions, peer at screens, and shout enquiries.

The woman inspector points to the line of chairs. 'Wait over there, please, while I get the paperwork sorted.'

They settle at the end of a row.

Sophie can contain herself no longer. In a furious whisper she demands: 'For God's sake, tell me what you've done!'

Beside them, a man in paint-covered jeans turns and stares.

'Nothing – I promise you.'

She lowers her voice. 'Then why are we here, Miles? You're being accused of this terrible thing' – she can't bring herself to name it.

He turns to her, his eyes wide with shock. 'Can't you understand that whatever they're saying is a lie?'

His face wears such a hurt look that she's immediately filled with remorse. She's lived with him for over twenty-five years, for heaven's sake. It's inconceivable she wouldn't have picked up on something like this.

She gives a slow nod. 'I'm sorry.'

He squeezes her hand. 'We must get hold of Marshall.'

'Of course. What do you want me to say?'

He swallows. 'Just ask him to come straight over.'

She moves over to a relatively quiet corner and looks up the number on her phone, her hands shaking.

'I'm afraid Mr Marshall is tied up in a conference call,' a woman's voice says. 'I'm one of the clerks.'

'Could you interrupt, please? It's urgent.'

'I'm afraid that won't be possible, Mrs Whitaker. But I'll pass your message on to one of his colleagues – Raymond Hewitt, who also deals with criminal matters.

He should be with you within the hour. Meanwhile, it's important your husband says nothing to the police until he arrives.'

Sophie ends the call, trying to control her panic. *Criminal matters.* My god!

Miles is sitting where she left him, head in hands. He looks up as she settles beside him.

'Rupert Marshall's not available, but they're sending someone else.'

'I never dreamed it would come to this. He said it would be all right. I can't understand how—' He breaks off.

The tough-eyed policewoman is coming towards them. She gestures to Miles. 'I wondered if you could come through to one of the interview rooms, Mr Whitaker?'

'My husband's solicitor is on his way,' Sophie protests. 'We've been advised to wait until he arrives.'

DI Benson ignores her, turning to Miles and pursing a small, determined mouth.

'We can certainly wait, Miles, if that's what you'd prefer.' For a moment her eyes soften. 'It *is* OK to call you Miles?'

He nods.

The policewoman waves a hand at the queue behind her. 'As you can see, things are pretty full-on and it would help *enormously* if we could at least make a start with the formalities. I imagine you'd like to get them over with as quickly as possible?' She pauses. 'Of course, you're entitled to wait for your solicitor, if you'd prefer.'

To Sophie's alarm, Miles says, 'No, by all means let's go ahead.'

'But—' Sophie begins.

'Much appreciated,' the policewoman says, as if Sophie hasn't spoken.

'Are you sure, Miles?'

He gives the ghost of a smile. 'I just want to get this whole matter cleared up as quickly as possible.'

DI Benson gives a brisk nod. 'The desk sergeant will bring your solicitor through the moment he gets here.'

Sophie watches Miles follow the policewoman through double doors, walking like a man in his sleep.

A few seats away, a harassed-looking woman is wiping a small child's nose; an elderly man in the middle sits with head bowed, apparently asleep, and beside him a teenager talks into his mobile.

Two young policemen approach the desk, supporting a grey-haired, emaciated man. 'Harry James again. Pissed as a newt,' one of them yells to the desk sergeant.

'Shove him in the end cell, Stu. He can have some tea when he sobers up. Get him up before the bench in the morning.'

At St Thomas's, she'd had her share of down-and-outs, and the foul language and violence, especially at the start of her training, had been difficult to handle. Eventually she learned to let neither pity nor repugnance get in the way of helping those who could be helped.

She glances about her. Almost without her noticing, the seats around her have emptied, leaving only the woman and child, absorbed in some game on his tablet.

What's happening in that interview room?

A man, in his early thirties, dressed in a business suit, a document case under one arm, has come through the main door. The solicitor – at last! She moves towards him.

'Mrs Whitaker? Raymond Hewitt. Came as soon as I could.' He has a small moustache and the slight upward slant to his eyes gives his face a Far Eastern look. He glances about him. 'Your husband?'

She points towards the swing doors.

'Don't tell me he's started without me?'

Her face must be saying it all, because he spins round, heading for the desk, where he elbows his way to the front of the queue. She can't hear what he's saying, but one of the policemen leads him through the far doors.

Now she can only wait.

It takes her a moment to realise her mobile is ringing. She roots in her bag.

'Sophie? How are you doing?'

The voice is unmistakable.

'*Rach*! I – I'm fine thanks.'

'Sorry not to have got back to you, my lovely. It's been full on here.'

'I can imagine.'

At the front desk, a group of youths are shoving and pushing one another.

'So how's the London pad? Settling in OK?'

'Oh, yes – fine. The house is fine.'

'Oi!' The desk sergeant's voice is at parade-ground volume. 'Any more of that and

I'll bang the lot of you up!'

'What was that?'

'Oh – nothing. I'm out in the street. It's rather noisy.'

'Could do with some of that excitement here.'

'I wondered, Rach…' Sophie walks over to the far corner. She could always ask her to call back, but better seize this opportunity while she can. 'It's just Miles and I left in such a rush. There wasn't really time to say goodbye to anyone and I wondered – you know – what's being said? About us?'

There's a pause.

'I'm hardly ever in the staffroom, Sophie.'

'Oh.'

'You know how things are, my lovely.' She gives a short laugh. 'In Murdo's time we actually *talked* to one another. Now it's all form-filling and ticking boxes.'

Why is Rach being so evasive? We've been in and out of each other's houses, she thinks, letting off steam over members of staff and pupils – little horrors some of them. Rach's son, Dillon, now doing his A levels, has grown up with the twins. All that surely counts for *something*?

'You still there, Sophie?'

The end doors are opening and Miles reappears, flanked by the woman inspector and Raymond Hewitt.

'Got to go, I'm afraid.'

'Once all this has blown over, my lovely, we'll have a good catch-up. I promise.'

Sophie ends the call.

Miles walks over to her. 'It went fine,' he whispers. 'Really fine.'

She studies him, longing to believe it.

The policewoman passes a sheaf of papers to Raymond Hewitt. 'We'll let you have more details as soon as they're typed up. Bail conditions still apply, but I can't imagine the magistrates will oppose them.'

'Bail?' Sophie says.

'A formality at this stage, Mrs Whitaker. Your solicitor will explain. Thank you again for your cooperation, Miles.'

'No problem.'

Raymond Hewitt consults his watch. 'I have to get back to the office, but Rupert Marshall will be in touch.'

Miles holds out his hand. 'Sorry to drag you over here.'

The solicitor's gaze flickers over him and then away. 'A pity all the same you didn't wait for me.' He shakes hands with them both before disappearing out into the street.

'What did he mean – "a pity"?' Sophie asks. 'You said it went well.'

'I'll fill you in once we're out of here.' He's staring about him as if in a daze. 'Look, why don't we grab some lunch somewhere? I don't know about you, but I'm starving.'

They find a curry house, empty apart from two elderly men seated in the window.

At Fordingbury, it's rare for them to go out locally and not bump into someone they know. At least we're anonymous here, she thinks with relief, as she and Miles are shown to a corner table.

He orders a bottle of wine, and a whisky that he knocks back in a couple of swift gulps.

She stares at the embossed wallpaper, the alcove with its arrangement of plastic flowers, and the paper tablecloths. In her student days, a group of them used to go to that Indian restaurant round the back of St Thomas's: Annie, the girl she roomed with in her first year, and the Irish girl, Breda, along with a couple of junior doctors and, of course, Alastair. She thought she'd forgotten all that, but suddenly she's filled with a sense of nostalgia.

The waiter brings their curry, which is surprisingly good, although she can only manage a few mouthfuls. She watches Miles dig into his chicken vindaloo, before refilling his wine glass. He's eating with such innocent enjoyment, it's impossible to believe that this man – her husband – has done what they are suggesting. And yet, what *are* they suggesting?

She sips her mineral water, trying to view him through a stranger's eyes. Although the cord trousers and blazer he wears at Fordingbury are shabby, they did fit in with the place. His manner, too, has always been confident, and parents invariably took to him.

As he helps himself to more rice, she realises that, away from the school, he might come across as somewhat eccentric – a little blinkered, perhaps, but without malice.

Certainly incapable of harming one of his pupils.

She reaches for his hand. They still haven't made love, and she misses it. Those Wednesday afternoons, she thinks, when the twins were at school, and the boys at away matches, and the two of us had South Lodge to ourselves. That closeness, the feel of skin on skin. The idea that he could enjoy that side of things, *and* be interested in young boys, was ludicrous. She wonders if that policewoman asked about his sex life. Surely that was a kind of evidence?

Miles gives her hand the briefest of squeezes before reaching for his glass again. 'Doesn't it feel good to be doing something normal? You do realise it's the first time we've eaten out since leaving Fordingbury?'

'I know.'

'More chicken?'

She shakes her head.

'Remember that Indian place outside Banbury? Dishes cooked at the table, a cracker of a wine list. Another world, eh?' He drains his glass. 'Though I must say, this isn't half bad.'

She hesitates. 'I know there's probably never a right time, Miles, but it's important I know what happened in that police interview.'

'Of *course.*' He drains his glass. 'But I don't want you worrying about any of this.

As I said to that young policewoman, the whole thing's a complete fabrication.'

She leans across the table. 'Yes, but what are they actually saying you've *done*?'

He thinks for a moment. 'That Tuesday afternoon. The class were in an uncooperative mood – especially Cunningham.'

'We had him in sickbay during the recent flu outbreak. He didn't exactly endear himself.' Yet fourteen can be a difficult age, she thinks, and he's always been such a pale, skinny boy.

'He goes around with Webb and Owen,' Miles continues. 'They can be pretty challenging at times, I can tell you.'

Luke Owen is the rather shy lad with a stammer, Sophie recalls. At nearly six foot, Chris Webb is the giant of his year, popular, excelling at sport. Both *seem* good-hearted boys. So what has made them behave as they have?

As if reading her mind, Miles said, 'Cunningham may come across as physically weak, but he has a strange hold over his friends. He knows how to divide and rule.' He takes another gulp of his drink. 'Anyway, as you'll have gathered from the police...' she can see him blushing '... he's accused me of – you know – touching him up.'

Sophie's stomach gives a flip. 'So where is this meant to have taken place? In a roomful of boys?'

He pauses. 'In the changing rooms.'

She stares. 'The changing rooms? But that's even more ridiculous – you never go in there!'

He hesitates, as if he's about to say something more. Then drains his glass again.

'Go easy on that,' she protests.

'It won't hurt for once.' Now he reaches for her hand. 'That policewoman seemed to accept my side of the story – that nothing happened. But as I've told you, I won't know the full details of the allegation until Rupert Marshall has more information.'

Miles is looking everywhere but at her, and she hates to see the hunted look in his eyes.

She strokes his arm. 'It's all too clear that Justin has made the whole thing up.'

He tips the rest of the bottle into his glass and she leans towards him again. 'I don't want to add to your worries, Miles, but the solicitors' fees are going to be pretty hefty, aren't they?'

He signals for the bill, catching the wine glass with his hand before righting it again.

'We are on a bit of a shoestring at present, but the school are still paying my salary, such as it is. This will all settle down once we're back at South Lodge.' He gives a small burp. 'Promise.'

She obviously won't get any more sense out of him in this state.

Outside, for the first time in days, the sun is shining, and above the rooftops, the London sky is a slate blue.

She thinks of the garden at South Lodge, with the magnolia in bud and the daffodils starting to poke through. The beech hedges will soon be in leaf, and the lawns ready for their first cut – all giving that wonderful sense of summer days ahead.

All she has to do now is hold her nerve.

TEN

EVERYTHING SEEMS DISTANT AND UNREAL. A CAR gives a vicious honk of its horn. 'Look out!' Sophie says, pulling him back onto the pavement. He links his arm through hers, trying to draw strength from her touch.

As they pass the skip piled with mattresses, still leaning at that impossible angle, he thinks back again to his police interview.

He was shown into a small, windowless room. It resembled a prison cell, so understandably he was pretty nervous. But the two police officers sitting across the table were civil enough, especially Detective Inspector Benson, who proved surprisingly sympathetic, listening without interruption as he described his difficulties in keeping the Remove Year in order.

'So you felt there was considerable tension between you and these boys?' she asked.

He felt it important to be as open as possible. 'It's an age group that needs both guidance and discipline.' He paused. 'The Cunningham boy's always been a bit tricky.'

She nodded in understanding. 'A teacher's job can't be an easy one. But you were able to take your concerns to your colleagues? I imagine the usual procedures were in place?'

'Procedures?' He took a sip of the tea they'd provided. 'Mr MacPherson, the previous headmaster, always encouraged us to stand on our own feet. So, no – I didn't see the need to discuss the matter with anyone.' Encouraged by the warmth in her eyes he continued, 'At Fordingbury, we address any issues that arise directly with the boys. It's all part of our aim to turn out well-rounded individuals, ready to tackle whatever life throws at them.'

'What we all want for our kids,' the po-faced constable said.

Then the grilling started. How often did Miles see Cunningham? How many disagreements had there been between them? Were they always alone during these detentions Miles imposed? Did other boys get given as many? And what about that Tuesday afternoon?

'They set me up,' he explained. 'Webb came rushing into the class to tell me there was an emergency in the changing rooms, so of course I went running over.'

'A medical emergency?'

'That's right.'

'And you didn't think to contact the school matron?'

'In hindsight, I can see that maybe I should have done, but it all happened so fast.'

He was fielding more questions when the door burst open.

'Raymond Hewitt,' the young solicitor announced. 'Here to represent Mr Whitaker.'

The inspector gathered up her papers. 'Then I have to inform you, Mr Hewitt, that we will be pressing charges. Meanwhile, this interview is terminated at eleven forty-seven.'

'But I thought, in the light of my explanation—?' Miles began.

'We'll look forward to receiving all the necessary documents,' the solicitor said and, putting a firm hand under Miles's elbow, steered him out of the room.

*

Now, walking back to the house, Miles is suddenly hit by a realisation: the police haven't believed him. And after he'd been so cooperative. Bastards! he thinks, pushing away a fresh surge of fear.

They're approaching the parade of shops, with the newsagents' board propped on the pavement. *Cigarettes and confectionury sold here.* The misspelling jars – Murdo would have picked up on it too. He still hasn't answered Miles's letter, but any day now, surely?

Sophie's phone is ringing. 'Miranda, darling. How're things?'

He waves his hand at her. The girls mustn't learn of his visit to the police station. Not just yet, anyway. 'Fine,' she's saying, nodding at him to show she understands.

'Your father and I have just been for a curry. Yes, really good. Uh-huh. And how are the exams going? That's great.' She listens for a moment, and then covers the mouthpiece with her hand. 'She's asking for another loan.'

'Tell her we'll think about it,' he whispers.

Sophie nods again. 'It's for what? You really can't manage? All right, darling. By the end of the week. Love you too!'

He sighs. 'How much this time?'

'A couple of hundred. A group of them are going to Madrid for the weekend.' She pauses. 'I didn't know what else to say. It's not as if we've ever refused her.'

'Oh, very well.' A wave of fatigue washes over him. 'All shall be well.' He gives a hiccough. 'And all manner of things shall be well.'

She shakes her head at him.

They're reaching the end of Stephen's Close with the house ahead of them. Its rickety gate and crazy paving seem like the grotty backdrop in some *film noir*. What was that old Hitchcock his father took him to, where Joseph Cotton played a suave conman, who turned out to be a murderer? *The Merry Widow*? That wasn't quite right, though he could have sworn the tune came into it somewhere.

'The key, Miles?' Sophie's saying.

He fumbles in his pocket.

'Hello there!'

The young woman from next door is stepping over the low fence and coming towards them. She has a carrier bag in one hand, and her nails are painted a startling blue. 'I've been keeping a look out for you. Just wanted to check you were OK.'

He stares at her.

'The police car and all.'

Sophie says quickly, 'We're witnesses – in a fraud case.'

'Must be serious if they send a car.'

'It's a real nuisance, but you know how these things can be.'

Kirsty is looking towards him.

'Oh, I don't think you've met my husband, Miles.'

He holds out his hand. She reminds him of a younger, slimmer version of Mrs Carter, the caretaker's wife.

'The last thing I want is to go poking my nose in, but if there's anything I can do?'

'No, thanks all the same,' Sophie says.

'See you later, then. And, if you feel like a fix of caffeine, Sophie, you know where to find me.'

He watches her long legs swing back over the fence. 'Phew, that was a close thing!'

'Ssh, Miles. She'll hear you!'

He leads the way indoors and hooks his coat over the banisters. God! He's completely shattered. 'I think I'll get my head down for a while.'

'Good idea. You need to sleep off that alcohol.'

He goes up the stairs and, kicking off his shoes, stretches out on the bed. He tries to spend as little time up here as possible – the chipboard furniture, the faded carpet, and the pineapple-shaped patch on the ceiling are too depressing.

He's about to nod off when he hears the shrill ring

of the phone reverberating from below. He sits up. Few people know the landline number here.

Sophie puts her head round the door. 'Rupert Marshall for you.'

He follows her down the stairs and picks up the phone.

'Ah, Miles. Glad to have caught you.'

Sophie is hovering beside him, but when he raises an eyebrow at her, she takes the hint and goes through to the kitchen, pulling the door to behind her.

He lowers his voice to a whisper. 'You heard about the police coming for me?'

'Yes. A pity – and I understand from Raymond Hewitt that they're pressing charges.'

'But in our last conversation, you told me the case wouldn't go ahead.'

'I think what I said was, that there was a reasonable chance of that because the police hadn't yet arrested you.'

He grips the end of the banisters. How can the man be so matter-of-fact? It's *my* reputation we're talking about, he wants to shout – *my* life.

'Just the way it goes, I'm afraid,' Marshall continues. 'Though I can assure you that when the time comes, our side will be well prepared.'

He looks along the narrow passageway, fighting off the urge to rush out of the front door, and head away somewhere – anywhere.

'Let's take it one step at a time, shall we?' Marshall is saying. 'We'll know more once the prosecution papers are served.' He pauses. 'Young people's evidence can be very unreliable. You'd be surprised how often trials like this crack.'

If anything were to crack, Miles fears it will be himself. It takes all his willpower not to howl down the phone – with frustration, with fear, with disbelief.

Somehow he manages to gather his thoughts. 'So what happens now?'

'The first hearing will be listed within the next three weeks. You'll need to be there, of course. The court will send you written notice, but the hearing itself will be a formality. Your plea will be taken and the bail conditions extended until the actual trial. We went through all these eventualities when we met.'

He doesn't remember any of it.

'Now, if there's nothing else—'

A terrible thought occurs. 'Suppose the papers get hold of this?'

There's a pause at the other end of the line. 'Press interest at this early stage is unlikely. And of course the school will want to avoid any adverse publicity. Now, you'll have to forgive me, but I do have a meeting to go to.'

Miles replaces the receiver and stands for a moment, willing himself to stay calm. He's been so sure that, as long as he kept his head down, everything would go away. Now it seems he's going to have to attend court – although maybe that's not the worst of it. For if Marshall hasn't foreseen these developments, what else might he have missed?

'Miles!' Sophie is handing him a coffee. 'What news?'

He takes it from her. If he tells her about his court appearance, it makes the whole thing all too real. 'Marshall has spoken to the police, and they're pretty confident that the charges will be dropped. Says they've overreacted, but that it will take time to sort.'

'That's brilliant, Miles. What a relief! And our return to South Lodge?'

'Ah – still up in the air, I'm afraid.'

'I spoke to Miranda earlier, and she assumes we'll be back there this week. We have to tell the girls what's been happening, so I've texted them both, asking them to come over here this Sunday.'

He opens his mouth to protest.

'No, Miles. We can't keep this from them any longer.' She fixes him with that stubborn look she's developed since leaving Fordingbury. 'We can't assume we'll be allowed back to the school before half-term. Think how dreadful it would be if they learn from anyone else that this isn't just a holiday break.' She pauses. 'And that you've been accused of something rather serious.'

He must go carefully. 'You're right.'

In the kitchen, he leans against the corner cupboard, his stomach churning. The shame of it all. These are his daughters – his girls. How on earth will they react?

He remembers when they were first brought home from the hospital – minute, squalling bundles – and how clumsy and awkward he'd felt around them. Luckily, it became easier as they got older. He could still picture Miranda listening round-eyed as he told her stories from the Greek myths – baby Hercules, who killed snakes with his bare hands; Midas whose touch turned his food to sterile gold; Icarus, who ignoring his father's warning, flew too close to the sun, and plunged into the sea.

Nowadays, she teases him "for going on a bit", but it's said with affection. Helena he's always been less sure of. She has a tendency to jump down his throat over the smallest remark. But he doesn't know how he'll bear it if either of them turns against him.

He must try to put as good a slant on things as possible.

'Miles?'

'I'm sorry – what did you say?'

'I realise how difficult all this must be for you. Let's talk about it again nearer the time.' She rinses her mug under the tap. 'Now, I want to give our bedroom another going over. Why don't you put your feet up in the front room? You still look done in.'

It's a relief to escape. He eyes the sagging armchair, before lighting the fire, the popping of the gas sounding a muted salvo. He was sitting here when that knock on the door came. It's no good – he can't settle. The sour taste is still in his mouth, but a small whisky will take it away.

He can hear Sophie moving about overhead.

In the kitchen, he lifts the bottle out of the cupboard. It's going down at quite a rate – he must remember to buy a replacement. He takes a large gulp.

On impulse, he unlocks the door into the garden and stands amongst the tangle of knee-high grass. A wooden fence to his left and the dilapidated shed on his right screen him from prying eyes.

Above his head the grumble of an aircraft sets off a flapping of pigeons on the shed roof, the sound echoing the clamour of his heart.

ELEVEN

H<small>E IS EIGHT YEARS OLD, AND IN HIS FIRST TERM AT</small> Fordingbury. One of the boys in his class has stolen his gym shoes, and the games master, a barrel-chested Welshman, ignoring Miles's stammered excuses, has imposed a detention. Miles has retreated to the cloakroom, crying.

The place has the damp, cheesy smell he associates with small boys. On pegs above his head, hang rows of shirts and shorts in the school colours of mustard and grey. Football kit lies in untidy heaps on the floor, and from somewhere comes the steady drip of water.

Then, as if from nowhere, a voice booms out. 'Whitaker, isn't it? Can't have you lurking in a corner like this. We must keep you and that brain of yours gainfully employed.'

He rubs his eyes, peering up at the thin figure looming over him.

'Half a page on the origins of the doldrums, accompanied by a geographical sketch. You'll find the relevant books in the library.' One bony finger points. 'On my desk by four thirty sharp! Agreed?'

'Y-yes, Mr MacPherson,' he manages to stammer.

He can't recall anything further about the incident, except that the task definitely numbed the pain of being away from home.

For leaving was more horrendous than he could ever have imagined. He can still recall the scratch of his new woollen trousers against his legs, the constriction in his throat from the too-tight knot his sister Anne made in his tie, and his frequent need to rush to the lavatory.

'Not again!' his other sister, Emily, joked, as he emerged from the bathroom. She was fifteen, and Anne two years older. Thinking of them now, he realised it was not that they were actually unkind to him. It was just they inhabited a different universe, forever giggling and whispering together about boys and lipstick colours and the latest pop releases – all out of their parents' earshot, of course.

Each week, when their father worked late and their mother attended her WI meeting, they would bring their record player into the front room, push back the rug and do a dance called a jive. Miles listened to the songs – Elvis Presley's *Wooden Heart*, Del Shannon's *Runaway* – enjoying his sisters' exuberance, even though he was never a part of it. At eight, his main interests were cowboy films, his collection of cigarette cards and a history of Rome that his father had recently bought him.

On that last day at home, his only consolation was that book, safely packed in the bottom of his trunk. He didn't dare think ahead to bedtime, and what it would be like not to have his father sitting beside him, smelling of forbidden tobacco, his moustache tickling Miles's cheek as he kissed him goodnight.

'Chin up!' he said now, as he passed Miles on the landing. 'Half-term will be along before you know it!'

Why are you sending me away? he wanted to ask. Yet already he knew the answer, overheard in a conversation between his mother and one of her friends.

'I thought I'd finished with all this, what with the girls being nearly grown up.' His mother's whisper carried easily towards the corner of the lounge, where he was sitting, cross-legged, sorting through his cigarette cards. 'You've no idea how humiliating it feels, Annie. The looks I get whenever I take him to school or the doctor's. I'm the oldest mother around.'

'Poor you,' his mother's friend said. 'But accidents will happen, more's the pity.'

'Anyone would think you were being sent to Siberia, Miles,' his mother said on his last day at home. 'And you don't want the other boys making fun of you, do you?'

She wore her hair in curls, as neat and shiny as if they were made of plastic. As a small boy, he used to reach up to see if they were real, but she always batted his hand away.

'Your sisters never had this opportunity, Miles. Think how very disappointed your father and I will be if you don't make a go of it.' Her smile didn't reach her eyes. 'After all we've done for you,' she added.

TWELVE

A FEW DAYS LATER, ALONE IN THE SMALL KITCHEN, he peers through the window. It's another overcast day – something he always associates with London. Nothing but grey buildings propping up a grey sky. From above, comes a high-pitched whine that he thinks for a moment is another bloody aircraft – until he realises it's the immersion heater. Sophie must be tackling another cleaning job.

Earlier, he found her scouring the sink yet again, before getting on her hands and knees to scrub away at the lino. All this, of course, is in aid of the twins' visit, although whatever she does will make little difference. The girls, rightly, will be appalled by this house.

He's just thinking that he could do with a drink, when he hears the slap of mail on the hall floor.

He goes along the narrow passageway and stoops to pick up a batch of circulars. He leafs through them, and then stops short. There, among them, is an official-looking envelope.

He tears it open and with shaking hands withdraws the printed form inside. He skims the contents, before leaning against the wall while he studies them in greater detail. *Sexual assault... vulnerable minor... duty of care...* he reads. The charge, listed in all its terrible detail, hits him like a body blow. He makes his way back to the kitchen, where he pours himself a slug of whisky.

How can he possibly show this to Sophie after he's told her the case will almost certainly not be going ahead? He stuffs the letter into his pocket. He'll take another look at it later, when he's feeling more able to deal with it. Then another thought strikes him: suppose, despite all Marshall's assurances, the papers have picked up on his court hearing?

He downs the rest of his whisky, before rinsing and putting away his glass. Then he climbs the steep stairs, willing himself to stay calm.

Sophie is in the spare bedroom, cleaning the window that overlooks the yellowing patch of grass. She turns, cloth in hand.

'I thought I might walk up for a paper.' He fights to keep his voice casual. 'I could do with some fresh air.'

She brushes the hair from her forehead. 'Fine. Lunch is at one. Oh, and could you pick up some butter?'

'Will do.'

Out in the air, he takes deep breaths, to steady himself.

He begins to navigate his route through the narrow streets, forcing himself to focus on his surroundings. Already the monkey-puzzle tree is a familiar landmark.

Araucaria araucana. He turns into the wider road that leads up to the high street. Here are older, pre-war houses, their front gardens hedged with privet or laurel. Although they are divided into flats and everything has a shabby look to it, you can see at once this is a step up from Stephen's Close. How much would the rents be? A small fortune, he imagines, even if he and Sophie were able to extricate themselves from their present contract.

Ahead of him, an elderly man in a brown suit is unlocking a battered-looking Ford. Something about the set of the stranger's shoulders reminds Miles of his father. What must it have been like to work for over forty years in the commercial world? At one time, Miles remembers, he was very keen for him to join the firm. 'It's really not a bad sort of life, Miles. Lots of paperwork, of course, but a company car and regular money coming in. You could do a lot worse.' There was a pleading look in his eyes.

Murdo's response, when his seventeen-year-old pupil reported the conversation, was as aghast as if he were on the receiving end of some foul expletive. 'You're not seriously telling me, Whitaker, that you intend to have a career *selling insurance*?' He clicked his teeth. 'What could possibly be more important than passing on classical and Shakespearean learning to the next generation?'

And Miles was overcome with shame, both for having made the suggestion in the first place, and for having a father with so little understanding of what really counted in life.

Now, watching the brown-suited man open the driver's door, he feels an irrational urge to look into the man's face, to see how content he might be with his lot. But by the time he draws level with the house, the Ford has pulled away.

The knack is simply to keep going. *You there, Whitaker! Put your back into it!*

Outside the newsagents, a group of youngsters is gathered, boys and girls alike in torn jeans and scuffed trainers. Were they at Fordingbury, he would be asking if they had nothing better to do than hang around all morning. Now he walks past, head down, an uncomfortable tightness in his chest.

The Patels' board is in its usual place on the pavement. In the World Cup, New Zealand is ahead of Sri Lanka. The information sits alongside the usual gloomy pronouncements: *ISIS militants execute more captives. All-out war in Libya predicted.*

The newsagents is dimly lit and smells of stale garlic. He's never been here at this time of day and, to his dismay, there's a line of people waiting to be served: mainly mothers with pushchairs and small children buying sweets. He joins the back of the queue. In his mind's eye, he can see the headline: *Public school master sexually assaults pupil!* Please God, don't let there be anything about it in the paper.

Each customer seems to take forever. The young woman immediately in front of him scrabbles in her purse before placing a handful of coins on the counter with maddening deliberation.

At last it's his turn.

Mrs Patel is dressed in a pink and green sari with an orange cardigan over the top.

The colours make his eyes ache.

'You've reserved *The Daily Telegraph* and the *Oxford Mail* for me,' he says, pushing his money across. His palms are sweating, and a dull thump has started in his chest. After muttering his thanks, he takes the papers from her, moving over to the corner, and leafing through the *Mail*. Thank God, he can find no mention of either Fordingbury or himself, though he'll go through it all with a toothcomb later.

He tucks both papers under his arm and is walking over to the door when a man comes barging in from the street, moving so fast that Miles isn't able to step aside in time. 'Hey! Watch where you're going!' he calls.

The man turns. 'Keep your shirt on! I was only—' Then he stops. 'Good heavens, it's not?' He comes closer. 'It *is*. Miles Whitaker! Fancy running into *you*!' He gives a loud laugh. 'And literally, too!'

Miles rubs his shoulder, casting around for what to say. Here, in front of him, is the last person he ever expected or wanted to see. It's as if he's been conjured up from thin air. Perhaps if he closes his eyes, he'll disappear. But no – he's all too real. Miles stares. Hugo Paget has always struck him as someone who *gleams*. Today, his pale pink shirt, his dark suit – silk surely? – and his well-cut hair, all bear the unmistakable patina of ostentatious wealth.

'I wondered what you were doing with yourself,' Paget says.

He was one of the people sitting across the table from Miles at that dreadful meeting in the school boardroom. He can still recall the man's knowing smile as Miles was ordered to pack up and leave.

He feels increasing alarm. What if he's followed him here?

Now the eyebrows, thick and bushy in a full fleshy face, lift fractionally. 'Don't tell me you're living hereabouts?'

Miles resists the impulse to turn and run. 'Good heavens – no! Just passing through.'

Hugo Paget smiles, showing large white teeth. 'Like me then. Nothing but roadworks everywhere. On my way back from a conference, and the buggers have closed the road and re-routed us all.'

Miles remembers him at sports days and concerts, his mobile phone clapped to his ear, talking of hedge funds and market forces. The man gave a generous cheque towards the new science block, and Miles can still hear Murdo's wry comment: *The arrivistes of the twenty-first century, Whitaker. Still, new money is as beloved by our bank manager as the old. And if it costs no more than a brass plaque on a wall, who are we to complain?*

He casts around for a means of escape. Perhaps if he just keeps quiet, Paget will leave.

'I was rather hoping somewhere like this might run to a coffee machine,' he's saying. 'But in this area it's probably too much to ask.'

Other customers are entering the shop – local people in trainers and anoraks, pushing their way between them.

Paget jerks his head towards the door. 'Shall we?'

The gesture leaves Miles no option but to follow. They stand in the doorway of the adjacent shop, to which Miles has never given more than a cursory glance. Although termed an antique emporium, the interior is filled with second-hand furniture and bric-a-brac. He can see a basket chair with a broken seat, and boxes filled with dusty-looking china.

He shifts his gaze, aware of Paget taking stock of him. Both his cord trousers and raincoat are in need of a sponging down.

He racks his brains for something to say – something that will bring this dreadful encounter to an end. 'My car's parked round the corner,' he says at last, his voice sounding unconvincing, even in his ears. 'I've exchanged the Rover for the latest Golf – handier to nip about town in. And Sophie prefers it.'

'Ah, yes – Sophie.' Paget sounds vague. 'She's well?'

'Doing splendidly, thanks.'

Paget is staring at him. 'You've got children, haven't you?'

'Twin girls. In their first year at university. And your—' he hesitates. Was Paget still with his second wife? 'Your family?'

'Just back from the Seychelles. You should try it some time.'

'I will.' He holds out his hand. 'Well, good running into you like this.'

Paget ignores it. 'I take it the enquiry is still ongoing?'

Miles nods, recalling Paget's whispered, 'The man's a bloody disgrace!' as the boardroom door closed behind him. He and all the others believe I did it, he thinks, with a rush of despair.

Paget flashes his teeth again. 'Well, better push on.'

As Miles turns away, the newspapers slip from under his arm. He tries to hold onto them, but too late – they fall to the pavement in a heap, the Oxford banner uppermost. He feels a rush of blood to his face.

Paget glances down. 'Keeping tabs on local events, I see.'

He leaves Miles scrabbling for the papers, and when he looks up, the man is across the road and climbing into a silver Porsche parked on the double lines opposite.

Miles is aware of a dryness in his mouth, and his heart is pounding. He's in no doubt that Paget will report this meeting to Sanderson and the rest of them. 'You'll never guess who I ran into the other day?' he can hear him saying.

And the look on the man's face as he asked, 'You've got children? Haven't you?'

THIRTEEN

H E CAN FEEL SWEAT TRICKLING DOWN HIS forehead. He glances behind him in case Paget is in pursuit, but of course the Porsche has long since disappeared.

He slows his pace, staring ahead to where the spire of St Saviour's rises above a ring of conifers. Sophie has been up to the church a number of times, but at least she no longer insists that he accompany her.

He pushes open the side gate, its hinges almost rusted away, and walks along a gravel path. Over to his right, yew trees are grouped alongside beeches and chestnuts, on which the early buds are showing. The ground is an unruly tangle of bramble and dead grass. Carter would have the place licked into shape in no time.

Now that he's able to take a proper look, Miles can see what a depressing sight the building is. Blackened by years of London traffic, the masonry has cracks running through it, and the stonework round the window arches is crumbling. Odd to think it's the same late-Victorian vintage as Fordingbury. He pictures again the tile-hung buildings, the rose-coloured bricks and gleaming paintwork – all of which he's taken so much for granted.

He catches a movement by the porch, and a figure in a long, shapeless anorak emerges. A pair of walking boots protrude from the hem.

'Hello there, Miles!' Webster calls, with a bouncy enthusiasm that sets Miles's teeth on edge. 'Good to see you again. Enjoying some fresh air?'

'Just passing through.'

'The churchyard's a bit of a shambles,' Webster says, as if reading Miles's earlier thoughts. 'But you should see it in summer. Foxgloves, bluebells, dog roses – you name it. All unplanned. Like so many of the best things!' He smiles. '"Long live the weeds and the wilderness yet".'

Miles thinks for a moment. 'Manley Hopkins!'

'Wonderful poet, wasn't he?' He points at the tangle of grass. 'People imagine they need everything neat and ordered, and maybe it's how most of us would like life to be. But it doesn't half have a way of tripping us up when we least expect it.'

Miles glances into the other man's face, but the eyes, the chestnut brown of a conker, seem innocent enough.

'Well, I *like* order,' Miles says, as firmly as he can.

'I try to think of this as everyone's place,' Webster continues, as if Miles hasn't spoken. 'We get all sorts – homeless, winos, illegals on the run from the police.'

Miles feels his chest tighten. 'Aren't you worried about them wrecking the place?'

'It is a problem, all right, but secure fencing costs a fortune, and probably wouldn't work anyway. Most of the trouble comes on weekend nights, of course. All we can do is try not to trip over the courting couples.' He sighs. 'And clear away the syringes the druggies leave.'

Miles can't hide his shock. 'I'd lock the lot of them up!'

The clergyman frowns. 'Not something I'd go along with myself.'

Webster turns to watch a black-clothed figure, rucksack slung over one shoulder, making its way towards them. It's only as the man draws nearer that Miles sees the dark skin and beard. He's wearing a tunic and trousers, so an Arab, then. He has a mental image of hollow-eyed men yelling slogans and shooting rifles in the air.

'Let me introduce you,' Webster says, extending his hand to the newcomer. 'Ali, this is Miles Whitaker. Miles, meet Ali Mahmoud.'

Miles nods at the stranger. He's older than he first thought, his beard and hair streaked with grey. The dark eyes, liquid in their intensity, are staring into his – surely a little too long for common politeness?

'Ali is one of our regulars,' Webster says.

'You attend the services here?' Miles tries to keep the surprise out of his voice.

The man smiles. 'Indeed, no. I am a Muslim. But Sebastian kindly allows me to sit in the churchyard.'

'It's for everyone's use,' Webster says. 'Anyway, I must

get going. I'll leave you two to get to know one another. Give my best to Sophie – and to Farah.'

Then he's off down the path.

'You are new to the area?' the man asks, shifting from one foot to the other.

The last thing Miles wants is to have to make polite conversation. 'That's right. I'm on a sort of sabbatical at present.' The lie, like all the others, seems to trip off his tongue.

'And let me guess! I would say you are from one of the top places. Oxford or Cambridge, no doubt?'

Despite himself, Miles feels a flicker of pleasure. 'Oxford, actually.'

'Ah. I thought as much.' He pauses. 'That must be a beautiful place.'

Miles thinks of Fordingbury in the summer – the flower beds filled with colour, and the beech trees casting their shadows over the lawn. 'Yes...'

'It is a very precious thing to live in peace.' Ali looks over his shoulder. 'You go to Sebastian's church?'

The directness of the question throws him. 'No – that is – it's not really my kind of thing.'

Ali regards Miles with solemn eyes. 'Many of the young believe that the days of Christianity are numbered.'

The cheek of the fellow! 'Oh, I wouldn't say that.'

'Yet I understand that churches in this country are poorly attended?'

'Oh, I can assure you that there's plenty of life in Christianity yet.' He pictures the Fordingbury chaplain, Wilson, with his emphasis on the importance of team spirit and standing on one's own feet.

Above their heads, the clock strikes the half hour. How long before he and Sophie are back in the school chapel again?

'That's something I miss,' Ali is saying. 'The *Azan*.'

'The what?'

'Our call to prayer. In my home country, it is sung from every mosque, so that all can hear it, and no one will be left out.'

There was that big row in Oxford a while back over a building application for a minaret. He and Murdo spent hours penning letters of protest to the local papers.

'They are such an integral part of life. I only realised the degree to which this was so when I came to England. Every time I walked around outside, I waited to hear the imam's chant, and...' he gives an apologetic smile '... although it's a strange thing to say, the silence almost deafened me.'

'You speak such good English. You've been over here a while?'

'A number of years.' He shifts his rucksack onto his other shoulder, clearly as uncomfortable with this conversation as Miles is.

'Well, I'd best be off. It's been good meeting you.'

Ali returns his smile. 'I hope there will be further opportunity to continue our discussion.'

'Of course,' he says, and makes his escape.

FOURTEEN

TIME TO GET SOME AIR INTO THIS PLACE, SOPHIE thinks, prising open the kitchen window. Outside, she can make out a line of blackened roofs and, high above them, an aeroplane the size of a silverfish crawls across a rectangle of sky.

She turns, as she hears Miles's steps in the passage.

'Lunch is ready. Shepherd's pie.'

He mutters his thanks, hanging his coat behind the door, and seating himself at the table.

'The butter? Did you remember to pick some up?'

He stares at her.

'Oh, never mind – I'll get some tomorrow.'

She's hungry after her morning's work, but for once he has no appetite, pushing his food around his plate.

'Sure you're all right, Miles?'

'I'm fine.'

'Oh, I almost forgot.' She hands him a cream-coloured envelope.

His face brightens. 'Murdo. At last!'

He slits open the envelope, and extracts the sheet of paper inside.

After a few moments, he looks up, and beams across at her. 'I knew he wouldn't let me down. Just listen to this, Sophie.

'*My Dear Miles,*

How splendid to hear from you. Not a day goes by that I do not think of the school, and of the boys. I wondered how you were getting on under the new regime. Not too much whip cracking, I hope.'

Miles looks up. 'He never took to Alan Sanderson, you know.'

She nods.

'*I continue along here in much the same vein, still enjoying my newfound leisure.*

When we meet we must resume our debate on Tacitus. I have found a fascinating passage on Tacfarinas' revolt in Numidia that certainly bears further examination, and—'

'But what does he say about this accusation?' Sophie interrupts.

'Sorry – of course. Let's just see. Ah yes.

'*Now, to turn to your little problem. I can't tell you how sorry I was to learn of it, Miles. You, of all people to be faced with something like this. Quite frankly, it beggars belief. I can't think what the world is coming to. It does indeed seem a wise move to distance yourself from Fordingbury until the whole matter has been resolved – in the very near future, I trust.*

Of course I would be more than happy to discuss things with you, and for you to draw on my experience, such as it is.

'You see!'

She nods again.

'*Perhaps you and the delightful Sophie could come over to tea? How would the seventeenth at 4.00 p.m. suit?*

Meanwhile, I assure you of my unwavering friendship and support.

Yours affectionately,

Murdo

'He still has pull you know.' Miles sounds euphoric.

'I thought you said that Rupert Marshall is seeing to everything?'

'And so he is.'

'So what exactly is it you're hoping Murdo can do, Miles?'

'*Do*?' She can hear the exasperation in his voice. 'You're speaking of a man who taught for nearly fifty years, who has been a highly respected headmaster for over a quarter of a century. You really think all that experience counts for nothing? That a word from him won't expose this fiasco for what it is?'

There's something about this that doesn't quite add up, but before she can ask him further questions, he smiles across at her.

'Let's take our coffee through. And, Sophie?'

'Yes?'

'I want you to know how much I appreciate all you do for me.'

He leans over, as if to give her a kiss, but she forestalls him, jumping to her feet.

He follows her along the passage.

'We still need to talk about the girls,' she says, when they're settled in the front room. 'They'll be here in the morning.'

'I was thinking: why don't we take them up to The Crown and Cushion? It's just off the main road, and the prices are reasonable.'

'I didn't realise you'd been in there?'

'I've only glanced at the menu in passing.' He sips his coffee. 'Or there's that curry place we went to?'

She shakes her head. 'I've already bought the food. Besides, the four of us really need to be able to talk in private.'

He peers at her over his glasses. 'You obviously still feel it's right to burden the girls with this?'

'How else do we explain being in this house? And suppose they were to hear what's happened from someone else?'

'Perhaps we could think up some explanation?'

'Lie to them, you mean?'

'No, of course not.'

There's a silence.

He reaches for his notepad and flicks it open. 'Just let me read through my notes.' She can see the page, filled with line after line of neat writing, like one of the meticulous lesson plans he spends so many hours drawing up.

'I needed to get everything clear in my own mind.'

'Good idea.'

'So, if I could just run it past you.' He pushes his spectacles further onto his nose. 'Let me see – I'm proposing to start with the outrageous way we've been treated – having to leave the school with so little notice, and so on. Then, I'll mention the teething difficulties with Alan Sanderson, and the challenges of teaching that Remove Year, and...' he skims down the page '... how the initial accusation of bullying was brought and then subsequently altered.' He pauses. 'To one of sexual assault.'

'And the decision not to go ahead with the court case?'

'Of course – if only to reassure them.' He isn't meeting her eye. 'Although, not to put too fine a point on it, Sophie, I still find the whole situation deeply humiliating.'

He may sound evasive sometimes, but that's just embarrassment. 'It's not as if you've done anything wrong!'

His voice is sad. 'Somehow that doesn't help.'

'I'm sorry, Miles. I realise how tough this has been for you. Although I imagine it's only a matter of time before we get the date for our return to South Lodge? They surely can't keep us cooped up here for much longer. Our names are on the lease – aren't they?'

He doesn't answer. 'I'll have another word with Marshall. See if he can chivvy things along a bit.'

She gets to her feet. 'I'd better press on. There's still quite a bit to do for tomorrow.'

'Can I give a hand? Help with the vegetables, perhaps?'

The last time she took him up on his offer, there was more potato left on the skin than in the saucepan. She shakes her head. 'More coffee?'

He smiles up at her. 'That would be splendid.'

FIFTEEN

'Mum!' Miranda, in dark jacket and jeans, is climbing into the front of the Rover. 'Didn't expect you to be as far out as this.' She leans over for a kiss. 'It's been quite an adventure getting here!'

Helena, wearing an orange tunic and green hooped earrings, settles into the back seat.

'All right, darling?' Sophie says over her shoulder.

A car behind hoots its horn.

'Grotty area, Mum.' She puts her mobile to her ear. 'Better get a move on.'

Sophie pulls out into the traffic. 'It does take a bit of getting used to.'

'And there was me thinking you were living it up in the West End.' Miranda smiles. 'It's so lovely to see you.'

'You too, darling.'

She turns off the main road and begins negotiating the maze of side streets.

'Everything *is* all right?' Miranda asks, as the Rover jolts over a pothole.

'We're just having a short break from the school. Dad will explain.' She pauses. 'So, what's new?'

'My course is really brill. Oh, and thanks again for that extra cash. You know a group of us is going to Madrid? We've agreed to speak Spanish the entire time. It'll be good practice for—' She breaks off. They're turning into Stephen's Close, the pavement to their left blocked by a pile of rubble. On the nearside, an old man in a plastic raincoat shuffles past in the drizzle. 'Please don't tell me...' Her voice tails away as a moment later Sophie pulls up outside the house. 'This can't be it?'

Sophie tries to keep her voice bright. ''Fraid so.'

'My god!' Miranda breathes. She follows Sophie out of the car, leaving Helena still texting in the back seat.

Miranda walks over to the front door and stands examining her surroundings, oblivious to the rain. 'Look at the state of the roof. And the net curtains. And this cracked paving.'

Sophie feels a moment's surprise. The house really doesn't seem quite so terrible any more. In a strange way, she's even starting to feel a mild affection for it, perhaps because it reminds her of her early days in London.

Helena comes up behind them. 'Fucking awful, Mum!' She narrows her eyes at Sophie. 'And you can't tell me you meant to end up in a place like this.'

'I made a mistake over the booking. Silly of me, but there you are. I'll explain when we're inside.'

Miranda holds out her arms. 'It's just so great to link up again, Mum.' As the three of them draw close, Sophie fights back tears. Whatever else happens, she thinks, being together is what matters.

'This rain.' She wipes her eyes. 'Come indoors, the pair of you, before you get soaked.'

She leads the way along the hall and into the kitchen. The house smells of roast chicken, and Miles is coming towards them, waving a tea towel in the air. 'Hello, you two! Anyone for a spot of Prosecco?'

She wishes that he weren't treating their visit as some cause for celebration.

She watches the twins greet him – Miranda flinging her arms around him, and Helena giving her usual peck on the cheek.

She seizes her sister's arm. 'Let's take a look around.'

They disappear down the passage to the front room, before climbing the stairs to the bedrooms and bathroom above. A few moments later they're back down again.

'Not very salubrious, I'm afraid,' Miles says.

Helena picks at a piece of flaking plaster. 'So, what's going on?'

They listen to the radiator emitting one of its regular creaks.

'We'll explain later, girls,' Miles says. 'But for now, let's go through to the front room.'

Miles hands round the drinks and the twins sit side by side on the sofa. Looking at them, Sophie thinks with a pang that it doesn't seem so long ago since they were little scraps of things, dressed in bright red Babygros, a patch of fluff on top of their heads, being wheeled around Oxford in the pushchair.

Miles clears his throat. 'So, how's life?'

'I'm loving Bristol, Dad,' Miranda says. 'And I've met some really great people. Thanks for that cash, by the way.'

Helena leans forward. 'I've got some news.'

'Oh?'

'I've decided sociology isn't really for me, so I've decided to switch courses – to law.'

'Law?' Miles looks alarmed.

'It's easy enough to change, if you don't mind my taking the extra time over it? I know there's the money side, but that should be all right, shouldn't it?' She sips her drink. 'The uni have got a great mentoring scheme, with a placement in the second year with a solicitor or barrister.'

'Well, I—' Miles begins, but Sophie cuts across her.

'We'll be back at Fordingbury soon and although things may be a bit tight, I'm sure Dad and I will manage.'

'That's great. Thanks.'

'But a brave move all the same,' he says. '*Audaces fortuna iuvat.* As Murdo would say: fortune favours the brave!'

Helena shrugs. 'What you really mean, Dad, is that it's a stupid choice. But I don't intend to be stuck in a rut all my life.'

Miles winks at Sophie. '"Buy one, get one free".'

Helena glares. 'That's *not* funny.'

Miranda puts a hand on her sister's arm. 'He's only teasing, Helena.'

She pulls a face. 'It didn't come across as a joke.'

'He doesn't mean anything by it,' Sophie finds herself saying.

'Of course he doesn't.' Miranda leans forward. 'So, how much longer are you two planning on remaining here?'

Sophie tries to catch Miles's eye.

'Dad? Mum? *Hello*?'

'We'll be returning to South Lodge any day.' He gulps his drink. 'Top-up, anyone?'

They shake their heads.

'Meanwhile, your mother and I are in the pink.' Miles takes another swig of his drink. '*Dum spiro spero,* or for the uninitiated: while there's life there's hope!"'

'Miles,' Sophie begins. 'I really think you need to go easy on that—'

He wrinkles his nose. 'Can I smell burning?'

She jumps to her feet. 'Oh, goodness – the gravy!'

Back in the kitchen, he carves the chicken, while the girls help Sophie dish out vegetables, muttering apologies as they bump into one another in the crowded space.

Miles spears a potato. 'I bet you've been missing your mother's roasts.'

'You're right. College food is never the same. But I don't know how you're managing, Mum,' Miranda says. 'That oven belongs in a museum.' She leans across the table. 'How are things at the school? Any word from old Murdo?'

Miles gives a broad smile. 'We're due to visit him next week. Isn't that so, Sophie?'

She nods, fighting a growing sense of anger. How much longer is he going to put off telling them?

Now he's talking about the changes Alan Sanderson is making to the syllabus, and the fight to retain the traditional staff drinks on a Sunday. Somehow she must steer the conversation in the right direction.

It's Helena who cuts through it all. 'So how soon is soon?' she says, as they begin on the fruit crumble. 'Before you return to South Lodge, I mean? I can understand your going on a cruise, or taking time out in Brussels or Paris, like normal parents. But staying on here is really weird.'

Once again, Sophie wills Miles to speak, but he refuses to meet her eye.

Helena glares at them. 'If you've been given the sack, Dad, then for God's sake, say so. Just so we know what we're all doing here, in this shitty little house?'

'Helena!' Miles begins. 'That's quite enough—'

Sophie draws in her breath. 'The truth is that your father's been asked to leave Fordingbury. But only on a temporary basis.'

'So, what are you meant to have done, Dad?'

He reaches for his drink, his hand shaking so badly that liquid slops onto the Formica.

Sophie can't bear to see the trapped look in his eyes. 'We didn't want to say anything to you both before this – not until we knew what your father was being accused of. But I'm afraid it is rather serious.'

'We've gathered *that*,' Helena says.

Sophie reaches for a cloth and begins wiping up the spilled drink. She hadn't expected to be doing the talking, and it's far more difficult than she imagined.

'There's been a formal complaint. Your father's been accused of – of misconduct.' She swallows. 'Sexual misconduct.'

Helena puts down her spoon. 'You can't be serious?'

'I'm afraid so.'

'With one of the boys?'

She looks at Miles. 'Yes.'

'I didn't do it!' Miles manages to get out.

'No – of course not. How could you have?' Miranda is on her feet and, coming round to the back of Miles's chair, puts her arms around him. 'Oh, poor Dad!' Sophie can see she's close to tears.

Miles remains speechless, patting Miranda's hand by way of a thank you, and after a few moments she returns to her seat.

Helena is staring at her father. 'So which boy was it? It is just the one, I take it?'

To Sophie's relief, he at last finds his voice. 'That's right, but I don't think it would be helpful for me to name him at this stage. Obviously, we've taken advice from my solicitor. That's the reason for your mother and I choosing London – so we could be within easy reach.' He gulps more of his wine. 'Rupert Marshall's a sound chap. His father was a friend of your grandfather's, you know. He's assured me all charges are being dropped.'

Helena leans forward. 'So there's no talk of a formal prosecution, then?'

He shifts in his seat. 'I've been assured it won't come to that.'

Sophie is aware of Helena's gaze, shrewd and assessing, moving between her and Miles. 'Coffee anyone?'

It's a relief to turn her back on the three of them, and busy herself with the kettle.

The important thing to hold on to, she tells herself, is that Miles is opening up at last.

So why does she not feel more relieved now the girls are in the picture?

SIXTEEN

'**Y**OU'RE NOT STILL FRETTING ABOUT THIS BABY business, are you, Sophie?'

They were in Miles's study and, watching him hunting around for some book or other, she was aware of only having half his attention.

'I mean, don't you think that maybe we have enough children in our lives?' In the distance a bell rang for afternoon classes.

'It'll be different with our own.' Talking about it felt very raw, but she knew that time was slipping by – they were already three years into the marriage. 'I must have a child,' she continued. 'It matters more to me than...' She broke off, realising that he could know nothing of her secret, of her loss. '... than anything else,' she finished, aware how lame she must sound.

Yet perhaps he picked up some of her intensity, because

he put down the folder he was carrying and looked across at her. 'It's quite a lot to take on. And I warn you, Sophie: I won't be any good at nappies, or getting up in the night – all that sort of stuff. In my book, Fordingbury and the boys are a full-time commitment – always have been, always will be.'

'I do realise that, Miles.' Well, if she had to manage on her own, so be it.

There was a silence. Eventually he said, 'If it means that much to you.'

And with that, she knew she had won.

The news that she was expecting twins came as a shock, especially as the babies took months to settle. But even in the early hours, the sight of them filled her with a fierce joy that increased each time she picked them up, delighting in their gummy smiles, their first teeth, their attempts to grab at anything which came into their line of vision.

And when she was at her most exhausted, there was the summer visit to Cornwall to look forward to – magical weeks that took her back to her own childhood.

Her father had worked for one of the big oil companies and was often overseas on business. Her memory of him was of a warm-hearted, ebullient man, breezing in and out of her life like a south-westerly. She loved her mother, but lived for her father's return when he seemed to light up everything around him.

Then, when she was fourteen, everything changed. Her mother dropped dead from an aneurism and, just over a year later, her father remarried and settled in the

Far East. He and his Thai wife made it clear that Sophie would always be welcome, but it was to Aunt Harriet that she turned, first on her own, then with Alastair, and finally with Miles and the twins.

All seemed so happy and it wasn't until the summer the girls turned eight that the problem became apparent. Helena – always the more argumentative of the two – grew increasingly fractious. 'No, I won't!' she'd shout, when asked to do even the simplest thing – help clear the table, or get ready for bed.

Miranda would be the one who carried her plate over to the sink or, changed into her pyjamas, would be smiling up at Miles as he read to her from a child's book on Shakespeare or the Classics.

Aunt Harriet jabbed a finger in their direction. 'I hope,' she whispered to Sophie, 'that Helena will get a turn.'

Sophie glanced at the child, absorbed in painting some abstract scene. Even from across the room, she could see the page of the sketchbook filled with jagged lines of orange and black.

'Oh, she's happy enough as she is,' Sophie whispered back, sensing that to try and push Miles and Helena together might only end in more argument. Yet a part of her longed for Miles to do something to ease the situation.

Then, one afternoon, the four of them went for a walk along the cliff-top, with clouds scudding overhead and a stiff wind blowing off the sea. The twins were running ahead when, over to one side, they spotted a rope bridge, slung across a narrow gully. 'Come on!' Helena called to her sister, and before Sophie could shout a warning, they'd taken off, bouncing along its length, which swayed from side to side under their weight.

It took only moments for their laughter to turn into shrieks of alarm.

Without stopping to think, Sophie went in pursuit. It was soon obvious that the sign: *Danger! Keep out!* was not one to be ignored. The rope handrail was only waist-high and badly frayed and, glancing down, she could see the waves crashing in green and white circles on the rocks below.

Slowly, she worked her way towards the girls, calling out to them to stay calm – that everything would be all right. They began walking back, clutching one another for support, shaking and sobbing. Eventually, she grabbed hold of them, and they slowly inched their way onto the path, where they stood, pale and shaken.

'Thank God you're all right, Sophie,' Miles said.

Suddenly it felt too much. 'A fat lot of use you were, standing here without lifting a finger.'

'I'm sorry.'

For once, his contrite expression did nothing to appease. 'And so you should be. Helena and Miranda might well have been badly hurt!'

She was too angry to say more.

As she set off along the path, Miranda's voice carried towards her on the wind. 'Don't look so sad, Daddy. Mummy was there.'

SEVENTEEN

MILES WAKES TO THE RUMBLE OF AIRCRAFT. IT'S not yet six, and he can hear Sophie's steady breaths beside him. He props himself on an elbow and leans over her. She's lying on her back, arms by her side. In the glow from the street light, he can make out the rise and fall of her breasts. Once, just a glimpse of them would have been a turn-on, but somehow these days he can't recapture the urge.

Quietly, so as not to disturb her, he dresses and makes his way down to the kitchen, taking his coffee through to the front room and switching on breakfast television. Another royal baby is due in a couple of months' time, and no doubt Fordingbury will be holding one of its famous tea parties to mark the occasion.

Miles pictures the sweep of lawn outside the main building, and the tables draped in crisp linen. He can hear the chink of Worcester china, and the burble of conversation as he moves from one group of parents to another, always with a ready smile and an appropriate comment about each boy.

He stares unseeingly at the screen. There's no way he'll be back in time for the celebration. The realisation is like a kick in the gut.

But then he remembers today's meeting with Murdo. The last thing he wanted was to disturb the old man's well-earned retirement, but whom else can he confide in? Already he regrets lying to Sophie, but still a sense of shame prevents him from talking to her openly. And besides, he needs to rehearse the sequence of events with someone who will believe them.

A new thought occurs, and his stomach gives a lurch. He's been keeping that court letter in his raincoat pocket, where it's all too easy for her to find. He needs to put it somewhere safe – somewhere she won't dream of looking.

He glances around at the corner shelves piled with Shakespearean texts and Greek and Latin volumes and the pot plant, its leaves yellowing, perched on the top. Stashed away inside his well-thumbed copy of the *Oresteia* are the unpaid bills he doesn't want her to see. No point upsetting her further – not until this whole court business is out of the way. But it still seems not a secure enough place – not for something as important as this.

There's not a sound from upstairs, so now is as good a moment as any.

He retrieves the letter and lets himself out of the house. It's still only just after seven, and other than that man walking his Alsatian, the street is deserted.

He unlocks the Rover, and climbs into the passenger side. He hasn't been in the car since their arrival and, breathing in its familiar smell of leather and oil, he feels his shoulders relax. With a sigh of satisfaction, he pushes the letter into the back of the glove compartment.

He gets out, and after a quick glance around to make sure there's no one about, climbs into the back, curling up on the seat, the leather smooth under his cheek.

For the first time since leaving Fordingbury he feels secure.

A bang on the side window wakes him. He opens his eyes to find himself staring into a distorted face pressed against the glass. He scrambles out, almost falling onto the pavement in his haste.

'Sorry to have disturbed you.' Kirsty, in T-shirt and jeans, turns to the child beside her. 'How many flaming times do I have to tell you, Henry?' She tugs at the boy's arm. 'Leave that car alone!'

'Just hunting for something I'd dropped,' Miles murmurs, feeling his face grow red.

The boy, spiky hair on end, wriggles away from her. 'Said he was too poorly for school,' Kirsty says, 'though from the way he's carrying on, I don't think there's much wrong. Well, I'd better get on.'

Before Miles can say anything further, she turns towards her house, dragging the boy after her. As Miles locks the car, the child's voice carries towards him – 'Mum, why was that man—?' The slam of the front door cuts it off.

In principle, of course, there's nothing wrong in having a snooze in one's car – it's really no one's business but his own. But, all the same, he wishes he hadn't been spotted.

As he re-enters the house, he can't shake off a sense of having been caught out.

EIGHTEEN

Iт's his second year at Fordingbury and he's sitting in Matron's office in his summer uniform of Aertex shirt and grey shorts. The room overlooks the sports field and he can hear the thwack of ball on bat and the shouts of the team. It's a Wednesday, so it must be the seniors. At the thought, he feels his stomach tighten.

'Now, Miles,' – although Matron's tone is soft, there's something about it he doesn't quite trust. As if the starch that makes her uniform rustle is lurking somewhere there in her voice. 'You know that an untruth always catches us in the end.'

Spit it out, a voice inside his head is telling him. But how can he, when that will only make things so much worse?

'We will sit here for as long as it takes.' When he looks up, her smile has become fixed. 'Well, what do you have to say for yourself?'

He fidgets in his seat. There's a scab on one knee that he itches to pick at.

'I don't want to be a sneak, Matron,' he mumbles.

'I'm sure you don't. But equally you won't want to be thought of as someone who has brought disgrace on Fordingbury. On yourself.' Matron pauses. 'And on your parents.'

He hasn't thought of the situation in those terms, but of course Matron is right to bring it up. He recalls his mother's dismay at having to take him to the local school alongside the other younger women; he can imagine his father's kindly: 'Never mind, old chap. Can't be helped, I suppose' – that feels even worse. Misery rises up inside him.

'You know, Miles, that anything you say in this room will not be passed on to any of the boys. So…' Matron's voice turns brisk 'let's put an end to this, shall we? A name, please.'

He pictures the prefects, all bigger and tougher than him and, as he's learned to his cost, capable of anything.

He picks at his scab. Let anyone take the blame, he thinks, just as long as it's not me.

He casts his mind around, but already he knows. Only one boy will not be able to defend himself. Only one boy is even more frightened than he.

He takes a deep breath. 'Inky,' he blurts out. 'It was Inky.'

Matron's eyebrows lift in surprise. 'Oladosu – The Nigerian lad?'

He nods.

She clicks her tongue. 'He seems such a gentle, polite soul. And the two of you such friends.'

We were, he thinks. We are.

'All the more commendable then for admitting the truth, Miles. Well done!' She leans forward and pats his knee, leaving him with an uncomfortable reminder of the praise his mother showers on the family spaniel.

'Of course, I shall inform Mr MacPherson of our talk. And Miles?'

'Yes, Matron?'

'As I've already said, how I came by this information will go no further than that.' She smiles again. 'I promise.'

He remembers walking out of the room, and then breaking into a run down the corridor and into the lavatories, where he throws up his breakfast. After that, his memory is a blank.

NINETEEN

THEY ENTER THE OUTSKIRTS OF EASTBOURNE JUST after three-thirty, travelling along tree-lined roads, with solid, well-kept houses on either side. At the top of a rise, they catch their first glimpse of the sea, the sun winking off the heaving mass of grey-blue water.

Sophie winds down the window, drawing in deep breaths of the salty air. 'Wonderful!' She turns to him. 'We must only be a couple of minutes away from the house. A shame there isn't time to go down to the seafront.'

He nods. 'Murdo's a stickler for punctuality.'

'Let's pull in for a while. That way we'll be sure to get to him on the dot.'

Now that they're here, he feels almost sick with anticipation. Though surely there's no need to be anxious? Murdo has never yet let him down.

He recalls again the old man's departure from Fordingbury the previous July. The other staff members had said their goodbyes, and the school was filled with the cathedral-like hush that always descended when it was emptied of boys. As he stood with Murdo outside the main entrance, Miles longed to find some way of acknowledging the years they'd known one another, and what the older man's support and friendship meant to him. But the words wouldn't come.

In the silence, the only sound was the click of Murdo's teeth.

When the taxi pulled up, he turned to Miles, his jaw working. 'Well, best foot forward, Whitaker. Tacitus and Ovid will be my companions now. But don't go forgetting this old man, will you?'

Miles looked away to hide his tears. Murdo had been such an inherent part of his life, seemingly as immutable as the buildings themselves. He still couldn't believe this was the end of their time together. 'I've got your address,' he managed to get out.

'I'll write – I promise.'

They shook hands, the older man's skin scratchy against his palm. Murdo's battered suitcases were loaded into the boot – his books and other personal items must have been sent on ahead – and Miles watched Murdo clamber stiffly into the cab. As it went off down the drive, he willed him to look round, but the old fellow remained, ramrod straight, staring ahead.

When the taxi disappeared round the bend in the drive, Miles returned to South Lodge. Sophie and the girls were out, and he wandered from room to room, unable to settle.

Now, waiting in the Rover with Sophie, he's filled with impatience to see his old friend again. 'Let's make a move. I'm sure Murdo won't mind our being early.'

They drive along a couple more roads, eventually pulling up outside a four-storeyed Edwardian villa. Sophie peers through the windscreen. 'Sea View House. This must be it.'

Miles studies the cream facade, the neat line of box hedge, and the window boxes filled with bright flowers. Although it isn't quite what he was expecting – in his mind he's pictured something a little more – well – gracious, he feels a kick of pleasure to see how well Murdo has done for himself.

Pushing open the gate, Miles leads the way up a brick path to the front door. Now that he's closer, he sees with surprise that the red and yellow flowers in the window boxes are artificial. Under the right-hand window a plastic garden gnome holds up a small lantern. Ahead of him is the front door, its brass knocker in the shape of a poodle's head.

He's aware of the tightness in his chest.

'Don't just stand there!' Sophie whispers.

He lifts the knocker, letting it fall back with a thud.

After what seems an eternity, the door opens and an elderly woman in a blue and green dress peers out. She's very thin, her white hair cut into a bob that resembles a faded version of the box hedge.

She regards them, the vertical line between her small eyes deepening.

'You'll be the visitors for Mr MacPherson,' she says in a pronounced brogue. She opens the door just wide enough to allow them both to edge their way into a pink-carpeted hall. 'Mr MacPherson has been lodging with me since last summer,' she continues, rather stiffly. 'You'll find him on the top floor. You'll need to bang quite loudly, mind – he's hard of hearing. Oh, and kindly remember this is a non-smoking household.'

She turns and goes off down the passage.

'Thank you,' Sophie calls to her retreating back.

Miles and she exchange glances, before he leads the way up the staircase. Every landing holds a glass-fronted cabinet crowded with china animals – cats, dogs, horses, mice, rabbits – and there are more plastic flowers on the window ledges. He feels disorientated, as if he's wandered into some child's nursery. His feet slow on the carpet.

When they reach the top floor, the door ahead of them – presumably leading to Murdo's sitting-room – is closed. To the left, Miles can see a bathroom, with lilac walls and green spotted curtains.

In his letters, Murdo described his new quarters as "first-rate" and Miles pictured dormer windows and the dull gleam of mahogany. Something more akin in fact to an Oxford college – or to Fordingbury. 'This must be it then,' he murmurs.

He raps on the door, and after a few moments shuffling steps approach from the other side.

The door swings open, and Murdo stands facing him, rheumy-eyed, thinner than Miles remembers, but still dapper in a grey suit and silk tie. He fights off an impulse to fling his arms around his old friend.

'Whitaker!' Murdo's smile reveals large discoloured teeth. 'How splendid of you to come! And Sophie too. Welcome to my humble abode.'

He ushers them into a square room with a bay window overlooking the street. Sophie hands over the bottle of dry sherry they've brought.

'Splendid!' Murdo places it on a side table and gestures towards a pair of pink velvet armchairs. He lowers himself onto the sofa opposite. 'Good journey?'

Miles nods, glancing around the room. There are a couple of prints he recognises as having hung in Murdo's study, and the bookcases along one wall are crammed. Otherwise it all seems strangely bare, the only other furniture a pair of upright wooden chairs and a low table, draped with a brown lace cloth, in the bay window.

Murdo crosses one long leg over the other. 'I take it you made it past the Hibernian hydra?'

Miles smiled. 'A hundred-headed dragon,' he explains to Sophie. 'Terrorised the neighbourhood before eventually being slain by Hercules.'

'As I've heard *many* times, Miles.'

'I insisted Mrs O'Dwyer remove her ghastly ornaments, so that at least some of my books could be put out. The rest are still in boxes.' Murdo clicks his teeth. 'Could be worse.' He turns to Sophie 'How are those twins of yours getting along? In their first year of university, aren't they?'

'Yes – Miranda's reading modern languages, and Helena's planning a change from sociology to law.'

'Splendid! Can't believe where the years have gone. Now, the hydra's left tea ready in the kitchen. Through that doorway. I don't suppose, Sophie, you would do the honours?'

'Of course.' She stands.

'That's the ticket! The lapsang's in the tin by the kettle.' As she moves towards the doorway, he says, 'I can't tell you, Miles, how appalled I am by this whole sorry—'

'You mentioned in your last letter that you've gained some valuable new insights into the Tacfarinian revolt in Numidia?' Miles interrupts, with a glance towards Sophie.

'Ah yes.' Murdo nods in understanding. 'Absolutely fascinating. Were you aware that one of the primary sources is being disputed by none other than…?'

But Miles can't concentrate. He listens to the hum of a kettle as it begins to boil. He needs to hone what he's going to say, so that it's neither too much nor too little. He's so engrossed in his own thoughts that when Sophie reappears in the doorway with the tray of tea, he experiences a momentary confusion – as if she were the hostess and he and Murdo the visitors.

'I still take a keen interest in the school, you know.' Murdo accepts a cup of tea from Sophie. 'Hope to make this year's speech day. But what a terrible business this—'

'These are delicious,' Miles interrupts, spreading jam on his scone.

'One thing to be said for the hydra – she provides a good spread. Only on Sundays, but she agreed to move the day in honour of your visit. The rest of the time I fend for myself. And manage splendidly, I might add. Do you take sugar, Sophie?'

She shakes her head. She's hardly eating anything, Miles notices. He himself tucks in – he hasn't had a tea like this for goodness knows how long.

'Takes one back a bit, doesn't it?' Murdo says, as if reading his thoughts. 'Now, did either of you see that article in the TLS about…'

Again, Miles struggles to give the subject his full attention. Suppose Sophie forgets their agreement to leave him and Murdo together? He can hardly force her out.

But, to his relief, as she returns from clearing up in the kitchen, she says, 'If it's all right with both of you, I think I'll walk down to the seafront. I fancy a breath of fresh air, and I'm sure you two have plenty to discuss.'

'Excellent idea!' Murdo says, levering himself out of his chair. He hands her a key. 'You can let yourself in again with that. We'll see you shortly, my dear.'

'A sound woman, that,' Murdo says, as they listen to her going off down the stairs.

He pours out two whiskies, and hands one to Miles. 'A little snifter to oil the cogs.'

'It's very good of you to see me like this,' Miles begins. 'Especially as it's not a matter I want to trouble Sophie with – not until absolutely necessary.'

Murdo taps the side of his nose. 'Best kept to ourselves.' He resumes his seat, crossing one bony leg over the other. 'The whole incident sounds most unfortunate.' He clicks his teeth. 'I remember young Cunningham, of course – always felt there was something a bit unreliable about him.'

Miles stares into the amber depths of his glass. Now

they've reached this point, he feels a return of his earlier apprehension. 'Sometimes I find it hard to recall exactly what *did* happen.' He gulps his whisky, taking comfort from the smoky warmth sliding down his gullet. 'As I explained in my letter, that Remove Year has been a particularly challenging one. Cunningham was the undoubted ringleader, although his two lieutenants, Webb and Owen, were not far behind.' He pauses. 'I dealt with them in the usual way – detentions, and the withdrawal of privileges.'

'The Fordingbury method,' Murdo interjects, 'and very effective it is too. Discipline, discipline – wherever would we be without it?'

Miles nods. 'The day there was all the fuss, the class had started, but not all the boys had arrived. I was just handing out a pile of homework, when Webb – you remember him?'

'Giant of a boy – stood head and shoulders above the others.'

'That's the one. Anyway, he came charging in, shouting something about an accident in the changing rooms. "Mr Whitaker, sir! Come quickly, sir!" he called.'

'So you did what most of us would do in the circumstances – dropped everything and went?'

'I wish to God I hadn't.' He's mortified to find himself near to tears. 'They set me up, Murdo. Cunningham was behind it of course – always resented any form of discipline. But I don't know how to make anyone, including Sophie and my daughters, believe me.'

Murdo shakes his head. 'Bad business. How about we take things one step at a time?'

*

Well over an hour later, Sophie returns. She's panting slightly, and is carrying two large bags of groceries.

'You should have left these in the car,' he whispers.

She gives a shake of her head, and it dawns on him that the shopping is not for them. He feels a moment's irritation. Heaven knows how Murdo will view this unwarranted charity. Fortunately, he has his back turned, and is thumbing through one of the books on the shelf.

Miles resumes his seat, initiating a hasty discussion on a recent translation of *The Iliad*. If Murdo hears the sound of groceries being unpacked in the kitchen, he studiously ignores them. How typical of him not to want to cause them any embarrassment!

When Sophie reappears, Miles stands up. Now it's time to leave, he feels a tug of regret. 'Well, we'd better hit the road, but you've been most helpful.'

'Think nothing of it.'

'Murdo is going to use his contacts on my behalf, Sophie. Isn't that wonderful?' He can't keep the relief from his voice.

'Yes, it is.'

She might sound more enthusiastic.

'Obviously I'll be in touch the moment I hear anything.' Murdo's voice is gruff.

'But come and see me again soon.'

'I will,' Miles promises, pressing the thin hand.

As he climbs into the Rover, he feels easier than he's

done in weeks. 'Murdo's promised to use his contacts – governors, a bishop or two, as well as a Member of Parliament.' He watches her switch on the headlights, and ease the car into the road.

She obviously hasn't been listening. 'Oh, Miles, all those empty cupboards.'

He's surprised by the note of distress in her voice. 'And you should have seen that fridge! A solitary egg, and a corner of mouldy cheese. You couldn't keep a child alive on that.'

TWENTY

MILES HAS TAKEN HIMSELF OFF – HEAVEN KNOWS where – so she's decided for once to spend time on herself. At the girls' urging, she's bought a hair colourant that promises to brighten the dullest look. She can't remember the last time she's used anything like this – obviously a while ago because the instructions are in such small print. A sign of the times, she thinks, giving a tch of annoyance. She rummages in her handbag for her glasses, before going through to the front room. She's already looked in all the obvious places, as well as those that Miles thinks she doesn't know about: the book with that hefty garage bill tucked inside it; the cupboard, where he keeps his whisky.

Of course she was worried sick when she first discovered them, but now she has his assurance that it's just a matter of time before they're back in South Lodge, there seems little point in challenging him. Alcohol is obviously his way of coping and they'll be able to sort out any debts once life settles down again.

She's going through one of the kitchen drawers, when she remembers their visit to Murdo earlier in the week. She must have had her glasses with her then.

The Rover is in its usual place, its shine covered in a layer of dust. Just as well, she thinks, recalling Kirsty's warning about theft. She brushes a dead leaf off the windscreen, before sliding into the driving seat.

As she'd feared, her glasses are not in her glove compartment, so she shifts her search to the passenger side, extracting some hand gel and a first aid kit. Then, right at the back, her hand closes on a crumpled envelope. She peers at it, registering the official stamp, and the fact that it's addressed to Miles. One more bill that he's hiding from her?

She takes the letter back to the kitchen, where straightaway she spots her glasses, propped behind the draining-board. She sits at the table and starts to read. After a few moments, she stops, staring ahead. Then goes through the document a second time, fighting off a growing disbelief. But there is no mistake. It's all there, in black and white – an order for Miles to attend court – next week, for God's sake! – on a charge of committing a sexual offence against a minor.

She sinks her head into her hands, recalling his assurance to both her and Helena and Miranda that the case was being dropped. Of course she believed him. Well, why wouldn't she? They've shared the ups and downs of school life all these years, have brought up the girls together, and have never had secrets from one another. Not like this.

It's too much. She'll think about it later. For now, she must have something to take her mind off things – a normal conversation to ground her in the everyday.

She seizes her bag and coat. Once outside, she replaces the court letter in the Rover, before walking round to Kirsty's front door. She presses the bell and, hears Big Ben chimes sound from inside. Please be in.

The door opens. Kirsty's eyebrows lift in surprise, but then she says quickly, 'Oh, good to see you, Sophie.'

'Is this all right?'

'Delighted to have the company. Come on in.'

She follows her into the hall, which is littered with an assortment of toys.

'You look a bit peaky. Hope you're not getting this bug that's doing the rounds?'

She forces a smile. 'I'm fine. Just thought I'd take you up on that offer of coffee.'

The younger woman is barefoot, in jeans and a glittery top. She's tied her hair back in a ponytail that shows off her long neck. She glances down at her own calf-length skirt, and the scuffed shoes she keeps meaning to replace.

'Henry and Ben are at school,' Kirsty says, 'so it's just Leo and me. You'll have to excuse the mess.'

'It's all right.' Sophie picks her way across the floor. 'My girls were the same at this age. It's good for them to rampage a bit.'

'Hello, Leo.' She stoops to retrieve a red spaceship that he's shot into the corner. She holds it out to him and, after a moment, he takes it from her before standing, thumb in mouth, regarding her. He has the same spiky hair as his brothers.

'He's sizing you up,' Kirsty says. 'He's very particular about his likes and dislikes.' She drops her voice to a whisper. 'Mike's mum is not exactly on his favourites list!'

Sophie smiles. 'When I was first married, my mother-in-law was so full of rules and regulations, she drove me up the wall.' She pauses. 'Perhaps that's why my husband relies on them so much.'

'Where did you say your school was?'

She feels herself colour. 'Outside Oxford. Can I give you a hand?'

Kirsty lifts Leo onto her hip. 'No, thanks. I'll just get that kettle on.' She points towards a doorway. 'Make yourself at home.'

The room Sophie enters is decorated in cream, with a polished wood floor, and a modern fire with a cream surround. The only splash of colour is from the print hanging above it – a couple dancing by the sea, the woman in a long scarlet dress. There's such a sense of lightness in the room, it's a surprise to look through the window and see the line of grey houses stretching into the distance.

She sinks onto a leather sofa. Through the archway she can see the kitchen's bright yellow walls and modern units. 'This is all really lovely, Kirsty!' she calls. 'What a difference it makes knocking the two rooms together.'

'Yes. We had a stroke of luck a couple of years back – a lottery windfall.'

'Goodness. I wasn't sure anyone actually ever won these things!'

'Well, they do. Though it wasn't one of the big ones, worse luck,' Kirsty says, coming through with the child in her arms, 'but enough to give us the deposit for this place, and for me not to have to look for work until Leo starts school.'

His eyes are beginning to droop. 'Would you mind?' she whispers, holding him out. 'If I try putting him down, he'll only yell.'

Sophie settles him onto her lap.

The younger woman goes back into the kitchen, and Sophie presses her face into the child's hair. She breathes in the smell of baby shampoo, recalling the twins at the same age – their round bodies and gappy smiles. Still, she wouldn't go back to all those sleepless nights, and being constantly on the go.

'If we're lucky we'll get five minutes to ourselves,' Kirsty says, coming back with a tray. She hands Sophie a mug of coffee. 'Flapjack?'

Sophie shakes her head.

Kirsty nods towards the sleeping Leo. 'How are your twins getting on?'

'Very well, thanks. It was so good seeing them. They're in their second term at university – Norwich and Bristol.'

Kirsty settles herself beside Sophie. 'I was offered a place at Birmingham, to do media studies. But in the end I turned it down.'

'Oh?'

'Decided to go for police training instead.'

Sophie gives a start. Kirsty was there, watching, as Miles and she were driven away in that marked car.

'Only in traffic, and I was glad to give it up when Henry came along.' She gives a wry smile. 'Well, Mike and I saw what those shift hours do to family life. He works in a leisure centre now – out in Watford. Bit of a commute, but at least it's a job. We were only in Victory House a year.' She sips her coffee. 'It was a tough time. All the drugs and smashed windows – no place to bring up kids.' She regards Sophie over the rim of her mug. 'Round here must be a bit of a let-down after Oxford.' Calling in like this was a mistake. She'll leave as soon as she's finished her coffee.

'I do miss it, but we should be away by the end of the month.'

Kirsty flexes bare toes. 'Mike and I have got plans too. Well, who'd want to stay in this area longer than they can help?'

Leo starts to grizzle, and Kirsty lifts him onto her lap, and reaches for the remote. '*CBeebies* – we'd be lost without it.' He puts his thumb in his mouth again, staring as a series of brightly-coloured birds hop across the screen. 'How did you manage with your twins?'

'Oh – I was lucky. I had plenty of help.' She sips her coffee. Just a few minutes more and she'll gather enough strength to stand up.

Kirsty glances out of the window. 'It's clouding over.' She turns to the child. 'We're going up to the swings in a little while, sweetheart, so Mum's just checking what the weather's going to do.'

She presses the control again, and the birds are replaced by a woman newsreader with a Northern Ireland accent. *In Downing Street today the Chancellor predicted tougher times ahead, but said he remains confident there will be no recession…*

All our unpaid bills, Sophie thinks.

The financial report is followed by pictures of another terrorist attack in the Middle East. Against the jagged backdrop of bombed-out buildings, fighter planes swoop out of the sky, while civilians stand, shocked and helpless, in the middle of blood-stained debris.

She feels exhausted watching it.

Suddenly, a fresh-faced male reporter is talking to camera.

At Winchester Crown Court, a forty-five-year-old man has been convicted on several charges of indecently assaulting children in his care. The abuse had been going on for a number of years, the chief superintendent confirmed. The victims' ages ranged from eight to fifteen. Passing a sentence of six years' imprisonment, the judge said –

Her mouth goes dry.

'Know what I'd do with him?' Kirsty drops her voice. 'String him up, and then cut off his balls!' She plants a kiss on the top of Leo's head.

Sophie is swept by a wave of nausea. 'Can I use your loo?'

'Sure. In the hall, on the right.'

Somehow she manages to get out of the room. She leans against the lavatory door, thinking back to Rupert Marshall's last phone call, and Miles's assertion that the case would not be going ahead. This letter is dated the following day, so he obviously lied to her. As he's lied about the bills and his drinking. And God knows what else besides.

She runs the cold tap and scoops water into her mouth. Why didn't I listen to Aunt Harriet? she thinks.

*

She took Miles down to Cornwall shortly after their engagement.

'Never heard of Fordingbury, Miss Ellacott?' Miles looked shocked. 'Of course it's not one of our mainstream establishments, but nevertheless we have built up a considerable reputation over the years.' He gave Sophie one of the wide grins she found so appealing. 'To begin with, the two of us will be in a flat in Oxford, but Murdo, my headmaster, is confident a house in the school grounds will come up soon. *Domus et placens uxor*,' he added. 'Horace – All a man needs for happiness is a roof over his head and a good wife.'

As Sophie was packing to return to London, her aunt took her to one side. The older sister of Sophie's father, she never married, although there had been a fiancé killed in the war. 'As you know, men were thin on the ground in my day,' she said now. 'You're lucky, my girl – spoilt for choice – so don't go throwing yourself away on just anyone!' She frowned. 'You should give yourself more time. There's something about Miles – all that strutting about the place – all those quotations.' She paused, before adding with a sigh: 'What I want to know is this: who is he?'

*

She needs to get out of here.

A burst of song informs her that Kirsty has switched back to the children's programme.

She pulls on her Burberry, and re-enters the front room.

'I'm really sorry about this, Kirsty,' she tries to keep her voice level, 'but I'm going to have to lie down.'

'You do look a bit off colour. Can I—?'

'No – it's all right – really.'

At the front door, Kirsty calls after her, 'Hope you'll soon feel better. Drop in again – anytime!'

On the pavement, Sophie pauses. It's starting to rain, but she can't bear the thought of re-entering the claustrophic gloom of number 49. Of being alone with the knowledge of the lies Miles has told.

TWENTY-ONE

A S SHE DRAWS LEVEL WITH THE MONKEY-PUZZLE
tree, a drop of rain bounces off her cheek. A few
yards further on the heavens open, the rain pounding the
pavement, driving against her face and soaking into her
hair.

The sensible thing would be to return to the house, but
she carries on, water splashing against her legs, the wet
seeping through the soles of her shoes.

In the road, the cars inch forward against the torrent
of rain, headlights on, wipers flicking backwards and
forwards. People are huddled in doorways, but she
continues at a half-run, past the newsagents, the chippie,
and the junk shop.

She goes down a side street, where the houses are set on a
ridge above the road. She has an impression of dirty pebble-
dash, mock mullion windows and steep front gardens.

She turns into a drive, overgrown with weeds, passing a disused entrance – the covered porch filled with cardboard boxes and piles of old newspapers – and round to the back, where an ancient Renault is parked. There's no bell or knocker, so she pounds the door with her fists.

After a few moments, it swings open and Seb stands facing her, barefooted, and dressed in a baggy jumper and jeans. He seems younger than she remembers.

She wants to smile her relief at seeing him, but she can't get her mouth to work properly.

He looks her up and down. 'You'd best come in.'

She finds herself in a square kitchen, lighter and roomier than the one in Stephen's

Close. A large dresser, crammed with an assortment of odds and ends, takes up one wall. In the centre, is a table strewn with paperwork that he pushes to one side.

She looks at him mutely.

'You're soaked through – let me take your mac.'

She obeys, wiping the wet off with the towel that he hands her.

'You look as if you could do with a hot drink.'

She nods.

He makes tea for them both, and sits opposite. 'There we go.'

She's grateful to him for not pressing her for information, when she can still barely get her words out.

They sip their drink in silence and after a while, she feels her panic subside. When she looks up, the eyes meeting hers are calm.

She begins with the phone call Miles received from Alan Sanderson, and the way the rest of the staff ostracised them; their ousting from South Lodge; Miles's continuing refusal to talk, and shutting her out of the solicitor's meeting; and, now, this shocking discovery that he's to face prosecution for a sexual offence. She tries, unsuccessfully, to hold back the tears. 'I keep telling myself there must be some good reason why he's kept his court appearance from me, but I honestly can't think of one. And because he's obviously lied about that, how can I believe his promise that he's innocent? And then there are my daughters...'

He pushes a box of tissues towards her, and she blows her nose. What on earth must he be thinking of her?

It's a relief when eventually he begins to speak. 'This is obviously a very tricky situation, Sophie, and you don't need me to tell you how important it is to get Miles to open up to you. The longer he withholds things, the more you'll continue to question his behaviour.' He tops up their mugs from a brown teapot. 'The shame attached to this sort of accusation can be very great.' He pauses. 'And, however it looks to the outside world, he may well be innocent.'

'You really think so?'

'Well, that's for you to discuss with him. But I think he deserves a fair hearing.'

She feels a renewal of hope. If Seb is not condemning Miles out of hand, then neither should she.

He glances at his watch.

'Oh, I'm sorry. I've taken up far too much of your time.'

'No worries. But I'm afraid I do have a meeting to go to.'

'Of course.' She gets to her feet.

'But I do think, Sophie, it might be a good idea for you to talk to a professional.' He roots amongst the pile of papers on the dresser. 'Ah, here we are.' He hands her a card. *Dr Ruth Madiebo, psychologist, psychotherapist.*

'The woman I met at the church?'

'The very one. I think you could do with more support than I'm able to offer. I'm sure you'll find her helpful, though it's up to you, of course.' He passes her coat to her. 'I'll just let my partner know that I'm going out.'

'Oh.'

'And here he is.'

A black man in a business suit has appeared in the far doorway. 'Hope I'm not interrupting?' He's strikingly handsome, with close-cropped hair and gold-rimmed glasses.

'No, I'm just leaving.' She forces a smile.

'I'll run Sophie home, Chuma, and go on to my meeting from there. No...' as she starts to protest. 'I insist – it's still chucking it down.'

A few minutes later, entering the damp house, she's relieved to find that Miles is still not back. She needs time to herself, to try and come to terms with all that's happening.

She changes out of her wet clothes and, returning downstairs, shoves the hair colourant in the bin.

Supper will be spaghetti bolognese. What a fool I've been, she thinks, as she chops onion and garlic, to have imagined, even for a moment, that Seb could rescue me from this mess.

TWENTY-TWO

I N THE SECOND YEAR OF HER NURSE'S TRAINING, there was a major pile-up on a local dual carriageway. It couldn't have come at a worse time, coinciding both with the weekend and with a staff flu epidemic.

A handful of students and junior doctors battled to cope with the stream of broken and bloodied bodies. Sophie, looking up from inserting an IV line, spotted a tall figure coming into the department in a shambling run. It was her first glimpse of Alastair, who admitted afterwards to being out of his depth – though you'd never have known it from the confident way he took charge. The team worked through that night and most of the following day, and Sophie remembered how his presence seemed to lessen both her uncertainty and her tiredness.

A week later she and bumped into each other in the canteen and he asked her out for a drink. She'd been surprised and flattered. He was a junior consultant, eight years older and about to make a name for himself, though neither of them realized it at the time. She had slept with two other men before him – brief relationships, mainly due to the long and erratic hospital hours. This was her first serious affair.

On their first date, she wore a black vinyl jacket, pedal pusher jeans and four-inch heels that brought her up almost to Alastair's height. They played every bit as hard as they worked, clubbing into the small hours, dashing down to country pubs in his green sports car and making love on the rickety bed in his Earl's Court flat.

'However did I get by without you?' he would murmur, stroking her body with his capable hands.

With his dark good looks and magnetic personality, he was always the life and soul of any party, flirting with the other women, joking with the men, but always with an arm around her, or a look that told her she was the one who mattered.

'I never dreamed life could be this wonderful,' Sophie confided to her aunt during one of the couple's visits to Cornwall.

'Well, in my day Alastair would have been called "a bit of a catch". And I'm delighted, girl, to see you so happy.'

'We're starting to talk about the next step – when I've finished my training and he has his promotion.'

'Just give me enough warning, so I can dig out my best hat.'

Things couldn't get any better, Sophie felt, until the morning she realised, with a sinking sensation in her stomach, that her period was over a week late.

She didn't break the news to Alastair until she was sure but, even then, she wasn't unduly concerned. After all, he wanted to specialise in paediatrics, and they were in love.

'You're *what*?' he demanded, his expression as incredulous as if he'd never heard the term, pregnancy. 'But you told me you were on the pill.'

'I'm sorry, Alastair. That Brighton weekend – I must have forgotten to take it.'

It was the early hours, and they were having coffee in the deserted canteen – not the ideal time or place, but for the past week he'd been working an eighteen-hour shift, and she didn't want to delay telling him, so he could share her excitement.

He looked across at her and, when she saw the coldness in his eyes, she could have wept.

'I've been thinking for quite a while, Sophie' – he spooned sugar into his mug – 'that perhaps it's time for us to have a bit of a breather.'

'But the baby?' *Your baby*, she wanted to say.

'Well, obviously it's up to you whether you want to keep it.' His tone was as clinical and detached as if he were giving a medical diagnosis to a stranger. 'It might be in your best interests not to, and if you go down that route, of course I'll support you.'

She was so shocked by his reaction that she could only nod; too stunned to speak, or to give any real thought to her unborn child. The grieving would come later.

The following month his sports car pulled up outside the clinic he'd chosen. 'Only the best for you, Sophie,' he said.

She slammed the car door in his face and, as she began walking up the ramp to the main doors, she heard him call after her: 'Good luck!'

A week later she fled, like a wounded bird, to her one place of refuge.

Aunt Harriet took one look at her. 'What you need, Sophie, is to get away from it all for a while.' She thought for a moment. 'I've always promised to visit my cousin, Muriel, in Christchurch. It'll take a fair bit of organising, but that's what we'll do.' And, as Sophie opened her mouth to protest, she added, 'And that decision, my girl, is final.'

Sophie was too numb to voice the query as to why so much organisation should be required, and it was only a couple of weeks later that it dawned on her that the Christchurch was not the town a few hours' drive away in Hampshire, but the one in New Zealand.

They went by ship, and night after night as she lay in her berth, she couldn't rid herself of the memory of being stretched out on the operating table while the baby – her and Alastair's child – was scooped out of her.

TWENTY-THREE

MILES STEPS BACK FROM THE MOTTLED GLASS OF the bathroom mirror, confident that his appearance strikes just the right note. His jacket and cords have been given a good brushing, and the touch of colour provided by his claret tie makes him seem more confident – less defeated.

The boiler gives a groan but, to his relief, there's not a sound from the bedroom. A part of him is relieved because Sophie has become silent and withdrawn once more, and he's not sure how to react.

Yesterday, hearing her key in the lock, he came out of the front room to see if she needed a hand with the shopping. But she wasn't carrying anything, and they stood facing one another in silence. He'd almost decided to come clean about his court hearing, but one look at her set expression decided him against it. Better to go on his own and anyway, he can't bear the thought of her being in court, witnessing his humiliation.

He straightens his shoulders. After all, Sanderson has assured him that today will just be a formality.

He gives his tie a final tweak, before creeping downstairs. He's catching an early train from Paddington, and will grab something to eat in Oxford.

He scribbles Sophie a note to say he'll be out most of the day and, after a moment's hesitation, tucks his briefcase under his arm. It's the one she gave him fifteen years ago on his promotion to senior master. Although somewhat battered, just having it with him will help his confidence.

He's walking away from the house, when he claps his hand to his head. He turns, and opening the Rover's passenger door, feels inside the glove compartment. The envelope is there, although he could have sworn he'd shoved it right at the back. Surely Sophie...? But of course not. She would have said something. For now, it's just a relief to have remembered it. He fights an urge to curl up on the back seat, contenting himself by giving the bonnet a surreptitious pat before setting off up the road.

He reaches Oxford in good time, forcing himself to down coffee and toast in a hotel near the station. A taxi drops him a few minutes' walk from the court – he needs the fresh air to calm his nerves, and to soothe the beginnings of heartburn.

There seem to be building works everywhere, and as he crosses a set of traffic lights, he thinks that at least this is an area where he's unlikely to run into anyone he knows

– although after that disastrous encounter with Paget, nowhere feels safe any more.

He finds the court entrance down a side turn, and ducks inside. At the security barrier his briefcase – empty apart from his newspaper – is searched. He walks up a steep flight of steps and approaches the reception area with trepidation. What if his name is shouted out? Or he's given a number, like some criminal? But the middle-aged woman behind the desk merely smiles politely before ticking him off on a list. 'Court 2 – morning hearing, Mr Whitaker,' she says, pointing him to the row of grey plastic seating on the concourse.

The wall clock says twenty to nine, and he's relieved to see that, apart from a trio of youths swigging cans of drink in the far corner, and a fat woman in earnest discussion with a man in a dark suit – her lawyer, Miles assumes – the place is empty.

He settles at the end of a row, glad of a chance to compose himself before Marshall's arrival.

A black-gowned usher walks past, clutching a sheaf of papers. He always associates those gowns with academia. My Oxford interview, he thinks. The early seventies it had been, and it still pains him to recall Murdo's confidence in his star pupil. Miles too felt well prepared, having boned up on all his favourite authors.

A gaunt, middle-aged woman, with metal jewellery that clunked alarmingly as she walked, showed him into a study, where he perched on the edge of his chair.

It was a room his mother would have described as being "in the best of good taste", and would have been intimidated by. There were a couple of oil paintings on the walls, a scattering of patterned rugs on the polished floorboards, and a view from the mullioned window of sloping tiles with, far below, a square of bright emerald lawn.

All so different from his parents' home, with its reproduction furniture and cheap prints, the neat bed of marigolds in the back garden and the fence his father coated in creosote at the start of each summer.

'So, Mr Whitaker' – the interviewer gave a shake of the head that set her necklace jangling – 'what makes you think you are a suitable candidate for this college?'

All his carefully prepared words evaporated.

After an agonising few moments, she crossed one skinny, black-stockinged leg over the other. 'Your views on the Vietnam War?'

At first hesitantly, and then with growing confidence, he began to talk about the importance of the West occupying the moral high ground. 'One has to concede that there is such a thing as a *jus bellum* – a war that is fought to achieve justice, and that—'

'The just side being?' the woman interrupted.

'America, of course.'

She gave a loud snort, pushing back her chair to indicate that the meeting – and the prospect of a glittering academic career – were at an end.

And still, all these years later, he finds himself wondering how on earth one could prepare oneself for the unexpected? How on earth—?

'Ah – Miles. You're here already. Excellent!'

Rupert Marshall stands over him, hand outstretched.

His grey jacket, toning with the silver hair, has the lustre of fine wool.

He scrambles out of his chair.

'I've secured a room, if you'd just follow me. I'm still optimistic the magistrates will accept jurisdiction. So plea before venue and a trial date.'

No doubt he has explained all this already, but yet again, Miles struggles to make sense of it.

Marshall peers at him over his glasses. 'Are you all right?'

He nods, fighting nausea.

'Some coffee, perhaps?'

He shakes his head.

'Wise decision. The machine stuff is pretty filthy.' He consults his watch. 'I'll leave you to it then. I need to have a word in the right ear – ensure things go smoothly. Won't be long.'

Left alone, Miles pats his pocket, where the summons is safely tucked away. It's a comfort to know that, as far as Sophie is concerned, this court appearance isn't happening. Yet as he stares around the small room, a part of him longs to have her beside him.

Perhaps he'll have a bash at the crossword to take his mind off things. He opens his briefcase, and takes out his paper. One across: *Old measure for convicted garden visitor? (4,4.)* He fills in the answer – *yard bird* – the word "convicted" dancing before his eyes.

Marshall puts his head round the door. 'Time, Miles. As I told you, I've gone for an early hearing. The press don't usually get going until later.'

Miles shoves his paper away and, keeping his eyes

fixed on the tiled floor, follows the solicitor across the busy public area and through a doorway.

The courtroom is smaller than he imagined, with wood panelling and dark blue chairs. The usher points to the glassed-in area of the dock. Marshall warned him he would have to enter it, yet still he feels a jolt of alarm.

Once inside, he stands, knees trembling, facing the three figures on the bench: a well-fed, bearded man of about his own age, flanked by two younger women, both in blouses and navy jackets. They could easily be Fordingbury parents, and at the thought his mouth goes dry.

In front of him are two rows of tables and chairs, all facing the bench. Nearest it, a short, bald man with an ear-stud, presumably a court official, is studying some papers. Behind him, beside Marshall, is the prosecutor, a young woman in black trousers and top. She looks harmless enough. Miles risks a quick glance at the rows of public seating. He had worried that the Cunningham parents, and Sanderson himself, might attend, but the area is empty. He feels his shoulders relax.

'Name and address,' the official says, and Marshall turns and gives an encouraging nod.

To Miles's relief, his voice remains steady. It feels as if he's taking part in some drama production and, so far, is managing not to fluff his lines.

After the chairman has given a warning about not identifying the alleged victim outside the courtroom, the bald court official speaks. 'Miles Whitaker, you are charged that between 3rd November 2014 and the 20th January 2015 you committed a series of sexual assaults upon a minor, namely Justin James Cunningham.' The voice continues, listing the charges in detail. How terrible they sound. He wishes he could stop his knees shaking.

'Has your client given an indication of plea?' the chairman asks.

'He has, Your Worships. It is one of Not Guilty.'

'Have a seat then, Mr Whitaker, whilst we hear the facts.'

He leans forward, trying to take in what the woman prosecutor is saying. 'On the face of it, Your Worships, this may not seem an offence that falls into the most serious category. Certainly no one is suggesting that it is at the top end of the scale. Nonetheless, given that the alleged victim is underage and a breach of trust is involved, the Crown does take a serious view.'

The court official and the magistrates are making notes, and the bearded chairman nods his head. Surely not in agreement?

Then Marshall is on his feet. 'My client is a man of impeccable character and standing, Your Worships. A man who has devoted his entire life to his school and to his community. As my friend has made clear, we are not talking about an alleged offence at the higher end of the scale. Even in the very unlikely event of my client being found guilty of this charge, he would not be facing a prolonged term of imprisonment.'

Imprisonment? Miles feels the room tilt.

'I would argue most strongly that this case is suitable to be heard in the lower court.'

The bearded chairman looks up. 'The bench will retire.'

Once the three have gone out, Marshall turns and nods at him, before talking with the young woman prosecutor. Surely it's not right for them to be smiling at one another? They're on opposite sides after all. When the usher comes up to ask if he'd like some water, he shakes his head. He's trembling too much to hold a glass steady.

After what seems an interminable wait, the official shouts, 'Court rise!' and the magistrates file back in. Miles sits as ordered, feeling his breakfast heavy in his stomach.

'Taking into account all the circumstances of the alleged offence,' the chairman announces, 'the bench is declining jurisdiction. The case will go to the Higher Court.'

Miles's insides lurch. He's clung to the hope that the magistrates would hear it, and surely Marshall thought this would happen? He wills the man to turn round, but he remains with his back to him.

'And the bail situation?' the chairman asks.

The prosecutor is on her feet again. 'The Crown is not opposed to bail, Your Worships, but in view of the fact that the alleged victim is underage, would ask for conditions – reporting, as well as residency and no contact. As you will be aware, the well-being and safety of young people must take precedence.'

'Your Worships,' – Marshall spreads his hands to convey his astonishment – 'through an administrative error, my client was not bailed by the police at the outset. When they eventually rectified the situation, he had already moved away from the school, and the conditions imposed were of residency and no contact. He has remained at his current address since leaving the school, and has turned up in court today. I respectfully request that the current conditions be allowed to continue.'

The magistrates go into a huddle again. Miles leans forward, but it's impossible to pick up what they're saying. They surely wouldn't – they *couldn't* – send him to prison at this stage?

After a few moments the chairman looks across at Miles. 'Could you stand please, Mr Whitaker?'

Miles stands, his shirt sticking to his back, his heart hammering in his chest.

'We are sending the case to the Crown Court for a Plea and Trial Preparation Hearing. In view of your previous good character, we are prepared to grant bail, with two conditions. You must live and sleep each night at number 49 Stephen's Close. And you must not contact, directly or indirectly, any pupil or staff member at Fordingbury School. Do you understand?'

Miles nods.

'Please ensure you keep in touch with your solicitor. Very well – you are free to go.'

With shaking hands, he picks up his briefcase and, released from the dock, follows Marshall out of the court, waiting for the chance of a private word. But the man is consulting his watch, moving along the concourse and down the steep stairs.

Once outside, Marshall pauses, his face expressionless. 'We do get bowled the occasional googly, I'm afraid. Another bench and the outcome might well have been different.'

'But you said my case would stay with the magistrates.' He can't keep the tremor out of his voice.

'No – what I said was that it was a possible outcome, but it was never a foregone conclusion.' He pauses. 'Of course, we're hoping these boys will prove as unreliable under cross-examination as most teenagers.'

'But—'

'Think of this as a setback only, Miles. And the good thing is the press haven't got hold of it.' Marshall extends a hand. 'I'll be in touch as soon as we have Full Case details. And I'll be briefing our barrister.' He glances at his watch. 'Now, you'll have to forgive me, but I have to be at the Crown Court in twenty minutes.'

Obviously the man must deal with dozens of cases like this, but the thought brings no comfort.

Miles begins walking along the road, the sun hot in his face, and the sweat trickling down his back.

There will be no getting out of telling Sophie now.

He feels dizzy and nauseous, not sure how much longer he can keep going. And then, like a miracle, a green space opens in front of him.

He goes down a path, with a bank of shrubs along one side, aware of the smell of damp earth, and – Bile fills his mouth, and he makes a dash for a far corner, puking up his breakfast into a bank of laurel.

After a while, he straightens up and heads for the station, the sour taste of vomit in his mouth.

TWENTY-FOUR

WHY WOULD AN INNOCENT MAN COVER UP THE fact he's facing prosecution?

'Did you do anything special today?' she'd asked, when he returned to the house. But he just shook his head, before disappearing into the front room. She could have pressed him further, but there seemed little point.

Now she hesitates, before reaching for her phone. After a few seconds, the familiar Welsh lilt comes down the line. 'Sophie, *cariad*. Is that really you?'

How wonderful to hear a friendly voice! 'Rach. How are you?'

'You've rather caught me on the hop, my lovely. The two of us had our hands full at the best of times, and now it's me on my tod, I don't know if I'm coming or going.'

She's swept by a familiar sense of guilt. 'They haven't found a replacement for me then?'

Rachel laughs. 'You know what this place is like. Takes months to change one item on the dinner menu.'

Is incompetence the real reason? Or has her job been kept open because Miles is telling the truth, and it's just a matter of time before they're back at Fordingbury? How she wishes she could believe it, but there's that court letter.

'So, how are things in the big smoke?' Rachel is asking.

'Well...' Sophie pauses to collect her thoughts. 'It's all been a bit of a roller-coaster, as you can imagine. We're still in the same—'

'Hang on a moment, would you? – *No, Daniel, you may not bring crisps into the sickbay. How many more times do I have to say it? Empty your other pocket. Now!* – Sorry, Sophie. You were saying?'

'You're obviously up to your eyes, so I won't keep you. But...' she draws in her breath, 'I'm ringing to see if there's any chance of our meeting up.'

'*Put them over there, Daniel.* Well, to be honest, life is pretty full on. All I can say is, thank God for the Easter break.'

'Which must start tomorrow. Any chance of your fitting me in for a coffee?'

'Well, if you're coming down here...'

'I was thinking London. I mean, the way things are at the moment, it's probably better if I give Oxford a wide berth.' She hesitates. 'I was wondering what you've heard – about us?'

'Nothing really, my lovely.'

A bell clangs in the background.

'I need to see you, Rach. It's really important. *Please.*'

There's a pause, and then she says slowly, 'Well, as it happens Saturday's clear. I could take the train up to Paddington...'

*

'You'll be out most of the day, then?' Miles says as they're finishing breakfast.

'Seb's short of volunteers, so I've offered to give a hand at the church.' She pauses. 'You can still come along, if you want?'

He purses his lips. 'Not one for me, thanks all the same.'

'I'll be in for supper. Oh, and there's the remains of that shepherd's pie in the fridge.'

'Thanks.' He scrapes his chair back. 'I'd better tackle some paperwork.'

He goes to give her a kiss, and she turns to avoid his lips.

An hour later, she's in the Tube, working out what she's going to say to her friend.

They've always confided in one another, but this situation with Miles feels different and, if she's honest, mortifying. Yet there was that time a few years back, when Rachel discovered Brian was about to move in with another woman. Rachel had been near breaking point. But I supported her through it, Sophie thinks now. 'I can't thank you enough, *cariad*,' she recalls her saying, when Brian eventually returned home. 'I hope you know I'll always be there for you.'

It's turned warm – for once she doesn't need her raincoat – and she's in her one good skirt and blouse. But how out of place she feels! Most of those around her look to be in their twenties, dressed in shorts and T-shirts, chatting and joking with one another.

She thinks of Miranda, on a culture trip to Paris with a group of friends, and Helena busy organising a debate on women and slavery. She's glad they're getting on with their lives, removed from all this worry – at least for the time being.

She's waiting at the barrier as Rachel's train pulls in, and her heart lifts as she spots the plump figure coming towards her. She's wearing the green crinkled skirt and orange top that she's had for years and, for a moment, as they exchange hugs, Sophie sees them through a Londoner's eyes: two dowdy, middle-aged women, up from the country.

'Thanks so much for coming, Rach.'

'No problem. I always enjoy a trip to town, though I'll need to catch the four o'clock back.'

'That gives us a nice long time for lunch. Hope you're hungry? I've spotted an Italian place near Praed Street.'

The restaurant, with its linen tablecloths and leather-bound menus is pricier than she'd have liked, but it's her way of thanking Rachel and, if she's being honest, of encouraging her to open up more.

They order fresh sardines, followed by a chicken salad for her and a clam and spaghetti dish for Rachel. Over a bottle of pinot grigio, Rachel fills Sophie in on the school news: Alan Sanderson has introduced a whole raft of rules and regulations; there's been a flu epidemic; and the third form have been gated for letting down the tyres of the science master's Volvo.

'I always thought from what Miles says that it was the Remove Year who were the unruly ones,' Sophie says.

'Yes, but it's a matter of knowing how to handle them.'

Do you see much of the Cunningham boy? Sophie wants to ask. But Rachel is launching into news of her son, Dillon, two years younger than the twins, who's been offered a place to read engineering at Birmingham.

'That's brilliant!' Sophie nods thanks to the waiter, who's topping up their wine.

'Miranda was asking after him the other day.'

'And how are the girls getting on?'

'They're loving their courses. Miranda's been offered a year's study in Barcelona, and Helena has been made secretary of the debating society.'

'And no doubt wiping out all before her!'

They both laugh. 'I do miss them.' Sophie sips her wine. 'And Brian?'

'Doing just great. Sends his love.'

In the pause that follows, Sophie registers that, whilst she hasn't yet mentioned Miles, neither has Rachel asked after him.

She watches her friend suck up strands of spaghetti, the sauce spattering the cloth.

Sophie picks at her food, suddenly uncertain. Although outwardly nothing has changed, both of them seem to have run out of things to say.

She leans across the table. 'I'm desperate for someone to talk things through with, Rach. Someone I can trust. As I know I can you.' She swallows more wine, enjoying the feeling of release it gives.

'Of course you can talk to me, my lovely.' Rachel wipes her mouth. 'God, that's delicious! Such a change after the bangers and mash we live on at home. Are you having a pudding?'

'Just coffee. But you go ahead.'

Rachel eats her tiramisu with obvious enjoyment and Sophie feels a prick of resentment. 'As I've said, Rach, I'd be really grateful for your advice.'

She puts her spoon down with a sigh. 'The truth is, Sophie, I shouldn't be here in the first place. We've been warned off you, you know. Brian would kill me if he knew.'

She pictures Brian – a short, sandy-haired man with an easy-going manner and a belly that shakes when he laughs. It's hard to imagine him getting angry with anyone, Sophie thinks. But then I always thought he was the last person to have an affair.

'So, what's being said about us at the school?'

'Well…' Rachel hesitates, 'nothing much really.'

'You mean Miles and I haven't been the subject of staffroom gossip?' *Do they believe that Miles has done this terrible thing?*

'The point is, Sophie, there's my job to consider. Brian and I aren't getting any younger, see, and there's Dillon's future too.' She sips her coffee. 'The staff has been given strict orders not to discuss the case, even amongst ourselves.'

Sophie raises her eyebrows. 'If only Murdo were still there.'

Rachel leans towards her. 'I'll be the first to admit that Alan has taken a bit of getting used to.'

'Oh?'

'He's not a bad sort, Sophie. Very straight down the line, if you know what I mean.

And we're all aware, of course, how much Murdo let things go.'

Suddenly, Sophie feels defensive of the old man. 'At least he'd have been loyal to his staff.'

'That's true. Especially to Miles.' She pauses, while the waiter places coffee in front of them. 'After all, they did have a pretty special relationship.'

Sophie stares at her. 'How do you mean, *special*?'

Rachel spoons sugar into her cup. 'Well, it's common knowledge that Miles was his star pupil; and then they went back such a long way. Remember how they used to be closeted together for hours at a time, even in the holidays? Brian and I often said how sorry we were for you...' She breaks off. 'I mean it must have been rather difficult...'

Sophie bangs her cup down. 'Actually, it wasn't difficult at all.' She pauses. 'I just felt glad that Miles had such a friend.' But the truth is, she thinks, I was too busy to give it much thought. What separate lives we led.

Rachel regards her across the table. 'That's all right then.'

But it clearly *isn't* all right.

She draws in her breath. 'Let me ask you something, Rach. Do the rest of the staff believe that Miles could be guilty of this?'

Rachel's cheeks flush. 'Of *course* not. But...' she hesitates, 'as Brian says, it isn't what *we* believe any more. It's what the court decides.'

Sophie recalls a white-faced Miles, informing her they had to pack up and leave, and later that day, she and Rachel weeping and hugging one another, Rachel swearing to do all she could to help.

'Between you and me,' Rachel is saying, 'I've always thought Justin Cunningham a bit of a toe rag. He was in sickbay again recently with a dose of flu and, although I shouldn't be saying it, I was glad to see the back of him.'

It feels good to have Miles's views on the boy corroborated. 'So surely, Rach, most people can tell Justin's not to be trusted?'

'But it's not only what *he's* saying, is it? The staff aren't meant to have got wind of any of this, Sophie, but, as you know, there aren't many secrets at Fordingbury.' She sips her coffee, studying Sophie over the rim of her cup. 'You do realise that two other boys in his year are involved, and are going to give evidence?'

The information feels like a kick in the stomach. 'I didn't know. Miles has had one court appearance that I'm aware of, but he won't talk to me about it.'

Rachel stares at her. 'Then isn't it about time you made him? And I know it's unlikely, but suppose he *were* to be convicted? Where would that leave you?'

'He won't be, Rach.' Does her voice sound as desperate as she feels?

'Yes – but just supposing he is. What will you do then? You really need to think things through.' She's speaking rapidly, as if afraid of interruption, or as if, Sophie thinks, she's rehearsed what she's going to say. 'For a start, there'd be no question of your returning to the school.'

'That would finish Miles. Fordingbury's his whole life.'

'I can see that. But what about Helena and Miranda?'

She puts down her wine glass. Why have her first thoughts not been for them? 'Well, obviously we've outlined the general situation to them, but Miles insists on playing everything down. I'm sure he's just being protective.'

Rachel's face creases with concern. 'Listen to me, Sophie. Even without the charges he's facing, Alan Sanderson is very much the new broom. He'll drag Fordingbury into the twenty-first century – and not before time, I might add. The school's in desperate need of IT equipment, as well as new sports facilities. There's even talk of selling South Lodge to bring in some extra capital.'

'Sell South Lodge?' Sophie is aghast. 'But it's our *home*!' A new thought strikes her. 'And what about Miles's pension? And the bonus Murdo promised him?'

'Miles will still get his state pension, won't he?' Rachel says. 'And he's not so far off retirement.'

'Yes, but—'

'You must have savings? I always thought you two did rather well out of Fordingbury.' She pauses. 'All that wining and dining, and the girls in private schools.' She gives an unamused laugh. 'Not like Brian and me, still in the same bungalow – working our socks off to pay the mortgage.'

Rachel couldn't possibly be envious, could she? Obviously on Miles's salary they'd never have afforded those school fees, which were paid for by Aunt Harriet.

But to admit that to Rach now might only add to her envy. She swallows. 'I'm sure we'll get by, one way or another.'

'There you are then.' Rachel glances at her watch. 'Heavens, will you look at the time. I must make a move.'

With a growing feeling of despondency, Sophie beckons for the bill.

'I forgot to ask: how's the London pad working out?'

Sophie thinks of the flaking paintwork, the cracked bathroom tiles and the garden that stinks of cat pee. She gives a huff of annoyance. 'You're talking as if it's some bijou residence in Kensington. The fact is, Rach, we've ended up in a real dump! You should see the place – you wouldn't want to spend even an hour there.' Suddenly she finds herself choking with anger. 'Thanks to Brian, we've been well and truly conned. The rent's exorbitant, and we're tied into the lease for months yet.'

Rachel glares at her. 'Brian was only doing his best. And at least he found you somewhere.'

'Well, we'd have been a sight better off if he hadn't bothered!'

She thinks again of how she stood by Rachel through the difficult patch in her marriage. Where was her friend's support for her now?

'But how on earth was Brian meant to know, *cariad*?'

'*Don't* call me that!'

The words echo round the small restaurant, and a diner in the corner looks up.

Rachel leans forward. 'Look, my lovely, I know you're upset. But all Brian did was put you in touch with his cousin. The rest was up to you, surely?'

The fact there's justice in what Rachel is saying merely adds to her stinging sense of resentment.

'I've really stuck my neck out meeting you like this.'

'So you've said.'

The waiter comes over with the credit card machine. Miles has promised his salary is still coming into their account each month, but how long will they get by on it?

When she's completed the payment, she says, 'So Sanderson must believe that Miles is guilty?'

'Can't you see that Alan's hands are tied? The three boys must be pretty convincing, or the police wouldn't be continuing with the case.'

You're reacting as if Miles has done this thing, she thinks. She stares past Rachel into the street, where the sun still shines and life continues as normal. 'You've known us both so long, Rach. You can't believe him capable of it, surely?'

She says slowly, 'No, I don't think I do.'

'You don't *think* you do?'

She bends down for her bag, but not before Sophie catches the guarded look in her eyes.

'What is it you're not telling me, Rach?'

'Let's just leave it there, shall we?' She straightens with a sigh. 'Look, I have to go, or I'll miss my train.'

They gather up their things and walk back to the station.

Once, they would have linked arms. Now the distance between them is like a chasm.

TWENTY-FIVE

Sophie looks around Ruth Madiebo's room, thinking what a welcome contrast it is to the dingy squalor of Stephen's Close. A rug, patterned in brightly coloured zigzags hangs on one wall, and facing it are two small masks, and a series of abstract photographs. A shelf in the corner is filled with an assortment of carved figures with, below them, a glazed urn, crammed with orange and yellow sunflowers. Although she knows little about African art, she appreciates the vibrancy of this space.

Ruth Madiebo remains impassive, and Sophie wishes she could shake off a lingering disappointment that Seb isn't the one sitting opposite. She's continued to attend the Sunday service at St Saviour's, and has dropped in at the rectory a couple of times. Although he's obviously not interested in women – or not in *that* way – still she knows herself to be attracted to him. She can see his hands

– long-fingered, with a slight fuzz of hair on the back; hear the rise and fall of his voice, and—

'I wondered where your thoughts are taking you?'

She feels herself blush. But she doesn't want to hold back in here – she's doing enough of that with Miles. 'I was thinking of Seb Webster, and how much I mind his being gay.'

'Ah.'

She stares out of the window again. A workman on a scaffold is gesturing to another and, a moment later, a bucket begins its slow descent, the sun glancing off metal as it twists its way to the level below.

'It's really bringing home the kind of life Miles and I led at Fordingbury.' She pauses to gather her thoughts. 'I've always had my hands full working in the sickbay, as well as running the house, and he's been absorbed in his teaching. Even in the holidays he'd be preparing lessons, or discussing school affairs with the headmaster.'

'You found the marriage rather a lonely one?'

'I suppose I did, although of course I had the girls. We've always been very close.'

'But now they've flown the nest?'

'Yes.' She feels the tears well up. 'Thankfully, they're shielded from the worst of what's happening. Though for how much longer, I don't know.'

'You say the worst, Sophie. What would that be?'

'Well – if Miles were…' She breaks off and, before Dr Madiebo can respond, adds: 'It was my decision to have children. Miles wasn't too keen. He felt the Fordingbury boys took up all his time and attention.'

'And what was it like to hear that?'

'Not easy. I wanted to explain how desperately I needed a baby after the termination I'd had before we met, but I couldn't seem to make him listen.'

She pictures the day she had yet another go at telling Miles. They had moved into South Lodge a couple of weeks earlier, following his promotion to housemaster, and were taking coffee in the study.

She drew in her breath. 'There's something I need to explain, Miles. Something that happened before we met, and—'

A look of alarm crossed his face and he glanced at his watch. 'Blast! Is that the time? Afraid I'm going to have to dash.'

She should have sat him down and forced him to listen, but once again she hadn't.

And it really didn't seem to matter all that much. He was not a man who disclosed his own feelings, remaining the same cheery Miles she'd always known, striding about the school, always ready with some pun or quotation. His enthusiasm for his work was one of the things she found most attractive.

Those Wednesday afternoons – the twins at school and the boys bussed off to away matches – when she and Miles had the house to themselves. All that tumbling on the double bed.

'The physical side was good – well, good fun. You know...' Her voice tails away.

'I realise how difficult it must be for you, Sophie, to focus on what's happening now, but if I get the picture right, you're left wondering how well you know the man you've been living with all these years.'

She gives a slow nod. 'The day of his court hearing, I lay in bed listening to him creeping around the house. He assumed I was asleep – that I didn't know where he was off to. If he'd explained he needed to be on his own, I would have understood. At least it would have been better than him sneaking off like that.' Her voice trembles. 'Why on earth didn't he tell me?'

'And it's obviously left you with questions?'

'Well, if he's hiding this, what else might there be?' She hesitates again. 'It could be all sorts of things, couldn't it? Nothing very much – or something serious.'

'Very serious indeed.'

Sophie swallows. 'Yes.'

'Something unspeakable – child sexual abuse.'

The shock of the words makes her catch her breath. 'I hope to God I'm wrong,' she murmurs.

'But you still won't confront Miles?'

'I have tried, but either he clams up or he tells me a pack of lies.'

'So the toughest part is that you're left not knowing what to believe?'

She looks across at the blue and gold African mask. The eye sockets stare blankly. 'Before all this happened, I'd have said Miles would be the last person to be accused of this sort of thing. There's never been any hint of it, and surely I'd have known? But then, the more I think about it, the more I wonder. I mean – how does one person ever know what someone else is capable of?'

Ruth Madiebo leans forward again. 'I do appreciate how very hard all this must be for you, Sophie, but we're going to have to leave it there for today.'

'Oh. I wondered – just before we finish. What would you advise?'

'Advise?'

'What should I do?' It's not an unreasonable question, surely?

Ruth Madiebo raises an eyebrow. 'Let's return to this again.' She walks over to the door. 'The same time next week, then.'

It's the lunch hour and the pavements are busy. A young couple are weaving their way towards her, hand in hand, and beside her, a woman in a business suit is laughing uproariously into her mobile. Sophie feels like screaming at them: 'If you were in my shoes, you wouldn't be so fucking pleased with life either!'

A stiff drink might help calm her, but she doesn't fancy going into a pub on her own. Then, down a side street, she spots a cafe with a striped awning. She turns into it, choosing an empty table at the back. The room is crowded, but there are fresh flowers on the counter and a delicious smell of freshly baked bread. What wouldn't she give to be sitting here with the girls, or with Connie and Marcia? To have her old life back?

She's not spoken with Rachel since their disastrous lunch, and although she's left several apologetic messages, has heard nothing further. Now, mixed with her sense of regret, is a growing resentment.

A young olive-skinned waitress takes her order and as she waits for it to arrive, Sophie's thoughts return to Miles.

He obviously eats out regularly. She can smell fried food on his clothes, and the other day she spent ages trying to remove ketchup from his tie.

Where does he go when he's not indoors, watching television and drinking too much whisky? And does he really think she doesn't know about the bottle he's hidden away, just as he hid that court letter? *What the hell are you playing at, Miles?*

The waitress brings her latte, and a prawn and avocado baguette. The therapy session has left her hungry and she takes a large bite, mayonnaise dripping down her chin and onto her blouse.

'Mind if I join you?' a voice says.

A man in jeans and a creased shirt is standing over her.

She dabs at her chin. The last thing she wants is to sit with some stranger, but the other tables are obviously full. 'Go ahead.'

The young waitress is taking the man's order, her smile becoming more pronounced. It's always such a giveaway when a woman finds a man attractive, she thinks. Not that this one is conventionally handsome. Probably in his late forties, he has dark eyebrows that contrast with the streaks of silver in his hair, and his otherwise regular features are spoilt by too big a nose.

He nods towards her. 'By the way, I'm Ian.' He has an accent that she can't quite place.

'Sophie Whitaker.'

When his food arrives, he begins eating in rapid bites. After a few moments, he looks up. 'Come in here much?'

'This is my first time.'

'Still getting to know your way around then?'

'Yes. I only moved into the area recently.'

He drains his coffee. 'Must dash. I have a meeting in half an hour.' He signals for his bill and the young waitress comes up, all smiles.

'Anything else I can get you, sir?' He shakes his head and she walks away, hips swaying, her bottom neat in its tight skirt.

Sophie fingers the frayed collar of her blouse. I was sexy too at that age, she thinks.

'Hope I'm not overstepping the mark.' He leans across and hands her a card. *Ian H. Carteret, Architectural Consultant.* 'I do tend to shell these out.'

'No, it's fine.'

He hesitates. 'Are you all right? If you don't mind my saying, you look a bit—'

'I'm OK – really.'

'Well, hope to see you around.'

'Goodbye.'

She watches him move over to the door, feeling unaccountably pleased when he ignores the smile the young waitress gives him.

TWENTY-SIX

MILES LEANS OVER THE BANISTERS. 'SOPHIE!' BUT apart from the creak of the boiler, the house is silent.

How much longer are they to remain in this state of limbo?

He hesitates, before going into the hall. The police still have his mobile and he hasn't felt brave enough to ask for its return. He lifts the phone and dials Marshall's number.

'As I explained when you last called, Miles,' – the suave tone doesn't quite mask a note of irritation – 'we're still awaiting the rest of the prosecution papers.'

'Yes. But I just wondered if—'

'Can't proceed without the witness statements, I'm afraid. Be in touch the moment I hear anything.'

'Well, goodbye then.'

But the man has already rung off.

He's aware of being treated like a not very bright pupil, as if he's missing something – something important. He doesn't think he's slipped up anywhere, but how can he be sure? He can feel the knot in his stomach that only alcohol seems to ease, but he must try and keep off the whisky until later in the day.

He sips his cold coffee, staring out at the tangle of grass in the back garden, trying to work out his next move. Top of his list is finding the courage to tell Sophie about the court hearing, nearly three weeks ago now. But how can he possibly open up to her when she's going out of her way to avoid him?

He rinses his mug under the tap. She's never given him cause to feel jealous before, but the plain truth is that, in all their years of marriage, he's never known her speak as warmly of another man as she does of Webster.

He glances at his watch. The boys will be halfway through breakfast. Assembly is at eight forty-five, followed by the first class at nine fifteen. The sense of loss is like a hammer blow in his gut.

It's no good – he has to get out. He'll walk up for the paper, and then head for The Crown and Cushion. A morning snifter will help settle his stomach.

Half an hour later, he's on his way to the newsagents, the sun hot on his face. For once, he's without his blazer, but even in shirtsleeves he can feel himself sweating.

He passes the usual collection of people – mothers with their rowdy children, the occasional dog-walker, and older women dragging their wheeled shopping baskets behind them. It's painful to think how at the school he knows everyone – would have been greeting all those he encountered.

The main road is as busy as ever, the sun catching the roofs of the cars and winking off windscreens and mirrors. He sees a gap in the traffic and darts forward. A horn blares at him, and then he hears another noise – a catcall.

Something is happening outside the newsagents. People are clustered on the pavement, and the traffic going past has slowed, the drivers leaning forward to take a closer look.

Although the memory of that encounter with Paget still makes him shudder, at least he's now able to view the meeting for what it was – an extraordinary coincidence.

It's only as he draws closer, that he spots two figures, standing apart from the rest – Webster, in jeans and T-shirt, and the Muslim, Ali, dressed in black, and still clutching that rucksack.

They're the last people he wants to spend time with, but already the clergyman has his hand raised in greeting.

'Hello there, Miles,' Webster says, as he joins them. 'Bad business, this.' He points to a jagged hole in the shop window. 'The second time in six months.'

'But that's terrible. Are the burglars still in there? Perhaps we could—'

'The police have been called, but the advice always is for the public not to intervene.'

'No doubt who's responsible.' He's aware of a growing sense of outrage. 'What these youths need is discipline!'

'What they need is employment, and a sense of self-worth,' the clergyman observes quietly.

Miles opens his mouth to reply, but Ali cuts in. 'Well, I agree with Miles. This kind of thuggish behaviour is inexcusable.'

Miles feels a surge of warmth towards the man. 'My old headmaster would be lamenting the days when the lot of them would have had a sound beating!'

Webster's eyebrows rise. 'But surely, as a former teacher, you can't believe in corporal punishment?'

Flogging wouldn't be good enough for Cunningham and his two friends. Aloud he says, 'I still maintain there's a place for it.'

There's a pause, and then Webster says, 'I hope to goodness Bindu and Lalit are all right. It must have given them such a nasty shock.'

'We will have to agree to disagree.' Ali leans forward. 'I have a suggestion. Why don't you both come back to my place? My wife has been baking. Your favourite chocolate and cardamom brownies, Sebastian.'

'It's good of you, Ali, but I can't stop. But Miles will go with you, I'm sure. It'll be an opportunity for him to sample Farah's excellent cooking.'

He'll think up some excuse to get out of it. He turns to the clergyman. 'Have you seen Sophie this morning?'

'Sophie? 'Fraid not.'

'Oh.' He's aware of the eyes studying him. How much will she have told him?

'That reminds me. She mentioned she was looking for work.' The clergyman extracts a business card from his pocket. 'I thought this might interest her.'

'Work?' Miles takes it from him. *Second Thoughts – Good as new clothing.*

Something inside him plummets. She obviously believes they won't be back at the school any time soon. And, equally, she seems to have forged quite a friendship with this man.

His thoughts are distracted by the wail of a siren. He spins round. What on earth is he doing lingering near a crime scene? Suppose that blonde inspector were to show up?

To his relief Webster says, 'The police'll have plenty of witnesses – best leave them to it. See you both later.' He walks a short distance away, before being brought up short by a girl in a skimpy skirt and laced boots that reach to her thighs. She rests her hand on Webster's arm, and begins speaking intently. She has pink streaks in her hair and looks younger than the twins. Webster presses a piece of paper into her hand – no doubt his phone number.

Ali gives a tch of disapproval. 'Why he has to bother with that kind of woman is beyond me.'

And not just that kind, Miles thinks, wondering if Sophie would be back at the house by now.

Webster and the girl part company, and the clergyman strides away up the road.

'My house is only a short distance from here,' Ali is saying, as Miles and he follow.

He really should be getting back so he can have that talk with Sophie. 'If you don't mind, perhaps I can take up your offer another time?'

'It's such a pleasant day.' Ali pushes open the side gate to the churchyard. 'Shall we at least sit together for a short while?'

Miles shuffles his feet. But the thought of the green space is tempting and, anyway, it makes a welcome change for someone to be almost begging for his company. 'Just a few minutes, then.'

They pick their way along the path, pushing back the tangle of brambles and greenery on either side. There's the usual scuffle of pigeons on the porch roof, and a rank smell of fox hangs in the air. As they settle on a bench, the clock above their heads begins its wheezing, before striking eleven.

Thursday. Latin grammar with the lower thirds.

He glances at the other man, who seems lost in thought. He makes a rapid calculation. Twenty minutes here, say, and a ten-minute walk to the pub. He should be there by half past.

Ali looks up and catches Miles's eye. 'So tell me, of what are you thinking as you sit in this delightful spot?'

'Oh, nothing much.' He wishes he could remember the cover story he's given. 'And you? You are still in employment?'

'I retired last year from my work as manager of a Muslim charity, and am enjoying my leisure. But you must miss your teaching duties?'

'I still keep pretty busy reading and doing research into the Classics.' He's relieved to have successfully deflected the conversation. 'I've been planning for some time to write a book on Romulus Augustulus, the last Roman ruler of the Western Empire.' He pauses, gratified by the

202

look of admiration in Ali's eyes. 'And of course seeing to the house takes up much of my time.'

He can picture the front entrance – the studded door leading to the vestibule, the tiled floor, everywhere smelling of polish and the indefinable odour of some two hundred boys. He forces a laugh. 'Though being here has given me a bit of a breather.'

'A well-earned one, I am sure.' Ali leans towards him – attentive, respectful. 'The system of education in the UK has always fascinated me. So many of your politicians and leaders are from public schools.'

'That's right. Fordingbury hasn't yet produced a Cabinet minister, but we live in hope.' He pauses. 'I think the system's success is due in no small part to structure and discipline. Each moment of the day is accounted for. And that way, of course, everyone ends up singing from the same sheet.'

Ali's forehead creases. 'I'm sorry?'

'Sharing the same values.'

Ali nods. 'How important it is that young minds are shaped in the right way.' He glances at his rucksack. 'What we learn from an early age stays with us.'

There's a silence.

'Can I tell you something?'

You're going to anyway, Miles thinks.

'Most days as I sit here, I picture myself somewhere else entirely.' He strokes his beard. 'And I sense that perhaps you also long to be in another place?'

He thinks of the front room in Stephen's Close with its orange sofa and sagging chairs. 'I must admit to missing

the school more than I thought I would. It was – is…'
Miles hesitates, '…very special.'

'It is indeed a terrible thing to be parted from the place
one loves. For me, it makes no difference whether I am
sitting here, or walking along the street. In my mind I am
back in my own country.'

Miles pictures camels and sand dunes. 'What part of
the Middle East did you say you were from?'

But Ali is staring ahead once more. 'I am in our
courtyard on a summer morning, listening to the splash
of the fountain, and breathing in the scent of lemons. We
had several trees and to my mind nothing compares with
the smell of the fruits ripening in the sun.' He pauses. 'You
would think I could stop yearning for my old life. But no.'
He gives a wry smile. 'No matter how hard I try, I can't
shake off the feeling that I am in the wrong place.'

Miles leans forward. 'It's the same for me. Well, not
exactly the same – there are no fountains or lemons in
the school grounds. Though Fordingbury – my school –
certainly has its fair share of trees. You should see the two
beeches by the tennis courts – great big fellows. Then there
are the cedars, and the chestnut on the seniors' lawn.'

He recalls the beech hedge along the drive, and the
pollarded limes by the path that leads to the science
block. He blinks back tears – then looks up. Suppose Ali
has noticed? But he remains oblivious, stroking his beard
as he continues to speak. 'And in the early morning, my
brothers and I would sit and drink coffee, and talk about
all we would do during the day. One of my brother's wives
would serve us – this was when I was still single, you

understand – and along with the coffee there would be fresh dates and almond biscuits – very sweet and good.'

'We had excellent almond biscuits once – in Tuscany. When we were first married, my wife and I holidayed outside Arezzo. A charming place. I don't imagine you know it?'

He shakes his head. 'I am afraid not.'

Miles leans back, crossing his legs. 'You were talking about food. At Fordingbury as a boy, my favourite meal was breakfast – porridge and kippers. A sprinkling of brown sugar – on the porridge, that is. A dollop of butter on the kippers – though not all the boys liked them on account of the bones. Well, you can understand that. Nowadays it's all cereals and croissants.'

'It was so hot.' Ali glances up at the pale sky above their heads. 'Not like here. A real scorching heat. Just outside our gate there was an alleyway that led into the central market.' He smiles into the distance. 'Stalls piled with mangos, limes, dates, eggplant, okra – you name it. And everywhere the scent of cardamom. We used to buy mint tea to clear the dust from our throats. The women bought fresh chicken and lamb, goats' milk and—'

'My wife's a splendid cook,' Miles interrupts. 'School chefs vary, but on the whole the standard is very good. Like you, we had plenty of meat. Always a roast on

Sunday. I like lamb too, but pork is my favourite, with crackling and apple sauce, of course.'

Ali clears his throat. 'That is not something I am permitted to eat.'

'How stupid of me. Of course not.'

Ali reaches for his rucksack. 'It is time I was getting home.'

Why did he have to go and put his foot in it, and just when the two of them were getting along so well? There should be something he can say to put things right but as with Sophie, the words elude him. 'Well, goodbye then,' he manages to get out.

Ali nods, unsmiling.

'Thanks for the invitation to your house,' he calls after Ali's retreating back, and is relieved to receive a wave in reply. He watches a magpie peck at a discarded food wrapper before forcing himself off the bench. He mustn't put off telling Sophie any longer. He just needs to find the right words to make her believe him.

TWENTY-SEVEN

THEY MET THROUGH A MUTUAL ACQUAINTANCE AT one of those unsatisfactory gatherings where everyone stood, elbow to elbow, drinking inferior Australian wine and trying not to drop peanuts on the carpet. By now, he was well established at Fordingbury, but little at ease in other settings. He stood in a corner of the room, listening to the babble of voices around him and wondering what on earth had possessed him to accept this invitation.

It was then he caught sight of her – a girl, of medium height, with a rounded figure and a shining curtain of hair that swung as she talked. Yet what struck him most was her air of warmth, and the poise with which she carried herself – so different from his mother's stiffness and his sisters' girlish giggles. He stood mesmerized.

He'd never been much good with the opposite sex. Used to a life surrounded by men and boys, women seemed remote, rather terrifying creatures. What on earth did one say to them for a start? There had been a few tentative fumblings, mainly in the back seats of cars, but no coitus. At thirty-seven he was starting to panic. Murdo might be content to go through life as a confirmed bachelor, but it was not what Miles wanted for himself.

Yet that first glimpse of Sophie, like the sighting of some promised land, awoke in him an almost miraculous confidence. When he pushed his way through the other partygoers to stand beside her, he saw his first impression was right – she wasn't one of those hard-nosed blondes, of which there was such a preponderance amongst the Fordingbury mothers, each one desperate for her son to be in the top stream. With soft grey-blue eyes and pink cheeks – perhaps due to the effects of alcohol, he thought later – she seemed like some Grecian goddess. When he quoted Ovid's description of Thisbe at her, she gave him a puzzled look, then threw back her head and laughed. In anyone else, that laugh would have felt like mockery. Instead, he found himself smiling back at her, so that for a moment it was just the two of them sharing a private joke.

He stared at her, imagining licking the red wine stain at the corner of her mouth.

Her low-cut dress revealed an expanse of creamy skin, and he was filled with an urge to burrow his head between her ample breasts. Back in his bachelor quarters that night, he fantasised about lying naked in bed with her, exploring what the school matron referred to as the "nether regions", and rogering her senseless.

It took him a week to summon up the courage to contact her, and he could hardly believe his luck when she accepted his invitation to dinner. However, the evening was not a success. She was paler than he remembered, with dark rings under her eyes – too many long stints at the hospital, she said. The sight of her filled him with a tenderness he'd never felt for anyone before, and he had to stop himself leaning over and putting his arms around her. At the end of the evening, they said a brief goodnight, and before he could plant even one kiss on her cheek, she disappeared into her flat. He wasn't surprised – what on earth did he have to offer a girl who obviously would have countless admirers?

All the same, he rang her number for days afterwards. There was never any reply.

He remembered walking around Fordingbury with a sick feeling in his stomach, knowing that for him, there'd only be one woman.

When, twelve months later, he received a phone call, saying she had just returned from a trip to New Zealand, and would he like to meet up, he had to stop himself punching the air in jubilation. Two years later, they were married, and his life – his real life, as he thinks of it now – began.

And now he must, and will, do whatever it takes to protect it.

He carries two chairs into the back garden, then turns as he hears the grate of the front door key. 'Out here!' he calls.

A moment later, she appears. Her hair is all over the place, and the top buttons of her blouse are undone.

'Whew! It's turned really hot.'

Despite all his good intentions, he can't keep a note of irritation from his voice. 'I thought you'd have been back by now.'

She puts her bag on the kitchen table. 'It took longer than I thought.'

'At the church?'

She pauses, fractionally. 'Of course.'

'I ran into Webster – outside the newsagents, and he asked me to give you this.' He hands her the card.

'That's good of him. Thanks.'

He stares at her flushed cheeks, but now is not the time for a confrontation. He swallows. 'There's something I have to tell you, Sophie.'

She sinks into the chair beside him, shifting away when their knees touch.

'The thing is,' he begins, 'and I'm truly sorry about this, but I haven't been giving you the full picture.'

'Oh?'

'About these charges. I haven't told you before, because I haven't wanted to worry you…' His voice tails away. He waits for her to help him out, but when she remains silent, he ploughs on. 'To be perfectly honest I thought the whole court thing would blow over.'

'And you're telling me it hasn't?'

He stares ahead to where a pair of cabbage white butterflies – *Pieris brassicae* – perform an intricate dance over the waist-high grass. 'The other week, when I told you I was just going out for a while…' – what reason had he given? He struggles to remember. 'Well, anyway, I went back to Oxford.'

'Oxford?'

'Yes – to the magistrates' court.' He swallows again. 'Marshall assured me it was all just a formality, but the bench simply wouldn't listen to his arguments. So...' he gives a shaky laugh, 'it seems I'm to be put on trial after all.'

Sophie regards him, grey eyes unblinking.

'For something I haven't done, for God's sake!'

'And what exactly is that supposed to be, Miles?'

Her tone is the one she uses with boys who have stepped out of line, and he feels his earlier confidence seep away. 'You see – it was like this...' He stops to gather his thoughts. The butterflies have flitted over the fence, and everywhere remains quiet in the sunshine. 'As I told you, the day it was meant to have happened, I was just about to start my Shakespeare class with the Remove set, when Webb came rushing in, shouting about an accident, and could I come at once.' He risks a glance at Sophie, but she remains impassive. 'I realise it sounds unlikely now – I mean, why didn't I question him more? But he was looking so panic-stricken that I didn't stop to think. I just went racing after him. Foolish of me, I know.' He draws in his breath. 'We ended up in the changing rooms. It was all pretty dark – I think a bulb must have gone again – so I didn't immediately see the boy. It was Webb, who pointed to a bench in the corner. And it was only as I got nearer that I saw Cunningham stretched out on his back.' He can't keep the tremor from his voice. 'He had a towel draped over him and as I bent down to ask how he was, somehow I lost my balance and fell on top of him. It was as I was struggling to get up, that I heard Laing's voice, asking what in the world was going on...'

Any moment, and he'll start blubbing.

Sophie leans forward. 'But why on earth couldn't you have told me this earlier, Miles? Why the lies?'

'I just never thought it would go this far.'

From the neighbouring house comes the slam of a door. 'Mu-um!' a child shouts.

'We'd better continue this indoors.'

She nods in agreement.

In the kitchen, he turns to her. 'You do believe me, don't you?'

She gazes at him for a long moment, and he can feel the thud of his heart in his chest.

TWENTY-EIGHT

E ARLIER IN THE WEEK, WHILE CLEANING THE FRONT room, Sophie discovered a new credit card statement tucked inside a book. No surprise that the bulk of the substantial debit was a payment to Marshalls. The concern was that Miles, as ever, hadn't told her.

'Excuse me. I wondered if by any chance you have another of these?'

A man, brown hair touched with silver, is standing directly beneath her ladder. She can't see his face, but he seems familiar. He's holding up a Willow Pattern dish. She can make out a faded pagoda, and a pair of birds hovering above water. Miles's mother went in for Willow Pattern, she recalls, for a moment back in his parents' claustrophic house, with Brenda, in her ridiculous hairdo – curls like a pile of meringues – pointing with pride towards a line of plates on the dresser.

Sophie glances out over the shop. The manager, Becca, is sorting something in the window. The other assistant, Steve – a boy in his early twenties with learning difficulties – is busy with a customer.

'I've had a good look around,' the man says, 'but I thought you might have more in your stockroom?'

Now she places him. Smiling to herself, she climbs down. 'Hello there!'

The messenger bag is slung over a rumpled shirt, and his feet are thrust into faded sandals. Nothing could be more different from Miles in his blazer and tie.

The man holds out the dish, as if for inspection. 'The Chinese legend is an English invention. That's late eighteenth-century branding for you.' There's that hint of a different intonation in his voice. He pauses. 'It's Sophie, isn't it?'

'And you're Ian.'

They smile at one another, the corners of his mouth creasing in the way she remembers from their previous encounter.

'Nice to run into you again.'

She smooths her skirt over her hips. At Becca's insistence, she's ditched her pleated skirt, and is still getting used to this shorter style. 'I'll just check. If you don't mind waiting?'

He nods, and she's conscious of his eyes on her as she walks away.

In the storeroom, the smell of stale clothing wafts towards her. She kneels beside a series of boxes, their contents covered in crumpled newspaper, and begins unwrapping pieces of china and placing them on the floor beside her.

From out of nowhere, a memory comes: Helena standing in the doorway watching Miles hand Sophie her monthly allowance. 'Honestly, Mum and Dad.' Helena rolled her eyes. 'It's like you're living in the Victorian era.'

Small comfort now to realise that her daughter had been spot-on. For what kind of a foolish woman goes along with an arrangement that leaves her, not only ignorant of her husband's finances, but also without any provision for the future? 'Murdo will see us right,' Miles always said. Why had she never questioned that?

'How's it going?' Ian's voice behind her makes her jump.

She looks up, embarrassed. She'd almost forgotten what she's searching for.

'Sorry if I gave you a fright.'

'No – it's OK. Really.' She gets to her feet, turning to him with her brightest smile. 'I've not found anything so far, but there's plenty more boxes to try. If you don't mind waiting?'

He runs a hand through his already rumpled hair. 'Can't stop, I'm afraid. I need to be somewhere.'

'Of course.'

They go back into the shop, and he hands her the dish he's been holding.

She moves behind the counter, wrapping the item in newspaper, and placing it in a plastic bag. 'That'll be £3.99.'

She waits for him to start rummaging for coins in his trouser pocket, as Miles would be doing. Instead, he opens the messenger bag, and takes out a wallet. There's quite a bit of grey in his hair that's brushed back from a widow's peak. Hard to place his age. Nearer fifty than forty-five perhaps.

'Thanks.' He takes the bag from her. 'Not often one finds a present that hits the spot.'

'For someone special?' She's not sure what makes her ask.

He looks across at her. 'It's my sister's birthday. Willow Pattern isn't something I'd give house-room to, but she loves the stuff.'

She smiles. He's not wearing a wedding ring, although of course that means nothing. 'As I said, there are quite a few more boxes to go through. If I come across another dish, would you like me to put it on one side for you?'

His eyes meet hers. 'That would be great.'

She blushes. Whatever's got into her?

He clears his throat. 'How about meeting up for a coffee?'

She hesitates.

'Friday, around twelve thirty? Usual place. If that would suit?'

'It would.'

He stares at her for a moment, before turning and walking to the door with that set of his shoulders that signals a man at ease in his own skin. Watching him, she's suddenly filled with a sense of elation.

The young assistant is at her elbow, asking about pricing. 'Sorry, Steve, I was miles away.'

He pulls one of his faces that she's learned is his substitute for a smile.

It's part of the agreement Becca has with the council that she employs a "disadvantaged person". Steve is a tall boy, dark-haired and broad-shouldered, his good looks marred by the way his mouth keeps twisting to one side in a nervous tic. He's only been here a couple of days, but seems to be coping well. Now, his question answered, he returns to writing out labels, forming the symbols with care, his tongue protruding between small, even teeth.

She calls across to him. 'Keep up the good work, Steve!'

He looks up at her with a crooked smile, before bending his head again. The exchange touches her.

Becca comes over. Her low-cut top reveals an ample cleavage. Emerald-coloured hoops, matching her eyeshadow, dangle from her lobes. She wouldn't hesitate about dating someone she fancies, Sophie thinks.

'The takings are up again, Sophie. At this rate, I might even treat Des to a night out.'

Becca's partner, a lanky black man, whose parents are in Barbados, dropped in earlier. 'Great little business,' he said to Becca. 'And you look pretty damn good too.'

'OK, Mr Charmer. I'll see to you later. Now, get out of my hair, will you!'

And with a laugh and a shrug, he wandered off again.

Sophie felt a flicker of envy, trying to remember a time when she and Miles were as easy-going with one another.

Now, once again, her thoughts turn to Ian. For, as she continues serving customers, she's aware of some change having taken place inside her. Hard to pinpoint though. Connectedness? Sexual frisson? That wasn't it. No, it was more that long-forgotten feeling she recalls from the heady days with Alastair: the sense of everything having come alive, of her surroundings changing from black and white to colour.

You're fifty-one. Stop being so adolescent! She chides herself, as she begins her lunchtime walk up to a takeaway place on the corner.

The afternoon is warm, the air like silk against her skin. Beyond the roofline, the sky is an illustration from a children's book – one single fluffy cloud pinned to a cerulean backdrop. The street is busy with others out enjoying the sunshine. A couple saunter towards her eating hamburgers, the pungent smell of onions catching her throat. An elderly man cycles past whistling a waltz tune. She skirts round drink cartons and cans spilling onto the pavement. A pair of pigeons scuffle in the gutter before launching themselves into the air in a fluster of feathers. All of it making her realise how much she loves the vibrancy of London.

She buys herself a sandwich and a latte, before heading towards what is referred to locally as "the park" – a large area of ragged grass, with a tired-looking chestnut tree in the middle. Usually the sight leaves her despondent, yet today its air of neglect seems charming.

She sits on a metal bench, sipping her coffee and watching a mother throw a ball to her toddler. The tan and white mongrel accompanying them gives half-hearted chase.

The young woman throws a stick to the dog, and the laughing child lurches towards it, arms in the air. She remembers the twins at the same age – what dear little things they were in their bright red Baby Grows – but she wouldn't go back to that stage for all the tea in China. For all the Willow Pattern dishes in the universe, she thinks. And smiles to herself.

The mother is lifting the toddler into his pushchair. Sophie glances at her watch. Time to be getting back.

As she walks along the road, she pictures the Willow Pattern man, as she calls him in her mind, seeing the faint stubble on his chin and his appraising look as she climbed down the stepladder. First Seb, and now him. Get a grip! she tells herself.

No doubt her feelings can also be put down to the fact that the physical side of her marriage has gone. Since the discovery of the court letter, she's taken to sleeping in the spare room. She can't bear the thought of Miles touching her.

A part of her would like nothing better than to walk away, but there are the girls to think about, and if she were to leave, wouldn't that be tantamount to saying she thinks him guilty? And she can't do that to him – not until she's more certain. Which means awaiting the outcome of the trial, which may now be only a matter of weeks away.

She turns into Stephen's Close with a feeling of dread, so it's a relief to push open the front door and be met with silence – no Miles in the front room, the smell of whisky hanging in the air, and that fixed grin on his face.

He says that he spends most of his time in the churchyard, but it's far more likely that he's in one of the local pubs. Although she can understand that. Away from the school, he has nothing to anchor him.

As she fills the kettle, her mobile rings. She glances at the screen and sees with a jolt of pleasure that it's an Oxford number. Rachel is at last returning her calls. She's still heard nothing from her since their difficult meeting. She clicks on the phone. 'Hello? Rach?'

A man's voice says, 'Mrs Whitaker?'

She can't keep the surprise out of her voice. 'Carter? I wasn't expecting to hear from you.'

'Sophie Whitaker?' the voice continues.

Something inside her plummets. 'Who is this, please?'

'And your husband is Miles Whitaker?'

'Yes – but—?'

'You don't know me, Sophie. It *is* all right to call you Sophie?' The voice doesn't wait for a reply. 'My name's Rod, Sophie, and I work for the *Oxford Mail*. I understand your husband is a teacher at Fordingbury School, Sophie, and is facing serious charges – charges of a sexual nature.'

'How did you get hold of this number?'

'I wondered if you and I could have a chat about things?'

She draws in her breath. 'No. We could not.'

'But can you confirm that Miles's case is due in the Crown Court in—?'

She grips the back of her chair. 'I have nothing whatever to say to you.'

'You can't hide away there forever, Sophie. I understand you and Miles are somewhere in London?'

She clicks off her phone. Then sits, staring at the floor.

She's realised for some time that Miles has been taking the Oxford papers – she found one crumpled in the bottom of the bin. Something else he's been keeping from her. Now she understands. For it's one thing to be coping with all this behind closed doors. Quite another for it to be out in the public domain.

She puts her head between her knees, wondering whether she'll faint or be physically sick.

After a couple of minutes her phone rings again – and goes on ringing.

TWENTY-NINE

'HELLO!' SHE CALLS, PUTTING HER BAG DOWN IN the hall.

The sun picks out a jug of cow parsley, its petals scattered like confetti over the side table. Underneath is the rag rug she made as a teenager, and in the corner is the grandfather clock, silenced since that summer when the girls knocked into it during a particularly rowdy game. And filling the space is the familiar sound and smell of the sea.

Home, she thinks.

She crosses the hall, the cool feel of the stone flags under her feet seeming to travel up through her body, releasing the tension of the past days. Already her headache is lessening.

She pushes open the door to the conservatory. It's a long room, filled with a motley selection of furniture. Pots of scarlet geraniums are ranged against one wall and the French windows opposite overlook a sea that rises and falls in the late April light.

Aunt Harriet turns in her chair. 'Oh, it's you, Sophie!'

She's never been one for shows of affection and now Sophie walks over, stooping to give an awkward hug. 'I should have let you know I was coming.'

'Don't be daft. And, anyway, I've been expecting you – ever since your last call.' She gets up from her seat with an alacrity belying her ninety-odd years. 'Expect you're hungry after your journey. Baked potatoes for supper?'

'That would be fine. Let me—'

'I'm more than capable, thank you. And, anyway, you're the one who looks done in.'

'I am a bit.' She hesitates. 'I'm sure you're wondering what—'

'We'll talk when you're good and ready, girl.' She points a finger. 'But for now, sit right there while I get the kettle on.'

Sophie eyes the nearest chair but, after her aunt has gone out, steps through the open French windows, round the side of the house and onto the cliff path. The sea pinks are in flower, and stems of tall grass brush against her legs as she passes. When she reaches the shore, she removes her shoes, walking into the shallows and emitting a gasp as the cold hits her. Then she stands, hand to her forehead to shield herself from the setting sun.

All the times of crisis when I've been at this same spot, she thinks, drawing comfort just from the fact that Aunt Harriet is here. Yet not even my mother's death, not even the termination, feels as terrible as what is facing me now.

223

And as she listens to the cry of the gulls and feels the lap of waves against her feet, she suddenly gives way to tears, great sobs that tear from her chest, as if a part of her is being ripped away.

She glances about her, but this stretch of beach is deserted. Just as well – she hasn't cried like this – not even when Miles was arrested or when she first discovered the extent to which he'd been lying to her.

She mops her tears with her sleeve. If only she could see an end to it all.

After a while, above her head, the light from the conservatory blinks on. Aunt Harriet will be waiting. She reaches for her shoes and begins the slow climb back up the path.

*

'I'm not sure what it is you're trying to tell me, Sophie.'

It's the following morning and they're in the side garden, Aunt Harriet staking up runner beans, while Sophie weeds the onion patch.

'I really don't want to burden you any more than I've already done.'

The old woman gives a snort. 'You walk in here, white as a sheet. Spend a good part of the evening in tears. Peck at your food. No…' as Sophie goes to interrupt, 'it really won't do.'

'I'm sorry.'

'So you should be. Since when have I turned into some frail creature who's going to have a fit of the vapours because you've got yourself into a mess?'

Sophie pulls a face. 'Another one.'

Her aunt fixes her with one of her stares. 'If it's any comfort, I was as wrong about Alastair as you. More fool me.'

There's a silence.

'Hand me that string, would you?'

'Here.' Sophie sits back on her heels. 'I don't know where to begin.'

'Well, it's obvious you're still undecided as to whether you can believe that husband of yours.'

'And it makes me think how you've never taken to Miles.'

'What's that got to do with anything?' Her aunt sighs. 'It's true I've never got through to the person underneath. But that's by the by. You're the one living with him. The question is: what do *you* think?'

'Yes, but you did try to warn me.' She tugs at a thistle. 'If only I'd listened. Although I wouldn't be without the twins, of course.'

'And now there's to be a prosecution.'

She nods. 'Sometime in the autumn, Miles thinks.'

'And he wants you with him in court?'

'To be honest, I can't seem to get my head around what's happening. It's as if I'm living in a fog. But I've decided to go along with what Miles wants because the best way of protecting the girls is by finding out the truth. And however terrible it may turn out to be, it's better to know.' She thinks back to the phone call from the Oxford paper. 'But even if Miles isn't found guilty, there'll be publicity. I can cope with it for myself, but for them—' She breaks off, before adding: 'Miranda especially has always been close to her father.'

Her aunt studies her. 'And after the trial? What then?'

She doesn't answer, bending to the vegetable bed again. 'I feel I'm being very selfish – going on about myself all the time.' She looks up. 'You've never spoken much of your love life, Aunt Harriet.'

'Of Bob, you mean?' She shakes her head. 'All those years ago. Hard to believe. You'd have liked him though. Also brought up by the sea – in Norfolk. He worked as a cook in one of the NAAFI canteens.' She laughs. 'I think I fell for his lamb hotpot before I ever took to him.'

'But you were in love?'

'Very much so.' She stares out over the bay. 'Then his unit got called up. We were never allowed to know exactly where they were posted, of course, but he hinted it was somewhere in the Middle East. He'd only been gone six months, when his mother wrote with the news. A bombing raid on the camp – no survivors.'

'I am sorry, Aunt Harriet.'

'Oh, you get over things, given time. As you well know. And remember in those days there was too much going on to allow for much navel-gazing. I became a land girl, doing much as we are now – though on a bigger scale, of course.'

Sophie hesitates again. 'Can I ask you something else?'

'Spit it out.'

'Did the two of you – you know – before he went away?'

'Why so coy?' She sighs again. 'Your generation thinks you invented sex. But I can tell you now that the war was every bit as swinging as the sixties.' She looks across at Sophie. 'But what is it you're trying to tell me?'

She runs a hand through her hair. 'The thing is, Aunt Harriet, I've met someone. He's Australian – an architect. He's been in London a good while. I don't know much else about him as yet.'

'But you want to?'

'Oh, yes.' She thinks for a moment. 'I know it sounds such a corny thing to say, but the couple of times I've been with him I've felt the way I used to with Alastair.' She throws back her head. 'So full of life – and optimism.' It feels odd to hear his name spoken yet again.

'And you're wondering whether it's all right to take this further?'

'Wondering if it's all right to hurt Miles and the girls, as it undoubtedly would were they to find out. And to put my marriage under threat.'

'Don't you think Miles is doing just that?'

'Yes – but that still doesn't justify my actions. And of course the whole thing is a huge risk, especially at my age.'

Her aunt snips off another piece of string. 'Let me ask you something. Do you regret your affair with Alastair? Wish perhaps you'd never met him?'

She puts her head on one side, considering. 'I did just after it ended, and for a quite a while later. But now – no, I don't. I guess it's part of who I am.' A part I've never shared with Miles, she thinks.

Aunt Harriet ties a bean plant to its cane. 'The week before Bob was sent overseas, we talked about sleeping together – don't look so surprised, Sophie. So many others were, and there was that sense, present also in the sixties of course, of being able to break the rules.' She reaches for the watering can. 'But in the end we decided to be sensible. Wait until his return – wait until the end of the war, we told ourselves.'

Sophie hesitates. 'So, do you wish…?'

There's a silence.

After a few moments, Aunt Harriet says: 'Time for lunch, I think.'

But as they gather up the gardening tools, she adds – and there's a hint of sadness in her voice that Sophie hasn't heard before – 'At least if you take the risk, you can look back and know you gave it your all.'

THIRTY

'SORRY TO BE LATE – LAST-MINUTE CALL.'

She lifts her eyes from the menu, which she's been pretending to study. She'd almost convinced herself that he wouldn't show after all. Now, seeing him standing and smiling down at her, she feels a fillip of delight. His hair is tousled, and he has a day's growth of beard that suits him. 'Designer stubble,' she can imagine Becca saying.

'Shall I order for both of us? You've decided what you want?'

She likes the way he takes charge. 'Soup and a roll, thanks. Here.'

She holds out a note, but he shakes his head, smiling at her again. 'The least I can do to make up for my late arrival.'

His eyes are a deep grey, the eyebrows above a dark brown. Probably the same shade as his body hair, she thinks, and feels herself blush, glad when he turns and walks over to the counter, his movements precise, yet fluid. He's wearing jeans and a faded T-shirt, the messenger bag slung across his chest. Miles would die rather than be seen in such clothes.

'They'll bring our food in a minute,' he says, seating himself opposite.

She leans her elbows on the table. 'I come in here a couple of times a week. It's hungry work sorting through all the stuff in the shop.' She pauses, remembering that he's not returned to Second Thoughts as he said he might.

As if reading her mind he says, 'I appreciated your help over the Willow Pattern.'

'The plate was a success?'

'You bet. My big sis was thrilled with it.'

She grins, a part of her registering his accent, which has a definite twang to it.

'You're from South Africa?'

He shakes his head. 'An out-and-out Aussie, for my sins. Haven't been back in years though. How about you?'

'Nothing much to say really. Brought up in the West Country. Nurse's training in London, and then Oxford, bringing up my girls.'

There's a clink of china as the waitress puts their food on the table.

Sophie spreads butter on her roll. She's on her second mouthful when she feels his eyes on her. He hasn't yet started his sandwich.

'Oh, lord – what a gannet you must think me!'

'Not at all. I like seeing people enjoying their tucker.'

As on the last occasion they met, she can't seem to take her eyes off him, glancing across from time to time, noting the set of his jaw, the large nose that should have made him look ugly, but somehow didn't; fascinated by the studied concentration with which he ate.

When, after a few moments, he catches her gaze and smiles, she feels her insides give another somersault.

There's so much she wants to ask: Does he have a wife? Children? How come he's in this country? For already she can tell how far removed he is from the public school men she's been surrounded by for the past twenty years. Most of them terrified of women, she thinks.

Suddenly she's filled with an urge to tell him about herself: Something – anything.

She puts down her spoon. 'When I was a student in London, I used to go walking on Hampstead Heath in the early morning. Barefoot, even in the rain. Can you imagine? A group of us would fall into a curry house for breakfast. It's still my favourite kind of food. All those spices, I suppose, and—' She breaks off. What on earth is she rambling on about?

He smiles. 'Sounds the total opposite to my wife, who's always on some sort of diet.'

Of course he's married. How foolish to have imagined otherwise. But at least their cards are on the table.

'I gave up long ago telling her not all men think skinny is beautiful.'

She fiddles with her earring, aware of his eyes moving from her face to the hollow at the top of her breasts. This new blouse that Becca insists suits her so well has a much lower cut than anything she would have worn at Fordingbury.

Her mobile starts ringing and, glancing at it, she sees it's Miranda's number.

'One of my daughters,' she explains. 'I'll get back to her later.' It's the first time since she's been in London that she hasn't picked up.

Whatever would the twins make of this flirtation, if that's what it is? Surprisingly, Helena might be the least disapproving of the two, but how will she react when she finds out about her father's trial? I've tried to shield her and Miranda from what's happening, Sophie thinks now, but have I been right to do so?

His voice cuts into her thoughts. 'So, what's brought you to this part of the world?'

'I'm sorry?' She gathers herself with difficulty. 'Oh, my husband decided to take a break from his work.'

He raises an eyebrow, and she adds quickly, 'You seem to enjoy life here.'

'I'll say. I've always liked the buzz of a city. I was in the centre for a while, but the rents were sky-high. At least out here they're a bit more affordable – I live just off the high street.'

'And you're an architect,' she says, thinking of his business card tucked away in the bottom of her bag.

'Yes. I specialise in converting old buildings into flats and offices. Mostly in run-down areas like this.' He makes circling gestures with his hands, his eyes alight with enthusiasm. 'It's a great feeling to breathe new life into a building. Though it can be a bloody slow process. But even in this neck of the woods, people are starting to realise the importance of hanging onto their heritage.'

She thinks of Oxford's medieval and Renaissance architecture. 'I wouldn't have thought there was much worth saving around here.'

'I guess we're all guilty of not seeing what's in front of us.' He leans towards her.

'Next time you go past the Tube, have a dekko at the electronics warehouse. It used to be an Edwardian music hall. A bit further on, there's that row of shops, tacked onto the front of nineteenth-century labourers' cottages. The upper storeys still have some original features. Then the other day, I spotted the remains of a Roman wall in someone's garden.'

'I'm obviously missing a lot.' She pauses. 'I've been away from London so long, it's quite a shock to see all the youngsters with their cigarettes and cans of lager.' She adds, 'And to adjust to the traffic and litter.'

'No offence, Sophie, but what planet *have* you been on?'

She pulls a face. 'I'm afraid I've led a pretty sheltered life. My husband was – is – a teacher at the private school where I work as assistant matron. We live in the grounds, and mix mainly with other masters and their wives. It's all very...' she hesitates, searching for the right word, 'cosy.'

'And you have daughters?'

'Helena and Miranda – both in their first year at university. And you?'

'A twenty-four-year-old son who's travelling the world before he starts his physics doctorate, and a girl, quite a bit younger.' He pauses before adding, 'My wife and I separated last year.'

She lowers her head to hide her smile. When she looks across at him, he's crumbling the remains of his bread onto his plate.

'So, are you going to tell me how you've ended up here?'

She fiddles with a strand of hair. 'It's rather a long story. My husband was asked to leave at short notice.'

'Surely an employer can't just do that? Or not without a pretty good reason.'

She swallows. 'I know – but they did.'

'So the move here must have been one hell of a shock?'

She should brush him off with some light remark.

'Didn't mean to pry.'

She shifts her gaze to the neighbouring table where the waitress is clearing away plates. Oh to be twenty years younger. She glances up and meets Ian's gaze.

'I hope I'm not sticking my neck out here, Sophie' – for the first time he sounds hesitant – 'but I'd really like to see you again.'

She can feel the pulse going in her throat. 'I'd like that too – very much.'

'How about tomorrow? Or later in the week, if that suits you better?'

This man is a virtual stranger. But, 'Tomorrow?' she finds herself saying.

THIRTY-ONE

IT'S JUST AFTER HALF NINE AND MARSHALL JUNIOR is coming towards him, hand outstretched. Miles returns the grip, thinking that there is no way this man will ever offer anything that doesn't have a three-figure sum attached. Though there are plenty of other things to worry about than the bill – this morning's session with the barrister, for a start.

Marshall pulls open the front door. 'Let's get going, shall we? It's only a few minutes' walk.'

Along the Embankment, the traffic is doing its usual nose-to-tail crawl. On their right, the wrinkled surface of the river shivers under a grey sky. Miles is thankful to turn his back on it all and follow Marshall up a side alley and along another street.

'Bill is very experienced in these types of cases,' Marshall is saying. 'I have every confidence in him.' He continues to talk, perhaps wanting to offer reassurance, but Miles can't concentrate. Already he can feel a knot in his stomach that tightens with each step he takes.

He and Marshall enter a modern building, and a lift takes them up to the second floor. A stocky man, with a shock of red hair above a round, freckled face, greets them. 'Bill Melbury Jones,' he says, as they shake hands.

His mouth is too dry for any words to come out.

'I'm just along the corridor. I'll lead the way, shall I?' He turns to Marshall. 'So, how's tricks?'

The two walk ahead, still chatting, and then they're in a room that at least looks like a lawyer's office, with files stacked against the wall and a scatter of papers across the leather-topped desk.

Melbury Jones seats himself behind it, and waves a hand at two chairs. 'No doubt Rupert's been putting you through your paces.' He smiles, showing a row of perfect teeth. 'Hope he's not been giving you too hard a time?'

Miles manages a shake of the head.

The barrister reaches for a notepad. 'Let's get down to business, shall we?'

Marshall leans forward. 'I have explained to Miles that you'll be going over the witness statements with him.'

'Indeed. But I'd like to start with your account, Miles. I've read it, of course, but if you could just talk me through what happened?' He consults his notebook. 'Let me see, it was back in January – the second week of term? And you were teaching the Remove Year.'

'Yes – Shakespearean tragedy.' Miles stares down at his feet, trying to put his thoughts into some sort of order.

More than ever it feels as if he's recollecting events from another world.

'And they were how old?'

'Thirteen – fourteen.'

'And you had something of a history with them?'

'As I've explained in my account, they were a pretty unruly lot.'

'Bloody difficult, by the sound of it.'

Miles nods, encouraged by the man's response. 'They also made a habit of being late. They have a sports session immediately beforehand, but there's ample time for them to change afterwards and get across to the main building.'

'Yet you began the lesson with a number of absentees?'

'Yes. I had made it very clear that I was not going to allow a few boys to hold up the entire class.' He pauses.

'But then one of them appeared' – the barrister riffles through his papers – 'Webb, wasn't it?'

That overgrown puppy, Miles thinks. 'He came bursting in, shouting and waving his arms. I could tell he was in quite a panic. He said something had happened in the changing rooms, and for me to go there at once.' Miles pauses. 'Looking back on it, I know I should have told him to fetch the school matron, Rachel Evans. Or phoned her myself.'

'We'll come to that,' Melbury Jones says. 'For now, just continue with what actually happened.'

'I went out of the building and began running along the path.'

'Did you at that stage ask him what was going on?'

'He was quite a way ahead – I was just trying to keep up with him.'

'So you entered the changing rooms separately?'

'Yes – at least I'm not sure. I remember pulling open the door, but I think Webb must have been standing outside. To begin with, anyway.'

'Go on.'

'It was very dark in there – I think a bulb must have gone – but eventually I spotted the Cunningham boy lying on a bench at the far end. I thought he must have been hurt pretty badly to account for all the fuss.' Miles pictures the metal lockers, the pile of sports shoes in the corner and, as he drew nearer, the towel half-draped over the boy's lower body. 'I remember running over and saying something like, "Are you all right, Cunningham?".'

'And was anyone else there at this stage?'

'Webb – he must have followed me in – and another boy, Owen. It was he who said something like: "He just passed out, sir. Do you think he's still breathing?".'

'Meaning Cunningham?'

He nods.

'So what was your response?'

'I didn't have my mobile on me, so I shouted at Owen, "Tell Matron to call for an ambulance. And get her to bring the first aid box."'

'There wasn't one in the changing rooms?'

'I didn't think – it's not somewhere I go to.'

'So – what are staff meant to do in situations like this?'

'I don't think there are any set rules, if that's what you mean.'

Melbury Jones is writing furiously. 'So then what happened?'

'I knelt beside Cunningham. He's always been rather pasty-faced, and in the dim light he seemed to me paler than ever. So I put my head on his chest.' He feels his face redden. 'To check if he was still breathing.'

'And then?'

'I don't know how he managed it, but suddenly he threw the towel to one side, hauled himself up, pulled me on top of him, and...'

'Take your time.'

'He forced my head close to his, and then he – he... kissed me.'

'On the lips?'

'Yes.'

'Any other contact? Touching of the genitals, for instance?'

'Certainly not!' His face is burning.

Melbury Jones gives a nod.

'It was then that I heard the door open, and when I turned round, there was the geography master, Laing—' He breaks off.

'How do you think he came to be there?'

'I honestly have no idea. One of the boys must have fetched him, I suppose.' He gulps, his breath tight in his chest. 'I managed to break free from Cunningham, and then I yelled across to Laing: "It's not what you think!"'

Marshall has been listening in silence. Now he leans towards the barrister. 'And I wonder, Bill, before we go any further, if I could just run over Laing's statement with you? He's the only other prosecution witness who'll be giving live evidence.'

'Of course.'

'Won't keep you a moment, Miles.'

It's a relief to have a few moments away from the spotlight, so that he can steady his breathing. He hadn't realised how tough this was going to be. God alone knows what these two men are making of him. The shame of it, he thinks, painfully aware that, however hard he tries, he'll never truly belong to this public school world, with its coded language and assumption of superiority.

'I think I've got the picture,' Melbury Jones says, when he finally finishes his questioning of Miles. 'The next step will be for you to enter your plea at the pre-trial hearing. All very straightforward, I promise you.' He taps a well-manicured hand on the desk. 'We'll run through all the details again nearer the actual trial – to ensure that you come over as well as possible, and that we avoid any googlies.'

'I just want the whole thing over,' he murmurs, 'so I can get back to my teaching duties.'

'Of course.'

Melbury Jones is consulting his notes again. 'Your wife and daughters will be attending the actual trial? It always goes down well with the jury when they can see the family giving support.'

Miles swallows. What will it be like to have them there, listening to every word?

Yet if Melbury Jones believes it's the best option, he'd better go with it. Thankfully, Sophie seems in a better mood since her unexpected trip to Cornwall – the break has obviously done her good. But he'll need to brief her and the girls, and soon. He folds his arms across his chest. 'Of course.'

'Excellent.' The barrister glances at Marshall. 'Anything else, Rupert?'

'Character witnesses?'

'Ah, yes. We need someone, Miles, either in a professional or a personal capacity, who'll be prepared to speak on your behalf. Emphasise your honesty and integrity – that sort of thing.'

He thinks for a moment. Aunt Harriet is out of the question, and the other names that spring to mind are Sophie's friends, rather than his. 'Other than my old head teacher, who unfortunately is rather frail, my closest colleagues are all at Fordingbury.'

'And under strict instructions not to get involved,' Marshall says.

'Well, I'm sure you'll come up with someone,' Melbury Jones continues. 'Now, anything you want to ask *me*, Miles?'

This is his chance to raise the point that's been haunting him for weeks. 'Just suppose for a moment I *were* to be convicted...?' His voice tails away.

The barrister leans back in his chair. 'I doubt you'd get sent down, if that's your concern. Most likely you'd be given some sort of community sentence, and of course your name would be on the sex offenders' register. But we'd appeal it.'

Miles swallows. All very well for this man to be so offhand, but it's not *his* life, *his* reputation. Why, this would be worse than being branded, because the whole world, including Sophie and the girls, would know. He feels sick.

'Let's cross that bridge when we come to it.' Melbury Jones pushes back his chair.

'Though I remain pretty confident that we'll see these young men off.'

Miles feels a glimmer of hope. 'You really believe things will go our way?'

The barrister nods. 'At that age, these boys are all mouth, but once they start to give evidence, they tend to crumble.'

The way his eyes glint when he smiles, makes Miles glad to have him on his side.

THIRTY-TWO

A GROUP OF JUNIOR BOYS WAS WHILING AWAY A wet Sunday afternoon in the common room, when three of the senior prefects entered.

'I say, Whitaker,' Huw Montgomery asked. He had a long, earnest face, with the shadow of a moustache above prominent front teeth. 'What post does your father hold?'

For a moment, Miles felt confused. Then, just in time, he realised this wasn't a reference to his father delivering mail.

'Management?' Montgomery prompted.

Miles thought for a moment. 'I don't think so. He travels around a lot, asking people to buy stuff.'

'A *salesman*, then,' Montgomery proclaimed to the group that had gathered around them.

'And your mother?'

'Oh, she doesn't work. Well, not outside the house, at any rate.'

'Too busy washing and cooking, I expect.'

'That's right,' Miles replied, baffled by the laughter his response evoked.

It took him a while to realise that other fathers had jobs in government, or law, or the City, and their mothers – when they weren't complaining about how difficult it was to find the right kind of domestic help – spent their days playing golf and bridge. There were also casual references to family trips to France and Italy, and visits to Ascot and Henley.

By the summer term, he had learned to gloss over his holiday activities – reading, walking the family spaniel in the nearby park, and going to Saturday matinees with his father. Yet deep down he knew that, whether he owned up to it or not, merely to live in a semi-detached in Croydon and take a fortnight's holiday in Weymouth each year, was to fall far short of Fordingbury standards.

And had it not been for Murdo, he might well have ended up a total failure.

'Ulysses,' the old man had proclaimed in his booming voice, 'if you junior boys can get anything into those thick skulls of yours – translated from the Greek into Latin. Renamed Odysseus. A seafarer and wanderer, blown about the world at a pretty brisk rate. Now, the Trojan Horse. Ring any bells?'

So that most of the class – Miles among them – were jumping about in their seats, waving an arm in the air. *Please, sir, I know! No – me, sir!*

In his second year, Miles turned into what the other boys referred to as "a swot", reading everything on Greek and Roman literature he could lay his hands on. At first, he ignored the various taunts that came his way, but then one day, seemingly out of nowhere, he found his voice. '*Labor omnia vincit*, or *sine labore nihil*,' he announced. 'That's to say, you ignoramuses, no one succeeds without putting his back into it.'

It was a voice not so dissimilar, perhaps, from Murdo's.

THIRTY-THREE

OUTSIDE, THE DAY HAS TRANSFORMED ITSELF, AND he walks back along the Embankment under a luminous sky.

The traffic is moving freely, and on the water, a red motor launch overtakes a line of barges that bobs to and fro in its wake. Around him, the shirt-sleeved tourists are out in number, clicking cameras and ambling along with the relaxed air of those who have left behind, however briefly, the stresses of everyday life. What wouldn't he give to be one of them?

Once this court case is safely out of the way, he must take Sophie off somewhere. She's always fancied a return to Tuscany, where they once holidayed years ago. Somehow they'll scrape together the money. And with the girls at university, and hopefully with a loan from Aunt Harriet to tide him and Sophie over, it will be a welcome change from Cornwall.

As he takes his seat in the warm belly of the Tube, however, he feels his optimism seep away. Although he and Sophie are getting on better, there's a change in her that he can't quite pinpoint. Some of it is obviously down to this new job, which has resulted in her acquiring a selection of shorter skirts and low-cut tops. She's also had her hair done differently, so that it now falls in soft fronds around her face. Although the change initially took him by surprise, he has to admit that it makes her looks younger, sexier.

How he wishes he'd found the guts to talk things through with her earlier. Yet now, just when he's ready to do so, it's as if their roles are reversed, and she's the one who doesn't want to know.

'I keep meaning to tell you, Miles,' she said over breakfast the previous morning. 'I've agreed to do more overtime.'

'Is that really necessary?' He tried to keep the panic out of his voice.

'I don't want to let Becca down,' she said, and, before he could reply, disappeared to the bathroom.

Now, as he gets out of the Tube and begins walking along the platform, a cold trickle of doubt creeps into his mind. Melbury Jones seems to think it unlikely the case will go against them, but supposing he's wrong? Would Sophie stay with him then?

He clutches the escalator rail, feeling beads of sweat form on his forehead.

He emerges from the Tube into bright sunshine, the empty hours stretching before him, and the only consolation his first drink of the day.

But then he catches sight of a black-clad figure walking towards him. How could he have forgotten their meeting?

'Ah, good. I was hoping to run into you before you reached the churchyard.' Ali holds up a hand as if to ward off argument. 'Now – absolutely no excuses are permitted. It is high time you came to my house for a coffee.'

It's like an answer to prayer. 'Well – if you're sure?'

'Absolutely.'

'Lead on, Macduff!' Miles says, and is gratified by the brilliant smile Ali flashes at him.

He follows him along what is now familiar territory – under the dripping railway arch, left and then right, with that ghastly tower block looming in the distance. They pass the entrance to The Crown and Cushion. He may drop in there on his way home – he probably won't be with Ali more than an hour.

After a few minutes, they turn into a quiet side street. The semi-detached houses are well maintained, and the pavements free of the ubiquitous dog muck and litter that characterise the area. That's one of the surprises about this neck of the woods: the pockets of poverty and relative affluence living side by side. Just his bloody luck to end up in one of the least salubrious parts.

Ali's house, the same 1930s vintage as 49 Stephen's Close, is halfway along the road and pristine in comparison, with cream walls and a bottle-glass bow window that gleams in the sun. With a feeling of shame Miles realises it will be out of the question to return this invitation.

Ali leads the way across the front paving and turns his key in the lock. 'I am home, Farah,' he calls, 'and we have a visitor.' Miles follows him into a small hallway that smells, not unpleasantly, of cinnamon.

Ali ushers him into a square front room, with a modern gas fire and a three-piece suite covered in a brilliant shade of peacock. Other than an Islamic-looking scroll over the fireplace, the cream walls are bare, although Miles is reassured to see that the alcove at the far end is filled from floor to ceiling with books.

'Ah, there you are,' Ali says, as a small woman appears, dressed in brown trousers and top, and wearing a head covering. 'Farah, this is my friend, Miles Whitaker.'

She gives a shy smile in his direction, before lowering her eyes again. She has a blunt nose, and round cheeks, which dimple as she smiles.

She pulls open the window, letting in a welcome waft of air.

'Coffee, Miles?' Ali is saying.

'Please.'

'And some of Farah's home baking?'

'That would be splendid.'

With another smile, she's out of the room, closing the door behind her.

'Do have a seat, Miles.'

He perches on the sofa, while Ali settles into a chair, placing his rucksack on the floor beside him.

Miles gestures towards the scroll. 'That looks interesting.' Bordered with gold and silver leaves, it's divided into four sections, each filled with lines of black writing – like the parts of some giant insect, he thinks.

Ali strokes his beard. 'The four Quls. They are prayers given to us by Mohammed, peace be upon him. They protect us from life's pitfalls, which unfortunately are never far away.'

Miles glances across, but Ali isn't even looking in his direction. He's rummaging in the rucksack.

'I spend much time studying.' Ali holds up several books.

How absurd to ever have imagined the bag could contain anything sinister.

'Literature mainly, but philosophy and history also. One of the things I miss most is the talks I used to have with my brothers and cousins.'

Miles thinks of the hours spent with Murdo: by the study fire on winter evenings, summer nights on the terrace with a G & T, their discussions ranging from Virgil to Wordsworth, Pliny to Thackeray, Plato to Betjeman. "Chewing the fat", the old man called it. He'll be down to see him again the moment this wretched court case is over.

'You left your country a while ago?' he asks now.

'Yes. No doubt with time, I will feel more settled here, *inshallah*.' He smiles. 'My brother-in-law has been in the UK for longer. Like you, he is a teacher, and the intellectual in the family. He is currently studying at the LSE.'

The door opens and Farah appears with a tray. The air fills with the smell of roasted coffee. She pours their drink into small cups, handing Miles his with a willingness that for a moment reminds him of Sophie – or of Sophie as she used to be.

Farah holds out a plate of dark cakes, decorated with sprinkles of green and pink.

'These look jolly good,' he says, selecting the nearest one.

She smiles acknowledgement, before leaving the room as silently as she entered.

He takes a cautious bite, the flavours of chocolate and spices melting in his mouth. 'I say, these are splendid!'

'Farah is an excellent cook.' Ali sips his coffee. 'But although I hold her in the highest regard, I have to confess it is simply not the same talking with a woman as with a man. To my way of thinking, there has only been one woman in recent history truly worthy of our esteem.' He glances at Miles for his reaction.

He's obviously speaking of some leading figure in the Muslim world.

'Your ex-prime minister, Lady Thatcher,' Ali continues, 'I admit to being one of her most fervent admirers.'

Miles gives a surprised laugh. 'And I thought I was the only Tory supporter for miles around!'

'Strength of character combined with a keen intellect – a powerful combination, don't you think?' He leans forward. 'Although I cannot claim to be a Shakespearean scholar like yourself, I have studied him since I was knee-high to a grasshopper. Why grasshopper, I wonder?'

'They're of the order *orthoptera*. From the Greek.'

Ali gives an admiring nod. Suddenly he throws back his shoulders, his voice resonating in the quiet room as he declaims, '"If you tickle us do we not laugh? If you prick us do we not bleed? If you poison us do we not die?"'

"'If you wrong us shall we not revenge?", Miles interposes. 'You forgot that.'

'There speaks the scholar!' Ali digs once more in the bag, holding up a well-thumbed paperback. 'I have here my favourite Shakespeare play. I wonder if you can guess which one it is?'

Miles shakes his head.

'*Antony and Cleopatra.*' He resumes his seat. 'Of course I don't need to ask if you're familiar with it?'

In the silence, Miles is aware of the thudding of his heart.

*

He's back in front of the Remove class, trying to work out how to handle this increasingly difficult set of boys. There are fewer than usual this year – only twelve – but in all his time as a teacher, he's never faced such a blatant challenge to his authority.

'The thing is, sir,' Justin Cunningham says, in his infuriating drawl, 'we're not too keen on the play that's been chosen.'

The boy is slouched over his desk in the front row. Miles can see the fair skin, almost paper-thin, the pale eyes and the cow's lick of blonde hair over the forehead.

There are mutters of agreement that Miles, like the alert skipper of some undernourished crew, interprets as the rumblings of mutiny.

This is Cunningham's second year at Fordingbury. His father apparently lost money in the City and had to remove the boy from his previous school, where the fees were almost double. Although Miles recognised from the start that the boy was a troublemaker, he's never been sure how to handle him.

'How do you find that Remove group?' he asked, cornering Laing in the staffroom one lunch hour.

'The Remove? A wee bit on the lively side, but that's all to the good. Why do you ask?'

'Oh, no particular reason.' For how could he possibly admit to the knot of anxiety in his stomach at the start of each teaching session with the group?

'What we want, *sir*,' Cunningham is careful to use all the right words, although the insolence in his tone is unmistakable, 'is something more relevant to our age group.'

'No doubt, Cunningham, you're thinking along the lines of *Romeo and Juliet*?'

'Well, it is about young love, sir. And sex, of course.' He pauses, looking around the rest of the group. 'And most other schools are doing it – the play, I mean. *Sir.*'

There is laughter from the others, the loudest coming from the two friends he goes around with: Owen, with patches of sweat under his arms even in cold weather, and

Webb, a good-looking lad of over six foot, who for all his size, is immature for his age. A follower, Miles thinks, who will do whatever is asked of him.

Now is the moment when he must take back control. If he fails, these boys will become unteachable.

'If you had an ounce of brains in your head,

Cunningham, you'd understand that *Antony and Cleopatra* is one of the greatest tragedies of all time.'

'Yes, but Antony *is* pretty well past it, don't you think?' Owen says.

Miles struggles to keep his tone even. 'Well, he doesn't seem to me to do too badly. He's co-ruler of the Roman Empire – no mean feat – and becomes the lover of one of the most beautiful and fascinating women in history. Don't just take my word for it. If we take a look at the text, we—'

'But he's still *old*,' Cunningham insists. 'Why would anyone waste time on someone like him?' He props his chin on his hands, gazing up at Miles with an innocent expression. '*How* long have you been teaching here, sir?'

There are more sniggers.

Miles pauses, before looking straight at Cunningham. 'In Shakespeare's day, it would have been usual for youths to have had their first sexual experience at eleven or twelve. So, by most standards, I imagine you'd be definitely "past it".'

Miles doesn't know what made him say such a thing. It was pretty much below the belt, in every sense of the word. Maybe it's because he senses, underneath the boy's bravado, a sexual insecurity, with which he was only too familiar at that age.

To his relief, his comment is greeted with shouts of laughter from the class, and for one gratifying moment, he feels triumphant.

Until, glancing once more at Cunningham, he catches the look of intense hatred in the pale eyes.

*

'Miles?' Ali is saying. 'I would be most interested in your thoughts on the play.'

He forces himself to concentrate. 'One of the whole points of the tragedy is that here is an older man who, as the result of a character flaw, loses everything – his status, the woman he loves, the respect of his contemporaries, and indeed of the world.'

'Well put. More coffee?'

He shakes his head. 'I really believed the boys I was teaching would take to *Antony and Cleopatra*, but they made their views very plain. I challenged them, of course, never dreaming it would lead to what it did.' To his dismay, his hands start to shake, slopping coffee into the saucer.

'And the difficulty, whatever it was, is causing you much pain?'

"Pain" – the word strikes right to the heart of Miles's misery. No one – not Marshall, not even Sophie – has used it. He draws in his breath and, before he can help himself, the words come tumbling out. 'I was found in a compromising position with one of my pupils.' He stares at the scroll, until the jagged lines of writing blur. 'A sexually compromising position,' he adds, his cheeks burning.

Ali blinks.

'The whole thing was a set-up. But who'll believe me? Apparently all three boys involved are giving the same story.'

He needs that slug of whisky to calm himself down. 'I've taken enough of your time. I'd better make a move.' He still can't control the quaver in his voice.

'To be accused of something of which one is innocent is very hard, my friend.'

Miles stares. Is it possible that here is someone who's not going to treat him like a pariah? Who is going to agree with his version of events?

THIRTY-FOUR

Sophie lies sleepless on the spare room mattress. The curtains don't meet in the middle, and the moon shines full into her face. At regular intervals, an aeroplane drones overhead, and she can hear Miles's faint snores from the other room. Yet through it all, her only thoughts are of Ian: his tousled hair, the quirk of an eyebrow when he smiles and his touch, delicate and sure, across her shoulders and inside her wrist – a touch that feels branded into her skin.

Just after five, she gives up on sleep and runs a bath, pouring scented oil into the water and, afterwards, smoothing on body lotion. When she's finished dressing, she tucks a set of clean underwear into her bag. Just in case, she tells herself.

She hasn't heard any movement from Miles, but when she goes down to the kitchen there he is, making coffee and hovering around – like a faithful Labrador, she thinks, hating her feelings of guilt and resentment.

'Busy day?' he enquires as they begin their cereal.

She nods. 'What about you?'

He spoons sugar into his mug. 'I thought I might link up with Ali again. It's good to have someone to talk to. Helps fill the time…'

He continues to speak, but she's only half-listening. Not long to go, she thinks.

'The thing is,' Miles is saying, 'there's something I need to talk to you about.'

'Not *now*, Miles.'

'Please?'

She hates that pleading look in his eyes. 'I'm sorry, but I'm late enough as it is.' She gets up, knocking over the remains of her coffee. He's on his feet in an instant. 'At least none of it's gone on you,' he says, as he mops up the spill.

Perhaps he wants to have a serious discussion about the court case? At last. 'Well, the girls need to know what's happening. Let's talk in the morning.'

After a pause, he says, 'Then the morning it'll have to be.' He eyes her linen dress and heeled sandals. 'That's a new outfit, isn't it?'

She nods.

'Makes you look really young.' He pauses. 'And sexy.'

'Thanks.'

He moves closer, and for one terrible moment she thinks he's going to put his arms around her. Instead, he says, 'I wondered if there's anything in particular you'd like for supper?'

'Afraid I won't be back in time, Miles. I'll grab a sandwich.'

At Fordingbury, no details regarding timetables or the boys seemed to escape Miles's eye. So now, without those distractions, is it possible that he's also spotted the difference in her – one that is not just to do with a new hairstyle and clothes? But the change that has taken place inside her? She hasn't felt this way since those heady days with Alastair when underneath the uncertainty, there was this same overwhelming pull.

Yet supposing her feelings for Ian are merely a figment of her imagination? And what if he were to change his mind? Maybe arriving late, as he did when they last met? A sign surely of reluctance on his part.

In the end, it's she who is running late, held up at the last minute by a white-faced teenager, complaining in broken English that she's been given the wrong change. Hearing the raised voices, Sophie turns back from the door. Steve is behind the counter, his face creased in alarm. 'N-no!' he shouts, so that other customers turn and stare.

Becca has gone to the bank, and by the time Sophie has calmed Steve down, and handed an extra fifty pence to the girl, precious minutes have gone by.

She runs the short distance to the Tube, her breath coming out in gasps as she pushes past the other pedestrians.

The afternoon sun is beating down, and she can feel her armpits damp with sweat.

So much for all the bath oil and lotion, she thinks.

She has what seems an interminable wait for her train, and when she gets out at her stop, she's already twenty minutes late. All the same, she pauses to glance about her.

She still isn't sure where Miles goes each day, and of course it would be a chance in a million if he were to walk past at this precise moment.

When to her relief there's no sign of him, she starts at a half-run along the main road, passing the fish and chip shop and the newsagents, and slowing her pace only when she reaches the turn that leads to the cafe.

As she draws nearer, she scans the pavement. All the tables are occupied, so if Ian isn't inside waiting for her, she'll take it as a sign that he's changed his mind.

She pushes open the door, and spots him immediately, sitting by himself at a side table. A look of relief crosses his face as he catches sight of her.

Her heart is thudding. 'So sorry. I got held up at the shop.'

'No worries. It could easily have been the other way round.'

He looks relaxed enough, yet she thinks she detects a waver in his voice.

She watches him push a hand through his hair, and longing for him flares up again.

'Coffee? Or a cold drink?'

She glances around at the other customers, laughing and chatting with one another.

'I'm not sure…'

He takes her by the elbow, staring into her face. 'We could go back to my place?' He hesitates. 'If it's too soon, just say.'

But that one touch sends a familiar shockwave through her. 'No. That'll be fine,' she says, speaking quickly so there's no time to change her mind.

They go out of the shop and walk in silence along the main road, turning down a succession of streets until he stops outside a narrow doorway. Sandwiched between a shoe repair shop and a chemist, the place looks run-down and seedy, not at all how she imagined. She feels a moment's hesitation. She doesn't know this man at all.

He reaches for her hand, and she allows herself to be led up a dark flight of stairs.

At the top, he pauses again, dropping her hand, and unlocking another door. She follows him through, and stands for a moment, blinking in a sudden burst of light.

She's in a large studio room, with sun pouring in through the sloping window at one end. She has an impression of uncluttered space, with a narrow chest along one wall and, above it, a painting in muted colours. Facing the window is a patterned screen. He moves towards it, pulling it back to reveal a double bed.

They stand facing one another, and then she steps towards him, reaching a tentative hand to his face. He turns her palm over and she feels the warmth of his lips in the curve of her elbow, and the hollow in her throat. She no longer cares that her hair is a mess, and that she smells of sweat. All she can think about is her need for him. Now they're bumping against one another, her elbow catching his face, a seam of his shirt tearing, and clothes tumbling in a heap to the floor. They fall back onto the bed, and she feels his weight moving on top of her.

Then there's the sensation of her body melting, and she calls out his name. A few moments later, they lie side by side, in a silence that seems to go on forever.

Later, they shower together, rubbing soap into each other's bodies, and towelling one another dry. Then he leads her back to the bed, and they lie with their arms around one another.

She must have dozed off, because the next thing she knows, he's propped on an elbow, smiling down at her.

She sits up, raising an arm to shield her eyes from the sun that still streams in through the window. 'All this space and light!'

He runs his fingers along her thigh. 'And there's me convinced I was the main attraction!'

He kisses the hollow of her throat, and she laughs, light-headed with pleasure in the moment.

'Fancy a glass of Sauvignon?'

'Just a small one, thanks.'

She watches him climb off the bed and head towards the kitchen, moving with that easy grace that still takes her by surprise. Already she feels she'll never get enough of him. She loves his square-tipped fingers, the fuzz of hair covering his legs and chest, and the set of his shoulders. She has a sudden picture of a pink-skinned Miles, hopping naked around the Fordingbury bedroom as he struggles to put on a sock. She pushes the image away, lying back on the pillows and studying the room.

Every item seems to have been chosen with care, and the simplicity of it pleases and surprises her. In the corner is a rectangular desk, its top a slab of grey slate on which a computer and a pot of pencils rest. A black lacquer chair is drawn up in front of it and a stack of papers piled neatly in a box on the floor. There's a long grey cabinet with drawers against the opposite wall, and beside it a row of square baskets containing folded items of clothing. The walls are bare, apart from the canvas of coloured squares – orange, red and purple. Maybe a Rothko copy – during her time as a student nurse, she visited all the major galleries and exhibitions. She must remember to ask.

Ian comes back in, carrying two glasses of wine, before sliding onto the bed beside her.

They sip their drinks in silence, his arm around her shoulders, listening to the flutter of pigeons on the roof opposite.

For the rest of my life, she tells herself, whatever happens, I will remember this moment: the voices wafting up from the street, the occasional bleep of a horn, and the way the bars of sun stripe his body with warm gold.

She looks at her watch. 'It's after seven. I'd better make a move.'

Perversely, she wants him to ask her not to go, but when he doesn't reply, she reaches for her clothes and begins to dress. Already she hates this leave-taking sensing that, away from this man, she will feel hollowed out and empty.

She turns and looks down at him. 'You do want to see me again?' God, how pathetic she sounds – like a needy child!

'What do *you* think?' He swings his legs off the bed, stepping into his shorts and walking her to the door. He puts his arms about her and she allows herself to relax against him.

In that moment, she's tempted to tell him everything: Miles's disgrace, their flight from the school, and the forthcoming trial that's only weeks away now. But just in time, she holds back. She daren't risk jeopardising things, not at this early stage.

He pushes a strand of hair from her forehead. 'Same time Thursday?'

She nods.

'Brilliant!'

Now *he* sounds childlike and, despite herself, she smiles.

'That's better.' He holds her at arm's length, looking into her face. 'See you soon.'

They kiss again, and then she's walking down the stairs, and opening the door onto the street.

As she mingles with the late shoppers, she thinks ahead to Thursday, which is also the day of her session with Ruth Madiebo. She'll make it the last one, she decides.

On impulse, she takes the turning that leads past the cafe, stopping to peer in through the plate-glass window. The place is closed, but there's the table, where, only two weeks ago, she and Ian sat together for the first time. *Our* table, she thinks, tearing herself away with reluctance.

She begins the walk back to Stephen's Close, skirting the potholes, and going past the monkey-puzzle tree and the overflowing skip.

It's only as she nears the house that her pace slows. How on earth is she going to face Miles? And what about the girls? What about the trial?

When she reaches the house, she stands transfixed. Only when she hears Kirsty's raised voice from next door, does she begin rooting in her bag for the key.

THIRTY-FIVE

'SO YOU SEE THE FAMILY STILL KEEP IN TOUCH AS best they can.' Ali strokes his beard. 'None of us ever forgets the place where we have been the most happy. It is Farah's and my fervent hope one day to return.'

'Nothing beats that sense of homecoming,' Miles murmurs.

They are in the churchyard, whiling away the time before they are due at Ali's house.

Miles glances at the clock, wishing that he could switch off, even for a short while, his thoughts of the coming trial.

Ali follows his gaze. 'Shall we make a move?' He leads the way out of the churchyard, still talking over his shoulder about family and home.

They reach the side street that leads past The Crown and Cushion. Here, the traffic is quiet, and there are few pedestrians about. Three men are emerging from the pub up ahead, and a young girl in a green skirt and blazer walks past.

'What a pleasant change to see a uniform,' Miles says. 'I wonder what school she attends.'

He waits for Ali's response, but his attention is fixed on the three men.

Now only a dozen yards away, they've spread themselves across the pavement, arms linked. They're white, Miles notes with relief, dressed in dark jackets and trousers, and with closely cropped hair. The one in the middle has a Remembrance Day poppy pinned to his lapel, and looks to be in his fifties, the lower part of his face covered in grey fuzz. He's more solidly built than his friends, who seem barely out of their teens.

Ali pulls at Miles's sleeve. 'Let's cross over, shall we?'

'It's all right, Ali. I bet they're ex-army.' *Our boys,* he can hear Murdo saying.

Miles waits for them to step aside, but the three have spread out again and are laughing together, not looking where they're going.

Ali drops back, just as one of the men, with pink cheeks and an ear-stud, barges into him.

Ali stumbles, grabbing onto Miles for support.

'Hey, look out!' Miles cries.

'No – your friend's the one who needs to look out.' The older man narrows his eyes. 'Fucking Muslim.'

'*What...?*'

In the moment it takes for the insult to register, the three have formed a circle around Ali.

'Terrorist cunt!' one of the men, snub-nosed and with a spray of freckles across his forehead, is saying. 'Get back where you fucking belong.'

Miles feels his throat go dry. 'Now see here…'

The man with the ear-stud raises his fist. 'Beat it, Granddad, or you'll get what's coming to him.'

In a sudden move, Ali ducks under the older man's arm and begins running across the road. There's a screech of brakes as a van swerves to avoid him. The two younger men are in pursuit, catching him halfway and dragging him back to the pavement. There's a scuffle, in which Miles makes out a flurry of arms and legs. The next thing he knows, Ali is on the ground, knees drawn up to his chest, his hands covering his face. 'Please, no. Please, no,' he whimpers.

Miles watches, paralysed, while the snub-nosed man kicks Ali into the gutter. There's another squeal of brakes, and a driver shakes his fist at them.

'Piece of shit,' the man says, watching Ali crawl back onto the pavement.

Miles feels his heart thudding. 'Leave him alone!' But what should have been an authoritative command comes out in a squeaky whisper.

The older man has stood all this time, arms folded across his chest, watching the proceedings. Now he steps forward and jabs a finger hard into Miles's chest, nearly throwing him off balance. 'You tell Mohammed here, if we run into him again, he won't get off so fucking lightly.'

With a nod to his friends they're off, heading down the road towards the Tube.

Miles leans over his friend. 'Are you all right?'

To his relief, Ali nods. 'Help me up, would you?'

Miles hauls him to his feet. A patch of blood oozes through his beard, and his tunic and trousers are coated in dust. He sways and Miles puts out a hand to steady him.

A thin man with a wispy moustache appears at Miles's side. 'I can't believe what I've just seen. Hadn't we better get him to A & E?'

'No hospital,' Ali says. 'Please.' He's shaking uncontrollably.

'But you might be seriously injured, mate,' the man says.

'I'm all right.' He rubs his shoulder, before looking up at Miles, who's embarrassed to see tears in his eyes. 'Just get me home, my friend.'

'I'll give a hand, if you like,' the stranger offers.

'Thank you. It's only a few minutes from here,' Ali says.

Miles and the stranger, supporting Ali between them, walk up past The Crown and Cushion. Ali's body against his feels surprisingly light. Other than a dazed look in his eyes, he seems not too badly hurt. They turn into Ali's well-ordered street, and when they reach the house, Miles leans forward and presses the bell.

After a few moments, the door is opened by Farah, who lets out a cry. 'Oh my goodness! What's happened this time?'

'He's been beaten up,' Miles says.

Ali remains silent, leaning against the doorpost, breathing heavily.

'Let's get him inside,' the stranger says.

They crowd into the small hall, manoeuvring Ali to the bottom of the stairs. He leans on the banisters for support. 'We will manage from here.'

'Would you like us to stay for a while, in case there's anything else we can do?' the other man suggests. 'Fill you in on what happened, perhaps?'

'That won't be necessary.' Ali's face is drained of colour.

'Well, *I* would like to know more,' Farah says. Miles can see the struggle she's having to keep herself under control.

'We could wait in the front room?' he suggests.

'Oh, would you, Miles? Thank you. I will be down shortly.'

He watches as the couple make their slow way to the floor above. There's the sound of a door closing, and then silence.

'In here,' Miles says, showing the stranger into the front room, with its peacock blue furniture and the scroll over the fireplace. It feels chilly, but he doesn't feel it's his place to turn on the fire.

The stranger extends his hand. 'Kevin Alsop. Kev to my friends.'

'Oh.' He returns the grip. 'Miles Whitaker.'

'This is a right old to-do, isn't it?' For the first time Miles catches the Birmingham accent. 'I mean, you see things like this on TV, but you never imagine it happening right there in front of you.' He settles in one of the peacock chairs, crossing one spindly leg over the other. 'You don't think he's concussed, do you?'

'God, I hope not.'

'Let's see what his wife says, when she comes down.' He looks to be in his early forties, with a snub nose and a receding hairline.

Miles sits on the sofa. 'Do you live round here?'

'No way. Born-and-bred Solihull, me. Have a wife and three kids there.' He leans forward. 'I'm down for a few weeks on a building contract. And you?'

He hesitates. 'Just visiting, like you.'

'You and this Arab know each other pretty well, though?'

'We meet up from time to time. Whenever I find myself in this part of the world.'

Suddenly he hates himself for telling yet another lie. 'Actually, we've become real friends,' he adds.

'Know what I think?' Kevin leans forward. 'I think you and me should go to the police. When you see something like what's just happened. Well, it's bloody disgusting, isn't it?'

'And I totally agree, Kevin.' He pauses. 'Although I'm not so sure about going to the authorities. In all honesty, what can they do?' He recalls the way that blonde-haired policewoman stitched him up on the day of his arrest. 'Those men will be miles away by now,' he adds.

'That's as may be. But we could have a go at identifying them. There might already be photos of them on file, and—'

The door swings open and Farah appears, her face grave. 'My husband is sleeping.'

'You should get your GP to give him a once-over,' Kevin says. 'That was quite a knock he took.'

'It won't be necessary.' She turns to Miles. 'Ali said you spoke up for him, for which he was most grateful.'

Kevin raises an eyebrow, and Miles feels himself go red. 'I didn't do very much, I'm afraid. There were three of them, and it all happened so quickly.'

She sighs. 'I've told him to report it to the authorities, but I'm not sure he will.'

Miles feels a wave of relief.

'That's just what I was discussing with Miles here,' Kevin says. 'We're both willing to go to the police, and act as witnesses. And your husband needs to have a doctor examine him and take photographs.' He pauses. 'It's the only way to nail these thugs.'

'You may be right,' Farah says. 'But try getting my husband to see it…' Her voice trails away.

'No doubt he has his reasons,' Miles says.

'Like what?' Kevin says. 'So he can sit around waiting for the next attack?'

Miles fights off a feeling of panic. 'All I'm saying, Kevin, is that it might be best to talk it through with Ali first.'

Kevin stares at him for a moment, before nodding agreement. 'You're right, mate. Sorry if I spoke out of turn.' He gets to his feet, turning to Farah. 'I'd best be off. How about if I leave my contact details, in case your husband changes his mind?'

'That's very kind of you.'

He scribbles a number on a piece of paper, and hands it to her.

'Well, cheerio for now,' he says to Miles, before following Farah out of the room.

Miles listens to their final exchange in the hall. 'You mustn't stand for this,'

Kevin is saying. 'Next time it might be really serious.' As Farah murmurs her thanks once more, Miles thinks of how swiftly life can change. One moment, he and Ali were walking along, talking happily together, and the next, this happened. Why didn't he do more to defend his friend? Suppose he's seriously hurt?

Farah is back in the room, her face pale. 'Can I offer you some tea?'

He shakes his head. He would like to go upstairs to check on Ali, but perhaps that isn't the done thing in Muslim households and, anyway, it's probably best not to disturb him. 'I'll make a move too, Farah. If you're sure Ali's all right?'

She gives one of her shy smiles that makes him think how pretty she is. 'I'm so glad you were with him, Miles. He never complains, but it isn't the first time this kind of thing has happened.'

'So I gathered. Though he's never said anything to me about it.'

'He gets pushed and sworn at, but then so do many Muslims. But today's attack is the worst so far.' She hesitates. 'That man, Kevin, thinks we should inform the police. My husband really looks up to you. So perhaps you could persuade him? They'd listen to someone like you, wouldn't they?'

He looks down at the floor. 'Well, one always hopes so.' He pauses. 'Kevin seems helpful enough, but it's hard to know whom to trust these days.'

'Indeed. Our son moved away to Bradford so he could

be in a Muslim community, where he feels he and the family will be more secure.'

'Well, I'll leave you to it, then. Please give Ali my very best regards. I'll phone in the morning to see how he's getting on.'

It's a relief to be out in the overcast day, heading down to the pub. It's the end of the lunch hour, and the pavements are busy. He pushes open the door, thinking how astonishing it is that the assault took place only yards away, and in broad daylight. He still feels shaken by the whole thing.

At the counter, he orders a steak and kidney pie, and a large whisky. He takes his drink into a corner. Most tables are occupied, and he's glad of the buzz of conversation around him, which makes him feel less alone.

He swirls the yellow liquid round his glass, replaying the attack in his head.

Supposing Ali isn't all right? He pictured his friend's dazed look. Supposing he's sustained some serious head injury? One reads of such things. He should have insisted on taking him to hospital, as that man Kevin suggested or, at the very least, urged Farah to phone the local surgery. What was it she said? 'My husband is sleeping.' Isn't that one of the signs of concussion?

He drains his glass and, with a rush of relief, realises what he must do. How stupid not to have thought of it before!

His meal arrives, golden pastry oozing rich gravy, with greens and a dollop of creamy mash.

When he's eaten, he consults his diary for the address.

Sophie's shop is only a few stops along on the Tube and, as a trained nurse, she's the ideal person to advise him if he's making a fuss about nothing.

THIRTY-SIX

H E EMERGES FROM THE TUBE, DUCKING TO AVOID
a cigarette butt thrown from a passing van. An
old man in a long raincoat is sifting through a litter bin,
staring up at Miles with rheumy eyes. What must it feel
like to be stuck here at his age, away from all that makes
life worthwhile? He has a sudden picture of the sweep of
lawn outside the main entrance at Fordingbury, but it's as
if he's looking down the wrong end of a telescope, with the
view at the other end very small and far away.

He reaches a hand to his collarbone, tender from where
that ringleader jabbed him. The memory of the attack still
makes him shudder. He wishes he'd asked Farah if she and Ali
had neighbours they could call on. He imagines they must
have, because Muslims are a community sort of people. But
all the same, he'll never forgive himself if anything happens
to his friend because he hasn't done enough.

He crosses the main road and, after a hundred yards, turns into a narrow, sloping street, with a building society on one corner and a florist opposite. The flowers on display provide a violent splurge of colour, and the cloying scent of lilies follows him as he passes a chemist, a betting shop and a building society. And there, a little further on, is a large plate-glass window, with above it, in green lettering: *Second Thoughts – Good as New – Fashion for You.*

He stares through the window, in the hopes of catching a glimpse of Sophie. But the display blocks his view. For a moment, as he studies the various dresses and skirts, arranged in unlikely looking poses, he's reminded of his sisters jiving in the front room of their parents' house. Anne died of breast cancer five years ago, and he and Emily, who's married to a Canadian and lives in Ottawa, only exchange cards at Christmas. Perhaps he'll give her a call? But he dismisses the thought as quickly as it arrives. From the beginning, the age gap turned her into a stranger.

The shop door opens and an elderly couple emerge, followed by three young women, all clutching carrier bags. Business is obviously brisk and, once again, he feels wrong-footed to have believed, even for a moment, that her decision to work longer hours was a cover-up, so that she could spend more time with that do-gooder, Webster.

Inside, the shop is more spacious than he imagined, and he can detect Sophie's hand in the shelves of neatly folded garments, and the general sense of order. He looks around for her, but apart from a few customers riffling through rails of clothing, the only people in view are a middle-aged woman at the counter talking to a dark-haired boy.

As Miles approaches, he looks up at him, twisting his mouth in a curious upward movement.

Miles puts on his best smile. 'I wondered if Mrs Whitaker was around?'

He shakes his head. 'Don't know anyone called that.'

He fights off a sense of disorientation. 'You must do. She works here.'

'No she doesn't!' The boy's face creases, either with anger or anxiety – Miles can't tell.

He has a moment of doubt. Perhaps there's another shop of the same name?

'Let me describe her for you. She—'

Before he can finish his sentence, the boy begins shouting: 'No! No! No!'

'What seems to be the trouble, Steve?' says a voice.

He turns. A young woman, with orange streaks in her hair, and wearing denim shorts over black leggings, is staring up at him. Silver studs glitter on her nose and eyebrows, and the eyes themselves are blackened with panda-like circles. Just the kind of outfit Helena likes to appear in.

'I'm sorry to bother you. I'm looking for my wife – Sophie Whitaker.'

'Ah – you must be Miles.'

'That's right. And you're Becca. My wife has talked of you. She said how well the shop is doing,' he adds, as more customers enter.

'Yes, I don't know how I'd manage without her.'

'Well, she obviously loves the work, and seems to be coping fine with the overtime.'

'Overtime?' Becca frowns, before saying quickly: 'You're out of luck, I'm afraid. Sophie's just popped out.' She hesitates. 'To the bank.'

He looks at his watch. It's not yet four. 'But she'll be back before you close?'

'Actually'– again, there's a slight hesitation – 'she may be a while. I've asked her to do other bits and pieces for me. Perhaps I can give her a message?'

'Well, I—'

A young black woman is holding up a pair of jeans. 'All right to try these?'

'Sorry, Miles,' Becca says, 'but as you can see, I'm up to my eyes.' She turns towards the customer, with what he could swear is an expression of relief.

The young man behind the counter leans forward. 'My name's Steve.'

Miles smiles. 'I'm very pleased to meet you, Steve.'

'If you'd said it was Sophie you were looking for, I could have told you she wasn't here.'

'Do you know how long she'll be?'

'Becca lets her work flexi.' He runs a tongue over his lips. 'She's gets in early and leaves before us. She won't be back till tomorrow.'

'She's gone to the bank?'

'Don't think so. Becca went earlier.' He looks vague. 'Sophie does other work – arranging flowers, or something.'

All Miles's old fears resurface. He knows exactly what those two words, "or something", imply. Impossible for flower arranging to take up three or four hours several times a week.

How can she do this to him, and at a time when he most needs her support?

'Say hello from me when you see her,' the boy is saying.

He pulls himself together with an effort. 'Oh, yes. I will.'

'She always smells nice,' the boy says.

On his way to the door Miles passes Becca, in conversation with another customer. She doesn't look up – definitely covering for Sophie, he thinks bitterly, as he makes his way into the street.

The rational part of him knows he should take stock of the situation before deciding what action to take. *Keep a cool head, Whitaker*. But it's not advice he's able or willing to listen to.

*

The vicarage is an ugly 1950s affair, with pebble-dash walls and greying paintwork. He passes a boarded-up entrance, trying not to think of Sophie following this same route. He glances up at the windows for any signs of life, but the glass only reflects the trees lining the road behind him.

A little further on, the path narrows, with just room on one side for an ancient Renault.

He can't see a doorbell, so he bangs with his fist on the panel. There's no response. He bangs again. After a few moments, he tries the handle and the door swings open. He steps inside, calling, 'Are you there, Webster?'

He's in a kitchen, with a wooden table and chairs, a dresser filled with an assortment of odds and ends, and a fridge that's making a loud humming noise.

He looks around for signs of Sophie. On the table are two half-drunk mugs of tea and a carton of milk, with a copy of the local paper spread out beside them. Not exactly a romantic scene.

In his imaginings, Miles pictured himself storming through the house, yelling Sophie's name. Instead, he sits at the table, staring round the room. Facing him is the dresser, crammed with a motley assortment of items: a statue of the Virgin and Child, thick-lipped and carved from dark wood, in that African style he's never cared for. Beside it, a small Picasso print, from his blue period, is propped against a pile of paperbacks. The stub of a candle protrudes from an empty wine bottle, and there's an untidy stack of papers on the shelf below. It all seems to fit with that unsettling quirkiness he associates with Webster. Yet he has to admit that even this room has a warm feel to it, in stark contrast to the squalid emptiness of the Stephen's Close house.

The door that leads to the rest of the house is half open, and he can see a passage, the floor carpeted in a pattern of bright orange and brown circles.

What on earth is he doing sitting here waiting for God knows what? Yet he can't bring himself to leave until he knows for certain what's going on.

Then he hears the sound of a door opening, and footsteps coming towards him along the passage. He stands.

'There you are, Webster!' he says, as the man enters the room, dressed in his usual cassock and boots. He's on his own, but no doubt any moment Sophie will be following him in.

'Oh. It's Miles, isn't it? I never heard you come in.'

He doesn't seem particularly surprised to see him, and neither is he exhibiting any signs of guilt. 'Coffee?' He moves over to the sink. 'Can't give you long, I'm afraid. Parish meeting in twenty minutes.'

Miles clenches his fists. 'Now look here—'

But Webster is pointing to the dirty mugs on the table. 'Mind giving those a rinse? I just need to make a quick call.'

In a trance, he obeys, listening as behind him Webster talks into his mobile.

When he's finished, he makes their drinks, placing the mugs back on the table. They sit. 'So – what can I do for you?'

His words, like his earlier bravado, have evaporated. 'Sophie,' he begins, feeling increasingly foolish. 'Where is she?'

Webster raises an eyebrow. 'She's not here, Miles. I've not seen her for several weeks. Other than at Sunday service, of course.'

He glances at the clergyman, who's as lean and flat-bellied as a greyhound.

Sophie has lost weight. Remembering the outfit she was wearing this morning, it comes to him that, over these past weeks, she has metamorphosed into a younger, more alluring version of herself.

'She said she was going to call in on you later.'

'Did she?'

No need for him to sound so surprised.

The brown eyes study him. 'So, why don't you tell me what's eating you?'

Miles picks up his mug and puts it down again. Webster is looking across at him, his face sympathetic. 'The long and the short of it is, we've not been getting along too well.' A part of him wants to tell Webster about the court case, blurt it all out, but as always, he can't think of the right words. And anyway, his main worry now is Sophie.

'Since she's had this new job, I've been seeing very little of her.' He's alarmed to realise how close he is to tears. 'And when I do, it's as if she doesn't want to know. She goes off in the morning all dressed up, and comes home later and later. She...'

He breaks off.

'I'm very sorry, Miles. Have you tried her at the shop?'

'I called in just now, and they told me she'd already left for the day.' He reaches for his handkerchief and blows his nose. 'She often says she's late home because she's been working with you.' He swallows. 'So I thought that you and she were – you know...'

To his surprise, Webster laughs. 'You've got the wrong end of the stick, I'm afraid.'

Miles fails to see what's so amusing. 'You give me your solemn word then, that there's nothing between you?'

Webster leans across the table. 'My solemn word.'

He doesn't want to believe him, but dammit all, the man is pretty convincing. For a moment, he visualises him at Fordingbury, and realises to his chagrin that the boys would probably warm to him. With a pang of envy, he thinks also that he wouldn't have stood any nonsense from the Remove Year.

'I've obviously made a complete fool of myself.'

'No worries. Can happen to the best of us.'

He gulps his coffee. 'To be honest, it's been a bloody awful day.' He pauses. How could he have forgotten the assault? 'Ali's been attacked, and—'

'Attacked?' Webster looks alarmed. 'When was this?'

'Earlier today. We were walking along the street, minding our own business, when these three men set on him.' He pauses. 'I did my best to fend them off, but they were too strong for us.'

'What a dreadful thing. But well done for doing your bit.' Now the eyes are filled with admiration. 'So, are you all right?'

He hesitates again. 'Fine, thanks, apart from a couple of bruises.'

'You called the police, I take it?'

'Ali was adamant he didn't want that.'

Webster sighs. 'Maybe just as well, given his circumstances.'

'Circumstances?'

'He's had a couple of run-ins with them. To do with their son. He and Farah are such a lovely couple. It's terrible to see how they've been ostracised – and by their own community.' He sighs again. 'Not a lot to be done about it, I'm afraid.'

'He's been knocked about quite badly,' Miles says, 'but he also refused medical help, which is why I went in search of Sophie. I thought she could advise about the risk of concussion.'

'Good idea, but—' There's a tap on the outer door, and Webster pushes back his chair. 'Leave this with me, will you, Miles? I'll give Farah a ring to check on things, and get them to contact their surgery.'

He feels as if a weight has been taken off him. This man will know what to do, whereas he himself feels drained, exhausted by the day's events.

There are voices behind him, and three people come crowding into the kitchen – two grey-haired women and a large black man.

'This is Miles,' Webster said. 'Miles, meet Frances, Carmela and Chuma.'

'Ah, Sophie's husband,' the black man says.

The words rankle. Everyone seems to know more about her than he does.

As he goes to the door, his eye is drawn to Chuma, who's moved over to Webster and is whispering in his ear. The clergyman gives a brief nod before the two men break apart.

Were they talking about me? Miles wonders, as he heads towards the road. And, if so, what on earth were they saying?

THIRTY-SEVEN

I T'S A RELIEF TO FIND THE HOUSE EMPTY – NO MILES
slumped in front of the television, or hunched over
the kitchen table. Now, there'll be no need to face his
questions about her day when all she wants is to hold on
to the physical sense of Ian. She can still taste him in her
mouth, and the smell of him is on her body.

Finding him feels like a miracle, she thinks, picturing
the line of his back, the arch of his brows and that confident
way he has of carrying himself – as if he owns the world.
Once, she also felt that way. Might it be possible to do so
again?

She walks through to the kitchen, staring out of the
grimy window and willing herself to be sensible. With
the court case so close, this is hardly the time for a
confrontation with Miles and, anyway, despite all that he
may or may not have done, she can't bring herself to treat

him in so brutal a way. Any parting that comes will need to be carefully planned.

For now, Miles will be back any moment. But how hot and sticky she feels. She decides on a bath and as she's towelling herself dry some twenty minutes later, she hears him calling her name.

She waits a moment, before replying: 'Up here, Miles.'

He doesn't answer and listening to the stairs creak under his weight, she feels her first moment of apprehension. When he appears in the doorway, she sees his cheeks are flushed, and he's panting, as if he's been running.

She holds the towel in front of her.

'Where the hell did you get to?' he demands. 'I've been looking for you everywhere.'

She steps back, startled by his unusual display of anger. He's so close that she can smell his breath, although she can't detect any alcohol on it.

'I actually went round to the shop, expecting to find you there.'

She stares at him. 'You went to the shop? Why on earth didn't you let me know you were coming?'

'Because it was an emergency, Sophie. Ali, my Arab friend, was attacked earlier. Quite badly, as it happens. I went to see you because I thought you might be able to help.'

'I'm sorry I wasn't there.' She fights off a feeling of panic. 'You spoke with Becca?'

'She just said you'd left early, but seemed to have no idea where you'd got to.' He pauses.

She imagines him combing the streets, maybe spotting her and Ian in the cafe, even following them back to the studio. She tries to control her panic. 'And after that?'

'I called in on Webster. Made a complete fool of myself, but that's another story.'

She turns away to disguise her relief, pulling on her clothes, her fingers fumbling with the buttons of her skirt.

'So where were you?' But already his voice has lost its aggressive ring.

'At the supermarket, and then back here.' She hangs the towel over the rail. 'And your friend, Ali. How's he doing?'

'I think he'll be OK. Webster is going to check on him.'

He lowers himself onto the edge of the bath. 'I've obviously got things completely wrong, Sophie. And not for the first time.' His shoulders sag. 'I can only say how very sorry I am. You'll think me crazy, but I really believed there was something between you and Webster.'

'Seb?' She laughs. 'Oh Miles. You do realise he's gay?'

'Gay?'

'That's right. His partner is the black man, Chuma.'

'But I thought he was married to that therapist woman.'

She suppresses a sigh. 'Ruth Madiebo's a widow, Miles. Chuma is her brother.'

'Oh.' She can see him absorbing the information.

'Look, could we start again, Sophie? I seem to have got the wrong end of the stick about so many things. I need to talk – really talk. And also to ask you something. If it's not too—'

He looks up as the phone sounds in the hall. 'I'll go.'

She leans over the banisters, trying not to think of that obnoxious reporter, and straining to catch as much of the conversation as she can.

'Yes,' she can hear Miles saying. 'It's really definite? But that's wonderful! Thanks – yes. I'll wait to hear from you, then.'

She follows him into the kitchen. He pours them both wine, and they sit opposite one another at the table.

He looks across at her and gives the ghost of a smile. 'That was Marshall. There's been a delay in the trial – due to some technicality. He says it's not unusual, but it won't be taking place until September.' He gulps his wine. 'It feels like a reprieve.'

And for me also, she thinks, because now I'll have more time to plan for the future.

'What we were talking about earlier,' he says. 'I can see what an idiot I've been. To go accusing you of…' He breaks off, and she can see the tears in his eyes.

She pushes away her feelings of guilt, recalling the summons hidden in the glove compartment and the countless other deceptions. 'Well, you have lied to me pretty consistently.'

'I didn't want to, Sophie. It's just that I've found this whole court business so utterly appalling. I honestly haven't known how to cope.' He leans towards her. 'I don't know if you can understand the humiliation – the shame of realising that the whole world may find out, and judge me for something I haven't done?'

He sounds so sincere – a part of her longs to believe him.

'I realise now that not telling you the full story was unforgivable.'

She forces herself to nod. 'So, now we know the trial is still to go ahead.'

He reaches for the bottle. 'I realise this is all very sudden, and that you may need time to take it in. But I wondered if, you know, if...'

She runs a hand through her hair. 'You're asking if I'll attend court with you?'

He looks at her, his mouth trembling. 'Would you?'

Is he only telling her this because he needs her by his side, in a public display of solidarity?

'I take it the case is to be heard in Oxford?'

'Yes. Marshall says to allow a week, although he thinks it will be over sooner than that.'

She thinks of Alan Sanderson and the Fordingbury staff, of all the parents they know, of Rach and Brian. How many of them will be there? And even if they aren't actually present, everything that takes place will be out on public display, as will Miles and she herself. She's struck afresh by the enormity of it all. It's not that she minds so much for herself, but what about Helena and Miranda? My darling girls, she thinks, who must be protected from this, at all costs.

'The barrister, Melbury Jones, seems pretty confident the witnesses will crack under interrogation.'

'Cunningham and his classmates, you mean?' She recalls the boy's sly glances when he thought no one was looking. He was perfectly capable of lying, of course, but then wasn't everyone? Just because he wasn't all that likeable, didn't prove a thing. But only by being in that courtroom has she any hope of getting at the truth. 'Of course I'll go with you, Miles.'

He lets out a sigh of relief. 'I can't tell you how much it means that you're prepared to stand by me.' There are tears in his eyes again. 'You see, when I went looking for you at Webster's place, I really thought I'd lost you. And I couldn't have borne that.' He squeezes her hand, and she has to stop herself flinching. 'You are my whole world, Sophie. You do know that?' A tear rolls down his cheek. 'When things are back to normal, I'll make it up to you. I promise.'

'Once we're back at Fordingbury, you mean?'

'Hopefully at the start of the Lent term.'

But surely he must see the sheer impossibility of that? What school will want to employ him, especially at his time of life, whatever the verdict turns out to be?

She hates herself for the coldness she feels towards him. Yet anything she says to ease his distress will surely only give him false encouragement?

She gets up and moves over to the sink. The dirty dishes from breakfast are still piled on the draining-board.

'I'll tackle those in a moment,' he says, getting up and coming to stand behind her.

'The thing is, Sophie, when I last saw Marshall, he stressed how much it would help if the girls could also be there.'

She dodges past him. 'I really think that would be a big mistake.'

His face falls.

'It will be such a public thing, Miles. I imagine that the

case, and perhaps our photographs, will be plastered all over the press. It will be hard enough for us.'

He lifts the bottle from the table and refills his glass.

'You really don't mind the girls hearing the details?' Whatever they are, she thinks.

'It won't be very pleasant but, as I've said before, I've done nothing wrong.' He pauses. 'Perhaps we could give them the choice?'

She still doesn't want them anywhere near that courtroom. Yet if their father is to be convicted, perhaps it's better for them to be prepared. 'They're both going travelling during the long vacation. Let's allow them to enjoy their summer.'

He looks relieved. 'You're right. No need to worry them at this stage.'

'Maybe if we leave it for a couple of months? It'll still give them plenty of notice.'

'Fine. And when the time comes, let's meet them somewhere in town. Well, we don't really want them here again, do we?' He glances around the dingy kitchen, and she senses afresh how ashamed he is to be in this house. And she also would rather they stayed away. She'll link up with them in town in between times.

She pushes back her chair. 'I'm feeling rather tired, Miles. If you don't mind, I think I'll turn in.'

'No, you go ahead. No doubt you've to be up bright and early again.'

He peers across at her, and she's momentarily taken aback by the haggard look on his face, that adds years to him. It reminds her of the dreadful morning when she found him crouched, white-faced, in his study at South Lodge, looking for all the world as if he were having a heart attack. Back then – and what an eternity ago it seems – she had no doubts about him. For a moment, she's filled with longing for their old, uncomplicated life.

'You seem pretty done in too,' she says now.

He gives a wan smile. 'It's been a difficult day, one way and another, but I can't tell you how relieved I am that we've talked.'

'I'm glad too, Miles – for your sake.'

'Sleep really well.' He reaches out a hand. 'I don't suppose…?'

'Sorry,' she says, moving away before he comes any closer.

Once upstairs, she texts both girls asking them to phone, and then sits on the edge of the mattress in her nightgown, trying to keep her thoughts away from Ian – the feel of his skin against hers, the intelligence behind the grey eyes.

I married on the rebound, she thinks, with painful clarity. Which is what Aunt Harriet warned me of at the time.

Suddenly she longs to hear the abrasive tones of the older woman.

She dials the number, picturing the old lady getting up from her chair in the garden room that overlooks the sea, and moving along the corridor to the phone that she still keeps in the farthest recesses of the hall. 'Can't be doing with all these new-fangled gadgets – laptops and satellite navs, or whatever you call them,' she often says, making the twins smile and roll their eyes.

'Hello,' the voice at the other end of the line says now. 'Is that you, Sophie?'

'It is indeed, Aunt Harriet. Just ringing to check how you are.'

'Still above ground.' She sniffs. 'Thought you might have upped and done a runner though.'

She laughs. 'No such luck.'

'The girls all right?'

'They're fine, thanks. They send their love.'

'And that husband of yours?'

She pauses. 'That's why I'm phoning – to keep you in touch with things, as I promised. The fact is, Aunt Harriet...' despite herself, her voice quavers, 'we've now got the date for the trial – September.'

'Ah.'

'I told you last time that the charge is an assault on one of the boys.'

'A sexual assault, you said?'

Her aunt is still as sharp as ever. 'That's right. There's bound to be something in the press, so I just wanted to warn you – so that it's not too big a shock.'

'When you reach my time of life, my girl, you're pretty well immune to shocks. But you, Sophie? How are you coping?'

I'm not, she thinks, but I must try and manage this on my own. 'It's obviously tough.' Despite herself, she can't stop her voice from trembling. 'But my main worry is Helena and Miranda. Miles still wants them at the trial, but my instinct is to keep them away.'

An aircraft buzzes overhead and then her aunt says, 'I

agree with you, although that'll leave you coping on your own.'

'I'll manage.'

'And your architect friend?'

'Still there. I'll keep you posted.' Without Ian, I'd be in pieces, she thinks.

After the call, she sits staring out of the window at the rooftops, their outlines blurred in the fading light.

THIRTY-EIGHT

THE JUGGLER IS STOCKY AND BOW-LEGGED, dressed in a check shirt and cut-off jeans, a mass of unruly hair tied back in an orange bandanna. The July crowds push and shove against one another, their chatter filling Miles's ears. In the distance, incongruously, a soprano is singing a Mozart aria. He watches as the man, teeth bared in a grin that seems both aggressive and shifty, sends batons arcing through the air in flashes of reds, greens and yellows. Miles imagines him in one of those Westerns his father took him to. 'Looking for trouble, gringo?' the man would be saying.

He averts his gaze, filled with sudden nostalgia.

He must have been seven when his father first brought him here. There had been a big fire the previous year, and he recalls vast, windowless buildings, their frames streaked with black. He was glad to have his father's hand to hold. 'Worse than a bloody bomb site,' his father muttered.

'Miles?' Sophie pulls at his sleeve. 'We mustn't be late.'

He detaches himself from the crowd, trying to focus on the coming meeting with the girls. As long as he has Sophie's support, it's bound to go fine but all the same, he'd give anything to be away from here.

He and his father took this same route all those years ago, he remembers. The ground then was littered with discarded fruit and vegetables while, around them, men in peaked caps pushed barrows, and shouted words to one another – 'Get the fuck out of my way!' and 'Pull the other one, you shit-faced git!' – words he sensed his mother would not like. Yet although he held tightly to his father's hand, the old market felt an exciting and alluring place. Its forbidden nature, akin to those cinema matinees, was borne out on the journey home, when his father tapped the side of his nose and said, 'Your mother thinks places like this are best avoided. We'll tell her the muck on our shoes is from the train.' Miles nodded. He had already learned that some things were best kept secret. Although looking back now, he wondered if perhaps his father's visit to Covent Garden provided an escape from their overly neat suburban home.

'The restaurant's just round the next corner,' Sophie says over her shoulder.

As they seat themselves at their table, he realises what a relief it is that she's back to her old efficient self.

'Chardonnay?' he suggests.

'Thanks.'

Sophie has her head bent over her phone. 'Helena's just texted. They'll be here in a few minutes.'

He can feel his stomach tighten. 'We want the jury to see you as a family man,' Melbury Jones said at their last meeting, adding, 'as of course you are.'

He looks across at Sophie. 'You still believe the twins will be on side?'

'Let's hope so.'

You're their mother, he wants to say. You know how to handle them better than me. He gulps his wine.

'Go easy on the drink, Miles.'

She's right. He needs to keep his wits about him, but he's struck by her air of detachment. He stares across at her. She has on another outfit, a black dress with gold earrings, that he doesn't recognise.

Perhaps it's not so much that she's being cool – more that she seems removed from him, her attention fixed on a neighbouring table, where a young couple are gazing into one another's eyes.

It pains him to realise how much her attitude contrasts with Ali's unfailing sympathy. 'British justice will prevail, my friend,' he said, when they last met. 'Meanwhile, you must stay strong.' The fact that Ali was not yet back to his old self after the attack, touched Miles the more. Yet the assault still worried him.

'You decided against involving the police?' he asked, trying to keep his voice non-committal.

'I thought it best to leave things as they are.' Ali leaned forward. 'And I have you to thank for notifying Sebastian. A truly remarkable man, don't you think? Although he's always so busy, he found time to visit me.' He paused. 'Just as he did when Farah and I ran into that difficulty.'

'Difficulty?'

Ali sighed. 'With our younger son.'

'The one that's overseas?'

'Yes.' He stared at the floor. 'Most parents would be pleased to see their child becoming ever more devout.' He gave a sad smile. 'Sadiq and I often played backgammon together, until he announced that it was a form of gambling and therefore forbidden. I kept telling him that in the Middle East we have been playing it for generations, but there was simply no arguing with him.'

Miles looked across at Ali. What exactly did he mean? It didn't do to pry, but some response was obviously called for. 'It must have been very hard, both for you and for Farah,' he managed to get out.

To his embarrassment, Ali gripped his arm. 'I knew you'd understand.'

*

Why can't Sophie show at least as much warmth as his friend?

Miles reaches for her hand. 'I wonder if you have any idea what these past months have been like for me.' She opens her mouth to speak, but he presses on, afraid that if he stops now, the words will dry up. 'If you really want to know, they've been pure and absolute hell.'

'You're hurting me, Miles.'

He releases his grip. 'I'm sorry.' After a pause, he says,

'Look, Sophie, I know I made rather a fool of myself over that business with Webster, and I have to admit I'd rather you hadn't started work in that shop of yours.' He takes another mouthful of wine. 'But I do realise that leaving Fordingbury has been tough on you, too.'

She doesn't respond, and he ploughs on. 'It sometimes feels as if it's not just Sanderson and the others who have turned against me, but the whole world.' *You included,* he wants to say, as she continues to stare impassively at him. 'And it's doubly hard since you've begun leading such a separate life,' he murmurs.

She looks away, her earrings catching the light as she moves.

He's aware of a constricted feeling in his chest. 'I swear to you that I haven't done this thing. We've lived together over twenty years, Sophie. You know me, for heaven's sake!' He longs to touch her again. 'The thing is, I need to be able to feel you're completely behind me on this.' God, he mustn't start crying – not here, not now.

She continues to avoid his gaze. 'This really isn't the time or the place, Miles. I mean, it's hardly going to help matters if the girls see us out of control, is it?' She's still not looking at him. 'It's bad enough that we're having to break the news to them about the trial, but please tell me you've had some thoughts over how to put it to them?'

Again, there's that alarming note of detachment in her voice. All he needs is a couple of words of encouragement to show she trusts him. Surely it isn't asking too much? He leans across the table again. 'You do believe I'm innocent, don't you? You—'

'Mum! Dad!'

Miranda, in a summer dress and sandals, dark hair pinned up, is smiling down at them. Helena, as always the least presentable of the two, has on a pair of ragged shorts, and a grey top, with "Save the Arctic" printed across it.

'There you are, darlings,' Sophie says, jumping up.

'Lovely outfit, Mum! You look really great.'

'Thanks.'

Miles stands up to greet Helena, but she's already slumping into a chair. 'I'm wiped! I was up writing debating society minutes until gone two!'

'Hello, Dad.' Miranda gives him a hug, and he feels some of his tension slipping away.

'Mum giving you a hard time, then?'

'I'm sorry?'

'Dragging you up to town.' Miranda laughs. 'Do you remember when we used to come to the Christmas shows?'

'I remember all right,' Helena says. 'He couldn't wait to get home again.' She helps herself to some wine. 'But let's organise some food. I don't know about the rest of you, but I'm starving!'

The waiter takes their order, and he signals for another bottle. The girls, as always, are talking nineteen to the dozen. He hates the thought of disrupting the happy atmosphere, yet the longer he and Sophie leave it, the worse it will be.

He watches her lean towards the twins, one hand up as if she's saying something she doesn't want him to hear. And it is in that moment that the realisation finally comes. He's going to have to do this on his own.

'So, I'm definitely going to Spain in October,' Miranda is saying. 'Only for a term, but it should really help with the language.'

'All right for some,' Helena grumbles. 'I don't see myself getting further than Cambridge.' She turns to Sophie. 'Any chance of a bit more cash, Mum? There's a course on women's rights that I'd love to do.'

'Well, I—' Sophie begins.

He needs to come in now, before they're touched for money they simply don't have. 'I'm sorry to interrupt, but your mother and I – well, *I* – have something important to say.'

'I know.' Miranda's smile of delight turns his heart over. 'You've been given a date for our return to South Lodge.'

'With a pay rise?' Helena adds.

He feels the familiar knot in his stomach. 'The thing is, girls, there's been a change of plan.'

'Meaning?' Helena's gaze is appraising.

'This assault business that your mother and I mentioned...' He glances at Sophie, but she has her head bent over her plate. 'Well, cutting a long story short, there's to be a trial after all.'

The girls stare.

'But you told us—' Helena begins.

'I know what I said.' He hasn't meant to sound so sharp. 'And, at the time, I spoke in good faith. My solicitor assured me that the boy concerned would be dropping the charges.' He pauses, relieved that the words are continuing to come. 'The whole thing is a complete fabrication, of course. But now it seems the boy has changed his mind, no doubt as a result of pressure from his parents.'

Miranda pushes her half-eaten food to one side. 'I still don't understand, Dad. What are they still saying you've done?'

He feels his face grow hot. 'I'm being accused of molesting this Cunningham boy.'

He pauses again, forcing himself to meet the girls' horrified gaze.

Helena's voice rises. 'So, what you're saying is that it's still a *sexual* assault?'

He's been vaguely aware of the restaurant filling up around them, but now her words drop like a stone into the background conversation. The couple at the neighbouring table turn and stare.

'For God's sake,' he hisses, 'keep your voice down!'

The waiter comes over. 'Everything all right, sir?'

'Oh, fine, thanks. Although maybe a whisky? Anyone else?'

They shake their heads.

'Just for me then. Make it a large one, would you?'

'Certainly, sir.'

'But this is *terrible*, Dad,' Miranda says, and he sees with a pang that there are tears in her eyes. 'And for you as well, Mum.'

He glances at Sophie, who remains silent, biting her lip.

'To look on the bright side,' he continues, 'I've got one of the best legal teams in London, and they're pretty confident that this whole business will be thrown out of court. No question.'

'You said that the last time,' Helena reminds him.

He forces a smile. 'I know I did, and you must forgive me. It's all been rather a lot to take in. One hell of a shock, to be honest.'

'Poor Dad!' Miranda says, with a meaningful look at her sister. 'And of course we'll support you in whatever way we can.'

The relief is tremendous. 'Thank you, Miranda. I really appreciate that.'

Helena scoops up a last mouthful of food from her plate. 'You want us to attend the trial, don't you?'

'Actually,' Miles says, 'that's the last thing I want.'

Sophie glances sideways at him, and he senses her surprise.

'What I mean is,' he spreads his hands in a gesture of appeal, 'I have no right whatsoever to ask anything of you girls. To be perfectly honest, if it weren't for my barrister saying it would help matters to have you both in court, I wouldn't dream of saying anything. I feel bad enough about it, as it is.'

Miranda looks across at Sophie. 'You'll be there, Mum?'

'Yes, darling, I will.'

'So when is the trial to start?'

He takes a deep breath. 'Not for a couple of months – towards the end of September.' He leans towards them. 'And I do realise it's a lot to ask of you both. Especially as it may last the week.'

'Well,' Miranda says, 'just tell us the time and place, Dad, and we'll be there. Won't we, Helena?'

She gives a hesitant nod.

'Thanks. I can't tell you what this means to me.'

'Of course, there may be repercussions,' Sophie says, speaking for the first time.

Miranda frowns. 'What sort of repercussions?'

'Mum means the press,' Helena explains. 'They're bound to pick up on something like this. We may well find ourselves plastered all over the media.'

'So what do *you* think, Mum?' Miranda asks.

Sophie pushes a hand through her hair. 'I have to admit I'm concerned about the impact of all this on you and Helena. As you know, any online coverage will be out there forever.' She pauses. 'To be honest, I'd far rather you stayed away from the trial. But it's entirely your decision.' Again, she's not looking at him.

'But Dad *will* be cleared,' Miranda says. 'So what's the problem?' She turns to Helena. 'We'll definitely be there, right?'

To his relief, Helena says, 'And we can't have you sitting in court on your own, Mum.'

Miranda gives a hesitant smile. 'That's sorted, then.'

'I knew I could rely on you both.' Miles pauses again.

'But what about our return to South Lodge?' Miranda's face is puckered.

'One step at a time, darling.' Sophie says.

There seems nothing more to say.

Helena picks up her bag. 'I'd better get going. I need to be back before seven.'

'I'll walk up to the Tube with you,' Miranda says.

For a few awkward moments, they stand in silence by the table.

'You realise you've stopped doing your quotes, Dad,' Miranda says, as she gives him a farewell hug.

'Have I?'

'Thank goodness for small mercies!' Helena mutters, darting forward to peck his cheek.

The girls are swallowed up in the afternoon crowds, and he and Sophie follow slowly after.

They're almost at the Tube when, through a gap in the crowd, he spots a familiar figure. A boy, slim and narrow-shouldered, with that unmistakable shade of pale blonde hair reaching almost to his collar. Surely it can't be?

He feels his mouth go dry, and quickens his pace, hearing Sophie's surprised, 'Miles?' as he shoots ahead of her.

The gap has closed around the boy, but he pushes his way through, elbowing others out of his way in his haste. He catches up with him just outside the Tube entrance. 'Cunningham!' he shouts.

Several heads turn, including the boy's, but instead of those pale eyes and the lock of hair falling over the forehead, a girl's face is staring up at him – a pretty girl, with a startled look in her brown eyes.

With a muttered, 'Sorry!' he steps back.

THIRTY-NINE

'GOODNESS, IT'S HOT!' SOPHIE SINKS INTO THE chair in Dr Madiebo's attic room. Specks of dust dance in the afternoon light, and the building opposite shimmers in the heat.

She glances surreptitiously at her watch. In under an hour, she'll be on her way to see Ian. The thought fills her with elation, as it's done throughout these past months. Nearly the end of August, she thinks, realising that she doesn't want this time in London, and all those precious hours with him, to end.

She clears her throat. 'I don't want to waste your time by continuing to come here.'

Ruth Madiebo tilts her head to one side. 'Waste my time?'

'I know that in our last session I was really worried about the twins. As I think I told you, Miles's solicitor has advised it would look better if they were at the trial. Better for him, that is.' She pauses. She really doesn't want to think about any of this, not today. 'But they want to be there, so I've just got to accept their decision.'

'I see.'

She sighs. 'All I want is to be able to get on with my life.'

'And, if I get the picture right, a life that no longer includes Miles?'

'I realise what you must think of me.' She braces herself for the criticism that will surely come. Aloud, she says, 'I didn't plan any of it, you know.'

'You mean, your affair with Ian?'

She looks down at her nails, which she's painted a deep red. Scarlet woman, she thinks. 'I honestly never imagined I'd feel this way about anyone again. Of course, I've agonised over telling Miles, but I don't feel it would be fair, not while there's all this uncertainty hanging over him.' She pauses again. 'Obviously it's still early days, but it feels as if I've known Ian all my life.'

'He's certainly taking up a great deal of your thoughts.' Dr Madiebo leans towards her. 'But the accusation against Miles is what brought you here, and the trial is, when?'

'Less than three weeks away.'

'So perhaps this relationship also tells us just how impossible things have become for you?'

Sophie looks across at the sunflowers. They should have died off long ago. It was only when you examined them closely that you realised their perfection could not possibly be real. She sighs again. 'Just when he seems ready to talk, I'm the one who doesn't want to.'

'Oh?'

'Well, for a start, how can I ever trust anything he tells me? He's done nothing but shut me out.'

'So you're still convinced he's hiding something?'

How well did you know your husband? she wants to ask. 'I always believed Miles and I had no secrets from one another – apart from the one I didn't tell him at the beginning.' She gazes out of the window to where a crane swings a metal arm against the pale sky. 'Goodness knows I wanted to.'

'You were afraid of his reaction?'

'Partly that but, as I've told you, it all felt too raw.' She bites her lip. 'I was on the point of collapse after the termination.' She's surprised to feel the tears welling up. 'That's when Aunt Harriet whisked me off to New Zealand. By the time we got back, I just wanted to put all that time in London behind me.' She fishes for a hankie, and blows her nose. 'And Miles was there waiting. Well, he always made it clear he was keen on me.'

And what a shy and awkward thirty-seven-year-old he was, she thinks, yet what a welcome relief after Alastair's unwavering self-confidence.

'You've said you never told Miles the real reason for going to New Zealand?'

'He assumed it was a holiday trip. He never pressed me about my past, you see, which I was only too happy to go along with.' She looks across at Ruth Madiebo. 'Maybe I was afraid that if he found out, he would ditch me, and I couldn't stand the thought of another rejection.' She pauses. 'Was that so terrible of me?'

'It's certainly understandable.' Dr Madiebo leans forward again. 'But it would seem, then, that Miles is not the only one to wear a mask?'

'I can see that it wasn't fair not to be honest with him, and I did agonise over it at the time. But then we just got on with our lives.' She pauses again. 'Until this crisis, when I glimpsed a different side to him.'

'Different?'

'It's as if I've been living all these years with some cardboard cut-out.' She glances again at her watch. They're already well into this session, and suddenly there's so much to say.

'I see now that he's probably put a lot of people's backs up – other members of staff, for instance. And Aunt Harriet took against him from the start. Miles and Murdo were always close, of course.' She paused. 'The school matron, Rachel, hinted at something unhealthy underlying their friendship, but surely one can't read too much into that?'

'Although it leaves you even more uncertain?'

'It's been a shock to discover this secretive side to him – the hidden whisky bottles, and that court letter in the Rover's glove compartment.' She studies her nails again. 'There would have been plenty of opportunities for cover-ups at Fordingbury.'

She pushes a strand of hair from her forehead. 'I know you're suggesting I began this affair with Ian out of a sense of desperation. But there's more to it than that.'

'Yes?'

'This isn't a very easy thing to say, but Miles and I haven't made love since coming to London – seven months ago now. I miss that side of things and, if I'm being honest, I was desperate for Ian to reassure me I was all right.' She feels herself flush. 'I mean, if Miles has been involved with a boy in the way it's being alleged…'

'If he has sexually abused him?'

The words still shock. 'What I'm trying to say is, if that were the case, then what would that make me?'

'What *would* it make you, Sophie?'

She watches a fly buzz around Ruth Madiebo's head, and settle on the windowpane. 'Culpable.'

FORTY

'EVERYTHING ALL RIGHT?'

Sophie comes to with a start. Becca is peering at her. Behind them, comes the background hum of customers, and at the counter Steve is serving a Chinese woman in a plastic raincoat.

'Sorry – I was miles away.'

'Planning your week off? You look as if you could do with the break.'

Nothing much gets past Becca. 'I think I'll have another go at that stockroom.'

Becca seems as if she's about to ask something, but all she says is, 'Good idea. Keep a lookout for summer clothes, would you? We need to shift them before the cooler weather sets in.'

September, bringing with it a new school year – and the trial. What will be the outcome, she wonders – for

Miles, for the girls, and for me? She pushes the thought away.

In the stockroom, boxes and plastic sacks are stacked alongside each other. She opens the nearest bag and begins sorting through the contents.

That day, when she knelt here hunting for Willow Pattern china, aware of Ian's presence behind her: Was it really possible to have an overwhelming sense of connection with someone from the beginning? She certainly had with Alastair, but look where that had got her.

And suppose Ruth Madiebo were right, and this is just a passing fling, embarked on as some kind of escape? Just as she rushed into her marriage as a way of dealing with loss? Yet she can feel her longing for Ian, like some hidden undertow, pulling her ever closer towards him. Twice, sometimes three times a week if she can manage it, she leaves the shop early to spend precious hours with him. Still, they never seem enough.

'Excuse me, Sophie.' Steve is in the doorway, shifting from one foot to another.

'Hello,' she smiles, and watches his mouth twist sideways in response.

'Is it time for coffee, Sophie?'

She looks at her watch. 'Still half an hour to go.'

His face falls.

'Do you remember I showed you the difference between quarter to the hour and quarter past?' She points to her wrist. 'Have a look. The little hand needs to be on the eleven, and the big hand on the three.'

He gives a satisfied nod, before wandering out again, and she returns with a sigh to her work. Although she tries to keep her mind on it, it's a relief when Becca sends her to collect change from the bank.

The day is a typically London one – everything a dull grey, and the sky holding a hint of rain. She passes hairdressers, a pizza parlour, and a shop plastered in orange stickers advertising Chinese medicine. *Look up!* she can hear Ian saying, and there, above the shop fronts, is a row of Georgian windows, set into mellow brick.

In a few hours from now she'll be on her way to see him, and at the thought, she's seized with a longing that makes her catch her breath. She only has to feel the touch of his hand, or see the tenderness in his eyes to be convinced of his feelings for her; but away from him is another matter. Afraid of discovery by Miles, she's asked Ian only to text or phone her in an emergency – a decision that she's now regretting. If anything were to go wrong – well, it didn't bear thinking about.

But for now she must force herself to concentrate on the trial. She turns into a doorway, and dials Miranda's number.

'Mum! Great to hear from you! How are you doing?'

'Fine, darling. This is just a quick call to say I'll be texting you and Helena the details of where to meet in Oxford. It's in some solicitor's office.'

'Oh, Mum – I was so hoping the trial mightn't go ahead.'

'Me too, darling, but that's the way it is. I'm really sorry.'

'No – it's far worse for you. Having to cope with being away from Fordingbury on top of everything else. How's Dad?'

'Oh, you know him – managing as he always does.'

'Give him my love.'

'Will do. Look, I'm afraid I need to get back to the shop.'

'Talk again soon, Mum. Love you!'

'Love you too, darling.'

If my girls suffer over this, she decides, as she clicks off her phone, I'll never forgive Miles. He would have been perfectly happy, of course, for it to be just the two of us and, somehow, the fact that the decision to have children was hers alone, makes her protection of the twins now all the more important.

*

She thinks back to that time when she still secretly hoped Miles might take to fatherhood, but it was a hope that was quickly dashed. He remained as good as his word, doing no actual hands-on care. She sometimes confided to Rachel what a battle it was to keep her resentment in check. All those sleepless nights, the non-stop feeds and nappy changes, she thinks, as she makes her way back to the shop. Yet Miles gave her fair warning, and there again, she knew she was lucky: Mrs Carter had been on hand to help during the twins' pre-school years, and there was always a master's wife available to babysit, although Sophie made sure she was there most evenings for the routine of bath and bed.

Only now she allows herself to imagine what it would have been like to have married someone more involved with his children. Someone like Ian, who has spoken of picking up his daughter from nursery school, of taking his son to football matches, of going camping with them in the summer holidays. Someone who seems to love both his children equally.

She looks at her watch. It's not yet one, so she still has several hours to get through.

If the thought of the twins attending the trial has left her unsettled, she's equally anxious about what to tell Ian. Although up to now she's put it off, she recognises that she can do so no longer. Yet whatever she says: 'My husband's been accused of molesting one of his pupils'; 'Miles has been charged with sexually assaulting a minor', it still sounds terrible. But she mustn't pretend, not with Ian. If he were to drop her, as Alastair did, better she find out now than later. For with the painful clarity of hindsight she thinks: my pregnancy was just the catalyst. He must already have been tiring of me so he would have ditched me eventually.

Just thinking of all this is unsettling and she arrives at the studio an hour early. Whatever happens, I must stay calm, she tells herself, but as she presses the bell, she can feel the pulse beating in her throat.

After what seems an interminable wait, the door opens, and Ian stands there, his hair rumpled, bare feet thrust into sandals. Just the sight of him makes her heart lift. 'Oh, good – you're in!'

He looks thrown. 'Sophie! And you're early.' She leans forward, and they kiss.

'All right to come in?'

'It's not a brilliant time, to be honest. I'm in the middle of something.'

'Ian,' a woman's voice calls from the floor above, 'who is it?'

Her face crumples, despite herself. 'Oh, look, I'll go and grab a coffee, or something.'

'No, it's OK.' He stands to one side. 'You'd better come on up.'

The realisation that all her hopes and dreams may be in pieces seems all too horribly familiar. She goes ahead of him into the studio.

A woman is sitting by the window.

'Let me introduce you,' Ian is saying. 'Annabel, this is Sophie. Sophie, meet my big sis.'

'Hello,' Sophie says, weak with relief.

Annabel holds out a thin hand. She has the same slight build and grey eyes as her brother, but her face is lined, and her hair almost white. She must be the one who collects Willow Pattern china.

She knows she should make conversation: ask Annabel about herself, or maybe make some comment on the trouble Ian took in finding the dish. But how tired she is! All she wants is to sink into a chair.

'It's all a bit of a mess, I'm afraid.' Ian waves his hand, and for the first time she takes in the spread of paperwork scattered across the desk. What on earth was she thinking of, barging in like this?

She turns to him. 'I'm really sorry to interrupt. I'll come back later.'

She reads concern in his eyes, and her agitation must be more apparent than she realises, because Annabel gets to her feet, glancing from one to the other. 'No, it's fine. I've plenty to be getting on with.' She gathers up the papers. 'Maybe finish this later in the week, Ian?'

He nods. 'I'll give you a bell.'

Annabel turns to Sophie. 'Ian's talked a lot about you.'

'He has?'

She smiles. 'All good, I promise. And it's been great meeting you.'

Sophie listens to the two of them going down the stairs. There's a muttered exchange, and then the sound of the front door closing.

'Now,' he says, as he comes back into the studio, 'tell me what on earth's up.'

Although she's glad he can read her so well, it also feels alarming. If he can see this in her, what else might he see? A woman who's prepared, quite callously, to abandon her husband, just when he needs her the most?

'How about a drink?' he asks.

'Something soft, if you've got it.'

He goes through to the kitchen, emerging a few moments later with two glasses. 'Elderflower all right?'

She takes the drink, aware of his eyes on her. They sit at the slate-topped table, and she runs her fingers through her hair. 'I've something really important to tell you, Ian.'

His eyes widen. 'To do with us?'

'No – with Miles.'

He lets out a sigh of relief. 'Phew! For a moment there, I thought you were giving me the push.'

She strokes his cheek. 'Never that.'

He pulls her closer. 'What then?'

She sips her drink. 'Miles is facing a charge – a criminal charge.'

He raises an eyebrow. 'Let me guess – he's turned bank robber?'

She smiles, despite herself.

'You *can* trust me, Sophie. I want you to know that, whatever happens, I'm on your side.' He rubs his hand along her back. 'Did I ever tell you that one of my great-uncles from Queensland was a famous counterfeiter? So whatever crime Miles may have committed, it can't be as bad as you think.'

But even murder would feel better than this. And how on earth will Ian view her now? As the woman who's chosen a child abuser as a partner? As someone who should have spotted what was going on? 'What he's being accused of...' she feels her voice waver, 'is molesting one of the boys.'

'Sexual stuff, you mean?'

'Yes.'

'At the school?'

She nods.

He lets out his breath. 'Oh, god – that *is* serious. How old is the boy?'

'He was fourteen at the time.' Her cheeks feel on fire. 'It's all come as a huge shock.'

'Small bloody wonder!' He stands, and begins pacing the room. 'But Miles is pleading Not Guilty – right?'

She nods again.

'Do you know what will happen if he's convicted?'

'I'm not sure – I don't think he'll go to prison. A probation order, I suppose.'

He stops beside her. 'It sounds pretty bloody awful, Sophie. But I guess the only question that matters here is: do *you* believe he did it?'

Her eyes fill with tears. 'That's just it. I'm not sure. Until fairly recently, he simply refused to tell me anything.'

She begins to cry.

'Hey!' He sits beside her, drawing her close. 'It's all right. Take it easy.'

She sobs into his shoulder, and after a few minutes, feels herself calm.

As she rests against him, she's aware for the first time of the rumble of evening traffic in the road. 'Before all this happened, I never had any reason to doubt him. I mean, why would I? But as time has gone on, and he's changed his story, I've become more and more suspicious.'

Ian strokes her hair. 'Sometimes a bloke can be secretive because he feels under pressure. It doesn't necessarily make him guilty.'

And oh the relief if he weren't.

She thinks for a moment. 'Miles and the new head, Alan Sanderson, clashed over so many things: the syllabus, the funding for the retired headmaster's portrait, keeping up the tradition of staff drinks on a Sunday.' She sighs. 'So when Miles was summoned to a meeting with Alan, I never dreamed it was anything really serious.'

'So what happened?'

'He says he wasn't given any chance to put his side of the story. We were simply given the weekend to pack our belongings and clear out.'

'Sounds like pretty shabby treatment.'

She nods. 'The worst of it was that none of the other staff came near us. It felt like being in quarantine for some terrible disease.'

'You didn't try to argue your case with the headmaster?'

'Miles kept saying that there'd been some dreadful mistake, but that he'd explain everything later. It all happened in such a rush, and there was so much to organise.'

'But he wasn't arrested at this stage?'

'That came later.' She gives a short laugh. 'The proverbial knock on the door a fortnight after we moved into this area.'

Ian looks thoughtful. 'So what did the police have to say? And I take it he has a solicitor? What has he told you?'

She thinks of Miles's insistence on going into the police interview on his own, and of how he's excluded her from the meetings with Rupert Marshall. 'I keep asking myself if I could have handled things differently, but Miles shuts me out all the time.'

He nods. 'It's a pretty tough thing to be dealing with, Sophie.'

She strokes his arm. 'The trouble is, he's lied so much already – hidden so much from me – that I'm not sure I'll ever trust what he says.'

'That's tricky. And he still doesn't know about us?'

'I thought about telling him, but the timing seems too brutal. I've decided to wait until the trial is over.'

'That makes sense. But I'm truly sorry, Sophie – what a thing to have on your plate.'

'You don't think any the worse of me for it?'

'Don't be a bloody idiot!'

She hesitates. 'And you're still sure about us? Because if you're not, I need to know now.'

He's suddenly stern, a vertical crease forming between his eyes. 'I've never felt this way about anyone, Sophie. Can't you believe that?' He draws her closer. 'I promise I'm not fooling. Well, what's the point at our stage in life?'

She bites her lip. 'I feel the same way about you – I have done from the moment you walked into the cafe.'

'There you are, then.'

But this kind of thing doesn't happen in real life, she thinks. Yet it had been this way with Alastair.

'And,' Ian begins unbuttoning her blouse, 'if whatever I say can't convince you, maybe this will.' He pulls back the screen and draws her onto the bed.

A while later, she lies in his arms, listening to the steady thud of his heart.

He glances at his watch. 'I'm really sorry to be doing this, when obviously it's such a tough time for you. But I've an important deadline to meet – a client with a big contract that I can't afford to lose.'

'No, it's all right. I'll get going.' She swings herself off the bed.

'You can still make Friday?'

She forces a smile. 'Of course.'

An evening sun has appeared, filling the room with splashes of gold. What wouldn't she give not to be returning to Miles and that dark, claustrophobic house?

She and Ian kiss goodbye, but already she can tell his mind is elsewhere. As she goes down the stairs to the street, she can hear him talking into his mobile.

FORTY-ONE

SOMEWHERE IN MILES'S MIND HE'S BEEN CLINGING to the belief that the case against him will be called off at the last minute. So as he wakes on the morning of the trial, he's swamped by a tidal wave of terror.

His earlier visit to the Crown Court to enter his plea was several weeks ago now and remains a curious blur, due perhaps to the double whisky he downed before leaving the house. Although the drink helped him get through it. Now, the thought of being back in the dock, and this time before a judge and jury, makes him long for the merciful oblivion of alcohol.

He stares up at the ceiling where a large spider dangles at the end of its thread, blown helplessly backwards and forwards by the draft from the window.

The room is filled with the orange glow from the street light. God knows, he's complained about it often enough

– just as he's made no secret of viewing this house as little better than a slum. Now, as he forces himself out of bed, he realises there might be worse places in which to end up. A prison cell, for instance.

In the bathroom he stares into the mottled mirror. He needs to wash and shave, but feels incapable of movement. Why hasn't he taken more time to think through what he's going to say, going over in his mind all the advice and instruction that Marshall and Melbury Jones have given him? He picks up his shaving brush. All very well for the man to say the worst-case scenario is unlikely to be prison. How can he know that for sure? For that matter, how certain was anything in this post-Fordingbury nightmare?

He can hear Sophie's tread on the stairs and turns with relief.

'I've ironed your shirt.' She places a mug of tea on the edge of the bath. 'It's in the wardrobe with your suit.'

'Thanks.'

'And I'm doing scrambled eggs. We'll need something to keep us going.'

If only she'd give just one smile, or put her arms around him and tell him that somehow, together, they'll get through this day. Yet it must be an ordeal for her also. They should have discussed it.

'I'm really sorry to have brought this on you, Sophie, but I promise that once it's behind us, I'll—'

'Not now, Miles.' Her brusque tone makes him cringe. 'Keep an eye on the time. We need to be out of here by seven.'

He listens to her going back down the stairs. After all, the fact that she's making breakfast, and organising his clothes, just as she used to do at Fordingbury, are surely signs that she's on her way to forgiving him? And what a comfort it is that the twins will be supporting him too.

As he dips the shaving brush into the soap, he has a sudden picture of Miranda as a very small girl, watching in fascination from the bathroom doorway as he ran the razor over his face, raising her chin in the air and puffing out her cheeks in imitation of his own. 'Don't cut yourself, Daddy!' she used to say, her dark eyes anxious. And he'd give a thumbs-up that made her smile, and go running off again.

He dresses with care in the one suit Sophie brought from South Lodge. The moment this court business is out of the way, he'll ask Sophie to take it to that shop of hers, although hopefully she won't be working there much longer.

They breakfast in a silence punctuated only by the gurgle of the pipes and thuds from the other side of the party wall.

'Leaving in five minutes,' Sophie reminds him. He nods, pushing his uneaten food to one side.

He's comforted by the fact they're taking the car to Oxford each day – the trains are too unreliable – and travelling in the Rover will be like bringing a part of home with him.

He puts his mug on the draining-board and goes to fetch his briefcase from the front room. In only a few hours' time, he'll be back here again, able to settle into one of the ropey armchairs, with a large glass of claret. Just a small drink now would help calm his nerves, but Sophie will go mad if she smells alcohol on him.

'Time to go, Miles!' she calls from the hall.

He squares his shoulders, following her outside and banging the front door shut behind him.

They're halfway across the crazy paving when Kirsty emerges from next door, barefoot, in jeans and T-shirt, carrying a bag of rubbish. From inside the house, comes the discordant voices of breakfast television. 'Hello!' she calls, walking forward and dumping the sack in the bin. 'You two look all dressed up. Off somewhere nice?'

'Visiting friends,' Sophie says, unlocking the Rover.

'In Oxford, I suppose? All right for some!'

'Mike and the boys OK?' Sophie asks.

'Fine, thanks. But I haven't seen you in weeks, Sophie. How are things?'

'Sorry about that. The shop's kept me really busy.'

'Don't forget your promise to call round!'

'I won't!'

As they drive off, he sees the young woman staring after them. If his case were to be reported in the press – although Marshall seems to think it would be local coverage only – the truth would emerge soon enough. He needs to talk to Sophie about moving out of Stephen's Close as soon as possible – but now is not the moment.

He stares through the windscreen. How strange it feels to be travelling the reverse of the route they took back in January! Now, as they turn into the main road, passing the newsagents, and going under the dripping railway arch, it all seems, if not exactly home territory, then at least not as alien as it once did. And of course, he thinks, as they draw up at a set of lights, if they hadn't ended up here, he would never have met Ali.

'Keep me in touch with how things are going,' he said, as Miles was taking his leave the previous day. He pressed Miles's hand. 'Whatever the outcome, you can always count on my friendship.'

Miles was moved. To have one person backing him without reservation was more than he dared hope for. True, Marshall and Melbury Jones seem to be on side, but then they were paid to be.

He reaches for a CD. 'All right with you?' he asks. Sophie nods, and he slots the disc into the player, listening to the opening stutter of Beethoven's Fifth.

Ninety minutes later, they're in the outskirts of Oxford, driving down treelined streets towards the centre. Already he can see the outline of the Magdalen Tower.

Each year, through a connection of Murdo's, he and Sophie have been invited to tea at the college, and he's spent many happy off-duty hours in the town, visiting the Bodleian and browsing the bookshops. Now, he can't wait to be away from the place.

'This must be it,' Sophie says, pulling off the road, and driving into a car park behind a half-timbered building.

A slim, middle-aged woman in a grey suit lets them in, leading them along a passage into a low-ceilinged room. There is an immaculate cream-covered sofa and matching chairs, and a side table with a neat array of bottles and glasses. It all has an artificial feel, as if he's stepped into some stage set.

Even more disconcerting is the thought that, just a few miles away, Fordingbury will be gearing itself up for another day. He would have finished breakfast, and be walking through the grounds, past the lawn and the beech trees, to assembly in the main building and…

He brings himself up short. Of course! It's still the long leave. The place will be all but deserted. What on earth is he thinking of?

The woman is saying something.

'I'm sorry?'

'Are you all right, Mr Whitaker?'

'Fine, thanks.'

'Please, have a seat.' She motions him towards a circle of armchairs. 'Mr Melbury Jones and Mr Marshall are just going through some documentation. They'll be with you shortly.' She pauses. 'Can I get you anything? Tea, coffee?'

He and Sophie shake their heads.

They wait, the tick of a carriage clock on the side table filling the silence.

He looks across at Sophie. She has on the same black linen dress she wore when they met the twins at Covent Garden. She looks very elegant, and very remote. He watches her flip through the pages of a glossy magazine, as if there's nothing out of the ordinary in being here; as if, in just over an hour's time, he won't be standing in the dock. He feels his stomach tighten. 'Sophie? You do—?'

The door opens, and Melbury Jones appears, Rupert Marshall at his heels.

The solicitor extends his hand. 'Ah, you must be Sophie. Good to meet you at last.'

'And you,' Sophie says, with a look towards Miles as if to remind him that this delayed introduction hasn't been of her choosing.

'Bill Melbury Jones.' The barrister shakes hands with them both. 'How are you, Miles? Bearing up? That's the spirit!' He pulls up a chair. 'We thought it would be pleasanter for everyone if we went through the preliminaries here.'

'Fine.'

They can hear voices in the passage.

'This must be our daughters now,' Miles says, realising how afraid he's been that they mightn't show after all.

As they exchange greetings, he registers with relief that for once Helena, as well as Miranda, is in more formal clothing – black jacket and trousers. He's not sure how her ripped jeans and slogan T-shirts would have gone down in court.

The barrister turns to him. 'Although the trial is listed for the week, I hope to have it wrapped up earlier. But we'll have to see how it goes.' He tucks a gold pen into his top pocket. 'We must be prepared for the local press to be there, both at the start, and also when the verdict is announced.'

Miles feels his mouth go dry, only half listening as the barrister continues issuing information and instructions. At some point, he finds himself drinking a glass of water, although he has no recollection of it being handed to him.

Somehow, later, he's sitting with Sophie and the girls in the back of a large hire car that smells strongly of hair oil. The two lawyers are in front, talking together in low whispers.

Miranda touches his knee. 'Are you OK, Dad?'

He nods, too dazed to speak.

They pull up outside the large cream building and Melbury Jones springs out, beckoning Miles to follow. With Marshall close behind, they push past a handful of people – thank God not the vast horde of his imaginings. A man in a check jacket yells something that he doesn't catch, and a moment later, he's safely inside.

Once through the security barrier, Marshall leads him up some stairs into a side room, with wooden furniture and light filtering in through a long window. Sophie and the twins follow.

The barrister turns to them. 'It'll take some time for the jury to be sworn and then the prosecution will have the floor for the rest of the day and most of tomorrow. So you probably won't be called on to give evidence, Miles, until midweek.' He pauses. 'Hopefully, we'll have put some dents into their case by then. Any questions?'

He shakes his head, wishing the man would sound more certain.

'I'll leave Rupert to show you into the courtroom.' He turns in the door. 'We can convene back here in the lunch break.'

'Let's go on in then, Miles,' Marshall says, when the barrister has left. 'Perhaps you and the twins would give us a couple of minutes, Sophie, and then follow? The court room is at the far end on the left.'

Miles glances across at her. She has her phone to her ear and doesn't look up. Helena remains impassive, but Miranda mouths: 'Good luck, Dad!' and he finds himself blinking back tears.

He follows Marshall along the concourse. Will Alan Sanderson attend? Most certainly the Cunningham parents will be here. He recalls her as being a rather dumpy, innocuous woman although Cunningham senior is a different matter. He has his own business, something to do with IT, and doesn't suffer fools gladly. Miles pictures the angular face, with thick eyebrows that arch in the middle, giving the man the look of a bird of prey. Cunningham junior bears little physical resemblance to his father. Only the eyes, blue with that droop to the lids, are his.

He feels sick.

Marshall pauses outside the courtroom door. 'All right?'

Miles nods.

'Remember to let the usher know if you recognise any potential jury members. And if you're feeling at all uncertain, it's best not to smile or look at any of them directly. A nervous expression can often come across as a guilty one, and that's the last thing we want.'

Miles doesn't need the reminder. He intends to keep his head well down.

Marshall pushes open the door and a middle-aged woman usher beckons them forward.

'If you'd follow me, Mr Whitaker, I'll let you into the dock.'

FORTY-TWO

Sophie isn't sure how she expected the jury to look, but as she watches them file in her initial feeling is one of relief. They seem such an ordinary group: a mix of men and women, most of them in casual clothes. The youngest-looking is a black girl with a shaved head, and the oldest a grey-haired man in a pink shirt. Although it's a comfort to have the girls with her, what comes home to her as they sit in the back of the court, is how much all four of them are now at the mercy of strangers.

She glances across to where the Cunningham parents, the only other people attending, sit on the opposite side of the gangway. She has only ever exchanged a couple of words with them on speech days, but Don has always come over as strong-minded and determined – not someone you'd want to pick a fight with.

At least there is no sign of the press. The barrister has said they may only appear when the verdict is being announced, and she prays he'll be proved right. Although, thinking the unthinkable – which makes her catch her breath – if Miles is found guilty, there will be no hiding from them.

The judge, in a neat wig and with a red sash over his robes, peers over his glasses as he answers a point raised by the prosecution lawyer, a stoop-shouldered man, whose wig is coming away at the back. The jury is concentrating on what's being said, and Melbury Jones and Rupert Marshall are deep in discussion. No one seems to be taking any notice of Miles, who sits in a glassed-in cubicle, like some dangerous species of wild animal.

It's only when the clerk asks him to stand that heads turn towards him. She can tell from the way he runs his tongue over his lips how nervous he is. I'm only here, she reminds herself, because I need to get at the truth. Yet as he gives his "Not Guilty" plea, she sees with an unwelcome return of pity, that he's trembling. Beside her, Miranda reaches for her hand.

The judge gestures towards the prosecutor. 'Ready to proceed, Mr Weatherspoon?'

He gets to his feet. 'Your Honour, ladies and gentlemen of the jury: as you are aware, the defendant, Miles Francis Whitaker, stands before you charged with a series of sexual assaults against a minor, Justin Cunningham. I make no bones about it, this is a serious matter.' He extends his hands, palms uppermost, to emphasise his point. 'At the time of the alleged offence, Justin was a boy of fourteen, a pupil at the public school where Mr Whitaker has taught for the past four decades.

'The prosecution alleges that over the course of several months, Mr Whitaker bullied and intimidated Justin. Furthermore, that this behaviour included the making of inappropriate sexual advances towards him on a number of occasions.'

Sophie feels Miranda's grip on her hand tighten.

'Too afraid to speak out for fear of the repercussions,' the prosecutor continues,

'Justin eventually found himself cornered by Mr Whitaker, and subjected to an indecent assault – an assault that was witnessed by two other pupils, as well as a master, who will all be providing evidence.'

To hear the allegations being voiced in public like this fills her with dread. Boys may well lie, she thinks, but surely not Laing? Is this why Miles has refused to tell her anything? Because the case against him is so damning?

'The prosecution maintains,' the lawyer continues, 'that the alleged offence was particularly serious, given Justin's vulnerability, and the fact that Mr Whitaker was in a position of trust.' He pauses. 'You are being asked to decide, ladies and gentlemen of the jury, whether Mr Whitaker committed this offence. He certainly had the opportunity. The prosecution maintains that he seized that opportunity to exploit a vulnerable young boy. And when you have heard all the evidence, I have no doubt that you will find Miles Whitaker guilty as charged.'

Sophie glances at Helena. Silent tears are trickling down her daughter's cheeks. She puts an arm around her.

This is precisely what she has been desperate to protect her daughters from. 'Do you want to go out?' she whispers, but Helena shakes her head.

'I will now call on Justin Cunningham.'

The judge leans forward. 'One moment, Mr Weatherspoon. For the jury's benefit, I understand Justin has been offered Special Measures.'

'He has indeed, Your Honour, but is adamant in his continued refusal of them.'

'And you have tried every means to convince him?'

'I have, Your Honour.'

'Very well.' The judge pushes his glasses further onto his nose. 'May I remind the court that Justin will be giving his evidence by live video link, and that the guidelines for the questioning of underage witnesses are to be adhered to at all times.'

'Of course, Your Honour.'

An usher steps forward and switches on a screen. There's a crackling noise, and then Justin's face swims into view. He's sitting behind a desk, blue eyes startled under the blonde hair that falls across his forehead. Sophie is shocked to see how much thinner he seems from when she last saw him in sickbay, his face drained of colour. She can hear a woman offering him a glass of water.

The judge is speaking again. 'Everyone here appreciates what an ordeal this must be for you, Justin. It takes a great deal of courage to agree to testify as you have done. So, if at any stage you are not comfortable with any of the questions, please let your intermediary know.'

The boy nods.

'Thank you, Your Honour,' Mr Weatherspoon says. 'Now, Justin, you understand why we are all here?'

'Yes,' he murmurs.

'I would like, if I may, to take you through the events of last January. You were in your second year at Fordingbury, I believe? So, could you tell the court, Justin, how Mr Whitaker treated you during that period?'

'Whatever I did or said wasn't right.' The boy is staring at the floor, his voice barely audible.

'Could you be more specific?'

'If I didn't understand something, he'd start walking up and down the classroom, spouting Latin.'

'Spouting Latin? How much of that did you understand?'

'Not a lot. But I was too scared to say anything back, in case he gave me another detention.'

'Ah, the detentions.' Mr Weatherspoon consults his file. 'How many do you say there were?'

'I don't know exactly. I had one most weeks.'

'I have here a copy of the school record from the start of the September term. It shows a total of nine. Did other boys in your class get detentions, Justin?'

'A few. But I was the one who got the most.' He hesitates, and a faint flush comes to his cheeks. 'All I know is that Mr Whitaker and I were often alone together.'

'I see. And what are you saying happened on those occasions?'

'Well, he would shout at me – tell me to pull my socks up, or I'd be in even worse trouble.'

'Worse trouble. What do you think he meant by that?'

'I don't know. He kept telling me what a bad influence I was.'

'A bad influence?'

'That's right. And that as far as he was concerned, I was a total waste of space.' He pauses. 'And after he'd been going on a bit, he'd come over to where I was sitting, and he'd touch me, and...' His voice breaks.

Sophie glances at the jury, most of whom are leaning forward, listening intently.

'I realise this is difficult, Justin, but if you could describe to the court in what ways

Mr Whitaker touched you?'

The boy lowers his voice. 'He'd, like, put his arm round my shoulders, and try to kiss me.'

'I see. Anything else?'

'Sometimes, he'd rub the outside of my trousers, and...' His voice tails away.

Sophie cannot bring herself to look at Miles. She recalls how often he's talked about keeping the boy back after class. But surely he wouldn't have spoken so openly if this kind of thing were going on? Yet as the prosecutor is only too keen to point out, the opportunity was there, and Justin's distress is all too horribly convincing.

As the boy continues to speak, she feels bile rise into her throat.

'So, Justin,' Mr Weatherspoon is saying, 'you've described to us the incidents that occurred when you and Mr Whitaker were alone together. I would like now, if I may, to turn to the events that occurred on the afternoon of January twentieth. You remember that afternoon?'

The boy nods.

'So, if you could tell us in your own words what took place. You had been playing football, I believe?'

'Yes. We have a practice session every week, and after the game, Chris and Luke and I were in the changing rooms.'

'That would be your friends, Chris Webb and Luke Owen?'

'That's right. We had Mr Whitaker's Shakespeare class to go to, but we had to change out of our kit first. We don't have long to get ready, and I realised I wasn't going to get to the class on time.'

'Any special reason for that?'

'I got an attack of cramp – a really bad one.'

Mr Weatherspoon smiles. 'Something that many professional footballers suffer from. So then what happened?'

'Well, the rest of the class had already left the changing rooms. So I asked Chris to run and tell Mr Whitaker that I would be late. And to ask him to get help.'

'Because you were suffering from cramp?'

'Not just that. I also had a stabbing pain in my side. It was so bad, I couldn't move.'

'And this pain. What has been the outcome?'

'The doctor says I've probably got a rumbling appendix.'

'And I have here a copy of his report.' The lawyer produces a document that is handed to the judge. 'That must have been frightening, and accounts for your desperation to get help. But to get back to the changing rooms. You were on your own when Chris went to call Mr Whitaker?'

'No, Luke stayed with me. I felt so bad, I lay down on one of the benches.' The boy bites his lip. 'I thought I was going to pass out with the pain.'

'It must have been terrible for you. So what happened next?'

'Mr Whitaker came in and told Luke and Chris to wait outside. I was lying stretched out, crying because it hurt so much. I simply couldn't move, and he came towards me, and...' the boy's eyes fill with tears, 'he bent over me. And then he – he...' The boy hesitates.

'And then, Justin?'

'He put his hand under my towel, and began stroking me.'

'Stroking you? Where exactly?'

'You know – on my dick...'

'On your penis?'

'Yes.'

The boy lowers his head and begins sobbing, a heart-wrenching sound that makes Sophie catch her breath. 'It was the worst moment of my life!' he adds.

She can hear the woman intermediary murmur reassurances.

'Your Honour,' Mr Weatherspoon says, 'might I suggest that the court takes a short break?'

The judge nods. 'An early lunch would seem sensible. Any objections, Mr Melbury Jones?'

'None, thank you, Your Honour.'

'Very well. We'll reconvene at 2 p.m. sharp. The jury is

reminded not to discuss the case, either amongst themselves, or with anyone else. Stand please, Mr Whitaker.'

A few minutes later, Miles joins Sophie and the girls in the side room. He's as pale as Justin, Sophie thinks.

'How are you doing, Dad?' Miranda asks, but she doesn't look at him.

'Not so bad, thanks.'

Marshall comes bustling in. 'Coffee and sandwiches are on the table behind you.' He turns to Miles. 'This is just the opening round. We'll soon get a chance to knock some holes in the evidence.'

Miles gives a tentative smile.

'I need to sort out one or two things,' Marshall continues. 'The usher will fetch you when it's time.'

When he's gone out, Miles turns to Sophie. 'I've always maintained what a good liar the Cunningham boy is. But I reckon he deserves an Oscar for that performance.'

Helena pushes back her chair. 'I think I'll get some air.'

'I'll come with you,' Miranda says. She pauses in the doorway. 'We're all behind you, Dad.'

'Thanks.'

Sophie can see a vein throbbing in his temple.

'Sandwich?' he offers, when they've gone out.

She shakes her head.

'I can't tell you how much your being here means to me, Sophie.'

'Obviously it's not easy for any of us.'

'No – of course not.'

For a moment, his face wears the expression of a small and very frightened boy, and she feels another unwelcome tug of pity. But there seems nothing more to say and for the remaining time, they sit in silence.

Back in the courtroom, the prosecutor finishes taking Justin through his evidence.

The boy is far more composed which, Sophie realises, makes what he says all the more compelling. She doesn't want to look at Miles.

Melbury Jones gets to his feet.

'If I may, Justin, I'd like to go over one or two points with you. If that's all right?' The voice is silken.

The boy nods.

'You're saying that these difficulties with Mr Whitaker began from the moment you entered Fordingbury?'

'Yes.'

'Which was the September before last?'

A nod.

'And that Mr Whitaker lost no opportunity in giving you detentions and extra homework as a punishment?'

'That's right.'

'But my question, Justin, is this: punishment for what?'

The boy hesitates. 'I've already told you – he said I was a troublemaker, and that I stopped the rest of the class from working.'

'A troublemaker? How did you feel about that?'

'It wasn't true, and I told him so.'

'I see.' Melbury Jones whispers something to Marshall, who hands him a sheet of paper. 'I have here a report from your previous school, Justin. The school you attended immediately prior to Fordingbury. You remember it, of course?'

'Yes.'

'It says here that you were reprimanded on more than one occasion because, and I quote: "At times the boy has proved virtually impossible to teach, taking every opportunity to disrupt lessons and—'

The prosecutor jumps to his feet. 'Your Honour! Justin Cunningham is not the one on trial here!'

'Your Honour,' Bill Melbury Jones says. 'I am merely seeking to establish the credibility of the witness.'

'I'll allow it.'

'Thank you, Your Honour.'

'But please be aware of the guidelines, Mr Melbury Jones, and moderate your tone.'

'I will, Your Honour. Now, Justin, let's put your past misbehaviour to one side for a moment, and turn to the incident in the changing rooms. You obviously remember what took place that day?'

His reply is a mumbled, 'Yes.'

'I know this is difficult, Justin, but please try and speak up. It's important that the jury can hear you. Now, we've heard you testifying that you were in those changing rooms after a game of football, and that you lay down on a bench because you were overcome with an attack of cramp?'

'That's what I said.'

'And you've had these attacks before?'

'Yes.'

'And you dealt with those, how?'

'By walking up and down. They weren't as bad before, and this time I had this pain in my side.'

'So you've said. But on this occasion, you asked your friend,' Melbury Jones consults his notes, 'Chris Webb, to summon Mr Whitaker?'

'Yes.'

'Wasn't that rather a strange request?'

'I don't know what you mean.'

'I'm sorry – I'll try to make myself clearer. My question is this: why turn for help to a man whom you say is out to get you? I'm wondering why you didn't ask Chris to fetch the school matron? Surely she's the person who deals with injuries, and her office is much nearer the changing rooms.'

'I don't know.' Justin's face wears a look of defiance. 'It just seemed the best thing at the time.'

'The best thing at the time.' Melbury Jones pauses. 'You see, Justin, I need your help here, because I'm really struggling with this. Because none of it makes sense, does it?'

'Not to you, maybe.'

'Not to me. And, I suggest, not to anyone else in this courtroom. Because what I think, Justin, is this.' Melbury Jones points a finger. 'That this whole story is a pack of lies. A pack of lies from start to finish. There were never any sexual assaults, were there? Either when Mr Whitaker supervised your detentions, or in the changing rooms.'

'That's not true!'

Sophie can see the boy shrink back in his seat.

'That when he made it clear to you he was not prepared to stand any more of your insubordination, you decided to take your revenge.' Melbury Jones's voice rises. 'And what better way of taking revenge than to accuse a long-standing and highly respected teacher of an offence that, if taken to its ultimate conclusion, would almost certainly lead to the end of his career?'

'He did it! He did it!' The boy is sobbing again. 'Why can't you believe me?'

One or two of the jury are leaning forward, a look of consternation on their faces.

'Mr Melbury Jones.' The judge points his finger. 'I have warned you before about this style of cross-examination.'

'Your Honour, I am only trying to—'

'I will not warn you again.'

The prosecutor is on his feet. 'Your Honour, I strongly object to my learned friend's manner of questioning.'

'And I agree with you, Mr Weatherspoon. There will be a short adjournment, and I will see both advocates in my chambers now. No need for the jury to retire.'

When he and the lawyers have gone out, Sophie listens to the murmur of conversation that has broken out around them. She daren't look over to where the Cunningham parents are sitting.

Miles remains seemingly impassive in the dock. At one point, he glances towards Sophie and the girls, and Miranda gives a small lift of the hand that he returns.

Ten minutes later, the lawyers are back.

'Mr Weatherspoon,' the judge intones. 'I understand that you have an application to make to the court?'

'Yes, Your Honour. I have spoken with Justin. He is, understandably, highly distressed by the manner of questioning to which my learned friend has subjected him.'

'Quite.'

'So I am requesting a longer adjournment to allow time for him to recover from what has been an undoubted ordeal.'

'Twenty-four hours?'

'Thank you, Your Honour.'

'Mr Melbury Jones?'

'No objections, Your Honour.'

'Very well. The court will reconvene then at 10 a.m. Wednesday. Stand please, Mr Whitaker.'

As Miles's bail conditions are extended, and he's released from the dock, Sophie isn't sure whether to be glad or sorry for the respite.

The four of them hang back to allow time for the Cunningham parents to leave.

Then they retrace their steps along the concourse and down the stairs.

'Bill's had to dash,' Rupert Marshall says, as they gather outside the deserted front entrance, 'as indeed must I.'

Miles seems bewildered. 'It went all right, didn't it?'

'Put it this way – I don't think the boy will stand up well to further questioning. And I can assure you I've by no means finished with him.' He shakes their hands. 'We'll meet again on Wednesday. I'll let you know, of course, of any developments.'

'He and Melbury Jones are worth every penny,' Miles says, as he flags down a cab.

'Could you drop us off at the station?' Helena asks the driver.

'Oh—' Miles hesitates. 'I thought perhaps we might go for a meal?'

'I don't think any of us is very hungry, Miles,' Sophie says.

'And I've got work I need to be getting on with,' Miranda adds.

'Of course. Let's save it for when all this is over.'

The taxi pulls up at the station and the girls say their goodbyes to Miles. Sophie stands with them on the pavement, fighting back tears. In all her worst moments, she hasn't imagined things would feel this ghastly, but most dreadful of all is the drawn look on the girls' faces.

'Please say you'll stay away on Wednesday. There's nothing to be gained by your being here.'

'But what about you, Mum?' Miranda says.

'I'll be fine, darling.' Whatever happens, they mustn't see her cry.

Miranda's voice drops to a whisper. 'I thought Bill Melbury Jones was out of order – browbeating the boy like that. I can't see how that will help Dad.'

'He's only trying to get at the truth,' Helena says.

And I'm still no nearer to finding it, Sophie thinks, watching the twins disappear up the station steps.

Fifteen minutes later, she and Miles are in the Rover, heading back to London.

FORTY-THREE

'WE FORGOT TO WATER IT.' SOPHIE HOLDS UP THE house plant, its once glossy leaves reduced to a dried-up stalk.

'Dead as a doornail,' she adds unnecessarily, walking over and dumping it in the bin. She turns. 'I've promised Becca I'll help her out.'

'*Today*?'

'Afraid so.'

'When will you be back?'

'Early evening, I imagine.'

'But she's already given you the week off.'

'I know, but she's rushed off her feet.'

'It would do us good to have this time together.' He tries a smile. 'We don't have to talk if you don't want to. We could go up to that Indian place for an early bite?'

'Sorry, Miles.' She stoops for her bag.

But I'm the one having to be back in that dock tomorrow, and the day after, he wants to say. I need you here.

'There's plenty of food in the fridge.'

As she moves past him, he catches the trace of that new scent she's using – musky and alien. It makes her seem further away than ever.

She turns in the doorway. 'I won't be late. We've to be up at five.' Her words are coming out in a rush. 'Try and take it easy. Perhaps there's a film on TV?'

The front door closes behind her and he stands listening to the creak of the boiler. Is she really going to that shop?

Yet he's got so many things wrong – he mustn't let his suspicions get the better of him. He's still mortified to recall the fond look – so obvious in hindsight – between Webster and the black fellow, Chuma. The recollection fills him with unease.

So many of my boyhood memories are a blur, he thinks. But he can still recall the levels of terror the senior prefect, Fothergill, evoked; can still remember the delicate-looking boy, whose name he has long since forgotten, sobbing into his pillow after lights out.

The kitchen smells musty and he steps into the garden, lifting his gaze to where the block of flats looms, a brooding presence beyond the fence. It's another warm day, and the balconies are draped in washing. In one of them, a man sits cross-legged, smoking. Above a steady thump of music, a baby is bawling its head off. I'll never get used to this way of living, he thinks – not just because it's an affront to civilised standards, but also because it's so bloody soul-destroying.

A movement makes him jump. A black cat, skinny and with a torn ear, emerges from the grass. It stares at him for a moment, before clawing its way over the fence.

All those times Carter's ginger tom got itself shut into South Lodge, he recalls. And to think that not so long ago, he believed he and Sophie would be back in Fordingbury for the start of the autumn term.

Christ! He could do with a drink.

But as he retrieves the whisky bottle, he hesitates. He got through a bottle of wine yesterday evening and must try and keep his wits about him. Even if the barrister keeps up the pressure, young Cunningham isn't the sort to cave in. He'll pursue this to the end. Yet he can see why Sophie and the girls were upset by the way Melbury Jones confronted the boy. But they don't know him like I do, Miles thinks.

'All this Latin makes you a good teacher, does it, sir?' Said with that insufferable note of insolence.

And then his own response: 'Detention for you, Cunningham,' followed by the sniggers of the class.

Yet in court, the boy's hysterical outburst was all too convincing. Miles feels a vein throbbing in his temple as he recollects Don Cunningham glaring up at the dock. He feels his mouth go dry. How in God's name will he get through it all?

He stares at the garden's waist-high grass on which the sun still shines – as it will be doing on the churchyard. How good it would be to spend time with the one person who doesn't doubt him.

He dials Ali's number and after a few rings, the familiar voice says, 'Miles! I wasn't expecting to hear from you till the end of the week.'

'There's been an unexpected break in the trial. I don't suppose there's any chance of our meeting up?'

'But of course. This afternoon will suit me very well. Farah and I are travelling to Bradford tomorrow to visit our son, so we can't offer you a meal, I'm afraid.'

'No, it's fine.'

'I will see you in the usual place, then.'

As he clicks off his phone, he almost weeps with relief.

*

In the deserted churchyard, a pair of blackbirds peck at the rough grass and the conifers cast long shadows across the ground. Someone has planted orange geraniums outside the porch. He's never much cared for them, associating them with municipal flowerbeds. Now, the splash of colour strikes him as a symbol of defiance and of hope. How far away that courtroom seems now!

'Oh good, you're here,' Ali calls, walking up the path, and settling himself on the bench. 'I've been very much thinking of you, my friend.' He puts his rucksack down beside him. 'So, tell me, how did it go?'

Miles hesitates, thinking of all the bland responses he could give. Instead, he finds himself blurting out: 'To be honest, it was pretty ghastly.'

Ali's face creases in sympathy. 'I am sorry. At least you are having a bit of a breather now.'

He's aware of the other man observing him. God knows he's been the object of enough scrutiny in that courtroom, but this feels different. The gaze is warm and accepting.

'I brought along the backgammon. I thought a game might be in order?'

He feels his shoulders relax. 'Excellent idea.'

Ali places the board between them. 'So, let's see how many of the rules you remember.'

'I am getting the hang of it, although I still don't see how I can start off so well, and end up so badly.'

'And in that, my friend, lies the skill of the game! And—'

A shout interrupts their talk. 'Good morning to you!' Webster calls, emerging from the porch. 'Can't stop!' He strides off in the direction of the lych-gate.

Miles looks across at his friend. 'I used to think he was just a leftie do-gooder.'

'I'm sorry?'

'Someone without any real principles,' he explains. 'With no substance.'

'I would say that he is a man of much substance.'

'Yes, I can see that now.'

'You wish to be white as usual?'

'Please.'

They begin placing their checkers on the board.

'How is Farah?'

'Very well, thank you. And Sophie?'

'She's decided to go back to work today.' He gives a small laugh. 'I was rather hoping she'd put her feet up. Yesterday was pretty exhausting for both of us.'

'I can imagine.'

And she still remains so aloof, he thinks, recalling the day of the attack on Ali, and Farah's look of horror when she opened the door and saw him propped between himself and that man, Kevin. She wouldn't have left Ali coping on his own like this. He feels the familiar sinking sensation inside.

'You and Farah have been married long?'

'Over twenty-five years. You to start.'

He moves the first of his checkers. 'Three years more than Sophie and me, then. So how did you meet?'

'Her mother was a cousin of my father's.'

'It must make things so much easier – coming from the same background. Sophie and I met at a party.' He pauses, remembering that first glimpse of her, beautiful and sexy, then as now. He thinks of the term-time round of lessons and of their Wednesday afternoons of love-making. Despite their differences, the two of them hit it off, didn't they?

'The trial must be a strain on you both.' Ali strokes his beard. 'Sometimes, if Farah is tired or out of sorts, I devise some treat for her. An outing, or a small gift – to show how much I appreciate her.'

'We've never really gone in for that sort of thing.' But that's not strictly true, he thinks, recalling the various offerings he used to find on his desk at South Lodge: a bar of his favourite chocolate, a pen, an initialed handkerchief. He recalls his last-minute searches for her birthday and Christmas presents. In recent years, Miranda has come to his rescue, but has he ever bought anything for Sophie in between? He struggles to remember.

'Your move,' Ali is saying.

'It's the kind of advice Miranda would give.' Miles shakes the dice again. 'As I may have told you, the twins couldn't be more different.'

'Ah, yes. Helena is the – how did you describe her?'

'The prickly one.'

Ali nods.

'Whatever I say or do, is wrong.'

'Sons and daughters. When all goes well, everything seems right with the world. And when it does not...' He moves one of his checkers.

'Your other son is still overseas?'

'Yes, indeed.' He sighs. 'Sadiq used to be such a kind boy, always willing to help others, never giving any trouble.' He lifts one of Miles's checkers onto the bar.

'Blast! I never saw that!'

'It is a game that demands much concentration. Even when I was a boy, and not always willing to sit still for long, my father and older brothers never let me win. The only way to learn, they said, is to work out the various moves for oneself.'

'My old headmaster was a firm believer in letting people stand on their own feet.' *Half a page on the origin of the doldrums, Whitaker!* He should get in touch with Murdo, although for the first time, the thought holds less appeal.

Aloud he says, 'Your youngest boy sounds rather like Helena, although mind you, she was never easy from the start.'

'I often wonder whether I could have done more to help Sadiq see things differently.' Ali pauses, staring at the ground. 'He hasn't been in touch for a while.'

He thinks of the comfort of knowing Miranda is on his side. 'That must be hard.'

'It is, especially for his mother. We believe he's got himself involved in an organisation we do not approve of.' He rolls his dice again. 'I often ask myself: what did I do that led him to being as he is?'

'But it's surely not your fault?'

Ali rubs a hand over his chin. 'When he was younger, I was rather strict with both him and his brother. I've always believed in the importance of good manners, and of showing consideration to those around one.'

Miles nods agreement.

'Sadiq never rebelled, so I assumed there wasn't a problem.' He moves another of his checkers. 'It was such a shock to have him suddenly announce that he considered me a bad Muslim. Me – who has always followed our imam's teachings, who has believed in the importance of tolerance and respect!' He pauses again. 'But the hardest thing is the way he has cut himself off from his mother and me.'

'Perhaps it's just a passing phase?' But some children are born troublemakers, he thinks.

'We can but hope. Sadly, Farah and I are no longer welcomed as warmly at the mosque, so we tend to keep to ourselves.'

'All very tricky,' Miles says, but now he's only half-listening, his attention caught by the sight of Ali's brown fingers hovering over the board.

Forgive me, my friend, for the terrible thing I did to you.

In those first terms in Fordingbury, Inky had been very keen on card tricks that he spent hours practising. Miles could still see the excited look on the round face, and hear the high voice. 'Come over here, Whitaker! Bet you can't spot how this one's done!'

We were together every spare moment, Miles thinks, swapping marbles and cigarette cards, sitting beside one another in class, and helping each other with homework.

Now an unwelcome memory comes that he feels powerless to wipe away. Mrs Burrell, starched dress rustling, looking around the common room and beckoning Inky over. 'The headmaster wishes to see you, Oladosu. *Now!*'

Inky puts down his latest card trick with a look that is both puzzled and anxious. He raises his eyebrows at Miles, as if to say: 'Do you know what this is about?' But Miles pretends not to see.

When the door closes, Fothergill ambles over to where Miles sits, head lowered in his book. 'So, Inky's been the naughty boy, then.' Fothergill is short and squat, his muscular forearms covered in dark hair. It's known that he can see anyone off in a rugger scrum. Now he stoops so close that Miles can smell his sweat. 'Pinning a sketch of his dick on Matron's door. Who'd have thought it!'

'And in such a girly pink,' Phillips says, from the opposite end of the room. He's a lighter build than Fothergill, but he is the prefect Miles fears the most. His stare is both mocking and suggestive – of what, Miles does not as yet understand. Only later does he piece together the haunted look on the faces of some of the younger boys, and the whispered comments: 'Phillips is a bit of a shirt-lifter'; 'Phillips likes the pretty ones.'

Miles is aware that the room has emptied, leaving him alone with the two prefects.

He fingers the marks on his wrist from the Chinese burns Fothergill inflicted on him the previous week. Mercifully, the bruises on his chest and upper arms are fading.

'What colour's yours then, Whitaker?' Fothergill is saying.

He feels his mouth go dry.

'Murdo's not going to like it. Not one little bit.' He snatches Miles's book from him and rips out several pages. 'But, as I think we've made pretty clear, it had to be either you or your nigger friend.'

Miles remains silent, eyes squeezed shut, until Fothergill saunters back to his seat.

Two days later, Miles also receives a summons from Murdo and feels his insides plummet. How on earth can he begin explaining something like this to his parents? He pictures his mother's stiff curls and her smile that is only for the spaniel, Tillie. He thinks of the sacrifices his father has made to send him here, and of all those Westerns they've gone to together. He can see now that they were also an important part of his education – a way of drumming into him that any boy with an ounce of backbone should be able to stand up for himself.

In Murdo's study, he's so busy fighting back tears that it takes him several moments to realise that, far from being angry, Mr MacPherson is nodding encouragingly at him. 'It's been a long time since I've come across a boy with as good a grasp of the Classics as you have acquired, Whitaker, and in such a short space too. So,' there's a click of teeth, 'I am moving you to the upper stream, and inviting you to join a select group, who meet with me on Sunday evenings to discuss classical literature and the arts.'

As Miles makes for the door, the headmaster calls him back. 'Oh, and Whitaker?'

'Yes, sir?'

'I hear some of the older boys have been throwing their weight around.' He clicks his teeth once more. 'You can take it from me, it won't happen again.'

'Thank you, sir,' and he shoots out of the room before Mr MacPherson thinks to ask anything about Inky.

After that day, Miles drops his friend, turning his back when he approaches and refusing to talk to him. In the dorm that they share with eight other boys, he lies awake listening to Inky sobbing into his pillow. It feels shameful, but what else can he do? There are his parents to think about.

When Inky did not return the following term, Miles had a sense of having been let off the hook. Especially as Murdo was as good as his word. As if by magic, the bullying stopped, and—

'You've been hit, my friend,' Ali is saying, placing Miles's checker in the centre of the board.

Miles stares. 'So I have.'

FORTY-FOUR

I AN PUTS AN ARM ROUND SOPHIE AND SHE FEELS some of her tension dissolve.

The studio window is flung wide, and outside it's one of those perfect September days, the russet leaves hanging in the still air that, even in London, carries a hint of wood smoke.

He brushes a strand of hair from her forehead. 'So, how did it go?'

She feels the tears well up. 'Pretty grim.'

'Hey! Come and sit.' He leads her to a chair. 'I'll put the coffee on.'

'Thanks.'

She watches him walk through to the kitchen with that way of moving that, despite all that's happening, makes her heart lift. Whatever the outcome of the trial, there is still this, she thinks.

The burble of the percolator takes her back to term-time, and Miles dashing back to South Lodge for his mid-morning shortbread. Now that ritual feels as if it belongs to another lifetime and another Sophie.

Yet she knows how differently Miles will be viewing things.

The abrupt break in the proceedings took them all by surprise and, after the painful parting from the twins, she and Miles drove back from Oxford in silence.

Although it was obvious that Melbury Jones's aggressive stance was out of line, the lawyer hadn't seemed in the least abashed by the judge's reprimand. A Rottweiler, she thinks, wishing she could be more glad on Miles's account, when what's uppermost in her mind is the memory of the Cunningham boy, white-faced and sobbing.

Back in Stephen's Close, she and Miles ate a supper of cheese and biscuits, before he took himself into the front room with the whisky bottle. At least he was no longer trying to hide it.

She'd gone upstairs and run a bath, lying in the cooling water for nearly an hour, trying to tell herself that everything would work out. Although she no longer knew what that meant. Only the thought of Ian held her together.

Yet she'd been nervous about phoning him. He has a business to run, she told herself, and he's not expecting to see me until the end of the week.

But when he answered her call, there was no mistaking the pleasure in his voice.

'Tomorrow would be great, Sophie. I should be clear by lunchtime. If that's OK with you?'

And now, here she is, feeling that skip of delight as he reappears from the kitchen.

'God, you look done in.' His forehead creases in concern. 'Want to lie down for a while?'

She nods. She managed only a couple of hours' sleep, tossing on the spare room mattress, haunted by the events of the day.

She slips off her sandals, and lies back on the bed, watching the play of sunlight on the Rothko painting.

In the South Lodge border, the Michaelmas daisies will be a mass of purple, and the late roses in flower. How can she tell the girls that they won't be returning to the only home they've ever known?

She closes her eyes. The one comfort is that yesterday's proceedings must surely have convinced Miles that, whatever the outcome of the trial, there is to be no return to Fordingbury. Regardless of whether or not he's convicted, how can either of them hold their heads up there again?

*

She wakes with the sun still filling the room. From the kitchen comes a waft of garlic and chilli.

Ian is sitting writing at the desk. He must sense her eyes on him, because he turns. 'Hi! You're awake.'

'Hello.'

He comes over, slipping a hand inside her top. 'Any more rested?'

'Mm.'

'I thought you could do with some food. I'll just put the pasta on.'

'Need any help?'

He raises an eyebrow to indicate that some men were perfectly capable of preparing a meal.

She walks through to the bathroom and, by the time she re-emerges, his papers have been cleared, and two places set at the table.

'Now,' he says, handing her a glass of rosé. 'Let's eat.'

She didn't think she'd have much appetite, but the food – pasta, with mushrooms and Parmesan, and a tomato salad – is delicious. She clears her plate, and then looks up, aware of his eyes on her. 'That's the best meal I've had in ages.'

She stares into her glass.

'Come, thou monarch of the vine,
Plumpy Bacchus with pink eyne!'

'Come again?'

She looks up, embarrassed. 'It's from *Antony and Cleopatra*, I think. Just something Miles used to quote.' Then, realising what she's said, adds, 'Oh, God.'

He hesitates. 'Look, Sophie, if you don't want to talk about the trial, that's fine. I don't want to poke my nose in where it doesn't belong.'

The edge to his voice warns her she mustn't shut him out. 'No, I want to tell you.'

She thinks back to the courtroom. 'It was a godsend having the twins with me.'

'And thank God you didn't have to cope on your own.' He kisses the top of her head, and she leans against him.

'One of the things I was dreading most was having to face anyone from the school, especially Laing, the geography master.'

'The arrogant sod who ordered you out of your house?'

She gives his arm a grateful squeeze. 'That's the one. It turned out I needn't have worried. As he's to give evidence in support of the boy, he's not allowed into the courtroom.' She takes another mouthful of wine, before adding, 'Although the parents were there – sitting opposite us, in fact.'

'That must have been bloody awkward!'

'It was.' But how on earth did they cope with hearing their son's evidence? How would she have reacted if it were either Helena or Miranda in his situation? I'd have wanted to murder whoever was in that dock, she thinks.

'And Miles?' Ian is saying.

She pictures him behind the glass screen, shoulders pulled back in that familiar gesture of defiance.

'He still denies he's done anything wrong. But why then the evasiveness – and the lies?'

'He might still be innocent.' Ian pauses. 'Although I'm not sure you believe that?'

She sighs. 'I don't know what to believe any more. Though at least the solicitor says that, even in the worst-case scenario, it's unlikely Miles will go to jail.'

Ian strokes her arm. 'And if he's cleared? What then?'

'Obviously that would be a huge relief.' She's aware of his gaze. 'Oh, that's not what you meant, is it?'

He shakes his head.

'You're asking if I've come to a decision about the marriage?'

'Yup.'

She detects a note of uncertainty in his voice, and draws in her breath. 'Whatever the jury decide, I can't go on living with him. My trust has gone.'

'So when are you going to tell him?'

'Not yet.'

'For God's sake, Sophie!'

'What?'

He gives an exasperated sigh. 'I know you Brits tend to pussyfoot around, but you really haven't given any hint about your leaving him?'

'What would you have me do?' She swallows her tears. 'Tell him in the middle of the trial? Announce it to the girls, when they don't yet have an inkling of it?'

'OK, I'm sorry. Point taken.'

She props herself on an elbow. 'But I do have something else to tell you, Ian.

It's serious.'

He stares into her face. 'There's nothing you can say or do that will put me off, Sophie. Surely you can trust that?'

'The problem is that someone else said the same thing to me once.'

'Another man, you mean?'

She nods, surprised by the wave of pain washing over her. 'We were both young, and working in the same hospital. We'd been together for over two years, and he'd made it clear that the minute I finished my nurse's training, we'd get married.'

'But he let you down?'

'I let myself down.' She struggles to talk about the secret she's kept hidden all these years. 'It was a moment's stupidity. I forgot to take the pill, and of course the inevitable happened.'

She can still picture Alastair pointing towards her belly. *I really can't be doing with any complications, Sophie.*

Is that all our child is to him? she remembers thinking. 'I was so sure of him, so certain of our future together.'

She's back, watching the green sports car drive away, too stunned to cry. Instead, she's walking through the clinic doors, which swing silently shut behind her.

She's sobbing now, tears streaking her face. Ian holds her to him. 'What a bastard! But it wasn't your fault.'

'Although this was the early 1980s, and times had moved on, I was ashamed, and so dreadfully guilty. I don't know if you can understand that? Even eighteen months later, when Miles and I married, I never said anything.'

'It can't have been easy holding back on something as important.'

'I knew deep-down Miles didn't want to hear. To be honest, I think he had me on a bit of a pedestal. But it still doesn't excuse my not telling him.' She blows her nose. 'And the habit of not discussing how I felt, just went on from there.'

'My poor sweetheart!'

'Hardly fair to Miles, though.'

'Maybe not. But you've been a pretty devoted wife, haven't you?' He brushes away a tear with his finger. 'All those bells and timetables.'

'I've tried to be.'

'Well then.' He gestures towards the bed, and they lie down beside each other.

'So, since we're sharing secrets, let me fill you in on a couple of things.' He strokes her arm. 'Felicity and I also met when we were very young – too young, I realise now. I think we both knew it was a mistake. Oh, we tried, for the sake of the kids, but in the end we agreed we'd be better apart.'

She thinks for a moment. 'We're such different people in our twenties and thirties. No one tells us that.'

'You're right there. I've had a couple of relationships since – the most recent ended over a year ago. Felicity's back in Sydney, and has been with someone else for a while.'

It takes her a moment to absorb the information. 'And the second thing?'

'I'm putting the studio on the market.'

'Oh.' She swallows. 'Are you moving far?'

'Only a mile or two up the road.' He smiles. 'A friend has given me first offer on his place. It's a three-bed conversion I did for him a while back and, even though I say so myself, it's got a great feel to it. Plenty of light and space, and I can use one room as an office. Plus there'll also be somewhere comfortable to talk other than on a bed.' He runs a hand along her thigh. 'Nice as this is.'

'I thought perhaps you'd had enough of me?'

'Are you kidding? You must know how I feel about you, Sophie? I want us to be together. Permanently, I mean.'

Relief floods through her.

'So,' his voice is trembling, 'what do you think?'

'I want to be with you too, Ian. Please believe that. It's just I need a bit of time to sort things out.'

He nods. 'Fair enough.'

'So once the trial is over, I'm going down to my aunt's in Cornwall – just for a couple of months. The twins can visit me there. They'll be needing my support, and it's a place they also feel at home in.'

He draws her to him. 'That'll work fine – I should be settled into the new flat by the time you get back.'

She smiles. 'You might want to come down and meet Aunt Harriet. I'm sure the two of you would hit it off.'

'That would be good.' He smiles. 'I shall ask my sis for tips on mildew and blackspot.'

'Ingratiating yourself with my aunt will get you everywhere.'

'Glad to hear it.'

Sophie feels his hand move further up her thigh, and she reaches up and eases his T-shirt over his head.

'So, we're agreed to take things one step at a time, are we?'

'Yup.'

He begins unbuttoning her blouse. 'Nice and slow. Like this?'

'Uh, huh.'

Outside in the street, the evening traffic is building. A car hoots its horn, and she can hear laughter, and footsteps running along the pavement.

FORTY-FIVE

H E'S AT THE TOP OF THE STAIRS WHEN THE landline, loud as a fire alarm in the early quiet, sounds in the hall. Who else but Marshall uses this number?

He can hear Sophie lifting the receiver. 'Fine,' she's saying. 'Of course I'll tell him. Love you too.'

'Oh.' He'd been so hoping to hear that the trial was off. He walks slowly down, the weight of what lies ahead pressing on him.

Sophie turns to him. 'That was Helena. She and Miranda have a lot on, so they've decided not to come to court today.'

'Oh.' He'd been banking on their presence, wishing now he'd told Miranda how much her wave of the hand had meant to him.

'It seems a sensible decision, Miles. They'll be back in court for the verdict.'

As he follows her into the kitchen, he thinks of the other news for which he's been secretly hoping. He hasn't spoken to Aunt Harriet in weeks, but Sophie's reported that the old girl's heart condition has flared up again. If she were to die – peacefully of course, since however difficult he finds her, he wouldn't wish her a painful end – all their financial problems would be over.

Whatever have I come to? he thinks, as Sophie places a cooked breakfast in front of him. Yet if things go against him this week, the legal costs will be sky-high. But that is to accept that Cunningham will get the better of him. He stabs his fork into the egg, the yolk oozing across the plate in a yellow puddle. Over my dead body, he thinks.

*

Yet as he and Sophie are shown into the room off the concourse, he feels his earlier resolve disappear. All he can think about is facing that judge and jury once more.

Marshall appears. 'Good morning to you both.' He gives a brisk nod. 'As I've said, Miles, I think it highly unlikely you'll be called on today. We've a way to go still with young Cunningham, and the prosecution witness, Laing, is still to give evidence. But if you are required to testify, I'll be requesting a short adjournment, so we can go over the key points.'

'Thank you,' he mutters, wondering what the hell the key points are, and how on earth in his present state, he'll be able to take them in.

Bill Melbury Jones, in wig and gown, puts his head round the door. 'No need to look so down in the mouth,' he says cheerfully. 'I've got the measure of the boy, and I can assure you I've not finished with him. Not by a long chalk!' He nods at Marshall. 'We have paperwork to go through. The usher will fetch you when it's time, Miles.' He smiles across at Sophie. 'See you both later.'

The barrister's confident tone was reassuring, so it's only as Miles walks across the blue-carpeted concourse towards the courtroom, that he remembers Don Cunningham. Almost the worst part of that first day was looking over and catching the man's hostile stance, arms folded across his chest, his eyes fixed in a belligerent stare. One heard about parents turning violent in cases like this, although surely he'd be mad to try anything in such a public place?

All the same, Miles enters the court, looking neither to right nor left. The usher locks the door of the dock, and he sinks into the seat, wiping a trickle of sweat from his forehead. He can hear the low murmur of conversation and, after a couple of minutes, risks a glance at the public seating area. To his relief, Sophie is the only occupant, and he's heartened to receive a smile from her.

As on the previous occasion, the clerk gives the order to stand, and the judge enters, peering over his glasses at the jury.

Miles is surprised a smarter dress code isn't insisted on. He himself would have been much more comfortable in blazer and cords, but Marshall was adamant. 'A jury warms more to a defendant who doesn't appear down on his luck.' He paused before adding, 'Especially with the type of charge you're facing.'

Now, Miles is aware of one juror, a young man in a grey T-shirt, staring up at him. Remembering the lawyer's advice, Miles looks away. Yet Ali believes in him, as does Miranda and suddenly the panic by which he's been gripped is replaced by a feeling of outrage. How dare a mere schoolboy put him, Miles Whitaker, who has devoted his whole life to education, in this position?

He leans forward. He will not allow these proceedings simply to wash over him. Instead, he will follow everything that's being said. Only then will he be able to put up the best fight when it's his turn to give evidence.

'The defence is ready to continue cross-examination?' the judge asks.

Melbury Jones is on his feet. 'We are, Your Honour.'

'I hope I don't need to remind you, Mr Melbury Jones, of the guidelines regarding the examination of underage witnesses.'

'No, Your Honour.'

'Good. As on the previous occasion, the live video link will now be activated.'

On the television screen, the figure of Cunningham swims back into view. How young and fragile he seems, Miles thinks. No wonder Sophie and Helena feel sympathy for him. If only it had been that strapping lad, Owen, making these allegations things would be very different.

'Now, there's nothing to be afraid of, Justin,' the judge is saying. 'All you have to do is to answer the questions as they are put to you honestly and truthfully. You have your intermediary beside you if you need support at any time. Is that clear?'

The boy gives a cautious nod.

'Good morning, Justin,' Melbury Jones begins, 'I hope you're feeling better?'

The boy gives another nod. He's always been on the pale side, but today there is a spot of colour in each cheek.

'I want to take you back again, if I may, to the afternoon of January twentieth.' He's obviously taken the judge's warning to heart, because his tone is conciliatory. 'You remember that in your evidence you said that you had suffered an attack of...' Melbury Jones consults his papers, '...of cramp.'

'And a pain in my side,' the boy mutters.

'Quite so. Now,' Melbury Jones rocks back on his heels, 'the previous account you gave the court was obviously upsetting, and the last thing any of us would wish is to cause you undue distress. But it is important that we get at the truth here. You do understand that?'

Another nod from the boy, who for the first time looks directly ahead of him.

'I wonder, Justin, if you could describe everything that took place between you and Mr Whitaker on the occasions when he gave you a detention?'

'I've already said.'

'Of course you have.' Melbury Jones pauses. 'And you've stated that you were given a detention nine times in a matter of months. That does seem rather a lot, doesn't it?'

'Chris and the others thought so.'

'So, Justin, you'd have been a bit fed up about these detentions, and understandably so. I mean, it must have been pretty annoying to be cooped up indoors, when your friends were enjoying free time?'

Another nod.

'So what exactly was it that Mr Whitaker expected you to do during these detentions?'

'Do? Oh, the extra homework, you mean. I had to read a passage from a Latin text, and then write a one-page essay on it.'

'It sounds as if he really made you work. And at something you weren't all that keen on. I mean, Latin isn't everyone's cup of tea, is it?'

The prosecutor is on his feet. 'Your Honour!'

'I agree, Mr Weatherspoon. Can you please get to the point, Mr Melbury Jones?'

'I apologise, Your Honour. All I'm trying to establish is the nature of the relationship between Justin Cunningham and my client.'

'Very well, then. Proceed.'

Melbury Jones smiles across at the boy. 'He sounds like a teacher who takes himself very seriously. Too seriously perhaps?'

'He did go on a lot. You know – spouting quotations at us all the time.'

'And I believe you and your friends had a nickname for him?'

Justin looks blank.

Melbury Jones consults his papers. 'Let me remind you. A Latin-sounding name?'

'Oh, yes.' The boy lowers his head.

'Which was?'

He mumbles something that Miles can't catch.

'Could you speak up, please, Justin?'

The boy's face reddens. 'We used to call him Fartimus maximus.'

'Fartimus maximus,' Melbury Jones repeats, and there are titters from the jury. He frowns. 'But this is no laughing matter, is it, Justin? You see, what we are talking about here is the reputation of a man, who cared very deeply about his work, and was only doing his best to keep order in what was often an unruly class.' He pauses. 'And, if the number of detentions are anything to go by, you were one of his most unruly pupils, were you not?'

'I don't know what you mean.'

Melbury Jones consults his notes again. 'We have already heard something of your conduct at your previous school. I quote: "This boy has proved virtually impossible to teach. He takes every opportunity to disrupt the class." What would you say to that?'

'It isn't true! Mr Whitaker gave me the detentions so that he could touch me up.'

The jury are leaning forward, eyes glued to the screen.

This is terrible, Miles thinks.

'Touch you up?' Melbury Jones repeats. 'And were there any witnesses to this alleged touching up?'

A shake of the head.

'No witnesses. That's a pity.' Melbury Jones looks across at the jury. 'So, Justin, you seriously expect this court to believe that you bore no grudge against Mr Whitaker? A teacher, who made it very clear he was not prepared to tolerate your unreasonable behaviour?'

A movement catches Miles's attention. The door leading to the concourse is opening, and Don Cunningham and Sanderson enter. He presses himself back, glad to be safely behind the glass screen.

'It wasn't unreasonable,' the boy murmurs. His face, Miles notes, has reverted to its usual pallor.

'That's what you say. But what I am suggesting, Justin, is that you have been motivated solely by a desire for revenge.' He points a finger. 'Revenge, for the justifiable detentions that were imposed on you. Revenge because you were faced, and not for the first time in your life, with a teacher who refused to tolerate your appalling behaviour.' His voice rises. 'Revenge strong enough for you to cook up these preposterous charges against a dedicated member of the teaching profession, a man who has only ever had the best interests of his pupils at heart.'

Thank God that at last Melbury Jones is fighting his corner. Miles risks a quick glance at the jury. One man in the back row is nodding his head, as if in agreement.

'But he did it!' the boy suddenly shouts, all traces of composure gone. He stares ahead, tears running down his cheeks. 'You're trying to make me say he didn't, but I'm telling you: he did!'

A woman juror gasps, and others shift uncomfortably in their seats. The prosecutor is on his feet.

'I agree with you, Mr Weatherspoon.' The judge points a finger. 'Mr Melbury Jones, you have already been warned and I have tell you that—' He breaks off, as the boy's cries fill the courtroom.

Don Cunningham jumps up. 'My son may be many things, but he's not a liar!' he shouts.

'I will not allow this kind of interruption in my court.' the judge yells. 'Any more of this, and you will be removed.'

Alan Sanderson tugs at Don Cunningham's sleeve, and after a moment's hesitation, he sinks back into his seat.

'Your Honour?' the prosecutor begins.

'A further adjournment, Mr Weatherspoon? I think not. There is the court's time to consider.' He leans forward, addressing the boy directly. 'I realise how difficult this is for you, Justin, but nevertheless, the law requires you to answer all reasonable questions put to you.' He switches his gaze to the barrister. 'Reasonable being the operative word here, Mr Melbury Jones.'

'Yes, Your Honour.' Melbury Jones is on his feet again. 'So, Justin,' the voice is once again soft, 'you have told the court that Mr Whitaker lost no opportunity in giving you detentions?'

'He was always picking on me! All my friends said so.'

'Which must have been pretty tough.'

'It was.' The boy fights another sob.

Miles feels a return of his earlier dread. For a moment there, things seemed to be going his way, but Justin is too convincing by half.

'So perhaps you can help clarify something, Justin?'
'Yes?'

'I'm sure everyone in this courtroom, yourself included, is familiar with the term "paedophile"?' He pauses. 'Someone who grooms children for his own sexual satisfaction? Whose behaviour no one in their right mind would condone. You agree with that?'

'Yes.'

'Someone like Mr Whitaker, perhaps?'

'He's a real pedo. Everyone in my year says so.'

'But everyone in your year isn't in court. You are. And you see, Justin, here's the puzzling part. Because a pedo, as you term it, would go out of his way to treat his victim well, to lure him with kindness, and promises of treats.' He pauses. 'Did Mr Whitaker ever do any of that?'

'I've already told you – he was really mean to me.'

'Which rather makes my point, doesn't it?'

Miles can see the jury eyeing the lawyer intently.

'You know what the truth of this is, Justin? The truth is that you are a liar. A liar with a proven history of troublemaking. An accomplished liar who will do anything to bring down a teacher he hates, who—'

Justin lets out another sob. 'Whatever I say, you're not going to believe me!'

'– A teacher who saw you for what you are, just as I believe everyone in this court will see you. And that—'

There's the sound of a chair being overturned. A moment later, the boy disappears from the screen.

In the silence that follows, Miles digs his nails into palms slippery with sweat. What will all this mean?

'Your Honour?' the prosecution lawyer is saying.

'Yes, you'll want a word with your client, Mr Weatherspoon,' the judge says. 'The court will adjourn – thirty minutes.'

Miles watches the jury file out, followed by the lawyers, and to his relief, Sanderson and Don Cunningham also leave, but not before Don casts a look of fury in Miles's direction.

The minutes tick by. An usher offers him some water, but he shakes his head. He's trembling too much to be able to hold the glass steady.

Sophie's head is bent over her phone. Perhaps she's sending a message to the girls, to let them know what's happening. Although what is happening? He isn't sure any more. His shirt is sticking to his back, and he's in desperate need of a pee, but daren't ask, for fear of running into Don Cunningham.

At last, over an hour later, Melbury Jones reappears, glancing across at Miles, as if to signal something. But there's no time to make sense of it because the clerk is giving the order for the jury to stand, as the judge comes back in.

The prosecutor gets to his feet.

The judge leans forward. 'Mr Weatherspoon. You have an application to make?'

'Yes, Your Honour. I have to notify the court of a new development.' He pauses, rocking back on his heels. 'Justin is adamant that he does not wish to continue with the case.'

Miles is not sure he's understood correctly. He presses his forehead against the glass, fighting off another bout of nausea.

'You have done everything possible to explain the situation to him, Mr Weatherspoon?'

'I have, Your Honour.'

'And he has been given every opportunity to discuss it, both with his advocate, and with his family?'

'He has, Your Honour. But he's determined that all charges be dropped.'

Miles still can't believe what he's hearing. He looks across at the jury, who remain impassive, apart from a man in a green shirt who stifles a yawn.

'Mr Melbury Jones?'

'In the light of this information, Your Honour, I make an application for the case against Mr Whitaker to be dismissed.'

It's true, then. Miles's shoulders sag with relief.

'Very well.' He turns to the jury. 'You have heard what the prosecution has said. This trial cannot now proceed, and you are free to go.' He looks across at Miles. 'Stand, please, Mr Whitaker.'

He gets unsteadily to his feet.

'As you have heard, the prosecution is not pursuing this matter, so there is no case to answer. You are free to leave the court.'

Miles stares. This is really it, then? Yet already the woman usher is unlocking the dock. Immediately behind her Melbury Jones is grinning from ear to ear. 'Well, we did it!'

'I – I can't thank you enough.' To his embarrassment, he finds tears running down his cheeks. He mops at them with his handkerchief, before following the barrister onto the concourse, where Sophie stands waiting. He puts an arm around her. 'Can you believe it?' She shakes her head, looking as bemused as he feels.

A hand grips his shoulder, and he is spun round, coming face to face with Don Cunningham. 'What kind of a monster would do this to a fourteen-year-old boy?' He spits out his words, the hooded eyes reminiscent of some bird of prey. 'Wrecking a young person's life for your own perverted pleasure!' He turns to Sophie. 'And tell me this, Mrs Whitaker: what kind of person does it make the wife of such a man?' His grip on Miles's shoulder tightens. 'You think you've got away with this, but let me tell you—'

Marshall has stepped forward, and an usher is coming up on the other side. 'That is enough, Mr Cunningham. If you don't leave this instant, I'll call the police.'

The man hesitates, before dropping his hand, and walking away.

'He'll calm down, given time,' Marshall says. 'But a highly satisfactory outcome, Miles. Nothing more to add at this stage. I'll be in touch when we've sorted out the administrative details.'

Miles is too numb to do more than nod.

'All right if Bill and I leave you to make your own way back?'

He nods again, watching the lawyers walk off down the stairs.

It's only some twenty minutes later, as Sophie drives them out of the car park, that it finally sinks in. 'So, it's finally over, then.'

'Yes,' she says. 'It is.'

FORTY-SIX

THE SOLICITOR'S WAITING ROOM IS AS SOPHIE remembers from that first visit – the same arrangement of magazines on the glass-topped table, the padded seating and the still-life prints on the walls that couldn't be more different from Ian's Rothko.

The desk lamps are switched on. Outside, the early October afternoon is muggy and overcast, with streaks of rain running down the tall windows.

Opposite her are two men in that indeterminate category of young middle-age, with greying hair and unlined skin. Every so often, they cast an affectionate glance at one another. In the corner, an elderly woman in a fur coat puts out a trembling hand to stroke the dachshund that lies curled on the floor beside her.

Miles has made no recent mention of Murdo, but suddenly the old man comes to mind. He would be at ease in this room, Sophie reflects, for like Fordingbury, it seems determinedly in a time capsule of its own.

What a lifetime ago since she sat here, fuming with resentment over the way Miles shut her out of his meeting with Rupert Marshall. Now she realises, with both surprise and sadness, it seems unimportant. Yet looking at Miles, she feels an unwelcome qualm of conscience.

After the collapse of the trial, he developed a high fever. The doctor prescribed antibiotics and plenty of fluids, and she tried to curb her annoyance that here she was, having to run up and down stairs with trays and medication; and, worst of all, unable to have any meaningful conversation.

She still managed to snatch precious hours with Ian, but during her last visit to the studio, there was a definite note of impatience in his voice. 'Well, have you told him?'

She shook her head. 'I'm sorry. I need to wait until he's up and about again.' She paused, anxious that he might not understand. 'I know this is hard, Ian, but please don't give up on me.'

He cupped her face in his hands. 'Just as long as you're definitely going ahead with this?'

'I promise.'

He smiled. 'That's all that matters, then.'

Two days later, when Sophie returned from the shop, she found Miles out of bed and sitting by the front-room fire.

He grinned up at her. 'As you can see, I'm on the mend.'

Say something *now*, she told herself.

Before she could open her mouth, he said, 'Marshall's just phoned. He's slotting in a meeting tomorrow. Apparently he has some very positive news on the financial front.' He paused. 'I'm sorry I never discussed the money side of all this, Sophie. The truth is, I didn't want to worry you, but I'm pretty confident that at least we won't have any costs to pay. And, although he wasn't very forthcoming, I'm hopeful also of a return to Fordingbury.'

She stared at him. Surely he couldn't still want to go back there? Not after the way the Cunningham father had behaved? But it would be a huge weight off her mind if Miles were to be reinstated, if not there, then perhaps at another school? Whatever he had or hadn't done, she couldn't bear to think of him with no work or a decent roof over his head.

She knew that she and Ian would manage. Becca was keen for her to go full-time, and his business was doing well.

For God's sake, Sophie! she could hear Ian saying. *Just bloody well spit it out!* But better to wait, she decided, until after the solicitor's meeting, when Miles would know where he stood.

Now, in Marshall's office, she resolves to break the news to him the moment they are back in Stephen's Close. He'll be upset, of course, but he'll get over it in time. 'You're allowed your own life,' she can hear Ruth Madiebo saying, but the words don't convince. Is she really entitled to be this selfish? To destroy, not just her marriage, but her family also?

All she wants is for the twins to come out of all this with as little anguish as possible. It was good to see their smiles of relief after the collapse of the trial. But how will they take the news about Ian? As a signal that Sophie believes their father to be guilty?

Miles must have felt her gaze on him, for he looks up and gives a grin. As far as he's concerned, she thinks, it's as if these past months have never been. No doubt he'll be suggesting a meal to celebrate – something she's determined to fend off.

A young assistant in a navy suit puts her head round the door. 'Mr and Mrs Whitaker? Mr Marshall is ready for you now.'

'Splendid!' With another broad smile, Miles is on his feet. Sophie follows, watching him stride along the corridor to the end room. As he enters, she can hear back-slapping and congratulatory comments.

'Sophie!' Rupert Marshall comes forward, leaning towards her, so that for a moment, she wonders if he's going to kiss her cheek. 'Come on in. Bill's here too.'

Melbury Jones, equally effusive, shakes her hand. 'Good to see you, Sophie. I popped by because Rupert and I thought a celebratory drink would be in order.' He turns to Miles. 'So, what's your poison?'

'Whisky, please.'

'Shall we make that a double? You look a bit off colour, if you don't mind my saying so. Rupert said you haven't been too well?'

'Just some bug or other. But I'm fine now.' He smiles across at her. 'Thanks to some splendid nursing care.'

'Excellent! And what for you, Sophie?'

The last thing she feels like is alcohol, but she doesn't want to be a killjoy. 'Vodka and tonic, please. Just a small one.'

They sit, while Marshall hands round the drinks, and then settles himself behind his desk. Through the window, she can see a row of plane trees, still thick with foliage, although the edges of the leaves are turning a mottled brown. She hopes this meeting won't go on too long. The sooner she's out of here, the sooner she can tell Miles. Yet, sitting in this room with these men, the idea of a new life with Ian seems distant and improbable. For a moment, she experiences a feeling of panic.

Melbury Jones leans back in his chair. 'All in all, a highly satisfactory outcome. Though I must admit, I wasn't expecting the boy to cave in quite so easily.'

'You did a really marvellous job,' Miles says.

Sophie stares out of the window again. She can still picture the fear on Justin Cunningham's face as he was being cross-examined; can hear the father's impassioned cry, 'My son is not a liar!' How could anyone think of it as a marvellous job?

'It's astonishing how common these allegations are becoming,' Rupert Marshall is saying. 'Of course all this Jimmy Savile business is another matter. All most unfortunate, but often – as in your case, Miles – these sorts of charges are brought by hysterical teenagers, no doubt influenced by material on the Internet.'

'I blame the parents for not keeping them under tighter control,' Melbury Jones adds.

'I couldn't agree more,' Miles says.

384

'Quite.' The barrister smiles. 'Anyway, enough of all that. What did you think about…?'

As so often in staff meetings at Fordingbury, Sophie feels an outsider in a male world. She studies the two lawyers. Both have the same suave manner as Alan Sanderson. Yet whilst there's no denying either the intellect or the confidence of these men, they seem to her to be blinkered, with a curious inability to empathise with anyone outside their own social group. She thinks of Ian's relaxed air of confidence that belies a steely determination to succeed in whatever he undertakes. Yet she couldn't imagine him browbeating Justin Cunningham, however much was at stake.

'Sophie?' Miles is saying.

'I'm sorry?'

'Bill is suggesting a toast, so how about raising our glasses to our first-rate legal team.'

'Oh – yes. Of course.'

They sip their drinks, and then Marshall begins telling some joke about a judge and some missing briefs, at the end of which Miles laughs uproariously.

'Well,' Melbury Jones replaces his empty glass on the desk, 'I'd better get going.'

'We can't thank you enough,' Miles says, as they shake hands.

'Just doing my job.' He turns to Sophie, and she's aware of his shrewd gaze. 'It's obviously been a challenging time, both for you and for Miles, but I think when you hear what Rupert has to say, it'll sweeten the pill considerably.'

'Now, to business,' Marshall says, when the barrister has gone out. He consults his notes. 'I have here a document from my colleague, Tony Murphy, who deals with the employment side of things. He can't be with us, but he's asked me to set out the financial position. And I must say that the outcome is highly satisfactory.' He settles his spectacles on his nose. 'In brief, your private pension has been reinstated, Miles, and all court costs and legal fees will be paid for by the school.' He looks across at them. 'The last thing they want is any adverse publicity, which of course would have been the case if we'd counter-sued, as I was proposing.' He shakes his head. 'Unbelievable in this day and age that none of the child protection regulations was in place.'

Miles gives another grin. 'I asked Rupert not to go into all this detail over the phone, Sophie, so we could hear the good news together.'

She forces a smile. 'Of course.'

'So, Miles,' Marshall continues, 'the school has also agreed to make you a substantial *ex gratia* payment – to compensate for the stress and inconvenience to which you've been put.' He smiles across at them. 'And although you had no formal contract, Sophie, the total includes compensation for your loss of earnings.'

He names a six-figure sum, and Miles gives a sharp intake of breath.

'Golly. That's marvellous.'

She feels a weight lift off her. At least he'll not have to share Murdo's fate, and spend his remaining years in some pokey bedsit.

'I just wondered?' For the first time Miles sounds tentative.

Marshall peers at him over his glasses.

'Now this ridiculous accusation has been withdrawn, would there be any chance of the school offering me a post of some kind? In view of all my years with them.'

Marshall studies his fingernails. 'I have to advise that it really would not be in your best interests.' He pauses. 'And of course the settlement on offer is linked to your immediate retirement.'

'Oh.' Miles's face crumples. 'I was still hoping. You know...' His voice tails away.

Has he really not understood the stigma that is now attached to him? Sophie leans forward. 'But with all the changes taking place under Alan Sanderson's regime, Miles, do you honestly think you'd be happy there?'

After a pause, he mutters, 'No – I suppose you're right.'

Watching him, she thinks again: how on earth will he manage away from Fordingbury? Away from me? Yet she can't go on living with him.

She glances at her watch. With any luck, in just over an hour they'll be back in Stephen's Close. She'll sit him down at the kitchen table. 'I've got something important to tell you, Miles,' she'll say. 'Something that may come as a shock.' She can't imagine how he'll react, but at least things will be out in the open.

'It is a very generous offer,' Marshall says. 'Far more than even I dared hope for.'

Miles squares his shoulders. 'Well, if Fordingbury doesn't want me, to hell with the lot of them!'

The solicitor's eyebrows rise fractionally. 'Quite.' He closes his notepad. 'I trust all this meets with your approval?'

She catches a hint of reproach in his voice that Miles must be picking up on too.

'We're both extremely grateful,' he says, but his voice sounds flat.

She should be adding her thanks to Miles's – after all, the solicitor has done his best by them, but she just wants to be away from this room.

Marshall is gazing from one of them to the other. 'Shall we leave it there then?' He pushes back his chair and says, with what sounds like forced bonhomie, 'And how will the two of you be spending the rest of the day?'

Miles turns to her with another of his wide smiles. 'I have a surprise for you, Sophie. I've booked us into a rather splendid hotel in the West End.'

'Hotel?' she echoes, feeling her stomach plummet.

'Just for a night.' He turns back to Marshall. 'She's been working so hard recently, having to nurse me as well as keeping her job going. I thought she could do with some spoiling.'

How long will it take to get from the West End to Ian's flat? she wonders.

'Sounds marvellous!' Marshall says.

'It's my way of saying thank you – for standing by me.'

She can feel the solicitor's eyes on her, but she simply can't bring herself to respond.

'Well, if you need our help in the future, you know where to find us.' Marshall holds out his hand. '*All's well that ends well*. Eh, Miles?'

Outside, it's still raining, the passing traffic sending up sprays of water. Beyond the embankment, the Thames is hidden in a fine mist.

'I hope the hotel bit hasn't thrown you too much?' Miles says, as he flags down a passing cab. 'You deserve only the best, Sophie. You always have done – you know that, don't you?'

'Thank you, Miles.' What else can she say?

They climb into the back seat. 'This is more like it.' He puts an arm around her, and she resists the urge to slap it away. 'I packed a bag for both of us. Oh, and I've reserved a table for dinner. I must say I'm looking forward to a decent meal. Apparently they do an excellent chateaubriand.'

'Miles, I—'

He reaches for her hand. 'No need for thanks. I've arranged for the girls to join us for lunch tomorrow. Between us, we'll be able to decide the best way forward.'

A part of her is saying: Coward! Tell him and get it over with. But he's looking at her with such a delighted expression she doesn't have the heart to disillusion him.

The taxi deposits them outside the hotel entrance, and a frock-coated doorman steps forward with an umbrella.

'The hotel will supply anything I've forgotten,' Miles tells her. 'No need for you to lift a finger!'

She watches him exchange pleasantries with the doorman, and then she's following Miles across a marble floor, with the glint of chandeliers overhead, and the rich scent of lilies in the air.

They check in at the desk, before a bellboy escorts them to a lift. The doors close, and they're borne upwards.

Miles beams across at her. 'This is more like it!' Then, maybe picking up on her mood, whispers, 'I know this isn't really our style, Sophie. All a bit OTT, but I thought it might be rather fun for once.'

She forces a smile.

'It's an odd thing,' he says, as they follow the bellboy along a thickly carpeted corridor, 'but in some ways, this business with young Cunningham has done me a favour. I mean, money's never been that important, but who would have dreamed we would ever end up with this much?'

The hotel room is done out in beige and gold, with plush curtains and button-backed chairs. As Miles starts unpacking his bag, she's suddenly reminded of their honeymoon in that dreary coaching inn and, even in her drunken state, her gratitude to him for putting her life back together after Alastair.

I'll give Miles this evening, she thinks. I owe him that much. And the truth is, I simply can't face telling him. Later, she promises herself.

He comes out from the bathroom and hesitates, looking across at her hopefully. 'I don't suppose you fancy–?' he begins, pointing to the double bed.

She shakes her head. 'I'm sorry, Miles, I feel really done in.'

She resolutely ignores his disappointed expression, slipping off her shoes, and sinking onto the bed.

Somehow she has to get through the next hours, but suddenly her exhaustion is overwhelming, and she feels herself sinking into the merciful oblivion of sleep.

FORTY-SEVEN

A FTER ALL THESE MONTHS OF SLEEPING IN
separate rooms, it's wonderful to have Sophie in the
same bed once more. He walks over to her. The curve of
her body under the sheet and the spread of her hair on
the pillow takes him back to his first glimpse of her at that
long-ago party. You're still so beautiful, he thinks.

He gives her a gentle shake. 'Time for dinner.'

She struggles onto an elbow, gazing up at him with
bleary eyes. 'I'm not sure I can manage any.'

'Nonsense. How long since you've enjoyed a gourmet
meal?' When she doesn't answer, he continues, 'Not since
Oxford. And,' he smiles, 'I've managed to bag the best
table.'

She nods, albeit with a certain reluctance, so it's a relief
when they're at last seated at their table. He's chosen the
wines in advance – her favourite Gewürztraminer, and a

decent Bordeaux for himself. He raises his glass. 'Well, here we are, back in civilised surroundings. Amazing, isn't it?'

'Yes, it is.'

He tries not to be put out by her lack of enthusiasm. 'I know this isn't quite our thing.' He waves a hand to take in the glittering chandeliers, the expanse of starched table linen, and the grand piano in the corner at which a young black musician is seating himself. 'But it is rather splendid, all the same.' He pauses. 'Especially after that hellhole of a house.' He wishes she'd volunteer a remark. 'We can discuss future plans in the morning,' he continues. 'The world's our oyster, I suppose. Talking of which, we might order some for when the girls join us tomorrow. Good to give them a first taster.'

Her continuing silence is unsettling. 'How's your chicken?'

'Fine, Miles.' She sips her mineral water. 'It's just I don't have much of an appetite.'

'Not to worry. Plenty more of this ahead.'

She's placed her mobile beside her, and as it starts to ring, she glances at the screen. 'Oh, it's Helena.'

He pulls a face. Sophie has already informed both girls about the outcome of the trial and he really isn't in the mood for another run-in with his cantankerous daughter. Not here, not now. Besides, they'll be seeing the twins in the morning.

'So, how did your interview go?' Sophie is saying. 'Wonderful! I knew you'd do it!'

They're obviously talking about Helena's new course. He mouths across the table. 'Can I have a word?'

Sophie stares in surprise. 'Here's your father for you, darling. See you soon,' she adds, handing him the phone.

'Helena?' Miles begins, wishing he were feeling less nervous. 'Your mother and I have just come from the solicitors, and we've had some really marvellous news.'

'Yes?' The voice is cautious.

'I don't think your mother's told you yet, but it seems we're in funds again. So there's no longer any problem about your switching to law.'

'I didn't know there'd been a problem.'

'We didn't want to worry you.'

'Well, while we're speaking like this, Dad, there's something I wanted to say.'

He swallows. 'Yes?'

There's a pause. 'I know I haven't always been the easiest person to get along with, but now that this trial business is finally over, I think we should try and put all that behind us. Make a new start.'

He feels his shoulders relax. 'I'm very glad you feel that way, Helena.'

'And, for what it's worth, Dad, I didn't think the boy's evidence was all that convincing.'

Oh, the relief of it! As long as the twins and Sophie believe his account, all will be well. 'Thank you for that, Helena.' He hesitates. 'See you tomorrow then.'

'Tomorrow,' she echoes.

He clicks off the phone, and leans over the table. 'What a miracle! She's offering to let bygones be bygones.'

He'd resolved not to bombard Sophie with any more talk of the future, but suddenly everything is falling into place. 'All that money. More than enough for us to make a new start.' He reaches for his wine. 'I know it's still early days, Sophie, but I've been thinking that, once we start house-hunting, it should be well away from Oxford. East Anglia maybe or, better still, the West Country. You'd like to be near Aunt Harriet, wouldn't you?'

She fiddles with her earring.

'So what do you think?'

'I'm just relieved you've accepted the break from Fordingbury, Miles.'

He smears mustard onto his steak. 'You were right. It would never have worked out.'

There's a pause.

'I'll be paying Murdo a visit soon. Obviously he'll be delighted with our news.'

'Yes.'

'He never came back to me as he promised.' He takes another mouthful of wine.

'But somehow that isn't important any more. Oh, by the way, there's someone else I'd like you to meet.'

'Your Arab friend?'

He experiences a kick of delight that she's able to read him so well. 'That's the one.'

'He sounds a real ally, Miles.'

'Yes. He's been a tremendous support through all the recent...' he hesitates, 'difficulties.' He reaches for her hand, and when she doesn't respond, he continues: 'I've been telling him all about Fordingbury.' He pauses. 'And the thing is, Sophie, I may have been in some small way to blame.'

She frowns, twisting her table napkin between her fingers. 'To blame?'

'Yes. You see, I really came to hate young Cunningham.' He takes another mouthful of wine. 'Well, he was so arrogant, such a troublemaker. He turned that Remove Year against me, you know.' He hesitates again, but there's no need for caution now. 'So I admit that I tried my hardest to bring him down a peg or two.'

'But he's just a boy, Miles.'

'I know. But that didn't stop him being such a...' he hesitates again, 'such a complete shit.'

'Well, it's over and done with.' Her gaze is dispassionate. 'I suppose,' she adds.

Her response is disconcerting, but he can't think of what else to say.

'Pudding?' he asks, after a pause.

'Not for me, thanks.'

'I rather fancied some port and Stilton. And we could have our coffee in one of the lounges.' He leans forward again. 'My other thought, Sophie, is how about planning that break together? Just the two of us? You've always fancied going back to Italy, and I—'

'Would you mind very much if we talk about this in the morning, Miles? I'm not in the mood right now.'

He swallows his disappointment. He so much wanted this evening to be one, not just of celebration, but also of reconnection. Behind her, as if in sympathy, the pianist is playing "Smoke Gets in Your Eyes". 'No – that'll be fine,' he says.

'I think I'll go on up. I feel really wiped.' She pushes back her chair. 'There's such a lot to talk through, isn't there?

Perhaps we could do it immediately after breakfast, so we've got time to sort everything out before the girls arrive?'

'Good idea.'

She waves a hand around the room. 'It was kind of you to arrange all this.' Her voice sounds sad. Obviously she's completely exhausted.

'No problem.'

He watches her walk away, a young man seated alone at a table, turning to look at her as she passes. At Fordingbury, he'd rather lost sight of what a very attractive woman she was. My Sophie, he thinks.

He finishes his meal, and wanders into the lobby, deserted, apart from two businessmen in city suits. For a moment, he's reminded of Paget. How good it feels to be able to hold his head up again amongst such people.

The businessmen are heading towards the lift, but as he goes to follow them, something snags his memory.

He turns and approaches the desk. The receptionist, a young Far Eastern-looking boy, sallow-skinned, with a fringe of glossy black hair, gives a deferential nod.

'Can I help you, sir?'

'I don't suppose you have newspapers covering the Oxford area?'

'Not hard copies, sir, but you can always access them online.'

'Well, maybe I won't bother.'

'No bother, sir. We have facilities for guests who do not have laptops with them.' He beckons to a bellboy, with the same black hair and slanting eyes. 'Tony here will show you.'

Miles follows the boy across the lobby and into a side room. It contains two desks that are surely Chippendale, with a computer perched incongruously on each. The boy switches on the nearest machine, motioning him to the chair in front of it.

'Here we are, sir.' The screen lights up. 'What is it you wanted to see?'

'A newspaper, please. The *Oxford Mail*, going back for the past month.'

As he watches the young man's fingers move over the keys, Miles is reminded of Murdo's resistance to the introduction of computers. 'Horrible, newfangled things,' he declared, but in the end having to bow to parental pressure. Although at least the boys still had to produce handwritten essays.

'Here's the one for the current week,' the boy is saying. 'If you follow the links, you can access earlier copies. Is there anything more I can help you with, sir?'

'No, that will be fine, thanks.'

He stares at the banner, recalling his final visit to the newsagents earlier in the week. Mrs Patel, in a lime-coloured sari with a pink cardigan over the top, was in her usual place behind the counter. He was struck by the dark circles, like bruises, under her eyes. She obviously worked all hours. Just as Sophie and I might have had to do, he thought, with an inward shudder.

He wanted to tell the Indian woman that he felt for her, but was anxious about giving offence. In the end, he said, 'My wife and I are leaving the area soon, so I just wanted to say goodbye and thank you.'

Unexpectedly she smiled, and the transformation was startling, as if years were suddenly knocked off her. 'I wish you both well,' she said.

Yet now, the earlier remark of Sophie's comes back to him: 'It's all over and done with, *I suppose.*' Although surely he's worrying needlessly?

He begins scrolling through the pages, forcing himself to read each one, and then to go through the earlier editions he's missed out on. He's almost finished when, suddenly, a paragraph jumps out at him. He reads it through twice, before sinking back in his chair.

A local teacher has recently gone on trial, accused of performing a sex act on a fourteen-year-old pupil in January of this year.

Miles Whitaker, 63, of Fordingbury School, near Oxford, denies the charge.

The male complainant, who cannot be named for legal reasons, gave his evidence in Oxford Crown Court.

Whitaker is on bail, and the trial continues.

The irony of the information being out of date is not lost on him.

FORTY-EIGHT

H E WAKES WITH A START IN THE EARLY HOURS. For a moment, without the orange glow from the street lamp filtering through the curtains, he struggles to remember where he is.

Then the hushed, scented atmosphere of the hotel room returns him to the present.

He clicks on the bedside light and looks about him. The inlaid furniture and velvet curtains seem more oppressive than ever. Through the archway, he can see the bathroom, done out in gold and cream squares. If he presses one of a series of buttons beside his head, an enormous screen will rise, Venus-like, from the shelf at the end of the bed.

He looks down at Sophie's sleeping form. Choosing this place has been a mistake. Small wonder she's so muted, for none of this is really her – or him – for that matter. Though what *is* Sophie? Once he thought he knew, but now?

In any event, he's going to have his work cut out convincing her of his version of events, but he'll book them into a *pension* with wooden shutters and a view over vineyards. The break will relax them both, and she'll come round in the end. After all, Helena has.

He swings his legs out of the bed, and going over to the window, peers into the street. Cars are parked bumper to bumper, and two women in waitresses' uniforms are huddled together, their cigarette ends pinpoints of scarlet in the semi-dark. In the distance a clock strikes, reminding him of the happy times with Ali in the churchyard. He will give him a call after breakfast to update him. 'Marvellous news, Miles,' he can hear him saying. 'We must have one of Farah's special meals to celebrate.'

He straightens, catching sight of his reflection in the window. Then he freezes as a pale face with a slick of fair hair hovers beside his own.

He's back once more in the classroom with this pupil – this one boy who has persisted in humiliating and defying him. Now, as he stares into the reflection, he is filled with a new sense of triumph. 'It was always your word against mine, Cunningham,' he whispers.

The image fades, but he's as far from sleep as ever.

On impulse, he pulls on his clothes and, letting himself out of the room, makes his way down to the lobby. It's deserted and as he looks about him at the leather chairs, the marble-topped tables and the arrangement of lilies, the quiet takes him back to that last dreadful morning in South Lodge. He squares his shoulders. He and Sophie are moving on to better things.

A liveried porter appears.

'Just going for a breath of air,' Miles says.

The man jumps to attention, pulling open the front door.

Murdo never grasped the true significance of money, Miles thinks, as with a nod of thanks to the doorman, he steps into the street. It's not the material things it buys you that matters – it's the respect.

Outside a fine drizzle has begun to fall, slanting against the street lights. He should have brought his raincoat, but all he wants is a quick turn around the block.

He walks, head bent against the rain, forcing his mind away from recent events. He pictures lunching with Sophie in some sunlit piazza, afternoon love-making in their *pension* with its view over rolling hills, and then there are the Roman remains at Cosa he's always wanted to visit.

He's so absorbed in his thoughts that it takes a few moments to register what's happening up ahead: the slamming of a door followed by shouts and the shattering of glass. Then figures tumble onto the pavement, swearing and kicking out at one another. He can't make out their faces, but from the way they're staggering about, they look to be very drunk.

Thugs, the lot of them, he thinks, recalling the attack on Ali.

He walks towards them, a reprimand forming in his head. *What on earth do you think you're playing at? You'll wake the whole neighbourhood!* Then he stops short, biting back the words.

The figures have spotted him and one of them begins weaving its unsteady way towards him. Miles doesn't hesitate, turning on his heel and going at a half-run back to the safety of the hotel.

*

In their room, Sophie sleeps on, a rounded form under the covers, one hand curled on the pillow. You're still so beautiful, he thinks, remembering his first glimpse of her at that long-ago party.

It'll be good to put the events of this past year behind us, he tells himself, and with Sophie beside me, I can tackle whatever life brings.

After a while, he returns to the chair, and sits waiting for her to wake, watching as the light of the new day leaks slowly into the room.

ABOUT THE AUTHOR

E. J. Pepper grew up in Worcestershire and Co. Donegal. She lives with her husband in Southern England.

Her first novel, *The Colours of the Dance*, was published as an ebook in 2020 and is due out shortly in paperback and as an audiobook.

She is currently working on her third novel.

To find out more about E.J. Pepper and her writing, please visit ejpepper.com

Matador

For exclusive discounts on Matador titles,
sign up to our occasional newsletter at
troubador.co.uk/bookshop